BUM'S RUSH

WHITE LIGHTNING SERIES, BOOK 2

DEBRA DUNBAR

J.P. SLOAN

debra dunbar

CHAPTER 1

BALTIMORE, AUGUST 1926

"Twenty cents, ma'am."

A portly bald man with mustaches that belonged in the last century handed over a package of salted pork, neatly tied with twine. Hattie smiled at him and dug in her pocket to pay the butcher, proud to be handing over real coin instead of wooden nickels that had been made to look real with her illusion magic. Lizzie's boat-legging business was hopping with a literal monopoly on booze distribution across the waterways off the Chesapeake Bay, and Hattie was finally able to fill her family's larder with plentiful and wholesome food, bought guilt-free with real money.

Stepping down from the curb and melding into the crowd, she dropped her illusion of a well-to-do Druid Hill lady, and grinned. She'd been bolder about using her light-pinching powers the last few months, practicing and sharpening her skills by altering her appearance for each encounter. Sometimes she broadcasted the magic to everyone who might look her way, and sometimes she narrowed the focus so only one or two individuals could see the illusion. It was fun, spinning a new story for every city block she strode, ensuring that her voice matched whatever persona she'd assumed at the moment, tailoring her magic to what might best suit the situation at hand.

Truth be told, it wasn't just for fun, it was to hone her skill. What had happened in May underscored the need to think and act on the fly when the sharks circled her boat. And what better way to practice than on a glorious sunny morning, when everyday folk were going about their business buying groceries for Sunday dinner, and there wasn't a shark in sight.

An elderly lady hobbled across the street, and in between cars winding through the intersection Hattie pinched herself into the guise of a strapping young lad, offering an elbow for the woman to hold on her way to the opposite side. One of her favorite grocers gave her a nod as she shopped for greens in the guise of a weatherworn matron in black. She'd considered coming up with names for these personas, but the point was quick thinking, not indulgence.

So many people were passing by as well as cars and trucks. A horse sometimes as well, though they were rarer than ever. There was a time not long ago when Hattie feared the city with all these eyes. She'd feared it would be too easy for them to see through her illusions, that there would be too high a cost to any magic she might need to perform, but after she'd tangled with the Baltimore Crew and its time pincher, she'd come to realize that all these eyes rarely ever saw anything. Her magic was actually cheaper in crowds than on the water.

That realization had changed everything.

Her last stop on her way home was always the flower stall. Ever since a young stranger had bought her flowers, allowing her a single moment of joy underneath that green canvas awning, she'd made a point to visit the stall every Sunday. The selection had evolved from the bright and dainty spring flowers to the bold bouquets of summer. Large, luscious sunflowers sat in rows, their cheerful color beckoning to her. Behind them, tubs of roses towered on thorny stems. Hattie hiked her basket of greens, potatoes, and packaged pork a bit higher up her arm and sauntered for the flower merchant, dropping her illusions and appearing as herself—a young Irish woman with bobbed red-blonde hair, freckles, and a hand-me-down gingham dress.

Two tall men brushed past her, checking her a step toward the red brick walls of the bank building. She scowled at them, sniffing at the pall of rank and tarry cigarette fumes that drifted in their wake. Such was the cost of spending so much time in the city. Rudeness. The odor of the masses. Coughs and sneezes.

She had none of that out on the water.

Hattie took a step to catch her balance, and her purchases teetered in the crook of her elbow. The package of pork slipped from her basket, and she released a quiet yelp.

A hand swept past her knee to grab the parcel before it hit the dirt of the street. A thick-boned boy of about twenty rose to her side, holding the paper-wrapped meat out to her.

She took it with a faint smile, and said in the lingering accent of her homeland, "Thank you, lad."

He replied with a deep resonance that belied his age, and in a language she did not understand. Then the boy hopped along to follow the men who'd sent her meat tumbling in the first place, and Hattie shook her head, amused that the three were together.

One of the ruffians reached behind him to grab the lad by the arm, jerking him forward a few steps. It must have been no small task, as the youth was easily twice their weight. These were clearly uncommonly strong men.

And they were stepping in a straight line for the florist.

The old Armenian who sold Hattie her flowers each

Sunday blanched as the men approached. His tiny shoulders lifted, and he pivoted around his cash table, busying himself by wrapping some long-stemmed carnations for no one in particular.

The taller of the two men lifted a hand to the others. "Is Sunday. Two weeks, Aram. You pay today."

A slick of sweat erupted across the florist's brow as he continued to focus entirely on the bundle of carnations in his hands. "It's a bad week."

"Two bad weeks," the brute groused. "We come back without money…is trouble, I think."

To underscore the threat, he reached over and snatched the entire bundle of flowers from the vendor's wrinkled hands, sending a flurry of petals scattering.

The florist recoiled, a tremor settling over his shoulders. "I have no money."

"Then," the brute declared with a nod to his compatriots, and a sniff of the carnations, "is trouble."

Hattie balled a fist, stepping closer. This was going to be a fine Sunday morning. Now she had a chance to put her powers to their proper use.

The polite young man flexed his fingers and cracked his knuckles.

Hattie eyed the mangled bunch of flowers in the other brute's hand, then smirked. With a wiggle of her fingers, she pinched light directly over that bundle of carnations. The man didn't notice, his eyes on the imminent violence as the young man moved forward.

She dug deep and added another two senses to the illusion—the sense of sound and touch. It wasn't cheap magic, but it was small, and hopefully would be quick.

The younger lad looked down at his own fist as he heard a hiss. Then he peered over at the flowers. They stirred. Something long and thin emerged with a slither.

His eyes shot wide as a green-scaled viper peered out from the center of the carnations, its head cocked back, mouth open to bare fangs.

The florist's stand erupted with thrown flowers and the blood curdling shrieks of the three thugs. The younger one tumbled backward into a side table, knocking it and its contents out onto the street. His enormous frame spilled over the upended table onto the pavement, and only when he got to his feet did his high-pitched screaming cease. The lad sprinted up Light Street, turning onto Lombard and out of sight with remarkable speed, the remaining ruffians close on his heels.

Hattie sucked in several breaths to stave off a wave of nausea, then rushed for the front of the stand as the florist struggled with the table.

"Need a hand, old-timer?" she asked, gripping the opposite end of the table.

They pulled it upright, and he smiled at her. "Thank you."

"You're welcome." She helped the old man collect the scattered flowers off the ground, watching as he spread them flat onto the table and began to rearrange them into bundles.

"What was that about, then?" she asked.

He remained silent for a long moment as he dropped the bundles of flowers into the cups that hadn't smashed when they hit the ground. Finally, he shook his head and shrugged. "This is business."

"Not the sort of business *I'm* used to," she replied.

He pulled the last bundle onto a sheet of paper and wrapped it into a cone for Hattie, holding it out for her. "For your help, Miss."

She smiled, then fished a nickel from her clutch.

He shook his head. "No, no. I insist. No one helps an old man anymore."

Hattie's brow drew tight as she considered the poor old

man. Then she set the nickel onto the table. "With hoodlums rolling you like that, you should take what you can get."

He sighed. "The Bratva won't be satisfied with nickels, I fear."

She squinted at the strange word. "Bratva?"

"They come from Russia. Since the Revolution, they have nowhere to ply their trade. So, they have come here."

"Their trade being two-bit protection rackets, I take it?"

"That and more, if they can get away with it." The florist handed her the flowers, and she took them, settling the bundle into her basket. Picking up the nickel, she pressed it into the old man's hands.

"We've got too much crime in this city, I think," she muttered half to herself. "Someone ought to do something about it."

He shrugged again, then pocketed the nickel.

Hattie fretted over it all as she returned home with her haul of food and flowers. Her mother stood in the kitchen stirring a large bowl of batter as the morning sunlight illuminated the lines on her face wreathed by her gray-streaked red hair.

"Brought some salt pork, Ma," Hattie declared as she set the basket onto the table.

The woman nodded to Hattie over her shoulder. "Put the skillet on, then."

Hattie put some pork into the skillet, then poured black tea leaves into the kettle. A voice boomed from the back of the apartment as her father emerged from the bedroom.

"'Attie? You get the bacon?"

"Aye, Da."

He sauntered into the kitchen with a broad grin. His posture was straight, with newly added lean muscle in and around his chest and arms. Now that his cough had eased and he'd been able to sleep nights, the man was on the road to recovery. He threw his arms around Hattie, she felt a blaze of satisfaction and relief at his strength.

As her mother started some flatcakes on a griddle, Hattie poured the tea. Pivoting away from the stove, she kept an eye on her father, who was absorbed in the day's paper. With deft fingers, she fished the tiny dram of Aqua Vitae from the space between her bra and her sternum and pulled the stopper free with a gentle tug. A glass stem rose from the bright blue liquid. One single drop lingered from the bulb at the end of the stem, slipping off and down into Alton's tea. Hattie replaced the stopper and double-checked that neither of her parents had seen.

One drop of the magic elixir each Sunday. Leon was true to his word. The magical draught had restored her father's health, and allowed him to return to day shifts. It had made all the difference in the world.

They ate breakfast at the kitchen table and Hattie's mother cocked her head as she considered the spread of flowers that were in a glass at the center of the table.

"You shouldn't be spending money on such frippery," she scolded gently.

Alton scowled. "They're nice, Branna. We can afford to liven up the place, aye?"

Her mother sighed. "There are better uses for what money we have, is all I'm saying."

"Best to enjoy them now." Hattie poked a griddle cake with her fork. "Soon there won't be any more flowers downtown, not if these Russian hooligans keep on strong-arming that poor old man."

Alton nodded. "They're a menace. We have a few Russian men at Bethlehem. They're all on about these no-good newcomers."

Branna frowned, "With the Italians running things here, you'd think there'd be some reckoning in store."

Alton snickered. "The Italians are big-picture sorts, love. These street brutes? They're nothing but two-bit wolf's heads. Not worth the Crew's time to go shielding poor florists and such from the parasites."

"For all the protection money they skim from the vendors, you think they'd actually do some protecting," Hattie grumbled.

Alton shrugged. "Best not to get twisted up about't. It's nothing to do with us."

Branna concluded, "Well, if the law meant anythin' in this city, someone would do something."

Hattie ate the last of her pork, nodding to herself. Perhaps someone would.

As if reading her mind, her father asked, "You still have the ear of that gangster you met at the wharf?"

She gripped her fork tightly, considering her response. She'd told her parents Vincent wasn't a threat, and that they'd parted amicably, but they had no idea she'd been meeting the time pincher here and there since May. "I imagine I could scare him up, if I had occasion," she replied, keeping her tone casual.

"Then scare the boy up," he bellowed. "Put those Baltimore Crew bastards onto these Russians. Problem solved in a fortnight!"

Alton shot her a smile, and Hattie responded in kind. Such was the way with her father, to jump directly to the most absurd solution, then ease away when it turned out crazy. It was a joke then, and not just him ranting into the wind.

He had no idea that Hattie was already meeting with Vincent Calendo once every two weeks, per the agreement they'd reached after dealing with Capstein and the Upright Citizens. They'd shared a near-death experience, and that forged something stronger than a mere connection. There was a mystery that lay in the unspoken bond between them —a mystery that was only partly unveiled by that demonic creature in Deltaville. The only hope they had to unravel it all was to work together.

Which so far hadn't been as easy as Hattie had hoped it might be.

Vincent *was* a gangster, after all. He had sinister masters holding court in the Old Moravia Hotel. The Baltimore Crew. Vito Corbi. Even Vincent's taciturn shadow, Lefty Mancuso. Especially Lefty. Vincent's "handler" enjoyed releasing Vincent outside his supervision as much as he'd enjoy a swift kick to the nethers. Which made every two weeks something more like every three. The two of them had only met four times so far to discuss matters concerning the Hell pincher as well as their strange connection.

Beyond that, they had very little in common. She was a free pincher. He was owned by the mafia. His story was the more common, since most pinchers on both sides of the Atlantic were identified early in life and scooped up by the various powers that be. In the New World, the real power right now was the mob, and they were who "owned" Vincent.

The one time Hattie had brought up her own upbringing, it had seemed to pick at a raw nerve inside the time pincher. He'd stormed off, only to offer a wounded apology the next day. Hattie knew she was an exception to the rule— the rule being that pinchers were born to serve. If it weren't for her parents sacrificing so much to keep her safe and free, she'd be just like Vincent—a tool for the crime bosses.

"Da?" she asked pushing aside her plate. "Back in the Old Country, before we knew what I was…" She took a moment to gather her thoughts as both of her parents stiffened. "Did anyone approach you? About me?"

Alton shot a look to Branna. Her mother silently shook her head.

Setting down his fork, Alton took a long pull of tea. As he put down the cup, he cleared his throat, and said, "Aye. They did."

"Who were they?"

Her mother wrinkled her nose. "What brought this on?"

"I'm curious. And I have a right to know, don't I?"

Branna eyed her sadly. "It doesn't matter. Some things are best left to lie undisturbed."

Alton grumbled, "Branna…"

"What?" his wife countered with a sharp tone. "Digging up the past is pointless. Nothing but bones underground. Best she lives her life, and we don't tempt fate."

Alton shook his head. "What's the harm in tellin' the girl? It's her history, no?"

Branna closed her eyes and lifted her hands. "Fine. Tell her everything. You deal with the consequences if trouble comes to our door."

"I have kept her safe so far. Haven't I?" Alton replied with a flat tone.

Branna opened her eyes, and her face softened as she looked at her husband. "Aye, you have. We both have."

Alton shoved his plate forward, then turned to face Hattie. "They claimed to be from the Church—a secret order dedicated to finding and securing sorcerous elements from among the laity. They were to take you away where you'd be raised in a convent and become a nun."

Hattie squinted. "They were priests?"

"That's what they said."

"A nun doesn't sound so bad," she mused. It seemed a better fate then a life of slavery to some mob boss.

"No, but we wanted you to have a choice in the matter," her mother said. "If you wanted to give up any ideas of having children and dedicate your life to the Church, I'd support it. But that needs t'be your choice, not a decision others make when you're a wee babe."

Hattie frowned in thought. "How did they know I was… how I am?"

Her parents shared another heavy look before Alton replied, "It was our fault. We didn't know, and we were worried for you. You have to understand, we had no one to turn to, when it all started."

Hattie asked, "How did it start?"

"It was your crib, is what," her mother said.

Alton chuckled. "Aye, that was annoying."

"You found your way out of your crib by twelve months," Branna continued. "Always were a climber. I'd come in and there you were lying in your crib like a proper good baby. I'd turn around and you'd be crawling around on the floor. I thought I was going mad. Then we'd take you outside in your pram and we'd get lost. Every time. Streets I've walked for years, but I couldn't decide if I was coming or going. And then came the cats."

Hattie blinked. "Cats?"

"Aye. Cats. Suddenly everywhere—wee kittens crawling up and over us."

Her father laughed. "We showed you a cat one day what had a litter. You were maybe two years. You played with the kits for an hour, and then we were up to our knees in kittens at all hours."

"Which was when you started getting sick," her mother added.

Hattie leaned back in her chair. "I was pinching light and didn't know when to stop."

"Who else could we turn to?" Branna concluded. "We spoke with Father Martin."

Alton grumbled, "The bastard. Next thing we know,

there's men at the door telling us they need to take you away to save your soul."

Hattie did her best to piece together the scene from a chapter in her life, of parents perplexed by their child's odd abilities and resulting sickness. Had Vincent's parents felt the same? Had they turned to a priest who'd gone to the mob rather than to some mysterious religious order?

"Would it have been any different here, though?" she asked. "In the States? Say you were a young couple in, oh, New York. And you find your child had these sorts of abilities. Would you go to the Church then?"

"Probably," Alton said. "Then I'd be running from a whole other bunch of people wanting the same thing—to snatch my baby away."

Branna smiled. "We'd run, but first I'd go see Seamus. Have him cook me up a fresh birth certificate before we headed out, just to cover our tracks."

Hattie nodded along, but the joke was lost on her. Finally, she asked, "Who's Seamus, then?"

"Your cousin, girl!" Alton downed the last of his tea.

"I have a cousin in New York?"

He waved her question off. "Your uncle Stephen moved to the States in '95. Seamus was born here. True-blooded American."

"He's the one who sends us those Christmas cards every year. Always says to visit if we ever come up to New York," Branna added.

Hattie nodded, remembering the cards. "And he could forge us vital documents if needed?"

"Not as such. He's the genuine article. Works for the records something or another...whatever it's called in Brooklyn. But I'm sure he'd do us a proper if pressed!" With a wink, her father stood up and gathered the dishes.

Hattie sat in her chair ruminating. Both her parents were

quick to the point regarding cousin Seamus. It was clear to her that he'd been a sort of fallback plan if things went sideways in Baltimore.

Records division. In New York City. Well, that was interesting. Brooklyn. Vincent was by way of Brooklyn. Vincent, who had no idea whether his parents were alive or dead, or even what their names were. She could offer…but then again, he was so touchy when it came to that subject that she hated to bring it up.

Branna stood and leaned over the table, cupping her hand over the flowers to take a sniff as Hattie's father washed the plates in the sink. "I know what that was all about," she said gently.

Hattie swallowed hard. "That a fact?"

"Aye. It's been on my mind, as well, the past few months."

Hattie turned to face her mother in surprise. "You're a mind reader, then?"

"No need to read minds. It's completely understandable."

Her fists gripped the sides of her dress, balling them up as she tightened her fingers. What exactly did her mother find "understandable"?

"I don't blame you in the least," her mother added, "and you shouldn't feel ashamed about looking to the future and wondering what that might hold for you."

"The…the future?"

"You're thinking of children," she stated.

Hattie's heart skipped a beat. "Well…I suppose the subject bears a second thought."

"You must wonder if you can have children. And the honest truth is that I have no more clue than you do. I don't have any idea either whether they'd end up with abilities like your own. Your father and I have wondered and thought on that one many a night."

Hattie released a breath, then smiled at her mother. "I've a long way to go before I show any interest in that sort of thing."

Branna gave her a knowing smile. "I was your age when I gave birth to you. And don't tell me there haven't been young men catching your eye lately. That's a good thing, as long as you're careful. I'm always here to listen and to help if needed. Although if you don't want my help, then that's fine, too. I'll just—"

Before her mother could turn away, Hattie grabbed her arm. "No, Ma. I appreciate it. Things are just too complicated right now. For me, for children, or anyone who might step up wanting to make that sort of thing happen with me."

Branna nodded thoughtfully. "When the time comes, we'll see you and your family are safe. You and your husband won't be raising a special child by stumbling around the way your father and I did. We'll help."

"Thank you, Ma." Hattie kissed her mother on the cheek, then withdrew to her bedroom. As she reclined onto her bed, she thought of Vincent's parents, and whether they'd turned to the Church. Would they have? Had that order her father had spoken of followed Hattie's kind all the way to America? Or had it always been the mob on these shores? Did they buy him outright, or had they strong-armed his parents into surrendering their child? Were they even still alive?

These were questions Hattie would need to know the answer to if she were ever to truly understand the man she met with once a fortnight.

And also if she ever wanted children of her own.

CHAPTER 2

On a day like this, Vincent Calendo would've been
enjoying the usual Sunday brunch with Lefty at
Alphie's. Bright sunshine filled the sky, and people would
have their windows open, ready to let in the breeze.
However, this was no ordinary Sunday. It was a business
Sunday, and Vincent was in Philadelphia.

He parked Lefty's car in front of a fish cannery on the
river bank, and the two left the brilliant summer morning for
the dank gloom inside the building. A pair of wingtips
clacked along the concrete floor to greet them. Filling those
shoes was a lean middle-aged man with close-cropped
brown hair and coal-black eyes. He offered a smile filled
with all the warmth of a shark's grin as he extended a hand
to Lefty.

"You Mancuso?" he asked.

Lefty nodded and shook his hand with a firm grip.
"DeBarre?"

"Glad you made it in so early. I gotta flatfoot it to the City
by sundown, and I wasn't sure how long we were gonna
chew the fat. If we can move this along, all's the better."

Lefty shot Vincent a cautious glance before the faintest smirk flickered in the corner of his mouth.

"I can't escape the notion that you're brooming us off, DeBarre," Lefty declared. "If this is a bad time, I'm sure Vito won't mind if we come back some other day."

DeBarre's eyebrows shot high, and he sucked in a breath. "Oh, no no. That's not it. We want no beef with the Crew. It's just been a hell of a week, you catch my shine?"

Lefty nodded mirthlessly. "These are trying times. And I assure you, we have no interest in wasting your day." He cleared his throat and stood aside with a flat-handed gesture to Vincent. "Loren DeBarre, you'll be pleased to meet Vincent Calendo."

DeBarre and Vincent shared a look, and they both smirked.

"Yeah, Lefty. We've, uh…we've met before," Vincent told him.

Lefty lifted his chin with a frown. "When?"

"About two years ago. Christmastime, I think?" DeBarre answered.

Vincent snapped his fingers and pointed to DeBarre. "That was it. Big gala up at the Yorkshire Arms."

DeBarre laughed. "They was pouring giggle-water like it was going out of style!"

"They were," Vincent agreed. "Volstead Act just passed, and the Treasury Men were pinching their seat cushions over every drop of grease flowing out of the City."

Vincent remembered that party. It was the first trip he'd taken outside of Baltimore in quite a while. The man had introduced himself to Vincent as a "down pincher." Vincent never figured out what that meant, exactly, but his status among the East Coast families was solid as granite, and Vincent never felt the urge to prod. It felt rude, somehow.

Lefty glowered at Vincent's side as DeBarre extended a hand for Vincent to shake.

"We pinchers stick together, Lefty. Don't get gloomy about it," Vincent told him.

"I would have remembered a Christmas gala," the man groused.

Vincent hid a grin. "That was the year the flu was making the rounds again. You caught it right in the chest. Lenin himself coulda marched an armored column up Light Street, you would've thought it was a three-man band."

Lefty nodded. "I remember that winter. Almost killed me."

DeBarre slapped Lefty's good shoulder. "Well, for what it's worth, I'm glad you're still with us. Come on, gents. We got some gin cooling off down in the poke."

The down pincher led the two deeper into the building, steering them past the canning line which sat dormant. DeBarre explained it was due to the new ownership who insisted on "keeping the Sabbath." The Philadelphia family took advantage of the owner's piety and used the cannery for official business while the workers enjoyed their day of rest.

As they descended a short flight of stairs into the basement and steam pipe tunnels beneath the building, a blood-chilling shriek echoed off bleak walls, muffled and indeterminate. It was like a cry from the bowels of hell itself.

Vincent cleared his throat as he peered at DeBarre.

The pincher shrugged. "Arnoud's here."

Lefty nodded thoughtfully as Vincent frowned, perplexed. "Who?" he asked.

Lefty sucked in a smug breath, then answered, "Seems you haven't met *all* the pinchers in Philly."

DeBarre chimed in. "To be fair, Arnoud is new."

"What's his flavor of cake?" Vincent asked.

"He's a touch pincher," DeBarre answered, just as another godless scream erupted from one of the rooms ahead. "Makes you feel what he wants you to feel. Which can put a sweat on your mop, if you think good and hard about it."

Vincent nodded as they strolled past what he'd deduced by the whimpering was Arnoud's torture chamber. Touch pincher? The power that implied was staggering.

DeBarre shoved aside a heavy steel door hung on a rail. Beyond the hulking panel of metal was a cozy space with red carpeting and Tiffany lamps set upon dark wood tables. A tiny service sat in the center of the room, its brass top sporting a silver bucket of ice chilling a bottle of clear liquid. DeBarre gestured toward the chairs arranged in random angles to create pockets of conversation space. The room was empty, save for the three.

Lefty took a seat without a word.

Vincent looked around as DeBarre poured three drinks, "Nice joint. Quiet."

"It's like a library in here on Sundays," DeBarre said as he squeezed some lime into highball glasses. "Most of the boys are downtown today. Me and Arnoud are stuck here doin' the business."

Lefty lifted his hand once again. "And we will be quick about it, don't you worry. Capo Vito has some concerns regarding trafficking up the Delaware, and he sent us to make nice."

DeBarre chuckled as he handed over the drinks. "Well, you can tell Vito that we're peaches and cream up here. What're his concerns?"

"As you may know, we've farmed out most of the boat-legging up and down the Bay."

DeBarre wrinkled his nose. "Don't you mean bootlegging?"

"Boat-legging," Vincent chimed in. "On boats. It's what

they like to call it. And it's a whole different set of skills from hustling hooch by truck."

Indeed, Vincent had become deeply familiar with those requisite skills this past spring when he'd spent a few days on a boat with the Crew's boat-leggers.

With Hattie Malloy.

Which was his other purpose in Philadelphia. Sure, Lefty had some shop to talk with DeBarre. It wasn't anything Tony or one of the other men couldn't handle though. But the word around the campfire was that a pincher in Philadelphia had experienced a run-in with a Hell pincher, and now that Vincent was aware of the new guy, Arnoud, the dots were connecting.

Lefty said, "Vito's concerns are security. On your end, to put it directly."

"What's wrong with our security?" DeBarre bristled.

"We don't know," Lefty replied. "But you're in a dry state. Feds are keeping their eyes peeled."

DeBarre asked, "Have you had any trouble shooting hooch up the river yet?"

"No."

"So, what's the beef?"

"No beef," Lefty responded. "We're just looking for you to paint us a picture. How you receive shipments, what you do to keep a toe-and-heel ahead of the G."

"I don't get it," DeBarre said with a frown and a wave of his gin. "Everything's running smooth as butter. What's with the third degree? Your people get the hooch up-river, and we get the particulars and the dollar bills into Vito's hands. It's a system, and it works—and you not shooting straight with me puts my teeth on edge."

"It's really more of a teaching situation, Lefty offered. "You do it right, so we'd like to share in your wisdom. Maybe we got other ports of call which aren't locked as tight as yours. Maybe it's just good business. This ain't no shake-down. We're just trying to pick your noodle."

Vincent eyed Lefty as DeBarre took a long sip of gin to contemplate the man's words. Lefty was privy to far more family business than Vincent. Hell, Vincent wasn't even considered *famiglia*. No pincher was. Though DeBarre seemed to be the closest thing to establishment any pincher could hope for.

DeBarre grinned, then set down his glass. "Let's cut to the fat, huh? Why are you really here?"

Lefty bobbed his head in equivocation, muttering his way through a bluff of some sort.

Vincent cleared his throat, then said, "We're looking to acquire pinchers."

Lefty shot him a disdainful glare.

DeBarre shifted his gaze to Vincent and nodded. "So, that's why Vito sent his pincher to Philly. You're in the market."

"It's a matter of priority for the Capo," Vincent added.

DeBarre lifted his hands. "Thank you for getting to the point. Long way around, maybe. But fine. I got good news and bad news for you. Good news is that you're making a proper request. There is opportunity to buy and trade pinchers among the senior families, and it's proper that the request be made by one of us."

"And the bad news?" Lefty grumbled.

"Bad news," DeBarre said scooping his drink back into his hand, "is that the market's lean. No pinchers to be had at the moment, thanks to this Bratva horseshit."

"Bratva?" Vincent repeated.

"Yeah. The Russians are hitting New York something fierce. Tempers are boiling already and it's looking to be a hot summer."

Vincent sighed. He was familiar with the Bratva, such as

they were back home. "We've taken care of the Brotherhood in Baltimore," he announced.

"Bully for you," DeBarre said. "Unfortunately the rest of us still gotta deal with these jokers. They lose their turf to the goddamn Bolsheviks, so now they become *our* problem. Which means all the major families are scooping up pinchers left and right. I know that's not what you wanna hear, but it's the truth. If you really did take out the trash down there in Baltimore, then you should count yourself lucky."

Lefty asked, "It's really that bad?"

"Could be, soon enough. We got our ears to the ground, and we don't like what we hear."

A noise sounded from the corridor behind the large steel door, and the three turned to watch as a gaunt, mouse-faced man entered the lounge. He ran fingers over his hair to restore its propriety, muttering something about people being so rude.

DeBarre stood up and motioned to the man. "Just in time to be awkward— Bradley Arnoud, this is Alonzo Mancuso and Vincent Calendo. They're from Baltimore, so dial it down a hair."

The touch pincher's face erupted into an unsettling grin. "Heya, fellas! It's a peach to meet the two of you!"

He hopped forward to extend a hand to Vincent.

Vincent checked it for blood before shaking it.

Arnoud giggled in an oddly infantile manner, then spun around to greet Lefty.

"Done with your toy?" DeBarre asked him,

The man shook Lefty's hand, then ducked his head sheepishly. "Gosh, no. He's just taking a moment. The poor boy passed out on me. I mean..." He slapped his thighs and cocked his head. "Rude? Right?"

Vincent stared at the touch pincher. "Rude. Yeah, I guess."

"Do you have anything besides gin, Loren?" Arnoud swept around them toward the table, inspecting the tray.

DeBarre shook his head.

"Well, would it kill you to put some juice on ice for once?"

"You don't partake?" Lefty held his highball aloft.

The touch pincher wrinkled his nose. "Can't abide the stuff. Not that I'm here to judge. Lord, no. Have at it, fellas. I've just never developed the stomach for hard spirits."

DeBarre gestured upstairs. "There's water a-plenty up top, Bradley. If you're gonna grouse about your liver, best do it elsewhere and leave us grown-ups to the business."

Vincent shoved a hand in to his pants pocket as he balled his fingers into a fist. This felt wrong. Yeah, the man seemed a real odd-ball, but DeBarre treating Arnoud like a child? It was…cheap.

The touch pincher returned a practiced grin and nodded to the rest as he turned back for the corridor.

"I'll join you," Vincent called out.

Lefty lifted a brow, but said nothing.

As Vincent stepped into the corridor after Arnoud, DeBarre and Lefty continued their business talk.

"I appreciate the company," the touch pincher told him. "This old cannery can get so gloomy."

Vincent trotted up to join him. "No sweat. Nice to meet another pincher."

Arnoud turned as he walked and clapped Vincent on the shoulder. "Feeling is quite mutual, my friend."

As they passed the interrogation room, Vincent stole a peek inside to find a seated, sweaty man slumped forward. A few lashes of jute held his wrists tight to the arms of the chair. There was no blood. No implements of torture. Nothing to indicate that the man had passed out from pain other than the pool of sweat that had gathered on the man's shirt. Vincent shuddered as he continued on.

They reached the steel grating stairs and ascended to the main cannery floor. Sunlight poured through filmy windows near the vaulted warehouse ceiling, sending hazy beams at angles into the space.

"So," Arnoud asked as he approached a work sink, "what brings you charming folks up to Philly on such a beautiful day?"

"Business for the Capo," Vincent replied. "Inquiring on the pincher market."

Arnoud snatched a greasy glass from the side of the sink and poured himself a splash of water. "Poor Corbi. Bad time to look into expansion."

"That's what I hear. To be honest, though…" Vincent peered at Arnoud as he took a long sip from the glass. "Mind if we cut to a delicate subject?"

Arnoud lowered his glass, eyeing Vincent with wide, mirthful eyes. "Well, this sounds positively delicious. Please, go on!"

"Rumor on the block is that you've had a run-in with a Hell pincher."

Arnoud's smile faded. "Ah. Well." He sipped more water, then dumped the rest back into the sink. "There are fun rumors, you know. Rumors about who's cheating on who, and what a dame looks like underneath her skirt, where someone got a tattoo, and whether his wife knows. Those sorts of rumors pass the time when we're short on work and long on hours. But this sort of rumor," he said with a lift of his finger, "isn't so much fun as it is troubling."

"You're saying it's all bunk?"

"No. I didn't say that." He stepped past Vincent. "I'm only offering you the opportunity to let this go."

"Why would I do that?" Vincent pressed.

"Because the business of a Hell pincher has a way of ruining lives."

"Well, I have a particular interest."

Arnoud spun around with a sharp grin. "You've had an encounter, haven't you?"

Vincent grimaced. "Maybe."

He snickered. "No, you have. I can tell. What was it? A demon? A golem?"

"*Golem?*" Vincent blurted.

Arnoud laughed. "So, it was a demon then. I apologize if I'm stringing you along, good man. We two are in an exclusive fraternity of sorts. Precious few stumble across the trappings of Hell pinchers and survive."

"So?" Vincent urged him on. "Tell me what happened."

"Before I joined the fine folks here in Philadelphia…" He paused to snicker at his own alliteration. "I found myself driving with a former associate west from Harrisburg. We were trying to beat a winter storm and we lost the race. Got mired up in some dreadful roads outside of Amish country. We holed up near a village of folk who, according to my companion's tortured German, weren't allowed to turn us away in the weather, but were disinclined to host us within their town limits. Thus, they escorted the two of us to a set of dilapidated old cabins in the woods." He gestured for Vincent to follow as he walked on. "They treated these woods like some sort of haunted forest. These cabins were their 'shame lands.' That's if my companion's grasp of the language was adequate. They sent people to these cabins when they were taken with the flu, or leprosy, or any other sort of devilry they couldn't stomach."

Vincent squinted at Arnoud. "I'm taking a stab, here. You ran into something unnatural in those woods."

"Quick study! Yes. A vicious, frightening thing. Eyes aflame. Able to summon fire at will. A beast."

"A demon," Vincent corrected.

"You know the sort. We barely survived. Happily, the

creature remained content if we left it alone—which by Jiminy, we did!"

"What did you learn, though?" Vincent prodded. "About the creature? And the Hell pincher?"

Arnoud paused and grinned, but the expression faded as he stared into space. "In the moment, precious little, though the remembrance clung to me like a wet sock. I couldn't shake the image of that…thing. What power had summoned it? How could it exist on this Earth? I had to know. And so, I investigated."

Vincent leaned against a tall steel tank and crossed his arms. "That's where I am, now."

"Then you understand the fever," Arnoud said. "The need to know. How can there be this sort of violent, Godless magic in our world?"

"You a church man?"

He shook his head. "I put no faith in any institution man has erected."

"Even the families?" Vincent jibed.

The touch pincher's face adopted a brief flicker of menace, before melting back into its previous geniality. "Well, we're talking religion here."

"How did you investigate? Where'd you go?"

"To New York," Arnoud explained. "Most of our history as pinchers has been chronicled by interested parties. Parties, I might add, that are privy not only to our existence, but to the existence of the Hell pinchers."

"You keep acting like they're different animals."

"They are," Arnoud stated. "Clearly. You and I? We were born with our abilities. Who knows why? But there it is. Those born without any special consideration—I suppose that's the only way to politely describe it—can choose to accept that we are powerful. They can crave our power. They sometimes look to usurp our power from us."

Vincent shook his head in confusion. "You a college boy, or something? I'm boiling only about half of what you're pouring."

Arnoud released a belly laugh, then covered his mouth. "I apologize. I've spent years with my nose down in books. I may come across a bit…artificial."

Vincent unfolded his arms and sighed. "If that's the worst you have to confess, then we're square, you and I."

"In the way of confession, I'll have to say it now: I have no idea who summoned that demon into the midst of Amish country, but I have learned that demons do not simply stumble into our world and do as they please."

"The Bible seems to disagree on that account."

Arnoud's brow shot toward his hairline. "Are *you* a believer?"

"I believe in what I see," Vincent replied. "And I've seen things."

The touch pincher nodded thoughtfully. "Whoever conjured that demon likely resides close by. I have theories—none of which I've been able to pursue. Not with my new masters." His eyes drifted to the floor.

Vincent reached out and gripped his arm. "I understand. This sorta thing needs to stay inside…what did you call it? The fraternity?"

Arnoud pursed his lips, then nodded. He whispered, "I believe this Hell pincher learned his craft in the South. Perhaps he moved north as of late, but I have a strong inkling that he yet lives, and that he lives somewhere near Wilkes-Barre."

Vincent leaned forward. "How sure are you?"

"As sure as anyone can be with these things. Alas, we might never know for certain who or exactly where this Hell pincher is." Arnoud released a long sigh. "I have business,

Mister Calendo. It's been a joy chatting, but alas. I must return to my duties."

Vincent stiffened, then nodded. "I'd like to pursue this. One day. You know, when things aren't quite so sticky?"

Arnoud smiled. "Sure." With a shrug, he moved back to the stairs. "Come on."

They descended into the bowels of the cannery, and proceeded back toward the hidden lounge. Arnoud paused by the door to the poor sap he'd been interrogating, and gripped the jamb with a sharp inhalation.

Vincent asked, "What's wrong?" Even as he asked it, he leaned over Arnoud's shoulder to spy into the room beyond.

One chair.

Several lengths of rope lying limp on the floor.

And nobody else.

The touch pincher spat a profanity that Vincent didn't recognize before bolting for the lounge. They both raced for the sliding steel door, slipping through to find Lefty and DeBarre sitting casually in their seats.

"Where is he?" Arnoud panted.

DeBarre lifted his glass to the ceiling with a smirk.

Vincent peered up to the low-hanging steel plates over their heads, where a panicked man in a sweat-soaked shirt gripped the light sconce. His body pressed against the ceiling, his eyes wide, searching the floor for some means of escape. He crawled away from the sconce as Arnoud approached, bustling on all fours along the ceiling as if it were the floor.

The touch pincher shook his head. "You naughty boy. I shall have to make you pay for this. Clearly pain isn't working. Something extra...perhaps an itch you can't scratch? Or..."

"Enough," DeBarre snapped.

The man on the ceiling whimpered in the corner,

releasing a string of babble in some language Vincent couldn't recognize before his body lurched into freefall, dropping ten feet to the floor. He landed with a heavy thump, his head twisting unnaturally as he hit the ground.

Arnoud scowled. "It sounded like he was confessing."

"Did you understand a word of it?" DeBarre asked.

"Given time, I might have—"

"He was done," DeBarre declared with the last swig of his gin. "And you need to work on your knots."

"Clearly," Arnoud confessed.

Lefty and Vincent made a courteous exit shortly thereafter, as the two Philly pinchers were left to police the body of their quarry.

On the road, Vincent caught Lefty eyeing him from the passenger seat.

"What?"

Lefty shook his head. "Nothing."

"You're givin' me the hairy eyeball."

"You were quick to duck out with that touch pincher."

Vincent nodded. "I needed to press the flesh, you know? Get the skinny on both of these pinchers."

"That's it?"

Vincent squinted. "That ball of wax you was rolling for DeBarre, shipping up the Bay, and such?"

"What about it?" Lefty grumbled.

"You weren't just stringing him along, were you?"

"Of course I was. Couldn't just jump directly into the subject of spare pinchers. Wouldn't be seemly."

Vincent sighed. "Tony coulda made this meet instead of us, if that's what we were here to discuss."

Lefty turned to stare out his window, offering nothing more.

As the road spread before Vincent, his thoughts were conflicted. On one hand, Vito's poking around the boat-legging business behind Tony's back filled him with a molasses-thick cloud of uncertainty. On the other hand, Vincent had finally contacted another pincher who'd survived a run-in with a legitimate demon. With any luck at all, he may have a direct lead on a Hell pincher. *That* would be something to tell Hattie on their next meeting—whenever that would be.

CHAPTER 3

Hattie stepped out of the battered Model T Runabout, and spied the Triumph two-seater parked in front of Lizzie Sadler's warehouse in Locust Point. The car had made more appearances during the day as of late. It belonged to one of the Baltimore Crew—Tony something-or-another. The man was their liaison, the mobster in charge of coordinating the bootleg trafficking on the water, or "boat-legging" as they called it.

But there was something more to the arrangement between Lizzie and Tony—something romantic. Well, romantic was most likely an overstatement. Either way, Hattie and Raymond had learned weeks ago that if they spotted the Triumph in front of the warehouse, and the warehouse doors were closed, they would do better to stick around outside until everyone inside was fully dressed.

A voice called from the empty lot beside the warehouse, "You gonna stare at that car all day, baby girl?"

Hattie smiled as she turned to find Raymond looming next to a stack of lumber, a tiny white ball in his hand.

"What've you got there, boy-o?" she called.

He tossed the ball to Hattie. "It's an egg!"

Hattie braced herself, wishing for a split-second that she could pinch time the way Vincent could. But this was the training she'd been working on with Raymond these past few months.

In the second that the tiny white orb floated in the air, Hattie pinched light around her body, reaching up to snatch the ball. Behind her, an illusion knitted into reality in the early summer sunlight. An egg smashed against the stone-dust pad behind Hattie, complete with a wet *chunk*.

"How did that look?" she asked as she dismantled the illusion.

Raymond nodded slowly. "Not bad."

She examined the ball in her hand. It was hard, with just a little give.

"What is this?" she asked.

Raymond shrugged. "Lacrosse ball, I think. Found it outside one a them Catholic schools up the pike."

Hattie tossed it back to Raymond. "Alright, so...let me have it. You said not bad. That means not good. What went wrong?"

He gathered his thoughts, then responded, "I saw the change."

"Ball to egg?"

"Yeah. Wasn't quite right. It was here, then it was there." He lifted his hand in the air, then dropped it a few inches. "You weren't lined up perfect."

She shook her head with a sigh. "Try it again."

He tossed the ball back to her, and she gave it another shot. Her illusion egg smashed against the gravel, and she sent Raymond a questioning glance.

He nodded. "Better."

"Better'n not bad?"

He shook his hand in equivocation, and she beaned him

with the ball. Raymond laughed as he tried unsuccessfully to sidestep the lacrosse ball, which smacked him in the hip.

"Hey, now! It was better than last time. Just a tiny bit off still."

"Alright, I'll work harder on lining things up." As she headed toward the stack of lumber, she thought of Vincent and the way he'd always kept track of things as he pinched time. This was here, this was there—it all had to be in the exact same place before he released his pinch. She wondered how many times he'd had to exercise that skill before he perfected it.

Raymond walked alongside her as they delved deeper into the maze of crates and wood that filled the back end of the empty lot. Glancing over her shoulder, she saw the Triumph still there.

"How long has that gangster been in there?"

Raymond shrugged. "'Bout five, ten minutes. Best to give them a half hour."

Hattie shook her head. "He's mighty quick, that one."

"A half hour? That's not so quick."

"You're kidding, right?"

"What? Time you make a little conversation and get your clothes off and back on, there's still a good twenty minutes left for what you came for." Raymond looked over at the car.

"Ten minutes for conversing and getting naked?" Hattie shook her head. "And twenty…you think that's adequate, do you?"

Raymond rubbed his eyes. "Don't wanna talk about this sorta thing with you, Hattie."

"What?" she teased with a shot of her elbow to the enormous man's ribs. "You don't want to think about me underneath some strapping young lad? Breathless. Frustrated because he's too quick to—"

"God! No!"

Hattie snickered. Raymond was too easy to bait like this. He was as good as a brother to Hattie—more so now that the two of them could speak openly about her gifts. It was his idea to take these stolen moments at Locust Point to train her abilities. It made sense. As a boat-legger hauling booze across state lines, she needed to be able to think fast on her feet.

That was a quality Vincent demonstrated in spades. His capacity to size up a deadly moment in a hair's breadth, then pinch time the way he did? That was skill honed through experience. Hattie might never be as good as the time pincher, but she was damned well gonna try. Which meant she needed to practice every chance she got.

"Alright, boy-o," she declared as she came to a halt. "What'll it be today? Besides eggs?"

Raymond rubbed his chin. "Yeah, I been thinkin' on this all week. Ya told me once about how expensive your magic was."

She nodded.

"How it costs more depending on how big it is, if it's more than just sight—like, sound and smell, and how many people saw these mirages?"

Hattie cocked her head. "What's the plan?"

"Take me inside one of these illusions, is what I'm thinkin'," he declared. "Spin me something real. Something I'd get lost in. But only me. Other people walking by would just see two people sitting on the ground."

With the illusion focused on just one person, she could really expand energy in making it realistic to all the senses. Hattie smiled. "What do you want me to create exactly? Someplace we've been before? Eating? Playing with kittens?"

"I dunno. Make it nice. Nothin' nightmare-like."

She nodded, then collected herself. Okay, she'd have to pinch light around the two of them affecting all senses. That would be expensive, on a magical level. But that was the other half of the training—it wasn't only about reducing reaction time. It was also about feeling out her limits. What could she do before she got too sick to keep the illusion going?

"Sure you're ready for this?" she asked.

Raymond took a breath. "It's just illusion, right? I can't get hurt?"

She snickered. "No, I'll be the one getting hurt."

He waggled a finger at her. "Not if you do it right."

Hattie kicked away some gravel from around her and took a seat on the ground, crossing her legs. Raymond followed suit, plopping down a few feet away.

The sense of Raymond's nearness helped propel her into the illusion. She pictured Raymond sitting at some slumped posture, his eyes deep set in his dark brown, sweat-beaded face. Then she spun a thought in her head—a thought she dwelled on with the full bore of her powers.

She pinched light, and that pinch was a massive theater around the two of them. Hattie stitched together every detail she could muster of Raymond's home. The wood plank floors. The weathered kitchen table complete with the tiny gashes Nadine had sliced with her paring knife as she made a Sunday feast. The little baby, Douglas, resting in a bassinet in the corner, cooing away to himself in his soft cotton clothes and bedsheets.

The smell drifted around them—a vegetable soup of sorts, with some crab meat. Raymond sat at the table, watching his wife as she stirred the pot. She peered over her shoulder at Raymond with a smile.

Raymond cleared his throat, and Hattie could feel a tug on her illusion. Something had happened. He'd fallen out of it.

She opened her eyes, sucking in a long breath and

shaking off a wave of nausea. That wasn't cheap magic, but it had been glorious to create something so detailed and exact.

"So? What did you think?" she asked.

Raymond shifted on the gravel. "That was…unsettlin'."

"What was wrong?" she frowned. Had she not gotten the table right? The soup? Douglas's little baby noises?

"Nothing. I mean…it was good. Like home. But…"

"But what?"

He shuddered, then gave her a sheepish grin. "Nadine don't look at me like that."

"Oh."

"Yeah. Kinda was like there was another woman in my kitchen wearing her clothes. That felt all kinds of wrong."

She nodded to herself. It was always a gamble, trying to recreate the life of another person. Hattie had enjoyed more than a few dinners with Raymond's family, but there were private glances, cues, shades of posture that could only be shared between two people. It was an ambitious pinch, and though Raymond dropped out of it, Hattie took solace in the fact she'd immersed him in something so involved.

She ran a finger underneath her nose, wiping a tiny trickle of blood from her nostril. "Worth a try, at any rate."

Raymond's brow wrinkled as he stared at her nosebleed. "Maybe that's enough for today?"

"Enough? We've hardly begun. Besides…" She eyed the front of the warehouse. Tony's car was still there.

Raymond sighed. "S'pose we ain't got nowhere better to be, huh? But still, you shouldn't be pushin' yourself too hard. That'll get you sick."

She wiped her finger on her pants. "That's the point, though. I need to train myself to work through the sickness. Build up a resistance."

He shrugged. "Okay. So, what's next?"

She thought about it for a moment. "Hmm. I tried your world. Let me try mine."

Raymond nodded as Hattie closed her eyes and pieced together the intimate details of her home. And as she opened her eyes, rather than an empty lot she found her own kitchen. Raymond stood across from her table, eyes wide.

"Now…that's somethin'," he gasped.

An illusion of Alton stepped through the kitchen. "Morning, 'Attie!"

Raymond stood aside to let Alton pass, then grinned. "That *is* somethin'."

Hattie held the illusion tight and controlled, though it had already begun tugging at her guts.

"This it? Your home?" Raymond asked.

"Aye," she wheezed.

"You okay?"

Hattie nodded. "This is too easy. I know all this. I need to involve your other senses."

She peered at the kitchen window, then squinted. With a tiny lift of her fingers, she dropped the outside world of her illusion into darkness. Nighttime. Moonlight sifted through the window.

Alton's illusion said, "Atta girl."

Raymond reached out for the table, then paused to give Hattie a glance.

She nodded for him to touch it.

As his fingers pressed against the wood of the table, he laughed. "I'll be damned. Feels like it's right here!"

As he pushed on the table, the illusion doubled in complexity. New sensation—touch, not just sight and sound.

Hattie conjured a bowl of fruit onto the table. Her favorite—apples.

"Give it a try," she said, balling fists to maintain focus.

Raymond plucked an apple from the bowl gingerly, then

lifted it to his lips. He took a tentative bite, snapping away the flesh with a tiny spray of juice. He chewed it, then nodded.

"Tastes real," he mumbled around the flesh.

The complexity of the light pinch doubled yet again, hammering down onto Hattie's brain with every chew.

But she kept it all held together.

Alton absentmindedly reached around Raymond to snatch a tea cup Hattie had just stitched into the illusion. A tickle on her lip called attention to the fact that the cost of this illusion was growing dangerously expensive.

Raymond dropped the apple back onto the table, where it disappeared. "You're bleedin' pretty good there, girl. Best pull this all down." He swung his hands around him. "I still can't believe none of this is real. That we're in an empty lot surrounded by crates and lumber beside a warehouse right now!"

As the words escaped his mouth, Raymond's mind probed deeply into the illusion, as if reminding himself that it was all only a dream. His moment of clarity tore through her, threatening to pull down the entire pinch. The illusion snapped taut around Hattie, like a noose around the neck of a body in freefall from the gallows, and she gasped.

Raymond disappeared, dropping out of the illusion.

Hattie clenched her fists so tight that her nails dug into the flesh of her palms. She squeezed her eyes shut, shouting against the sudden weight of reality trying to flay apart her illusion.

And then it stopped.

She opened her eyes to the sunlight. But there was no gravel. No warehouse. No Raymond.

Alton remained in the kitchen, leaning over to read a paper on the table. He looked different. Younger. The kitchen seemed brighter, and she took a long look around at the freshly cleaned cabinet doors, the sparkling floor tiles, and the glass in the windows which was smooth and clear. Wait, this wasn't her kitchen back home, this was someplace else—someplace that had only ever existed in her imagination.

Her father nodded to himself as he ran a hand through his hair. It was thick and full, a light chestnut brown without a hint of gray. His face was lean and firm, filled with youthful vigor. He was a handsome man in his mid-thirties, by the look of it.

"Alton?" a voice called from the living room. "Give us a hand, here?"

Hattie stepped aside as the young version of her father swept past her with a smile blossoming on his face. She followed him into a living room, and gasped at the sight of her mother.

Branna was younger as well. Her round face sat beneath a mop of reddish-blonde hair, spilling out from a loosely gathered bun. She peered up at her husband with glittering emerald eyes and gave him a warm smile.

On the floor between Branna's knees crawled a tiny baby.

"She needs changing," Branna declared. "And I'm due for a whisky."

Hattie released a snicker as her mother gathered the tiny infant to hand her off to Alton. Whisky? When had her mother ever partaken of spirits?

But even as the young woman eased around her husband to plant a kiss on his neck on her way to the sideboard, Hattie knew anything was possible in this illusion. It wasn't a view of the past. It was simply a version of the past that Hattie had created in her mind.

Unlike Raymond, however, knowing this was a dream did nothing to pull her out of it. She lingered in the doorway to the kitchen, watching her father cradle the baby, whispering to it as he reached for a folded diaper on the chair nearby.

"Hey there, little 'Attie! We'll get you sorted."

A tear fell from Hattie's eye as she watched, a smile creasing her cheeks. There was such warmth in this scene, such a sense of family—and of safety. There was no fear that someone would knock on the door and shatter their lives. There was no planning for how they might need to leave in the middle of the night with little notice. There was just love.

Alton cooed to the child, "'Attie. 'Attie."

Behind her, Branna coughed against the whisky. It was a choking cough, as if she'd swallowed too fast and inhaled some of it.

"'Attie. Hattie. Hattie? *Hattie!*"

More coughing. Choking.

Gasping for air.

The kitchen faded into bright sunlight, and the coughing erupted from Hattie's throat.

Raymond loomed overhead, his hand rubbing the sides of her cheeks.

"Hey, baby girl! Come on, now! Breathe! Breathe!"

Hattie sucked in a long gasp, then coughed hard. A spray of blood rose into the air, pelting the side of Raymond's face. Her lungs felt as if they'd been torn apart. Every breath bubbled with blood and bits of tissue. There was not enough air. She couldn't get enough air.

Hattie, panicked, clutching at Raymond's hands as she tried to sit up. She had no strength. Only the trickle of blood flowing down her windpipe and filling her lungs.

Dying. She was dying.

Raymond rolled her onto her side, pounding on her back. "Hattie, breathe!"

She pawed at her chest, tugged at her blouse, pulling it low nearly to the point of ripping stitches. Her fingertips landed against a tiny, hard lump tucked into her brassiere. She pulled it out between heaving gasps, and held it up for Raymond.

He cocked his head at her as he examined it. "What's this?"

His voice was fading, his face blurring as he knelt close. She held up a finger, and tried to drag air into her blood-filled lungs. "One…drop…"

Raymond fumbled with the stopper, his meaty fingers growing misty as she watched him struggling to unscrew the tiny cap. Finally, it came loose, and he lifted the stem and bulb into the air. The bright blue liquid gleamed in the sunlight.

Hattie closed her eyes, trying not to panic at the notion that she was rapidly suffocating on her own blood. Then she tasted something cold and sharp on her tongue, something that shot through her like a bolt of electricity. She closed her mouth and swallowed, trying to hold the precious liquid down along with all the blood in her throat.

Her head spun—but not with the usual nauseating vertigo of magic sickness. It was as if everything was being sucked back to a state of order. The shattered remains of her lungs flew into place with a wave of a Cosmic hand. The blood stopped tickling her throat, easing back into its rightful place with a gentle thump. Her stomach gurgled—that single hunger pang one gets when bacon hits the griddle in the morning. Her fingers tingled, stretching out to run against sharp bits of stone.

She took several calm breaths, then sat upright. Hattie ran a hand under her nose, pulling it back to show it was still bloody. Her nose, her shirt, Raymond's shirt, the gravel around her. It looked like someone had slaughtered a chicken in their midst, but in spite of the mess, she felt fine.

Raymond stoppered the tiny dram and gripped it like a hand grenade. "You…uh, you okay?"

She nodded. "Aye. But that was close."

Close. That was more than close. If she hadn't had that bottle on her, if Raymond hadn't been here to administer it, she would have died.

"What happened?"

She reached for the bottle, and he handed it back to her. "I think I got lost."

"Lost?"

"In my own pinch. Hell of a thing, it was."

He shook his head. "How do you get lost in your own magic?"

Hattie stretched her neck and held out a hand. Raymond helped her to her feet, and she raised her arms to stretch out her back. "It was a fantasy from my imagination, something I didn't want to end."

"Well, if it didn't end, it would'a killed you, so, don't do that again!"

She tucked the elixir back into her top and nodded. She'd never tried Leon's potion herself, determined to save every last drop for her father. It was as potent as he'd promised, and once again she sent out a silent thanks to the water pincher for his generosity.

The warehouse door squealed open, and Tony emerged from the dark interior to snap his hat onto his head. He ducked into his car, started the engine, and drove off at a casual pace. Lizzie stood at the opening watching as the car disappeared around the bend. Then her eyes found Hattie and Raymond in the vacant lot. She approached with an impatient glare. That glare became panic when she spotted the blood on Hattie's face and clothing.

"What in all hell have you both been doing out here?"

"Butchering chickens for supper," Hattie teased. "You two

finally done in there or should Raymond and I go home for the day?"

Lizzie flushed and grumbled something incoherent before leading them back to the warehouse to clean Hattie up. As she followed Liz, Hattie's mind spun with notions. Two of them, to be precise.

First, that the Aqua Vitae was a more useful potion than she'd originally imagined. Not only could it be used to heal her father's lung ailment, it could also be used to right the effects of magic sickness. That removed the upper limit to what Hattie could do. One drop, and she could stitch her wrecked insides back together again and start over. In a moment of desperation, that elixir could prove to be the difference between life and death.

And second, she now had a new weapon in her magical tool bag. Beyond illusions to draw attention away or toward, she could capture someone in a full-world light pinch. How long would it remain in someone's mind once she withdrew her magic? What if she created a world that someone didn't *want* to leave? Would it be like a prison? A den of opium sapping the body of the will to break free? Or would it be like an iron maiden, closing in with spikes of metal dressed in fond memories?

These were dark thoughts, but in times such as these, Hattie took comfort in the notion that she had something as powerful as a Tommy gun, should the need arise.

CHAPTER 4

"Y ou need the car tonight?" Vincent asked Lefty. "Mind if I take her for the evening?"

Lefty shot him a perceptive glance. "Sure. Might walk over to Hudson's on the water, but that's it. Spent too many hours today in this jalopy with your sorry hide."

Vincent grinned. "I'll leave you at the old folks' home. How's that grab ya?"

Lefty showed him a finger as he stepped out of the car and onto the curb in front of his home. Then he pointed at the car. "You scratch this, and you're floating in the Patapsco by sunrise."

Vincent nodded. "Fair's fair."

He watched as Lefty fished a key from his vest pocket to unlock his door. Once he was inside, Vincent hammered down the gas pedal, heading up the street to change for his evening.

Sunday night. Should be music at the Old Moravia. And he knew Ermanno was running the kitchen, so the food would be better than good. He sprinted up the stairs to his second-story apartment and showered off before putting on his charcoal gray suit, the one with pinstripes up the vest. It was an outfit he rarely found a use for. Once the cufflinks were in his sleeves, and he'd combed his hair into a raven wing, he snatched his fedora and trotted downstairs, trying to ignore the knot in his stomach.

He'd never had enough free time to consider having a steady girl, his relationships tending to be with women who made their living entertaining members of the opposite sex. It was easier that way. Vincent never had to explain missing a date because Lefty had shown up to whisk him away for a job. He never had to explain long absences or lie about what he did for a living or cover up the nature of his magic.

But Fern had grown up around the *famiglia*. She knew he worked for the Baltimore Crew, and that he was a pincher. After she'd tracked Vincent down and thanked him for sticking his neck out when Cooper had been hitting her, he'd thought maybe he'd found the perfect woman.

But that was months ago, and tonight was their first date. He'd had no idea the hoops he'd need to jump through, the permissions he'd need to secure just to take the ex-girlfriend of a member of the *famiglia* to dinner. And in the time it took to get the Crew's blessing, that spark he'd felt when they'd talked at the Fontainebleau had long faded, making this feel like an awkward date with a complete stranger.

After all the trouble he'd gone to in securing the necessary approvals, it seemed rather uncouth to cancel, so here he was, driving Lefty's Alfa Romeo, and feeling more like he was going to his execution than to dinner with a beautiful woman.

Several blocks uptown, Vincent parked in front of a white columned home overlooking Druid Hill Lake. This wasn't the two-bit row house he was used to, this was a house built on avarice. Most of the supervisors and managers along the waterfront took up their residence along this avenue. These broad, boxy mansions stood as resolute as a hunk of Sparrows Point steel, in defiance of the rest of the East Coast, in defiance of the old money. The American nobility. This was recent wealth that built angry monuments to its own cupidity.

He'd been surprised when Lefty had told him the Crew owned this mansion in Druid Hill—even more surprised when he'd found out Vito had turned it into a women's boarding house, smack in the middle of the wealthy neighborhood. From the outside, it looked the same as all the other stately homes on the avenue, but in the late summer heat, with all the windows open, the difference became apparent.

Somewhat raucous female laughter emerged from the house along with tinny strains of fast-beat jazz music. He could practically feel the other houses leaning away in disdain.

Vincent gave the bell a ring, and heard a shrieked, high-pitched, "I've got it!"

The door opened and a breathless blonde in a drop-waist dress with a huge bow at the collar ushered him in.

"You Fern's gentleman caller?" Without waiting for a response, the woman turned and shouted behind her. "Girls! Come see what Fernnie hooked on her line! He's a looker!"

Two women raced out from a side parlor, one wearing an asymmetrical skirt with a crisp, white blouse, the other a pleated dress. Their bobbed dark hair was disordered, a faint sheen of perspiration on their foreheads.

"Oh, he *is* a looker!" one exclaimed as the woman who answered the door tore up the stairs shouting for Fern.

"Do you know the Black Bottom?" the other woman asked in a tone of voice that would have made seasoned soldiers spill national secrets.

"Uh, a little," he replied, half afraid to admit he knew the complicated dance that bore some faint resemblance to the Charleston. Vincent had faced down armed gangs. He'd fought another pincher. He'd stared into the fiery eyes of a demon. But nothing was more unsettling and...well, downright terrifying as stepping into this bastion of bold, independent females.

"How many beats before the hip swings?" she demanded. "Is this it? Because Bea says it's not."

The woman twisted her feet to the quick rhythm, knees in and out as her arms undulated in time. Then she slapped her fists on her waist and hopped a tight circle, her hips in wide rotation.

Vincent cleared his throat, hoping that Fern hurried. "Uh, eight more beats of the...of the other...thing. I think. I mean, from the last time I saw.... And your fists need to be lower, I think."

"See!" Bea pointed triumphantly. "I told you!"

The record faded to a stop, and the women dashed back into the parlor, while Vincent sent an imploring glance up the stairs.

Finally, a clacking of footsteps captured Vincent's attention. He turned to find Fern descending the stairs, the blonde woman in tow. She wore a red-and-black gown which fell off one shoulder, pinned by a neat red rosebud atop a spray of baby's breath. Her face was made to perfection, eyes smoky but reserved, lips red but demure. As both women stepped down into the foyer, the blonde reached out and tweaked something on Fern's dress.

"Have fun, Fernnie-girl. And don't do anything I wouldn't do!" She winked and Fern laughed, an attractive pink staining her cheeks.

There was the spark he'd thought was gone. But then the blonde joined her friends in the parlor, and the Fern that turned toward him was beautiful and polished, like a perfect statue, not a trace of joy or emotion at all on her face.

The spark sputtered. Died.

She marched forward gripping a black-beaded clutch in black-gloved hands, lifting one to smooth a tidy curl of brunette hair held tight to her face by a velvet headband.

"Mister Calendo." She gave him a nervous smile. "I am ready for dinner."

It was then that Vincent realized he hadn't removed his hat. He popped it off the back of his head, sending it tumbling in a controlled line into an outstretched palm at his breast. He bowed with a wink.

"You're a sight!"

Her smile softened, reaching her eyes. "Thank you. Shall we?"

He opened the door for her, closing it behind them. She stepped across the portico, then took the few steps to the concrete walkway with Vincent's outstretched elbow in her hand. Once inside the car, and a block clear of the mansion, she released a long sigh.

Vincent eyed her quickly. "You okay?"

She blinked a few times, then nodded, her eyes remaining locked on the road before them.

Vincent cleared his throat. "So, uh…nice digs back there."

"Nicer then I should be able to afford." She shot him a quick sideways glance. "As long as I'm available to help patch up any of the Crew, I don't pay rent."

It wasn't any of his business, but Vincent was glad she wasn't living off some stipend from Cooper. Suddenly the reality of her situation hit him. She'd said her mother had passed, and he got the feeling she had no living family to help her out. A single woman, trying to make enough money to live on her own didn't have many options. It was a good thing she had picked up her mother's nursing skills, or Fern might have found herself having to rent a room in a much less desirable part of town.

His thoughts went to another young woman, one who put on pants and survived by working in a man's world, a smart, confident, strong, capable woman. But Fern wasn't Hattie, and it wasn't fair to compare the two.

"So the three other girls live there?" he asked, trying to focus on the woman next to him. "They seem…nice."

She released a single dry laugh, then shook her head. "There's eight of us, although one is…uh, leaving for other accommodations next week."

"Oh." Vincent set his jaw, knowing exactly what she meant. Was that what Cooper…

But he wasn't going to think about Cooper.

"It's a bit strange living with a group of women. I never had sisters or anything growing up. I always had my own apartment or…well, you know."

Yes, he knew. And he wasn't going to think about that either. Vincent gave his head a quick shake as he turned onto the cross-street. "I'm glad. It's a nice place and you deserve some comfort."

She looked away, staring at the darkening buildings as they passed by and they both fell into an awkward silence for the rest of the drive.

Vincent finally pulled up to the front of the Old Moravia Hotel. One of the valets approached, but stopped short as he spotted Vincent exiting the driver's side door. Vincent gave him a stern glare and tossed the keys to him. Even though he was Vito Corbi's only pincher, the Capo barely offered Vincent any more recognition than these valets. They knew it, too, and were used to seeing Vincent pop out of that same car with Lefty, his handler, not a beautiful woman—a woman who had until recently been attached to one of the actual *famiglia*.

That thought gave him a moment of pause. But Vincent couldn't worry about that. Not tonight. This was his first official date with Fern, since he'd ironed things out with Vito and Cooper. "Ironed" might have been a charitable way of putting it. There were, in fact, several wrinkles left in the fabric. One, that Vincent had effectively strong-armed Cooper away from Fern. Two, Vincent's lack of standing among the Crew. He was a tool, simply and completely. He was owned, not even considered a person, let alone part of the *famiglia*. He was not allowed to take the oaths to the Capo. There was simply no need. He was the property of the Crew, not a member.

Which was strangely the reason Vincent was here with Fern tonight. It was against the dogma of the family to poach a woman from another member of the Crew. As Vincent wasn't actually a member, he'd taken no oath, and thus had broken no such taboo. But when it came down to it, the real reason he was "allowed" to be here tonight with Fern was because no one liked Cooper. The man was a pig, and every woman he kept in his clutches would end up with fresh bruises of one sort or another. The Crew had always looked the other way. Vincent had been the first to call Cooper to account for his behavior.

And in a sheer stroke of luck, he'd survived performing what had basically been an assault upon a made member of the Crew.

This was his first public appearance with Fern on his arm. He'd chosen the Old Moravia specifically for this reason. He needed to demonstrate his autonomy in front of the others. If Vincent were ever to gain their respect, he'd have to seize it for himself, to show them he was more than just a well-trained attack dog, and that he deserved respect.

It had seemed like a good plan at the time, but now, he

wondered if he'd made a mistake. Perhaps a quiet, lesser known venue would have been a better.

He waited by the curb as the second valet guided Fern to the front of the hotel. With a nod, Vincent offered his elbow once again, and the two stepped through the brass-and-glass double doors of the hotel.

They were greeted immediately by the swells of fat, languid music. This wasn't the up-tempo beat of Fern's roommates or the music of Saturday night. No, this was Sunday. Older couples gathered at the hotel restaurant, tucked beneath potted palms and brass sculptures, indulging in the slow sounds of twanging bass and tenor sax as decadent as the food.

The maître d' nodded to Vincent, offering him a grin of recognition if nothing else. Still, Vincent had left nothing to chance. A reservation was waiting for them, and unless the Crew intended to openly disrespect its pincher, they should be guided to a table shortly.

They were.

Vincent moved to hold Fern's chair, but the maître d' beat him to the punch. Vincent returned a stiff nod as the man withdrew, and removed his hat, only to realize he had no one to offer it to. Deciding to slip it underneath his seat, he took his place across the tiny two-top from Fern.

She watched him, her soft eyes sparkling in the candlelight. The smell of seared beef and lamb swelled around them, mixing with the fume of cigar smoke and the pulse of the band on the opposite end of the hotel lobby.

Vincent smiled at Fern, searching for something to say.

"So, uh…here we are."

Her smile opened enough to reveal pearly-white teeth. "Yes. Here we are."

The waiter arrived with three menus…one each for food, and one for the wine. He offered the wine list to Vincent, who eyed it with trepidation. If a lifetime in the service of the mob had taught Vincent anything, it was to appear more confident than he actually felt. And as such, he sent a calm finger down the list until it found a Meritage from a vineyard in Havre de Grace.

Vito's vineyard. He ordered the wine, sending the waiter scurrying along. Again, he peered over the flickering candle at Fern.

"You look really nice," he announced, wincing at his clumsy verbiage.

She nodded. "I do like that suit you have on. It's sharp. You should wear it more often."

He replied, "Maybe I will."

A blush rose to her cheeks as she looked down to the table, inspecting the menu. Her eyes ran up and down the list quickly, rising again to take in the scene.

Vincent, for his part, found the menu to be utterly baffling. He'd eaten steak before, and there it was. Steak. Hard to mistake that. Everything else, on the other hand, was another language. Vincent knew that people ate duck…he simply hadn't had the opportunity. Nor was he likely to try it for the first time in front of Fern, in case he found duck to be unsettling in his stomach.

When the waiter returned, he opened a green-glassed bottle with several quick twists of a corkscrew. They were practiced motions, and Vincent wondered if waiters wouldn't be formidable opponents in back-alley knife fights. The man poured a finger of the red wine into his glass, then lingered with heavy eyes on Vincent.

Vincent took a moment, then realized the waiter expected some kind of response.

Lefty had brought him to proper dinners here perhaps twice in the six years they'd spent together. He dove deep into those memories to determine the next course of action.

Vincent lifted the glass, smelled it, then took a sip. He nodded to the server, who poured Fern a full glass, then Vincent before setting the bottle onto the table. When Lefty'd done it, the action had seemed like afterthoughts, as if he needn't even pause the conversation to go through these motions. Indeed, Lefty hadn't. This was normal for Lefty. This was far from normal for him.

Fern reached across the table with her goblet, holding it to the light.

"To the family," she declared.

Vincent took the glass and chimed it against hers. "The family."

They both took a sip. As Vincent set the glass back down, he spotted a table or two nodding in approval nearby. Thank God for Fern, he mused.

"So," Vincent said, "have you settled in?"

"Hmm?"

"The new address."

Her brow shot high, then she nodded. "Yes, I have. There's a matron there who is supposed to answer the door and look after us, but I think she's deaf. She rarely comes out of the back rooms unless it's to bring out a meal. Bea jokes that if she died back there, we wouldn't realize it for a week."

He chuckled. "At least a deaf matron means you can play the music without someone yelling at you to turn it down."

"True, although the neighbors do plenty of that. Actually, they don't yell, they just stand in their yards and glare at us. And you? Still at the old apartment?"

He nodded. Yes, he was still in the old apartment—the one in which she'd nursed him back to health. That one with three rooms—four, if you counted the bathroom. Unless the Crew decided to increase his stipend, that would be his address for some time to come.

"Are you practicing medicine now?" he asked. "You said you were taking care of us in a more formal arrangement?"

She laughed. "I've never practiced medicine." Before he could contradict her, she continued, "But yes, I stitch up knife wounds and take care of a broken bone here or there. Time to time I'll see to a poor fella who's taken a bullet."

"I'm glad. I owe my life to you." He shook his head at his own grandiose pronouncement. This was dinner...not the burial of some Viking king. "I mean..."

"I know what you mean." She nodded. "My mother taught me what she could after..." Her eyes drifted.

"The War," Vincent stated, more to continue her sentence than to ask.

She nodded stiffly, returning all of her attention to the wine. "And what about you? Was your father in the War?"

Vincent set his jaw.

Fern's eyes shot wide for a split-second, and she covered her mouth with her fingertips. "Oh...I am so sorry."

"No sweat there."

"I wasn't thinking," she insisted with a tilt of her head.

Vincent sighed. "Truth is, I have no idea. Maybe he was, maybe he wasn't. No clue if he's alive or dead. Whatever. It doesn't really matter, you know?"

Fern nodded, then buried her nose into the wine goblet.

Damn. Vincent had assumed this would be a safe subject, but on retrospect perhaps bringing up the War wasn't the best idea for a dinner date.

"Moving on," she declared with renewed composure. "What have you been up to these past few months?"

"Well, there's problems everywhere. Bootleggers from the mountains trying to run product around Baltimore and go direct. Grumblings in New York about who owns what and where. And now there's these Russians."

She cringed. "I meant...I didn't mean business."

He clenched his jaw for a brief second before answering. "That's pretty much all I do, Fern. Business."

"Oh." She picked at the tablecloth. "I just…should I even know the details of these things? Should you be telling me about this?"

He took a breath and let it out. How the hell would any relationship work if he couldn't talk about business? What were they supposed to talk about? The weather?

"It's been a hot summer," she offered. "We could sure use some rain."

The weather. "Yes, very hot." He searched for something else. "Did you see that pothole on Light Street? Someone needs to fix that thing."

"No, I didn't see it."

Silence fell. Vincent eyed his wine, wondering if he'd suddenly become more witty and articulate if he slugged it down. Probably not.

Fern sighed, then bit her lip. "Okay, business then. So you were saying something about Russians?"

He struggled, trying to find something else to discuss and coming up empty. Maybe if he kept it all vague, she'd be okay with it. "Yeah, thought we'd taken care of the Russian situation, but now I'm wondering if that's not the case."

The Russians. That was a memory Vincent had hoped to bury. Last year there had been an incident that had sparked a brief and bloody feud which ended with a whole lot of dead Russians and no dead Italians. It had been quick, violent, and when it was over the Baltimore Crew was the last mob standing. The fighting over those three months had been the final act of Vito's consolidation of power. Though the full extent of his control was still questioned in the shadows, it had never since been outright challenged.

The brief turf war was one thing, but that first incident? That haunted him. Yakov Dmitrivich had done some work for the Crew and had been caught with his hand in the till. Just a little bit of embezzlement, but Vito wasn't known for giving second chances to non-*famiglia*. The only problem had been that Yakov lived in a building filled with the Bratva—the Russian Brotherhood, and they weren't likely to hand him over without a fight.

So Vincent had frozen time, and there had been a slaughter. And over the next few months, there had been a whole lot of slaughtering, all of it aided by the Crew's time pincher.

He'd done his job, and he'd done it well. But that didn't help him sleep any better at night.

Vincent released a discreet sigh and forced a smile. "But enough about me, what about you? What's been in your bonnet these past few months?"

"Well, I've been patching up a few men here and there. I can't really go out much, because I have to be available and easy to locate in case I need to provide medical care."

He grimaced. "Surely you can go out sometimes? Let someone know where you are?"

Fern paled and sipped her wine, not offering a reply. Vincent suddenly imagined what would happen if one of the Crew pulled up to that mansion with an emergency that needed Fern, only to have to go haring all over the city looking for her. That…that would not be a pleasant exchange when they finally found her.

But still, did she have to be a virtual prisoner?

"You want me to talk to someone? I could," Vincent pressed.

"It's fine," she said.

Silence fell over the table, broken by the welcome arrival of the server asking for their order.

Vincent froze. It was customary for a gentleman to order for his lady, but they hadn't discussed the menu yet. Or, was he expected to just know what she'd want? His stomach gripped in a moment of panic as the server eyed him with thinning patience.

He reviewed the menu once again. The only dishes he recognized happened to be the most expensive.

"So, what're you thinking?" he asked Fern, venturing her opinion.

"Whatever you like is fine. You choose."

Wonderful. No help from her at all. Vincent took a breath and ordered a brie en croute as a starter and lamb for mains, hoping she ate lamb. Once the waiter disappeared, Vincent took another stab at conversation.

"You like the wine?"

"It's fine."

Vincent balled his toes inside his shoe, hiding a wince as he tried to keep the conversation moving along. "It comes from the Capo's vineyard."

"I know," she said with a hollow stare. "I was there."

"Oh. Right." Another unpleasant memory. That was the day she'd tossed him under the train. How much of that had been loyalty to Cooper, and how much had been fear, Vincent wasn't sure.

The arrival of food did nothing to improve the conversation. Every attempt at small talk was met with flat charm. Every effort at deeper conversation was met with dismissive silence. Everything was "fine." By the time they'd finished their mains, and Fern had excused herself to powder her nose, Vincent was left with the notion that she was bored... and so was he.

He peered around the atrium restaurant. So many familiar faces, though these were the Old Guard. Proud members of the Baltimore Crew, who remembered a time before Vito Corbi had taken the reins. They remembered Jim D'Urso, and the empire he'd scraped together with his own hands. Vito's tenure was still relatively new, by their reckoning. When they made eye contact with Vincent, he found little more than disdain. No one took him seriously among the Crew. Many probably felt it unseemly that he would spend outlandish amounts of money here, in their temple, dining a woman who had belonged to one of their own.

Vincent rubbed his forehead. This dinner was painfully expensive. What was he thinking? He could have taken Fern to any hole-in-the-wall. This had been as much about his standing among the family as it was about getting to know her, and he'd failed on both accounts.

When Fern returned, she pulled her chair around the table to sit closer to Vincent. He lifted his brow but said nothing. As the woman took a seat, she wound her hand around his arm, squeezing it tight.

Huh. Perhaps this wasn't a failed evening, after all.

"Dessert?" he offered.

She didn't respond. Instead, she just sat tight-jawed, staring at the candle as her grip tightened.

"What's wrong?" he asked.

"We should leave," she whispered.

Vincent repeated his question, peering over his shoulder at the path she'd taken through the hotel atrium. Near the wood-carved bar tucked into the side room Vincent spotted a ruddy-faced man nursing a martini glass. He scowled as his eyes latched onto Vincent's.

Cooper.

Beside him was a well-dressed man with a beak-like nose, gesturing with a glass as he made his way through what appeared to be a thick conversation. Cooper's eyes left that conversation as they bore into Vincent.

"Did he say something to you?" he snarled.

"No. But we should go."

Vincent nodded, then signaled for the bill. He tossed down more dollars than he'd been prepared to spend that night, then pulled Fern's chair for her. As they left the atrium, he shot a steady glare back at Cooper, who turned back to the fellow chewing his ear.

The mood inside the car was quiet and tense. Vincent knew better than to attempt to draw out the evening. Instead, he returned Fern to the mansion, and walked her to the door.

"Thank you for a lovely evening," she stated, leaning forward to kiss his cheek.

"Sure," he said. "I'll see you around."

Vincent returned Lefty's car, parking it on the street in front of his house and walking the rest of the way home in the humid night air. What a bust this whole evening had been. Frustration and indignation swirled inside Vincent's chest as he thought about Cooper. There was no sensible way to remove him from the situation. Cooper was Crew. He was there to stay.

Vincent grinned as he wondered if the Russians couldn't start back in the gambling business, just to put the boot to Cooper's gambling parlor. Maybe *they'd* remove Cooper from the situation?

Such dark thoughts evaporated as Vincent spotted a familiar Model T Runabout swinging down the lane. A young red-haired woman drove the truck past Vincent, not spotting him.

Hattie Malloy.

She'd be on her way to that warehouse of Lizzie Sadler's, probably returning from some liquor run up the Chesapeake. He was to have another meeting with her next week, and the remembrance lightened Vincent's mood. Hattie was a stubborn Irish river rat with spunk and a quick temper. Conversations with her were occasionally contentious, but he'd laughed more in the time he spent with her than he had in the sum total of his life. With Hattie he could talk about what it was like to be a pincher, about the Crew's business. She infuriated him, and sometimes left him speechless with her bold wit, but she was never boring. With her, he never had to resort to conversing about the weather, or the potholes on Light Street.

He'd just seen her a week ago, but found himself longing for next Sunday. Maybe he didn't have to wait for next Sunday. After all, he actually had some information, for a change. A demon in Amish country, possibly the location of a Hell pincher who could explain this strange bond between Vincent and that headstrong light pincher.

That surely warranted moving their meeting up a bit.

CHAPTER 5

*B*y Tuesday, a cold front brought a solid morning of rain to the city. The skies had only just cleared as Hattie exited her house to walk downtown. Side-stepping a puddle gathering in the mud in front of the pharmacy on Light Street, she sneered thinking on how long it'd taken her to choose her clothes that morning. It was a rainy mid-week afternoon, and the mud would be everywhere. There were no Bay runs for the Crew that day, but it made no sense to bother with one of her dresses. No sense whatsoever.

All she was doing was meeting with Vincent.

He'd left a message with Lizzie by way of a courier. Apparently, he'd made some progress on their personal inquiries so it would be an interesting meeting with the time pincher. Although if she were to be completely honest with herself, every meeting with him was interesting.

To date, their rendezvous had mostly consisted of spirited conversation peppered with speculation. Sometimes Vincent would go on and on about the "connection" they had, wondering how it was that they were immune to each other's powers when that had never been the case with any other pinchers he'd heard of. Did it have something to do with their particular abilities? Or did the mutual immunity have to do with that demon down in Deitaville? Vincent always seemed far more invested in this whole thing than she was. Although…she'd looked into that creature's eyes. She'd seen something vast, endless, celestial. There was beauty within that tortured being of flesh and flame.

Maybe she was just as invested as Vincent, after all.

In her reverie, she wandered near the edge of the street just as a car came swinging around the corner. Its tires slashed into one of the puddles pooling up in the muddy street. Hattie sucked in a breath as a wave of filthy water sprayed into the air. She clamped her eyes shut and turned her face.

The sounds on the street muffled, pulled long and dark like rubber. Then silence. Nothing but her heartbeat. The air was suddenly thick, nearly unbreathable. Hattie smiled. She hadn't felt this sensation for months. Not since Deltaville.

When she opened her eyes, she found the muddy water had crystallized in midair. Rather than a sheet of muck, the water glistened like tiny diamond beads hanging on invisible strings from the sky. The car stood still as a statue, its driver squinting through thick glasses at the street ahead. And just past the arch of suspended puddle water stood a dark-haired man in a gray suit and hat, hands in his vests pockets, a playful smirk painted on his face.

Hattie tried to say something, but her voice couldn't manage anything more than a muffled gurgle. She rolled her eyes and nodded. Right. Can't talk inside one of Vincent's time bubbles.

Stepping past the splash that would have doomed her to misery for the rest of the day, she wove around an older couple walking arm-in-arm, then stood before Vincent with a cock of her hip and a lift of her brow.

He took a hand from his vest pocket to hold it for a second in the air, then snapped his fingers.

The water careened over the side of the road, reaching clear across to the building. Car engines roared to life. The older couple continued their stroll, pausing as the mud washed along their path.

"I suppose I should thank you for that," Hattie said.

Vincent shrugged. "I'm just bein' a gentleman over here. They don't hand out medals for that sorta thing."

"Well, boy-o, you're my hero for the day then."

He chuckled and turned to walk alongside her as they approached a café. The outdoor seats were still beaded with rainwater from the morning's downpour, and the owners hadn't made an effort clean them off. Hattie suggested they move on, but Vincent held out a hand for her to wait. He stepped inside the café for only a minute, after which two young men hopped out with towels to wipe one of the tables dry, along with two chairs. Once they were done, Vincent held a chair out for Hattie, who took a seat with a snicker.

"I hope you didn't threaten their families, or anything," she said.

Vincent sat across from her, pulled off his hat to hang it on a chair post nearby, then shook his head. "I don't play with people's families. That's dirty work. No stomach for that sorta thing."

"Good to know." She knew better than to press the issue of family further. That was a raw nerve she had no interest in poking.

They ordered coffee from one of the panicked young men. When Vincent offered to pay for it, Hattie added a scone to the order. His eyes widened with the barest flicker of alarm, and she regretted the move immediately.

"No, forget the scone," she told the waiter.

"Bring the scone," Vincent told the man.

"I changed my mind. I don't want it."

"You do, or you wouldn't have ordered it."

The waiter's head was swiveling back and forth. Hattie resisted the urge to smother Vincent with her napkin. Drat the man. Here she was trying to let him save face, but his stupid pride wouldn't allow him to take the gracious out.

"I don't *want* the scone," she ground out.

"Well, you're *getting* the scone."

She fixed him with a glare. "If that scone shows up on this table, it's going right up your nose, boy-o."

The waiter sucked in a breath. She saw the corner of Vincent's mouth twitch up before he clamped his lips down tight.

"Fine. No scone. And can we possibly have one conversation where you don't get your knickers in a twist and threaten me with bodily harm? Just one?"

She sat back at batted her eyelashes at him. "Well, okay. Just this once. And only because I'm not wearing any knickers."

The waiter took off as if she'd set him on fire. Vincent's cheeks flushed, a disconcerted expression on his face. Hattie grinned.

"I...you aren't serious, are you? No! Don't tell me." He waved his hands in front of his face and shut his eyes tight. "I don't want to know."

"You sure?" she asked.

He sputtered, then opened his eyes and started to laugh. "What, are you going to show me, right here on the street in front of the café? Wait, don't answer that."

"You're adorable when you're flustered, you know?" She smirked. "So, time pincher, how's life in your corner of the city?"

He began by telling her about an issue at one of the gaming establishments, then went on about a situation in

New York that was rapidly escalating. The tension fell from his shoulders, the lines around his mouth easing as he spoke. By the second cup of coffee, he was imitating Lefty making a fuss over some subpar chowder, waving his hand around and duplicating the other man's dour tone and expression.

Hattie wiped the tears from her eyes, trying to catch her breath from laughing. "You shoulda been an actor. Either on stage, or the new talkies I hear about. You'd a been famous."

"Valentino famous?" he teased. "Probably not. I don't have his looks."

She opened her mouth to contradict him, then thought better. The man had a big enough head without her inflating it further. Although as she'd gotten to know him, she'd realized that his cocksure attitude didn't extend much beyond his pincher abilities.

"You'd have held your own," she told him instead.

His smile turned wistful. "Maybe if things had been different. What about you?"

"Me?" She shrugged. "I'm happy with what I do. I like being on the water, and working with Lizzie and Raymond. Can't imagine anything I'd rather do than be a boat-legger."

He reached over across the table and tapped the end of her nose with his finger. "Well, wear a hat then, girl. You've got a touch of sunburn."

She rolled her eyes. "I do wear a hat. It's the curse of Irish skin. Sunburn and freckles everywhere."

"Everywhere?" he teased.

And now she was the one flustered and choking on her coffee. "Wouldn't *you* like to know, mister."

He grinned, leaning back in his chair and cradling his cup of coffee in his hands. "Yes, I would. They're cute. I like freckles."

And now her whole face probably looked like it was sunburned. Her eyes met his and they both smiled, something warm and electric sparking through the air between them.

"More coffee?" the waiter asked, breaking the spell. Vincent nodded, and the man filled both cups to the brim, checking to make sure they had adequate sugar and cream on hand.

"So, time pincher," Hattie said once the waiter had left, "what's all this exciting news you were hinting at in your note?"

Vincent thumped his hand down onto the table for effect. "Right. So, there's a new pincher up in Philly by the name of Arnoud. I've been nosing around the campfire, digging up rumors and such. Most of it was bushwa, but time-to-time I got a nugget."

"What, you talk to people? Complete sentences and everything? Amazing."

He crossed his arms, leaned back, and with an exaggerated sigh asked, "You done?"

"Not even remotely."

"Anyway, this Arnoud let slip some details about a run-in with a sort of demon up in Pennsylvania. So, I decided to pay him a visit."

"And it turned out," she said, wiggling her eyebrows with conspiratorial mirth, "he was no more than a drunk old bastard who'd gotten pissed on country wine and was seein' things. Am I right?"

Vincent chuckled. "Not quite. He's a touch pincher, according to DeBarre."

"And who's he, then?" she asked.

"The old guard. Philly's original pincher. Met the man a while back. Good enough fella, though I think he and Lefty both got their charm from St. Cecilia's Finishing School and Knife Fighting Academy for Sour-pussed Heels."

Hattie nearly choked on her coffee. She set it back onto

the table gingerly, and leaned forward. "Is this Arnold for real, then?"

"Arnoud. I think he's from Canada, maybe. Anyways, yeah. This guy doesn't look like the type to spin a yarn."

"So, either he's real or he's insane."

Vincent nodded. "And he's no one either of us want to cross. Trust me on that count."

Hattie laughed. "Hell, boy-o. I've trusted you with plenty already."

His face darkened, and he unfolded his arms to lean in. "On that point, there's something you should know."

She took a breath and braced for whatever could draw him so quickly out of his good mood.

Vincent cleared his throat. "There's some heat out on the streets, right now. Things aren't so settled in the city as we'd like. It's probably best if you keep your head down, you know?"

"Head down?" she repeated.

"Up the coast, the families are getting some push-back from the Russians."

Hattie squinted. Russians. Bratva. "Is that a fact?" she whispered. "I thought you people put a good drubbing to those Russians a year or so ago."

Vincent closed his eyes. "Yeah. We did."

When he opened his eyes, they seemed more haunted than usual. Hattie sipped her coffee, letting the moment pass.

Vincent continued as he gathered himself, "Which is why it's not so much a problem in Baltimore. Up to New York? P.A.? Not as quiet."

"Well, if it's out of state, then what's with this storm crow harangue?"

"Problem is that when the heat gets turned up, the families start looking hard for pinchers."

Hattie's smirk faded. "Oh."

Vincent nodded. "Vito's trying to find pinchers through the usual back channels, but there are none to be had. Word is, there's a buyer's market on pinchers, so, free elements such as yourself are in demand." He added in a softer tone, "I want you to keep your light pinching to a bare minimum. You understand?"

She rolled the thought around a bit as cars passed on the street. "But there's nothing specific, eh? Vito hasn't put out a fresh new crusade?"

Vincent shook his head.

Hattie grinned. "Then you're just fretting your pretty little head over me, aren't you? Awwww. That's sweet."

Vincent pulled the spoon from his saucer and tossed it in Hattie's direction, drawing a squawk from her throat.

Then the jollity had drained from his face again. "The Crew will be on the lookout, though. If you're going to stay a free pincher, you'll need to keep your eyes peeled and your shoes light."

She bit her lip. "And if I don't?"

"Well then, we'd be happy to welcome you into the Baltimore Crew," he teased. "Shall I go over the many benefits again?"

"No," she drawled. "Your recruitment pitch is still shite. I thought you were working on that?"

He rolled his eyes. "Haven't found another free pincher to try one out on."

"Maybe you should send off for one of those Dale Carnegie courses?"

"I only had the one spoon to throw at you, but I'm sure there's more inside."

He moved to stand, and she kicked him under the table. They laughed together, then they caught their breath together. And then, came silence. It was weird and heavy and full of something neither one of them wanted to face at the moment.

Hattie cleared her throat, shifting awkwardly in her chair. "You really don't want me working for the Crew, do you?"

He glanced up at her with an odd smile. "That would be... a disaster."

"Agreed. Maybe I don't want *you* working for the Crew, either?" she added softly.

Vincent sighed, and she lifted her hands.

"Alright," she grumbled. "I know, I know. Something about having a purpose and the way things are, the way they should be. And none of that applies to me, but only to you."

"Yep."

She wrinkled her nose. "I'm thinking you're holding out for something better than a lowly light pincher, anyway. One of those mind readers maybe? Or like that crazy fool down in Virginia only less crazy?"

"Hattie, you're not lowly, and you're far more than just a light pincher." He ran his hands over his face. "You're...scary. Alright? What you do is so much more than illusions. It's... scary," he repeated.

She closed her mouth.

Vincent continued, "You're probably the second-most terrifying pincher I've ever met. Myself included."

"Who's the first, then?"

His eyes narrowed but he didn't reply.

"What about you, then?" she offered. "One second, everything's peaches, and then the next, you've done whatever it is you want to do to a person while you've pinched time. Something could happen at any moment, and a person would never see it coming, never have a moment to react or defend himself. I don't think you fully grasp how intimidating that can be to the rest of us."

He nodded. "I have, actually."

She watched him with interest.

Vincent returned her gaze. "But when it comes down to it I just stop time. You manipulate all five senses, not just light, not just visual illusion. When…whatever it was happened to the two of us in Deltaville? Those men. Those Upright Citizens thugs." His face blanched.

She crossed her arms and stared at her knees. "Aye." After a long silence, she added, "Even I don't know exactly what I did to those poor bastards. I gave them a nightmare come to life, but the source was their own fears, not what mine would have been."

Which meant she'd unconsciously read their minds. It was a disturbing thought. Vincent withdrew into personal contemplation, and Hattie afforded herself a measure of the same.

How could anyone hope to defend themselves, when their own mind had been stolen? That was what her illusion had done that night at Deltaville. That's the potential she had. She stole someone's senses away, twisted them and made them into what she wanted. And with the new immersive style of illusion that she'd been honing with Raymond down at Locust Point, it all begged the question of whether she was, indeed, perfecting some manner of evil.

And with the Aqua Vitae, that evil could be boundless.

That was a notion that broke her out of her own thoughts. Hattie peered over to Vincent. He'd suffered at the hands of his own magic, as did any pincher. Magic came with a cost, and a nasty cost at that. But for her to let him use this magical elixir that Leon had provided for her father's health? That would tip the balance of power unnecessarily.

She genuinely liked Vincent. He was by any reasonable measure a "good man." He acted out of a center of self-managed morality. And even *he* knew that he served masters who controlled and dominated and abused people. The facile justifications he'd attempted to perfect in pitch? That was all, as he liked to put it, "bushwa." She knew that deep down, he too believed that.

Which was why Vincent should never have access to that elixir.

He was a man owned. Vito Corbi literally owned the man. Perhaps not in a legal sense, but in every sense that actually mattered in these times. And he'd own Hattie if she let slip her true nature.

"I...need to tell you something," Vincent whispered.

Hattie leaned in.

Vincent roughed up his hair with his fingertips, then smoothed it back down again, gathering his thoughts as Hattie's trepidation grew.

Then he told her everything about the Russians. About how a young thief had sparked what had turned into a war, about the lives he'd taken, both directly and indirectly. He told her how that young thief's death haunted him, such a steep price to pay for a few dollars pilfered here and there.

Hattie watched him as he spoke, simply taking it all in. He'd told her about other incidents before, like the one in West Virginia where a young boy, their informant, had mistakenly got caught in the crossfire and died, but *this* felt like some manner of confession. As sympathetic as she was, Hattie felt ill-equipped to offer him any absolution. When Vincent staggered his way to a conclusion, he peered over the table at her with uncertain eyes.

"So?" he mumbled.

"I don't know what you want me to say. You're a gangster, Vincent. I knew that all along. The fact that you've made such an agony over these lives you've taken...well, if anything that tells me there's a bright and shining soul somewhere beneath those shirtsleeves."

A smile of relief arose on his lips.

She nodded. "I'll never judge a man for hating death. Quite the opposite. If you ever feel comfortable with't, then you let me know. I'll smack you hard."

"I will."

She shifted in her seat and needlessly rearranged her coffee cup and saucer. Vincent followed suit, defusing the moment.

Then Hattie looked up and chirped, "Well?"

"Well?" he parroted.

"What's next with this Amish demon?"

He shrugged. "I figured maybe when we get a moment, you and I could take a drive?"

Her lips curled into a devious smile. "Why, you old dog."

"Not…not like that," he stammered.

"No, you've gone and put it out there." She crossed her arms again. "You're practically salivating at the thought of getting me all to yourself. Alone. In a car. Where you'll conveniently get lost down some isolated road and proceed to take advantage of my virtuous self."

He scowled. "You done?"

"Not even remotely, boy-o."

They continued to banter until the waiters were surely thinking they would stay for dinner, then concluded their business with a handshake, and a resolution to meet back in a week to discuss the details of their road trip. For all of Hattie's poking, she felt fine with the arrangement. Strangely, she'd come to trust this gangster. It wasn't the fact he'd promised not to out her to the Crew. It wasn't his striking good looks. It wasn't even that boyish genuineness that emanated from the man like waves of righteous charisma from a holy saint.

It was his complete lack of guile. The man couldn't lie to save his own skin. He knew a thing or two, and he believed in far more things than he knew. That made him an idealist.

It also made him superbly easy to read.

As Hattie walked home, she thought about Vincent. His finely-chiseled Italian features. That mop of straight black hair that always found its way out from underneath his hat. He *was* the Valentino sort, she concluded, just as she spotted Raymond sitting in the Runabout in front of her house.

Hattie trotted up to the driver's side window.

"Hey," she grinned. "What's the skinny?"

Raymond replied, "Last minute run. Sorry, baby girl. We got work."

"Fine by me," she chimed. "Let me tell the folks and change clothes, and I'll be back down."

Raymond drove her down to Locust Point, where Lizzie was outside guiding a truck into the warehouse. It was laden with barrels of…something. Raymond parked the truck by the front, and the two stepped around the Crew's delivery goons to find Lizzie barking orders.

"Fresh delivery?" Hattie asked over the noise of the engine now well inside the warehouse door.

Lizzie nodded. "Last minute. I know it's your day off. I'll pay you five percent bonus."

Hattie squinted. "Make it ten."

Lizzie sighed. "We'll call it two dollars extra, and I don't put a deadline on it. How's that sail?"

Hattie nodded. "How many barrels? Can we use Winnow's Slip?"

"Ten barrels," Lizzie shouted over the truck engine, turning to slap the side of the vehicle before its driver ran over a pallet. "Raymond's boat should be enough."

"Fine, then."

"By the way," Lizzie called as Hattie turned away. "You have a package in my office."

"What?" Hattie blinked in surprise.

"Package. In my office."

She lingered for a moment, then turned with a nod to Liz. Vincent had taken to sending messages to the Locust Point warehouse by way of personal courier. Neither of them wanted Lizzie to know how deeply she'd stitched herself into affairs with one of the Crew. The arrangement worked.

Inside Liz's office, now a chaotic trash heap of paperwork and packing material tossed aside from bottle drops, Hattie found a tiny brown-paper-wrapped parcel tied up in twine.

She examined the parcel with a faint grin. Vincent had to have sent this prior to their meeting. What was that man up to?

Hattie pulled loose the twine and thumbed open the brown paper. Within she found a tiny folded card on white stock. She held it up to the daylight spilling in from the open warehouse door and unfolded it.

The writing was bold and florid. Neat calligraphy in ink. The handwriting presented a sort of refinement Hattie hadn't seen in any of Vincent's letters.

No…this wasn't from Vincent.

She squinted at the letter, taking in the words:

Did you get lost in your own illusion?

Hattie gasped and nearly dropped the note. Who…how?

She lifted the note again to read the second line. It wasn't any sort of English she recognized. Indeed, the glyphs seemed somewhat familiar, but she couldn't understand it.

Γνῶθι Σεαυτόν

The note quivered in her trembling hand.

Who sent this?

There was no signature. Nothing to indicate whether this was a message of warning, or a threat? Or was this friendly?

Regardless of its intention, Hattie realized as she peered out over the business within the warehouse, that someone was watching her.

And they knew what she was.

CHAPTER 6

Vincent inspected his eye shadow in the mirror, feathering the edge of his left eye with the pad of his pinky. Just dark enough to look haunted, but not so dark that it looked like stage makeup—which, of course, it was. He snatched the fez from its stand behind him, bending slightly to settle it upon his head in the cramped broom closet that doubled as his changing room. With a final adjustment of his jacket, he gave himself one last look.

He waved a hand in a tidy circle in front of his sternum, declaring with a mysterious squint, "I am...Damir."

He tried the word a few more times to get the R rolling properly.

With a confident nod, he muttered, "Showtime."

Stepped through the red velvet curtains covering the door to his changing closet, Vincent sized up the gathering at his séance table. This was always a moment of rapid calculation for him—the first face-to-face. He simultaneously had to portray the best, most mysterious first impression as a Levantine mystic, all while gauging the customers' level of skepticism. The old ladies were typically easy to convince. Often times, he'd find a young man or woman at his table, brought in by the word-of-mouth advertising he relied on. The younger ones tended to hold him to higher account, but he knew how to play the game.

Anyone who picked up on his former clients' referral would have been instructed to bring with them the name of their dearly departed written on a slip of paper somewhere on their person, and a personal item. They were advised to keep these "tethers to the living" hidden away in a purse, or a pocket. Easy pickings, if one could stop time and rummage through aforementioned purses and pockets.

Tonight's crowd consisted of two elderly women, one white and one black, and a well-heeled young man with a hawk's beak for a nose and brown hair slicked back against his scalp. His grooming was immaculate. Manicure. Shoes with a high spit-shine. His ice-blue eyes followed Vincent as he stepped into the room with his typical flourish, a thin brow lifting in consideration.

Vincent pinned this fellow to the front of his brain, then cleared his throat to begin his theater.

"Good ev-en-ing, I am the Great Damir. I am the purveyor of the Secret Knowledge. The keeper of the Hidden Flame. I see beyond the veil between the living, and the dead."

The two women seemed to have swallowed the hook, but the man folded his fingers together as the corner of his mouth lifted.

Vincent's faux Arabic accent faltered just a hair as those crystal glacier eyes peered through him, but he collected himself with a half-turn toward the shaded window.

"The mysteries of the beyond, the realm of the dead. You are all seekers, are you not? You have loved ones who have passed beyond our mortal prison." He lifted a theatrical hand to his temple, squinted, then nodded to some ancient voice calling from planet Cockamamy. "Yes. I see this. Each of you have an item. Is this true?"

The women nodded.

Vincent cast a quick glance at the man. He unfolded his fingers, then sighed. "Shall we kneel together at the altar of eternity?"

He took a seat at the table, palms flat against the surface, then began his chant.

"Al…leppo. Al…manna. Al…Jeddah. Khartoum." The tiniest of noises came from the man to Vincent's left. A sniffle? Perhaps even a stifled snicker?

This wasn't going to be a good night, Vincent could tell. Still, though. Even if this young man was a dyed-in-the-wool skeptic, Vincent had one more trick to pull—real magic.

As he throated the chant into increasing frenzy, the wide-eyed women stiffened, easing away from the table. With their tension at a peak, Vincent hammered his fists against the table, pinching time as they blinked.

The women blinked…but not the man.

Vincent froze, eyes hard on those glassy blues. He waved a hand through the murky, time-frozen air. The man's eyes did not respond. Vincent eased his chair away from the table, the typical twelve inches. He knew precisely where he'd hit the table with his fists. Where the chair was when he stopped time. Which expression his face held. All of this had to be perfect for the time pinch to go off unnoticed.

And with one of the customers watching the entire time, there was zero room for forgiveness.

Vincent eased around the table to his right. He fished through the old ladies' purses for the necessary info. Names of deceased husbands. A gold watch with an engraving from one of the major banks downtown. A hand-carved smoking pipe in the shape of a woman's face.

And then Vincent came to this unflappable gentleman in black patent shoes. He nudged the man's shoulder lightly, testing to be sure he was, in fact, subject to the time pinch. Confident that he was frozen like the others, Vincent slipped his fingers through his jacket pockets. Brushing against a stiff piece of cardstock, Vincent eased it from the jacket and held it to the light of the flickering candles in the corner of the room. Elegant calligraphy sliced across the card.

Nice pinch. Let's talk after.

Vincent's fingers tingled as his stomach dropped.

Who was this man?

Vincent pocketed the note as he paced back around the table. Whoever this was he had put himself into a weak posture, and very much on purpose. This wasn't a threat. That wouldn't make sense. It was a declaration.

An invitation.

The time pinch jerked at Vincent's guts, and he staved off the sickness as long as he could, attempting to formulate a plan for how to deal with this man and finally deciding it was best to simply play along.

He arranged himself at the table—chair in the proper position, hands on the usual spots. As he released the time pinch, the sounds on the street returned, and the hammer of his fists echoed off the walls. The old ladies jerked back, blinking in alarm.

A bead of sweat trickled down Vincent's cheek as he swallowed back the nausea. Dropping back into character, he avoided eye contact with the man. He spun a yarn of ghostly husbands calling from the hereafter, the banker expressing regret for focusing on lucre instead of a fuller life, the smoker with an eye for beauty calling on his widow to join him once her days had finished on this Earth.

And then, Vincent turned to this hawk-nosed man.

"And you," Vincent droned, "have a sweetheart. A young love…I see her."

The man's eyes crinkled with mirth, and he nodded with a half-shrug.

Vincent continued, "A flaxen-haired girl with eyes dark as mahogany. Her passing was unexpected, was it not?"

The man drew in a breath, then spoke with a snappy East Coast bounce, "She took a header off the side of a luxury cruiser outta New York City. Dropped in off the coast of Nova Scotia."

The older ladies clucked in sympathy.

Vincent grabbed a random name. "She was called…Marlene?"

The man nodded. "Marlene Cosecki."

"She was your lover, yes?"

The man tilted his hand. "We had some fun nights, but we was in more of a business relationship."

The old ladies leaned in with lifted brows.

Vincent jutted his chin. "I see. She tells me…warns me of betrayal."

"Yeah, that'd be the long and short of it. Got rolled by some East River confidence men. Shook her down for her pearls." The man added with an ominous tone, "Her *mother's* pearls."

"But she knew these men," Vincent corrected with a lift of his finger. "Else there could be no betrayal. Yes?"

"One of them was…"

He lingered to let Vincent pick up the thread.

"Her own brother," Vincent declared, actually enjoying the improvisation.

One of the old ladies lifted a hand to cover her mouth.

The man released an over-rendered gasp. "Amazing, Damir!"

The second lady whispered, "What does she want?"

Vincent turned to the women, his shtick in full force, and lifted fingers to his temples. "Justice, my friends. She cries for justice!"

Once the séance had concluded, and the women had left generous tips in the bowl before taking their leave, Vincent remained in the room to blow out the candles and pocket the bills destined for the neighborhood soup kitchen.

He pulled off the fez, ran a hand through his hair, and in his natural voice, asked, "Enjoy the show?"

"It was alright."

"Figured you wouldn't sit through all that if you didn't enjoy the theater of it."

The man squinted an eye. "You're not as good at this as you think. Your delivery was everywhere. Writing's a bit thick."

Vincent scowled. "I don't work off a script."

"It's just my opinion," he offered with a diplomatic grin. "For what it's worth. I think you can do better."

With a sigh, Vincent grumbled, "Can I get your name, at least?"

The hawk-nosed man smiled and leaned forward with a hand extended. "Smith. Alexander Smith."

Vincent considered the hand for a moment before shaking it. "You got me at a disadvantage, Mister Smith. If you wanted to talk business, you coulda found me during business hours."

He lifted his hands in apology. "Believe me, I've tried. But it's been a real bear trying to get around your one-armed keeper."

"You know a lot about me," Vincent muttered. "More than I know about you."

"That, my dear Mister Calendo, is precisely my business."

Vincent pulled the red velvet curtains aside to open the door to his dressing room. "Give me a moment, huh?"

As Vincent settled his fez onto its stand and hung his costume onto hangers on the back of the door, Smith poked around the séance room.

"You rent this party?" he asked.

"From the grocer, yeah."

"How much does this put you back?"

Vincent grabbed a white handkerchief to wipe away the stage makeup. "Not so much. Worked out a deal with the Crew to put him on protection. Been kinda busy so I only use this space about twice a month, anymore." He leaned over to eye Smith through the doorway. "I suspect you know this already?"

"You're a quick study, Calendo."

Vincent resumed his grooming. "I know your type, Smith. Answer Men. You broker in info, and you're not so particular in who you sell to."

"What makes you say that?" Smith asked as he crossed his arms with a smirk.

"Because I've never seen you before. And I've seen everyone in the family. That means you're an outsider. Which means you're looking to sell." He peered at Smith with heavy eyes. "And because you're here talkin to me, that means whatever you're selling, Cooper wasn't buying."

Smith's face betrayed the barest moment of surprise before a practiced composure slammed back down like a lead weight.

"You saw us at the hotel the other night."

"If you struck out with that deadbeat, don't think you'll do much better with me."

Smith shook his head. "You haven't even heard my pitch, yet. So quick to kick me to the curb?"

Vincent finished up and reached for the string to click off

the overhead bulb. "I'm quick to go to bed is what I am. Look," he said as he pushed aside the curtains and closed the door to the dressing room, "I'm no one to talk to. I got no use for your information, and I got no authority inside the Crew."

"I know that," Smith countered. "You're the pincher. The *only* pincher, actually. Which means you ought to have a place directly behind the Capo, whispering your dark secrets in his ear while he sends you on shadowed errands for well or ill. But that's not how it played out for you. Is it?"

Vincent brushed past Smith to blow out the candles on the corner table. He held the stairway door for Smith as he descended, locking up before they proceeded downstairs.

"So, what's your interest in me, then?" Vincent grumbled.

"An in's an in. And I want one."

"An in? To Vito?"

As Vincent reached for the door to the street, Smith leaned against it to capture Vincent's attention. "I'm a businessman, Mister Calendo. And I'm not easily rattled. I've got eyes and ears on every street corner in Baltimore already. I'm an information broker, which means I don't make this sorta move unless I've already got something to sell."

Vincent sighed and took a step back. "Sounds like the sort of thing you should bring to the family, but I'm not their doorman."

"The Russians are giving the East Coast families the red-ass. Am I wrong?"

Vincent squinted. "Most of them."

"But not here in Baltimore."

"Right."

"You think that's because Vito Corbi's got them thumbnailed? Because the Baltimore Crew puts the fear of god in the Bratva?"

Vincent pulled at the door hard enough to move Smith. "Yes."

As Smith followed him out onto the street, he scoffed, "Then you're dumber than a sack of biscuits. Listen to me. I have actionable intelligence for sale, here."

Vincent drew to a halt with a lift of his head to the sky. "Will you leave me alone? You don't get it, Smith. You're pitching to the wrong Joe. The Crew don't care what I have to say. They don't listen to me." He added with a hard swallow, "They don't care. You're better off with Cooper."

Smith snorted. "That gin-soused pig gave me less attention than you are."

"I'm just a pincher," Vincent declared, turning away.

"I know. Which is why I'm coming to you with this." He strode to catch up with Vincent as he walked away. "You say they don't listen to you? So, give them something they can't ignore."

"Go away."

Smith drew to a stop as Vincent kept walking. After several stops, Smith shouted, "Masseria's nephew is about to get black-bagged."

Vincent slowed, then paused.

Smith continued as he stepped toward Vincent, "I got sources in New York. They say the Russians have this planned like clockwork."

"Masseria?" Vincent whispered. "Are they insane?"

"They're looking to light a match on this powder keg between Salvatore and Masseria. Let the Italians soften each other up, then pick up the pieces."

Vincent stared at Smith, searching the man's face for hints and shadows of deceit. He found none.

"When?"

"Day after tomorrow. On his way to his sister's for

dinner. Man's got a routine, and they've got it mapped like Magellan."

Vincent stuffed his hands into his pockets. "That's a handy little bundle of bad news all wrapped up in a bow. If I deliver this to the Capo, and you're wrong, or lying, I'm gonna come out of this looking like a real stooge."

"So?" Smith countered. "Isn't that what you are already?"

Vincent balled a fist inside one of those pockets.

"Listen, Calendo. This is a no-lose situation for you. You take the gamble. If you crap out, then it's business as usual. Maybe a little egg on your face, but nothing that'll change your life. But," Smith chimed with a lift of his finger, "if it's bona fide, and Vito saves Masseria from sparking off a real Sicily-flavored family war? What's that gonna do to your cache? I'll tell you what. It's gonna send it through the roof."

"What's your price?" Vincent asked.

"You take that for free. Can't take it back now."

"Yeah, but what's the angle?" Vincent pressed.

"All I want is an introduction. Like I said, I'm a businessman. I'm offering a sample of my product, and I'm confident the Crew will find it satisfactory."

Vincent leaned into Smith. "Why us? Why not Philly? Or Pittsburgh? Or even Richmond? Why not go straight to Masseria with this?"

A razor-sharp grin lifted onto Smith's face. "Because Vito Corbi is the weak link. He needs me more than the other families, so he'll be willing to pay more for what I offer. Supply and demand, Calendo. I've got the supply, and I'm banking that Vito Corbi's got the demand."

Vincent stood silent for a long moment, turning it over in his mind.

Smith nodded. "It's in your hands now. Do with it what you like. If Masseria's nephew ends up floating in the East River, then I'll know you've passed on this offer. Then maybe

I'll give Richmond a tug. That pincher there is almost as desperate for recognition as you are."

Smith turned and sauntered back down the street.

Vincent called, "If it's solid, and the Capo wants to meet, how will I find you?"

"You won't have to," he replied without turning around.

blanket of tobacco smoke hugged the exposed timber rafters of a tiny wood-paneled cottage. The spicy cigar fragrance mixed with the fishy aroma of Nadine's seafood stew. The lithe woman stirred the cast iron pot slung on a hanger over the kitchen fire. Little wisps of curly black hair had escaped the bandana she'd tied around her head, creating a frenetic mane that haloed her face.

Hattie watched her cook as she sat beside Raymond. Nadine appeared so slight to Hattie, belying the fact she'd given birth only a few months ago. It hooked a twinge of worry into Hattie's stomach. Were they not eating enough, for her to be so thin, so soon?

The baby rested in Raymond's enormous arms, writhing his chubby hands within that nest of muscle. They'd named him Douglas after Nadine's father, and his cherub face was adorable if unsettling, as Dougie was, in fact, a baby, and Hattie had no experience with babies.

Raymond unwound his arms to bob the child on his lap.

"Now, don't jerk him around like that," Nadine chided from the fireplace.

"I ain't hurtin' the child," Raymond grumbled. "He's alright."

"Well, at least let her hold the baby for a hot minute," she added. "She's been lookin' at him with big ole eyes ever since she came in."

Raymond lifted Dougie for Hattie to take.

"I...I...er..." she stammered

"What?" Raymond muttered. "You don't wanna?"

She did. Well, part of her did. The other part of her wasn't sure what to do with a baby in the first place. They seemed so fragile. Too easy to drop when they squirmed. Too easy for their heads to pop off like Kewpie dolls.

And they smelled funny.

Nadine cocked a hip as she arched a brow at Hattie. "You ain't tellin' me that you don't wanna hold that baby, 'cause I know you do."

Hattie replied, "I'm just not used to babies, is all."

"Oh hell, girl," she snickered. "Ain't no one used to babies 'til they have one."

Raymond nudged her with his elbow.

Hattie reached for the infant, gripping him at the waist.

"No," Raymond said, "you gotta...here. Hand under the head like this."

So, she was right. Their heads *could* pop off.

Hattie followed instructions and hoisted the baby over to her lap with a tiny whimper of panic. She cradled him along her thigh straight out from her body. The child squirmed and arched his back, eyes shut tight.

"Bounce him," Raymond whispered. "Just a little."

She kicked her heel slowly, sending the child up and down. The squirming eased, and he opened his huge brown eyes to stare up at Hattie.

Something tugged inside her chest, almost like she'd used her powers—but that wasn't it. It was a deep stirring, thrilling and terrifying. Babies had powers too, it seemed. Power to captivate and to panic. Masterful little magicians they were.

Hattie grinned and made silly noises at the infant as he waved his little fists around. What a thing this was. A tiny human being, full of need and necessity, but also potential. She couldn't imagine the notion of another person being a blend of herself and someone else. Literal alchemy wrought in flesh.

She handed Dougie back to his father to help Nadine with the bowls. Halfway through dinner, Nadine nursed Dougie at the table while Hattie looked on.

Would she ever have a child? Hattie was about the same age as Nadine, as far as she knew. There were decades to go before having a child would no longer be an option. There was no rush whatsoever, especially with the mob families eager for more pinchers. What kind of life could she offer a child, at any rate? Every day, the child would be at risk of having its mother whisked away to serve some master in another city. Or worse, the child could be a pincher, too. Then they would both be in jeopardy.

Especially if the tales Vincent had spun about "stables" of pinchers were true. It was the lesser evil, to be sure, but if a pincher had to live a life of servitude to the masters of modern power, then keeping a family close would be the only way she could imagine surviving that.

She thought of Vincent and what his parents must have gone through. Hattie knew nothing of his parentage. She knew that pinchers beget pinchers, and as such the odds were that his parents were in the fold serving elsewhere. Then again, there was that small percentage—those who came into being with their powers without the benefit of their heredity. Hattie was of this ilk. If Vincent were the same, then his parents might have faced the same dilemma as hers—a child with magical powers, and a faceless establishment seeking to snatch him away. Only, Vincent's parents hadn't been able to make the same choices Hattie's parents had. Clearly. They were no longer in his life. Had they been compensated? Did they live like royalty somewhere? Or had Vincent been acquired with a payment not in gold, but in lead?

Hattie shivered at the thought.

Nadine asked, "What, stew's no good? Don't you like mussels?"

She lifted a hand. "Oh, no. It's wonderful."

Raymond nudged her with his elbow, giving her a knowing nod.

Nadine huffed. "Well, alright you two. Don't tell me nothin'. Let me just sit here like I was a toad on a log…"

Raymond chuckled. "Hattie's got a problem."

Hattie's eyes shot wide open. "What problem is that, then?"

With a face lifted in mischief, he said, "Hattie's got it bad for one of the boys in the city."

She squawked.

Nadine leaned forward. "What, now? Oh, no you can *not* let that just sit there. Tell me everything!"

Hattie rammed her elbow into Raymond's side. "He's a liar, and it's shameful."

Raymond said, "He's one a them pretty boy spit polish types. Suits. Hats. Whole nine."

Nadine snickered. "Money man? Oh, girl!"

Hattie licked her spoon clean, then reached up to smack Raymond on the top of the head with it.

After dinner, Nadine withdrew to the far side of the cabin to settle the baby into his bassinet.

Hattie pulled Raymond aside, nodding for the door. "A moment?"

Raymond nodded, then stepped over to a steamer trunk near the back wall. He opened the lid, fished for a moment, then produced two cigars. "Nadine, I'm taking a puff."

His wife rolled her eyes. "About time you took that outside. Make that a habit!"

Raymond opened the door for Hattie, and the two stepped out into the humid evening air. He handed her one of the cigars. She took it and considered it for a moment while he carved the end off of his own and punched a hole in the opposite end. He swapped cigars with Hattie, giving the second the same treatment.

"I don't smoke these, you know," she told him.

Raymond froze, then shook his head. "You could tell a person before he goes and cuts his cigar."

"That sounds like something you'd pay extra for in one of those Crew brothels."

He released a thunderous chuckle. "Alright. I'll pocket that one for tomorrow." Raymond lit up, puffing a heavy plume of spicy smoke into the air. It drifted up to the low-hanging oak boughs along the eaves of his cabin, shimmering with rays of moonlight.

Hattie eyed him for a moment then fished a piece of paper from her pocket and held it out.

"What's that?"

"The reason I wanted you out of earshot of your better half."

He took the paper and unfolded it, holding it up to the moonlight to read. "Hmm."

"Can you make that last bit out?" she asked.

"You and me have run boats down to the Carolinas for a year, now. You seen those ocean scows. The Greek ships?"

Her eyebrows lifted. "It's Greek, is't?"

"Looks that way." His brow dropped as he reread the note. "Wait."

"Right…"

"Who wrote this?" he demanded. "Where'd you get this?"

She held out a hand for him to lower his voice. "It was left with Lizzie. Picked it up just the other day."

"This was after…"

"Our last training bout? Yes."

He sucked on his cigar, eyes narrow with thought. "This that boy from the Crew?"

"I don't think so. He'd just come out and rib me about it to my face."

"Seeing a lot of his face these days?"

She scowled. "None of your business."

"So, it's someone else. Someone knows what you are. And they're watching you."

"They're watching us," she corrected. "Which means you're involved. That's why I brought this to you."

His body shook. Actually trembled. Hattie reached out for him, but he twisted away.

"We…we gotta find this…whoever this is."

"I know."

"Now," he spat.

She shushed him, trying again to make contact. This time she managed to stroke his arm. "We will."

Raymond took a few breaths before stuffing the cigar back into his mouth.

Hattie added, "This could be a threat, or it could be a simple hello."

"This ain't simple." He handed the paper back to Hattie. "You need to find out what that Greek bullshit is about. You best find out if it's a threat."

Hattie nodded as she pocketed the note. That much was certain, and it was difficult to view anyone with the knowledge of her powers as anything other than a threat.

"Don't suppose you have any Greek friends on the water?"

He shook his head. "Ask Lizzie. Maybe she does."

Hattie nodded. The plumes of smoke gathered beneath the oak tree, now illustrating several distinct beams of light as they filtered through the foliage.

"I didn't mean to upset you," she muttered.

"I'm not...I'm not mad at you, baby girl. Just whoever thought this—" he pointed at her pocket "—was cute." He leaned against the side of his cabin. "Best not use your hoodoo around the city, until we know who's who and what's what."

Hattie nodded again. That was a conclusion she'd already reached. The author of this message had clearly seen her in action. But until this anonymous peeping Tom made his intentions clear, it was best not to give him any more ammunition.

"Raymond?" she whispered.

"Hmm?"

"Next time I come over, let's have chicken. I'm not sure I can handle any more of Nadine's mussel stew."

His face drew stiff. A brow lifted. Then he leaned close to her and said, "Me neither."

Another chest-pound laugh filled the air along Curtis Creek as Raymond finished his cigar, and Hattie wondered how she would manage this new complication.

CHAPTER 8

*D*aytime at the Old Moravia stood in stark contrast to the frenetic jazz-and-gin nights, or even to the subdued Sunday evening cocktails crowd. The lobby bar of the hotel was packed with men in suits grumbling one to another, their cigarettes piping fingers of white smoke toward the ceiling. The mood in the room was anxious. As such, Vincent stepped carefully around the couches and potted palms to find Lefty scowling near the front windows.

"Something happen?" Vincent muttered.

Lefty shrugged. "Vito's late. No one knows why."

"He call a meeting?"

Lefty nodded.

"You didn't give me a heads-up or nothing?" Vincent grumbled. "What if I was sleeping one off?"

Lefty sighed. "It's Crew business. Doesn't require your input."

Vincent shook his head and stood beside Lefty. Precious little required Vincent's input these days. Never before had it been so clear that he was strictly a tool for the Crew to assert their power in the patchwork of East Coast families. But now he had something of value. Something that wasn't in his usual kit bag. This was information, and it could prove far more useful toward asserting that power than any time pinching he could pull off.

"Were you?" Lefty asked.

"What?"

"Sleeping one off. You look like something a cat chewed up then coughed back out."

"Haven't touched the sauce for a few days, now."

With the first hint of a grin Vincent had seen on Lefty's face for over a month, "Girl trouble?" he asked.

"Sure, Lefty. It's girl trouble."

"Don't have to snap my head off."

Vincent sighed. "No, I've got some truck on my mind is all. Don't sweat it."

Lefty raised a brow. "I'll sweat it."

"What's the business?" Vincent interjected with a wave to the room.

"Between you, me and the fence post, I think it's the Russians."

Vincent nodded thoughtfully. "They keep popping up, don't they?"

"Like mushrooms."

Vincent considered the moment. Vito would be arriving eventually to address the Crew, most of which seemed to be gathered in the room. He spotted Tony standing by the bar, his usual gin martini in hand. Cooper was conspicuously absent, Vincent noted. Maybe he was on the outs with the Capo? Maybe he had a whale show up at his poker hall?

But with this moment came an opportunity. The opportunity to give Smith's info to Vito. The opportunity to cash in this chip, hopefully raising his stock in the eyes of the Crew. And if it all ended up a bust, what was the loss?

When Vito finally entered the room, a tiny retinue of

aging gangsters in tow, the risks involved in this deal suddenly became real. Jesus…this was the Capo. If this info was a load of bushwa, and he'd made the Crew look like fools, Smith would be long gone and Vincent would be the one with the stretched-out neck.

Vito Corbi sauntered into the room with the best approximation of a smile on his face. The look sent chills through Vincent's guts. He never looked that happy about anything—not without some bombshell ready to drop.

The Capo took his usual position near the center of the bar, precipitating a shift in the men already lined up. Tony was forced from his stool, and ended up in the standing room near the far wall.

With a clearing of his throat, and a spread of his hands, Vito announced, "Gentlemen and friends, thank you for coming."

Hell's bells…what was with his chipper mood?

He continued, "As most of you know, we dealt with the menace from the Czar's lands with quick and decisive action last year."

Vincent sucked in a breath as memories of those skirmishes rang fresh in his brain.

Vito wagged a finger. "This was due to forethought. My sense of things to come. I moved quickly to pull this weed out by its roots." He pantomimed a weed-pulling motion. "And we have seen little from the Bratva this past year beyond desperate, pathetic grabs at protection rackets. These *Russi* persist in our memories more like vermin than predators."

This spawned a weak spattering of applause.

Vito lifted a hand. "However…" The noise immediately muted. "…our associates along the Coast have not fared as well. Perhaps it is a lack of foresight on their part." He smirked to himself. "Perhaps they suffer from a density of

Russi. Regardless, the families in Philadelphia and New York find themselves enveloped in a series of pointless battles due to these upstarts vying for power. Yes. You hear me true. We in Baltimore enjoy the benefit of peace, while our neighbors to the North are beset with conflict. I would thank each and every one of you for this state of affairs."

The crowd turned one to another half in bafflement, half in hope that this meeting truly meant a boon from the Capo.

Vito allowed the murmuring to subside before continuing. "This is our time to shine, my friends. This is our time to finally break the liquor traffic from Atlantic City that has been our primary competition."

Vincent peered to Lefty, whose face was stony and transfixed by the proceedings. Atlantic City had been the top dog when it came to liquor trafficking. Their booze had proliferated from Maine to Florida, and as far west as the Mississippi River. The benefit that Vito had enjoyed in Maryland, by way of the governor rejecting the Volstead Act, was limited by the sheer volume that Atlantic City had produced. Their organization behaved like a well-oiled machine, stepping left and right to grease palms, acquire shipping lanes, and secure muscle when necessary. They were what Vito seemed to aspire to.

And they were now distracted by the Russians.

"Are there any issues I need to address?" The Capo asked with an imperial sweep of his hand.

A voice came from the rear near the lobby. "The Southeast neighborhoods are being squeezed by some gang and they're screaming bloody murder."

Vito blinked in the direction of the comment, but he simply shook his head. "Who are these gangs? Polish? Irish? Or Jews?"

The faceless voice replied, "No. They're saying it's the

Bratva. The Russians are back and they're rolling my neighborhoods."

Vito nodded. "Easily dispatched. Giuseppe…" He eyed one of his retinue with gravity. "Deal with this. Are there any other concerns?"

This was it. Vincent's moment. He had only a few seconds to decide—would he roll the dice, or would he remain, as ever, nothing but a tool.

"Capo," Vincent said as he took a step forward. It wasn't enough to capture Vito's attention, so Vincent repeated it with more volume. He spotted Lefty reaching for his arm in his periphery, and so he took another half-step forward.

Eyes moved toward Vincent, including Vito's. The man's face drew long and stony. The murmurings in the entire lobby fell silent. Vito's expression betrayed no sense of approval or disapproval, patience or impatience. It simply stared across the space at Vincent.

"Capo," Vincent repeated, "I have something for you."

Vito didn't respond.

"A man has come forward with information."

Still, Vito remained silent.

Lefty whispered something, but Vincent resolved to block him out. No turning back.

"Information regarding the Bratva in New York."

One or two snickers threatened to pierce the silence, but Vito lifted a hand to strangle the murmurings back. He took two steps toward Vincent, wandering toward the center of the gathering.

With a flat tone, he said, "What sort of information?"

All eyes were now on Vincent, alive with the morbid anticipation of watching a man flame out so publicly that the rumor mills would turn for years. What to say? Give him everything now? Surrender Smith's name, so that anyone else could poach this opportunity out from underneath Vincent?

"There are plans for a hit," Vincent replied, voice creaking from a dry throat. "A hit on a member of Masseria's family."

No amount of gravitas from the Capo could stifle the wave of consternation washing through the room.

Vito snapped his fingers and pointed at Vincent. "With me." He half-turned and added, "You too, Alonzo."

Lefty stepped alongside Vincent, who refused to turn to face his handler. He didn't have to. He could feel Lefty's glare peeling the skin from the side of his face. Vito led the two men directly back into the midst of the gathering, gangsters fumbling to make a path for the Capo as he wove his way toward the bar. Vincent nodded to Tony, who gathered his drink while avoiding eye contact.

As the three stepped behind the bar and the bartender found a way to vanish without making Vito step aside, those standing nearest the bar shuffled away as many steps as they could. Vito sighed, ran a hand over his face, then turned to face Vincent.

"What is this, now?"

Vincent took a steadying breath. "A man by the name of Alexander Smith approached me the other night." As Vincent focused on the details, his voice strengthened. "It was after sunset. He came to me discreet-like. Said he was looking to trade with the Crew. Info for cash."

Vito nodded. "I know the sort, if not this man. Continue."

"He said that the Bratva were planning a move on New York. They put a hit out on Masseria's nephew, and were going to make it look like Salvatore was behind it. It's supposed to go down tomorrow night."

With a squint, Vito turned to Lefty. "Is this information worthwhile?"

Lefty straightened a bit, clenching his jaw before answering, "I don't know, Capo. This is the first I've heard of this."

"Do you know this…Smith?" Vito pressed.

"No."

Vito's squint sharpened. "Isn't it your job to keep people such as this away from my *stregone*? Is that not specifically your job?"

"It is."

Vito shook his head and turned toward the back wall, eyes narrowed in thought. After a nerve-baring moment of silence, he said, "I received good word from Philadelphia. The *stregone*, DeBarre, speaks highly of the two of you. It seems you've made a favorable impression with the family there." He turned to Vincent and Lefty with a softer face. "This is good. There may come a time when they prove to be necessary allies. The New York families seem destined for war. We should be ready when the time comes—and we are not yet ready. These Russians must not push New York to the tipping point. Not yet."

The room was dead silent. Vito's words, though nearly at a whisper, carried to several dozen ears nearby, eliciting a round of sober nods.

Vito cleared his throat and turned to Lefty. "Alonso. You will contact Giuseppe Masseria on my behalf. Inform him of this rumor."

Lefty asked, "You want…me?"

Vincent blurted, "Capo, I would be happy to do this for you."

Vito lifted a hand. "You failed to keep this outsider from my *stregone*, Alonzo. Therefore, I saddle you with this task. If this information is correct, then we will all benefit. However, if it is false—some prank, or worse—" he pointed at Lefty "—you will shoulder the consequences."

"Capo," Vincent urged, "I may be the better choice. The

odds that you'll lose face if this is a lot of bushwa are, well…
no one cares if I'm wrong."

Vito lifted his face to Vincent with a half-smirk. "I understand your words, Vincenzo."

A shot of energy flew from Vincent's heels into his skull.
Vito called him by name. That wasn't a common occurrence,
and every time the Capo used Vincent's name it felt like a
boon of some kind.

Vito continued, "And perhaps I even understand your
ambition. But we must consider both failure and success.
Alonzo has contacts in the city. He knows who to call. And
from the sound of it, we don't have a lot of time."

He rested a hand on Vincent's shoulder, sending another
thrill jolting through Vincent's chest, before turning to Lefty.
"Our fortune appears to be changing. It is my hope that this
Smith is part of these favorable winds. He is a businessman,
and that I can respect. But he is an outsider."

Lefty nodded.

Vito clapped his hands, turning to bellow to the rest of
the gathering, "Which brings me to our final business."

The sudden eruption of volume from the Capo made
Vincent jump. He eased away from Vito to stand beside
Lefty. The rest of the Crew turned from their tortured
postures, attempts to appear as if they were not overtly
eavesdropping on the private business.

Vincent spied Tony a few paces away from the bar, his
martini glass now drained. His face was downcast, eyes on
his shoes, misery heaping over his shoulders. The bleakness
of his posture was striking, and only as Vito continued with
his announcement did Vincent realize something was wrong.

"My friends," Vito declared, "as you know we have had
difficulties in the foothills with our suppliers as of late. This
has forced us to focus on these backwoods savages for many
months now. And with our neighbors in Richmond dealing

with some internal issues, business along the coast has been flush. It has forced us to rely on outsiders for our liquor distribution."

Vincent's stomach drew into a tight ball. He peered at Tony, whose forehead now sported a bead of sweat.

Vito continued, "I am happy to announce, however, that our difficulties with the West Virginia suppliers have been dealt with to my satisfaction. Product now flows in its proper direction—toward Baltimore, and out of Baltimore."

A couple weak cheers slipped from the back of the room.

"This brings renewed purpose, and frees up manpower we have lacked these past few months. Beginning immediately, we will no longer make use of outsiders for our waterfront distribution."

Vincent balled a fist before stuffing it into his pants pocket. No. No, this couldn't be happening. He pictured Hattie the other day, her red hair sun-streaked, her freckles, the burned tip of her nose, the expression on her face when she said there was nothing she'd rather do than be on the water, running booze from dock to dock.

She'd be devastated by this.

Vito spread his hands in a grand gesture. "No more middlemen. No more outsiders. Our business is now, and forever, entirely in our hands. Our destiny…is in our hands."

Fresh cheers, heartier than before.

Vito wandered back from behind the bar to address specifics, referring point men to Tony for this new arrangement. Tony remained stiff and passive, his eyes moving wearily from face-to-face. And Vincent now realized the source of the man's misery.

He would have to tell Lizzie Sadler that she, and her employees, were out of a job. This would be tricky for Tony, as he'd developed an intimate relationship with the Sadler woman. Those days, Vincent mused, were likely over. But

Tony would survive. If anything, he had become a more pivotal figure within the Crew. He would be marshalling forces, making arrangements, heeding logistics. His future was robust.

The future for Hattie Malloy, on the other hand, was far more uncertain.

Lefty leaned into Vincent. "Thank you so much."

"Sorry," Vincent grumbled. "It happened fast."

"You're supposed to tell me these things. Not shout them out in the middle of a meet."

"I know."

Lefty turned to face Vincent, his face painted in disdain. "What was this? Some grab? You booting for some position? Trying to make me the fool and climb over my back?"

"The fella came at me at my night job. He had me figured. Knew who I was. Knew *what* I was." Vincent added in a whisper, "He'd already hit Cooper up."

Lefty squinted. "If you'd come to me when this happened, I could have told you that I know every info broker between Charleston and Philly. I ain't never heard of no Alexander Smith. If Cooper had the good sense to kick this Jake to the curb, then what makes you think we should've given him the time of day?" Lefty pinched the bridge of his nose. "You have no idea how lucky you are that Vito was in a good mood."

Vincent eyed the Capo raising a freshly filled glass of red wine as others joined him.

"It was supposed to be me, Lefty. There was no risk that way." He added with a sigh, "I wasn't trying to put the screws to you. You have to believe that."

Lefty shrugged. "Well, it don't matter now. Does it?" After a long glare, he turned to walk away. "I have some calls to make."

CHAPTER 9

Hattie hopped onto a street car on Maryland Avenue, glancing back at the Cathedral of the Annunciation as she took a seat. The enormous circular edifice loomed on the corner, its granite blocks hewn into a bulbous knot of Greek architecture. She wiped a bead of sweat from her brow as the street car lurched forward, her stomach rumbling, and a wave of nausea sweeping through her body. She'd used a lot of magic inside that building, and now she was paying for it.

Her practice had come in handy. The long-bearded Orthodox priest inside had turned her away when she asked for a word, yammering something about women and rules. And so, she spied one of the young Greek men walking along Preston and followed him for a couple blocks to digest his voice and inflection. With that, she pinched light over her face to create the illusion of being a Greek lad. Whether it was because the old priest was hard of hearing and near-sighted, or whether the practice Hattie'd poured into performing her illusions had paid dividends, the man proved more cooperative the second time around. And Hattie had the information she wanted.

She fished the handwritten card stock from her pocket, eyeing the Greek text scribed with polished loops—text she had just translated.

Know thyself.

It wasn't a threat, after all. Rather, the message became an urging. An admonishment.

Perhaps even a rebuke.

Hattie had lost herself inside her own illusion because she'd underestimated how deeply the fantasy of a normal home life had rooted into her psyche. She'd always assumed that, should her powers overtake her, she would pass out before the magic levied a lethal price. She was wrong. It was a learning experience, and it could have been her last. Whoever had sent Hattie this note seemed to understand that.

And didn't want to see her repeat it.

Lifted by the line of thought, Hattie took the streetcar to the end of the line, stepping out near the harbor. The walk to the warehouse would be reasonable, and the weather was warm and clear. So, she set out along the dusty trail around the fingers of the harbor toward Locust Point, shuffling off the illness from her light pinching as a wave of optimism swept through her.

She caught sight of Tony's car as it kicked up a plume of dust on its way back up the road and into the city. Hattie waved the dust away from her face, tucking her shirt over her nose until she emerged into cleaner air in front of Liz's warehouse. The sliding door had been left ajar, and she spotted the Runabout parked in the front. Looked like the joint was open for business. Too bad. Hattie was looking forward to some private time with Raymond to discuss her findings at the Greek church.

She stepped through the story-and-a-half opening left by the sliding door, into the cool air of the warehouse. Twelve pallets of crated bottles sat in a neat row, waiting for transport to Winnow's Slip and points beyond. Probably two good runs, there—enough to keep them busy for the rest of the week. More business from the Crew would be along by Saturday. They always moved more hooch on the weekends, when the treasury men took time off for their families.

But something was wrong.

It was Raymond that Hattie noticed first. He paced in the center of the warehouse shaking his head, grumbling refusals to no one in particular. His eyes were narrow, and his forehead sported more sweat than usual. This was his nervous pace. She'd seen it before, specifically the nine months prior to the birth of little Douglas.

Was Nadine pregnant again? That was certainly possible, but there was an edge to Raymond's posture. This wasn't simple jitters. This was anger.

No, this was panic.

Before Hattie could clear her throat to ask what the hell had crawled up Raymond's shorts, she eyed Lizzie leaning against one of the hooch crates, arms folded in front of her. Liz's eyes were downcast, still, resigned—not full of calculation, as was her usual state. Her lack of movement was every bit as alarming as Raymond's pacing.

Finally, Hattie managed to ask, "What's the problem, then?"

Raymond nearly jumped out of his skin, pulling arms up to his face as Hattie stepped close enough to see. He shook off his alarm with an embarrassed sigh, then continued pacing. This time, he began swinging his arms.

Without making eye contact, or moving a single muscle, Lizzie replied, "We're sunk."

"Come again?" Hattie pressed. "What's this all about?"

Raymond began shaking his head and making noises like he was about to say something, but never landed on anything intelligible.

Lizzie said, "Just got word from the Crew."

"And that word is?"

"They're bringing all Bay traffic in-house."

Hattie stood motionless, waiting for Lizzie to look at her.

When Lizzie lifted her chin, eyes rimmed red, the weight of the words hammered Hattie in the chest.

"The what, now?"

Raymond barked, "They're cuttin' us off!"

Hattie shook her head. "That's insane. What do they know about the Chesapeake?"

"Nothing," Lizzie snapped, turning away.

Hattie stepped carefully around Raymond, reaching for Liz's shoulder. "How'd this happen? Wasn't that Tony, just now?"

"Yes," Lizzie replied with a sigh. "Yes, it was. You just missed him."

Raymond grumbled, "Shoulda snapped his neck."

Hattie lifted a hand to shush Raymond and glared at Liz.

The woman rubbed the bridge of her nose. "Seems old Vito was just waiting for the dust to settle with the bootleggers in West Virginia before cutting us out. He's convinced we're leaving him open to some sort of infiltration from outsiders. Hell, we *are* the outsiders according to him. And he's done with us. It's just that simple."

Hattie sputtered, "Well, no. No, it's not. What do his goons know about Bay trafficking? Fuel points? Treasury patrols? He's putting his business into the hands of amateurs because of his ego?"

Lizzie spun on Hattie, eyes filled with jagged glass. "Yes. That's it exactly."

Raymond stopped pacing, lifting a hand at Liz.

The three stood in silence, heaving breaths from Lizzie the only sound filling the cavernous warehouse.

Lizzie rubbed her face briskly. "Yes, that's the situation. Until I can figure out how to salvage it."

Raymond released a single dry chuckle. "Good luck! The Crew ain't known for bein' easy to talk to."

"I know people on the inside. Maybe I can sniff around, find out what our options are." Even as she said it, she knew Vincent wasn't in a position to help.

Lizzie sniffed. "I have an insider, too, unless you've forgotten. Fat lotta good that did."

Hattie tucked her chin and glanced at her shoes.

Lizzie continued, "Tony's broken up about this. At least there's that."

Raymond grumbled, "Shoulda broke his nose."

"Stop," Hattie urged. "This can't be happening. We have a contract with the Crew. Right?" She repeated to Lizzie in a lower tone, "Right?"

"There are no contracts in our line of work, Hattie. I think you know that. And even if there were, who would we go to? The government? We've been playing a game with Vito Corbi these past few years. And now he's changing the rules."

"Well, what'll we do then?" Hattie rasped. "I need this job."

Raymond threw his hands onto his hips, cocking his head in an angle of exasperation.

"We all need this job," Hattie added.

"I'm working on it," Lizzie crossed her arms and leaned once again against a crate, eyes burrowing a hole to China.

Raymond finally settled his breathing to resume a neat ten-pace route back and forth between the doors and the pallets.

Which left Hattie to stand alone, chills running up and

down her arms. How could the Crew simply pull the stopper like this? They'd relied on boat-leggers for years. Who else knew the ins and outs of the Bay and its tributary rivers like they did? Even when they were in competition with the Solomons Island Boys, it seemed obvious that water traffic was a specialized field. One couldn't simply farm the job out to any joker in a suit and fedora and expect him to know what days the Feds were sniffing north of Annapolis, or south of Richmond. When the Upright Citizens were transporting their own goods across your terrain, and when to let it rest. When the boys from Philadelphia were hot enough to ask for a run up the Delaware instead of going through Atlantic City like usual.

What would this mean for Hattie's parents? Her father had just gotten well enough to refuse night shifts. Life had settled into a regular rhythm. They all ate breakfast together. They took dinner together, even when Hattie was running an overnight haul. Sundays were fish. Saturdays were the movie house with her father. Fridays were reading time with her mother.

Now? Now, there was no more boat-legging money. No more fish on Sundays. Their entire rent was barely covered by Alton's wages, and the paltry sum that Branna brought home from the fabric mill wasn't enough to feed them all.

And finding a new job, especially one that paid like this one did, would be next to impossible. Hattie could count the number of employment opportunities open for women on one hand and most of them she wasn't skilled for. Jake had been enlightened enough to hire a scrappy Irish girl to help run product, but she was sure few others would be.

Losing this job wasn't simply a matter of missing out on that little extra they'd enjoyed these past couple months. It would mean hunger. Real hunger—the sort that made people sick enough to slip even further into poverty. There was no end to it, this vicious cycle of want and will. Hattie would eventually grow desperate enough to take risks.

And with a free pincher, risks meant doom.

But then again… Hattie patted the lump near her sternum, where the dram of Aqua Vitae rested snug in the strap of her brassiere.

Sometimes you had to take a chance.

Hattie shook her head. No. This was stupid. Risking her freedom for the sake of a few extra dollars per week was no sort of solution. Sure, she had the magical elixir which could extend her powers. But at what cost? Every dose she took of that potion was another month of health she'd be stealing from her father.

Then again, without this job, what sort of life would they have?

A pitiful noise filled the warehouse, a sniffling moan rose to the rafters, sending a couple pigeons flapping away in alarm. Both Hattie and Lizzie turned toward Raymond, who had hunkered down onto the floor Indian-style, his face buried in his hands. He released a long sob, undulating as his breaths heaved against the baleful noise.

Tears streamed from Hattie's eyes as if someone had turned on a spigot. This massive man had been brought low with a single slash of a pen. Despite his strength, his resolve, his knowledge of the Bay, he had no options, now. And he had a tiny baby to feed. As much as Hattie needed this job, Raymond and his family needed it a hundredfold.

Hattie covered her mouth with her fingers as her eyes stung with tears. She peered over at Liz, whose face remained dry, but was now further pinched in agony.

This wasn't just about Hattie. It was about all of them. These two were as much her family as her parents. How could she withhold her powers if it could save them?

"What about these crates?" Hattie asked, pointing to the

rows of cased bottles standing in a line behind them. "Are we not allowed to finish our standing deliveries?"

"Vito is sending men tomorrow to pick them up and take them to the wharf."

Hattie lifted a brow. "Are we forbidden to finish the job, is what I'm asking."

"I don't know, Hattie. Tony seemed to think they wouldn't cotton to us running anything over the water."

"But he didn't forbid it?"

"What're you getting at?" Lizzie asked.

"I…have an idea," Hattie replied.

Lizzie turned to face Hattie, though Raymond remained on the floor. "What?" The word was sudden and urgent. Clearly, she was grasping for something, anything, to make this right.

Hattie clutched the front of her blouse, gripping the dram of Aqua Vitae beneath the folds of fabric. "We have to prove to the Crew that we are better at distribution than they are."

Lizzie shook her head. "They don't care. We're not one of them."

"Yes," Hattie whispered, before clearing her throat. "Which means boat-legging isn't enough. We'll have to become better bootleggers, as well."

Raymond lifted his face from his hands with a long sniffle. "Huh?"

Hattie explained as she paced around Raymond. "Vito doesn't respect us. He sees us as less than. Less than him. Less than his men. It's a dogma to the man."

"So?" Lizzie pressed.

"So, we've already lost the fight for the water. We have to take the fight to the land. We show the Crew that we are the best. More than them. More capable. More efficient. More daring. We get the land-based distribution, then work our way back into getting the water."

Lizzie made a winding motion with her finger. "And how do you intend to do that? Get to the point, Hattie."

Hattie waved at hand to the pallets of booze. "Where are these going?"

Lizzie replied, "Virginia."

"Where in Virginia?"

"Alexandria."

Hattie nodded with a squint. "How long does it take to run these over water? Raymond?" She snapped her fingers to capture Raymond's attention.

He coughed, then replied, "'Bout a day. Three hours drive to the Slip. Six hours down the Bay. Then we have to wait for the tide, if we don't time it right. And if the Feds are on patrol."

"Rather a lot depends on the Feds, doesn't it?" Hattie posited. "Adds time to the job."

Lizzie groused, "It's the only way to get the hooch to Alexandria. It's right underneath the Feds' noses."

"Is it the only way?" Hattie asked with a smirk. "What if we simply threw these onto the truck and drove them down. How long would that take?"

Lizzie threw her hands in the air and spun away. "Don't be stupid!"

Raymond offered, "Could make the trip in three hours, one way. Might take a couple runs, though."

Hattie lifted a finger. "But if we weren't stopped, and we had the stones to run these right through D.C.?"

Raymond nodded. "We'd have it in half a day."

Lizzie turned back to face them. "What you're proposing is suicide. There's a reason the Crew won't bootleg hooch across the Potomac. The Feds know we're a wet state. They have every highway and byway into Virginia and the District locked down tight as a funeral drum."

Hattie took a step toward Lizzie, a distant smile on her face. "Yes. Well, there's one thing the Crew doesn't have."

Lizzie sneered at Hattie. "What?"

"A light pincher."

Lizzie shook her head. "Parlor tricks are one thing. But you've told me again and again that you can't hold down a broad daylight illusion big enough to cover a truck full of product without killing yourself."

Raymond nodded. "She's right, baby girl. You can't do this to yourself."

"Well…what if I could?"

Raymond cocked his head. "What're you talkin' about?" he blurted.

"I'm simply asking the two of you. If I could pinch light over the truck, both coming and going, would you be willing to take a gamble on me? Show the Crew that we're the better option, even against their own?"

Raymond peered up at Lizzie.

She glanced back at Raymond.

"Do I want to know how you plan to accomplish this?" Lizzie asked.

"You surely don't," Hattie replied. "But, what choice do we really have?"

Raymond nodded to Liz.

With a grand exhalation, Lizzie Sadler declared, "Fine. If the two of you are willing to risk your necks bootlegging two truckloads of white lightning down Pennsylvania Avenue, then I suppose I'm willing to let you do it to yourselves."

Raymond hopped up off the ground, dusting off his rear before reaching out to slap Hattie on the back. "We'll get it done!"

Hattie lifted a finger. "One thing—don't tell the Crew. Not Tony, not anyone. This has to be done before they have a chance to weasel their way back here and take the product back."

Lizzie nodded. "I get it." She added with a glance filled with doubt, "What's your plan? We all know you aren't strong enough for this sort of magic."

With a smirk, Hattie answered, "Maybe I'm stronger than you think."

After a long stare, Lizzie nodded. "Fine. We'll play it your way, as long as you realize that if this goes sideways, you're cooking your own goose."

Hattie knew that. She knew it all too well.

The three worked together to load the Runabout with as many cases as it could hold without peeking over the sides. Three cases by four, for a total of twelve. That was nowhere near enough. Raymond scared up some jute and started stacking them two-high, lashing the boards together with the rope.

"This'll be out in the air," he grumbled as he snapped a knot taut. "You sure you wanna do this?"

"What choice have we?"

"I dunno. Find some work in the steel mill?"

Hattie frowned. "They don't hire coloreds. Half the reason you got into this business with Old Jake was because you were treated properly. You had freedom to come and go. You're respected on the water. Why do you think Jake left you the boat in the first place?"

With a patient sigh, Raymond said, "Baby girl, you really think they respect me on the water? You don't see things the way I do."

"Well, these daft bastards from Richmond are one thing, but—"

"But nothin'. I get hell everywhere I go. From the Crew. From the other watermen. Fuelers. I gotta think twice and three times about everything I say before I say it, or else someone'll take offense. Assume I'm gettin' all uppity, and be ready to cave my head in or worse. I got a family I gotta take care of, you know."

She frowned. "I know that."

"Well, all I'm sayin'…it ain't just your goose that's gonna get cooked." He peered over his shoulder at the office, where Lizzie had withdrawn to soak her head in whiskey. "Lizzie? She'll be okay. She's got that gangster that's gone sweet on her. And she's a take-charge type. Maybe too much." He glanced back at Hattie with looming eyes.

Hattie whispered, "What are you getting at?"

"If we get nabbed," he replied, "she'll cut line on the both of us."

Hattie thought it over and couldn't disagree. Lizzie was always business first. She was a hard thinker. She'd managed to keep the business together after her husband, Jake, was gunned down on the Bay. Kept the contacts intact, blazed new paths into the Crew. She'd even figured out that Hattie was a pincher before Hattie ever thought of revealing her identity to the woman.

Lizzie was about survival. And if Hattie's illusions failed them at the wrong moment, then Lizzie would have a plan figured out to escape the blowback before Hattie and Raymond even felt steel on their wrists. Hell, she probably had a plan already.

Hattie whispered, "Then we won't get nabbed. Will we?"

"Damn straight," Raymond replied with a tight grin and a bump of his fist against her shoulder.

They loaded as much liquor into the truck bed as possible without creating a toppling hazard. The load was top-heavy to be sure, but the drive through D.C. wouldn't be a quick one. They'd take it easy. Nice and slow. They debated waiting until nightfall in order to take advantage of the darkness. It would make the cost of Hattie's magic a bit cheaper in the short run. However, the Feds doubled their patrols at night. The trade-off was more than Lizzie could accept. And so, they decided to head out immediately.

Hattie climbed into the passenger side door, pulling the vial of Aqua Vitae from her blouse, settling it in her lap for easy access. Raymond started the engine, and they eased forward, the jute rope creaking a bit as the cases of moonshine leaned their weight. They would take Route 1 due south, directly into the northeastern hinterland of the District. It was the quickest route, but it took them straight through the capital. In this case, fast was better than long.

The drive through Howard County was quiet, but not peaceful. Hattie kept her head on a swivel, eyeing forward and backward as Raymond focused on keeping the payload steady. The first real moment of tension came at the border of the District and Maryland. Two Model Ts sat on either side of Route 1, a clutch of young men standing at either side of the road. Hattie spotted them from a distance, but there was nowhere to go but through.

"What now?" Raymond asked.

"You know what to do," Hattie whispered.

"Okay, well, whatever you got cookin', best pour it outta the pot."

She watched as the Feds let two cars pass before flagging down a large Volvo truck. One of the goons harangued the driver while two more pulled open the tailgate and rummaged around what appeared to be wooden furniture. The shakedown lasted only a minute before the Feds waved the truck through.

Then came Raymond's turn.

Hattie recited her illusion through her mind as Raymond eased forward, only to have the lead Fed flag him down. Olive oil. It had worked before, and she was familiar with the illusion. She knew what it looked like, smelled like, even tasted like if it came to that. She waved her fingers in a tiny circle near her lap, and pinched the light around the rear of the truck, trying to keep the radius as discreet as possible.

Raymond slowed the truck to a stop as the trench-coated Treasury man approached his window.

"Afternoon," the young man declared, eyes flickering back and forth between them. His face tightened as he took in the sight of Hattie, and he eased his sharpening gaze back to Raymond. "Miss? You, uh…you alright?"

Hattie nodded twice. Just enough to answer the man. Not enough to break focus.

Raymond offered, "We're friends, is all."

The man's face snapped tight. "I wasn't asking you, boy."

Raymond dropped his gaze to his lap, knuckles gripping the steering wheel in panic.

Hattie risked turning her head, centering as much focus on her illusion as possible, though it was already tugging at her guts.

She cleared her throat and said, "Sir, this man is my driver." Her tone drawled with a humid Southern belle accent.

Raymond lifted his brow and stole a quick glance at Hattie. Hell…even Hattie didn't know where that voice came from. Playing with illusions in the market area had taught her several tricks these past few months. Adopting the mimicry of an Upright Citizen seemed appropriate under the circumstances.

The Fed nodded, then peered back toward the truck.

Hattie renewed her focus on the illusion as a wave of nausea racked her abdomen.

She heard the tailgate swing open. Eyes probed the illusion, searching the tops of the crates. Green glass bottles, she meditated. Green glass bottles. Hattie allowed a very subtle aroma of olive oil to leak out from the light pinch. It was a minor scent, but the added dimension of magic hammered her in the chest and throat.

Two men pulled a bottle out of different crates and Hattie gritted her teeth, expanding the illusion of touch, sight, and smell to both men. One cracked open the top of the bottle, sniffed, then took a swig. She bit back a moan, tasting blood in her mouth as she hunched over in pain.

Another bottle opened. The contents sniffed and tasted. If they didn't finish soon, she was going to puke blood all over the inside of the Runabout.

The Fed next to Raymond's window called out, "What's the word?"

The tailgate slammed shut, as a voice called out, "Nothin'. Bunch of oil."

A stream of warmth poured from her nose, tickling Hattie's upper lip. She turned her head to face forward, lifting a sleeve to her nose as casually as she could.

"Sir," she moaned with aristocratic impatience, "we have appointments to keep."

The Fed checked his tablet, lingered over Raymond for a brief moment, then nodded. "Alright, then. Have a good one."

Raymond released the brake and pushed the Runabout forward as fast as he could without raising attention. Once they'd reached two blocks, Hattie released the illusion, then clamped a hand over her mouth.

Raymond pulled the truck over, easing to a stop just in time for Hattie to shove open the door and vomit onto the side of the road. Spitting her mouth clear, she felt grateful that she'd skipped a meal.

"You okay?" Raymond asked, reaching for her arm.

She waved him away. "We did it."

"Well, we're just crossin' into D.C. Not there yet, and judging by the look of you, you're not gonna be doing that again."

He was right. That illusion had taken a huge toll on her. She might be able to hide the crates as they drove through the city, but another multi-sensory illusion needed for a second inspection stop would be beyond her.

Unless…she looked down at the vial in her hand. She needed to be stronger, to recover quicker. She needed to ensure this booze got to Alexandria. It was time to be bold, to make this happen, for all their sakes.

Hattie eased the stopper from the vial, dangling it over her open mouth. A single drop of the elixir fell onto her tongue, sending a wave of cold energy through her throat and chest.

The nausea melted away like fog on a summer morning. Her breathing eased into a normal rhythm. The nosebleed even stopped. She reached beneath the seat to fish out an old rag, and cleared her face.

Raymond watched in silent terror until she gave him a shuddering nod. "Okay. Let's go."

"That…that liquor, there?"

She dropped the vial back into her lap. "Aye."

"It's what I gave you last time you were so sick? Back in the field the other day?"

"Aye."

"What is it?"

"Distilled magic," she said. "Puts things to rights."

"I got that much," he grumbled. "But, is that your plan? Just about kill yourself, then nip on that magic potion?"

She stretched her neck, then turned to face him. "That's the plan, boy-o. I'm ready to do it again, if need be. And again. And again if I have to. That's the benefit of this little bottle of snake oil."

"Well, I don't like it, baby-girl." Raymond shook his head then put the truck into gear as she deposited the vial into her blouse. They made the drive through the District, coming close enough to see the Washington Monument and the cupola of the Capitol, with remarkable ease, all while Hattie hid the contents of their truck with barely a twinge of nausea.

After a half-hour's drive south, they crossed the Key Bridge into Virginia. Hattie eased up in her seat to look over the Potomac River. The enormous swell of muddy water flowed southeast toward its confluence with the Anacostia. Hattie had never boated this far inland along the Potomac. She'd only made it as far as Fort Washington, and that was with an empty boat. The old city sat just downriver of Georgetown, rows and rows of houses running at odd angles, all surrounding the cluster of governmental buildings huddled around the tall white obelisk near its center. It was a broader space than Baltimore and a bit cleaner. Its energy was fussier. Hattie was certain she wouldn't last very long in a city like this.

Just as her thoughts eased back into the present, Raymond shoved on the brakes, sending her bracing against the console.

"What is it?" she gasped.

Raymond stared forward at another roadblock, this one securing the border between Virginia and D.C.

"Well, shite," she muttered.

"Ya got enough gas in the tank for this?" he grumbled.

"Aye. I think I do."

As the line of cars crept toward the roadblock, this one a bit more invasive than the last, Hattie worked up another illusion. Same as before—olive oil in crates. The sun had begun its descent toward the west, but though the quality of light had changed, it wasn't enough to make the illusion any cheaper on Hattie.

They eased forward toward the new bevy of Treasury men.

Hattie pinched light and loaded her unpracticed Southern drawl.

These new Feds were a touch older, and certainly more mechanical. As Raymond nodded to a man with salt-and-pepper hair receding from his temples, the Fed simply asked, "What's in the back?"

"Olive oil," Hattie replied.

"Mmm, hmm," the Fed hummed, checking his clipboard. "Mind if we take a look?"

"That'd be just fine, sir," she cooed.

The illusion felt a tad easier this go around. The weight of power wasn't churning her intestines quite as hard as it usually did. As the tailgate swung open behind them, Hattie braced for the pairs of eyes probing into her magic.

"Looks like oil to me," one of the men said. Then he reached in and pulled bottles from the crates, squinting to look through the glass. Hattie held her breath and closed her eyes, concentrating.

The man muttered something, but she was afraid to open her eyes and break her concentration. The bottle clinked back in the crate, and Hattie squinted open her eyes to see the man pulling another out, unscrewing the top.

Sight, touch, smell. She waited for the nausea to hit her, for the blood to bubble up in her lungs, but she felt nothing beyond a mild abdominal cramp.

"Uh, sir?" the man's voice crackled from behind the truck.

The salt-and-pepper Fed offered a nod then withdrew to the rear of the vehicle. A conversation ensued, gathering in intensity.

Raymond peered through the mirror at the rear of the vehicle.

"Hattie?" he whispered.

"I've got this, Raymond." She lifted a hand, then added further dimension to the illusion.

"Hattie," Raymond urged in rising volume.

"What?"

She twisted in her seat to find a young Treasury man lifting a green bottle of olive oil to the sunlight as the older Fed made notes on his clipboard.

The illusion flickered, and for an instant the oil was a mason jar of clear liquid. The man holding it yelped.

Shite.

"We're nabbed," Raymond grunted.

"Can't be," she caught her breath. "Can't."

Oh no. Something was wrong. Something… Hattie squeezed her eyes shut, pushing hard at the light pinch. But if they'd caught that stutter, that might be enough to pull them out of the illusion.

A babble of excited voices came from the rear of the truck, and Hattie whimpered, realizing that Raymond was right. They were nabbed. Frantically trying to stitch the illusion back together again, Hattie opened her eyes and saw the younger man take a swig from the olive oil bottle.

The man released a paroxysm of coughing, nearly spraying his older cohort with high proof alcohol as he wiped his mouth. The older Fed raised a whistle to his mouth and blew.

Raymond sucked in huge breaths. "H-Hattie?"

"I'm sorry." Tears stung her eyes and she looked around, frantically trying to decide what to do. Make the truck disappear with themselves inside? The chances of that working with the Feds staring right at them were slim to none. What should she do? *What should she do?*

Feds trotted from across the street, ducking aside as a bicyclist nearly bowled into them.

Raymond grunted, "Hell with this," then hammered down on the accelerator.

The Runabout lurched forward, sending the crates of

moonshine hard against the jute. The load was too much for the rope, which creaked, whined, then finally snapped. Crate after crate of white lightning slipped out the back of the truck bed, smashing onto the road in a burst of smashed glass, and a spray of moonshine.

Raymond jerked the steering wheel hard, sending the truck down the bank toward the riverside, slicing through tall grass on their way to the Potomac.

Hattie gripped the window and the console, her eyes wide, chest heaving. How? How did this happen? Maybe physical health wasn't the only limit to her magic.

Or maybe she just wasn't good enough. Or good at all.

Feelings of shame spilled heavy into her chest as Raymond thundered through the brush alongside the river.

"Wh-where are you…going?" she wheezed.

"They're on us," he shouted. "Gotta get off the road."

Hattie turned in her seat, peering over a now-empty truck bed at a pair of cars slicing through the tall grass some few hundred yards behind them.

"Do you think they'll—?"

Before she could ask if they would open fire, gunshots rang out behind them. Raymond reached for Hattie, shoving her head below the seat. She clamped her eyes shut, adrenaline thundering through her arteries, and waved her arms over the front of her face. "Disappear!"

There was a familiar tug on her guts. The truck was gone, but she couldn't do anything about the sound. Maybe it would be enough. Maybe.

She opened her eyes, glancing up at Raymond.

He growled, "They still on us!"

A tear rolled down Hattie's cheek and she dropped the illusion.

"Hold your breath!" Raymond bellowed.

"What?"

"I said…" he jerked the wheel sideways. "Hold your damn breath!"

Hattie eased high enough to see out the windshield at the muddy Potomac approaching at alarming speed.

"Dive, girl!" Raymond shouted.

He kicked open his door and rolled into the grass as it gave way to water, cannonballing in a huge mass into the river.

The truck slammed into the Potomac, sending Hattie's head into the console. Stars shone in her vision, and little else. The vehicle twisted and bucked beneath her, and she grappled all around for purchase. The dizziness eased a bit as the ringing in her ears continued to whine, and she found the truck had plunged up to the hood into the water.

She pulled at the door handle and tried to push it open. Cold water rushed in around her waist, shoving her back against the door. With a scream, she kicked at the door, sending a spate of river water into the cab. The entire truck listed toward her head.

With frantic hands, she reached for the steering wheel as it rotated over her head. Water began spilling in through the driver's side window, and she realized the truck was half-submerged already. With great heaves, she pulled herself up to the driver's side of the bench, and up to the window opening.

There was a loud rush of wind all around her, and the golden sunset sky beyond the driver's side window snapped into a dark film as the truck slid completely underwater into the Potomac.

Hattie held her breath, kicking her feet as the rush of water finally stopped, sending her into a simple buoyant freefall. Her lean figure wriggled clear of the driver's side window and into the space of river water just beneath the surface.

She could hear muffled cries just above the surface so she lingered but the noise withdrew as the current of the river carried her forward.

And downward.

Hattie kicked her legs, pushing herself toward the surface as the water threatened to suck her down. Her face broke clear, and she sucked in a gasping breath, her hair plastered to the sides of her face as she bobbed along the surface of the river.

The two pursuing cars were now several yards away, the Feds wading ankle-deep into the river, still eyeballing the submerged Runabout. Hattie scanned the banks for Raymond, but she couldn't find him.

Finally, as the river neared a bend, and she worked to tread water in proper waterman fashion, a voice rasped nearby. Hattie pivoted with a rotating scoop of her hands to find Raymond's head bobbing a few dozen yards away.

His eyes were wide and wild, his mouth working against the water to keep his breath.

"You…you okay, baby girl? Can ya…get to shore?"

Hattie nodded and kicked her legs closer to the surface, then made overarm strokes, swimming toward the Virginia side of the river. The current eased as she made her way to the muddy bank, stepping onto semi-solid ground. Her feet squished through thick mire until she reached straw-like grass just above the bank.

Raymond's head continued downstream, easing its way toward shore as he dog-paddled his way inland. Hattie picked up the pace to catch up with him, finally reuniting almost a quarter-mile downstream. Raymond sat on the bank catching his breath, hands on his knees.

"Hey, boy-o," she said, uncertain how much of the water on her face was from the river or from tears.

"Guess that didn't go so good," he grumbled.

She sniffed, wiping her nose on a wet, muddy sleeve. "No." That it hadn't.

"Are you sick?" he asked without looking up.

She shook her head, then reached to her blouse for the vial. A familiar lump greeted her fingers near her sternum. Good. She still had it.

At length, Raymond caught his breath and got to his feet. Together they wandered through the brush, avoiding roads, until they reached Alexandria, negotiating a ride with a dark-skinned fellow with a truck full of fabric bolts. They hitched a ride farther south, carrying on and out of the reach of the Feds. At last, they ditched their ride and found their way to a friendly landing along the Potomac not far from Aquia Creek. There they talked their way onto a boat heading back to Baltimore.

The sun set while they were on the water. Raymond was quiet for the most part, as was Hattie. Crippling shame weighed on her shoulders. This had been *her* plan. Now, they'd lost an entire load of the Crew's moonshine, as well as Liz's Runabout. That alone would put her out of business.

By midnight, Raymond and Hattie found themselves at the Locust Point warehouse. No cars. No gangsters. Maybe word hadn't hit Baltimore just yet. If it had, Hattie figured there would be a trap waiting for them inside that warehouse.

"Well?" she asked Raymond. "Shall we face the music?"

Raymond reached for her hand, gripping in his massive fist. "Let's do this."

They marched up to the warehouse, sliding the door open on its squeaky rails.

They found Lizzie sitting in one of her office chairs in the direct center of an empty warehouse. Her face was leaden.

Hattie stepped forward. "So…"

"I've heard," Lizzie stated.

"We're alright, if you were wondering. All in one piece."

Raymond nodded his agreement.

"We lost the truck in the Potomac though," Hattie added softly.

"Doesn't matter." Lizzie stood up from her chair. "It's gone to shit anyway."

"Does the Crew know?" Hattie asked.

Lizzie released a laugh. More of a cackle. "Of course, they know! Everyone knows!"

"Everyone?" Raymond repeated.

Lizzie thrust her hands onto her hips. "Yes. They all know there's a bootlegger who tried to run a load of hooch through the center of D.C. and almost succeeded. They know this bootlegger was carrying moonshine that was magically disguised as olive oil."

Hattie caught her breath. "They know about the illusion?"

Liz's face finally fell into something approaching sympathy. "Yes. They know there's a free pincher somewhere in Baltimore. They know she…" she pivoted to Raymond, "…or he can create mirages. Illusions. Whatever."

Hattie's stomach dropped into her feet.

Raymond muttered, "That means…"

Lizzie completed his thought. "That means Vito knows Hattie exists. And he wants her."

CHAPTER 10

A curtain brushed against Vincent's cheek, wafting in the humid summer night's air as he sat in his open window. The city spread away from him, the avenue twinkling with gas lights and a few electric lamps toward the downtown. It was like some oil painting, murky and dark. A couple cigar-shaped clouds hung close to the harbor to the north. They eased across the sky, gossamer fingers lit from below by the city lights. Someone's phonograph scratched out the languid oboe strains of the Liebestraum, courtesy of Paul Whiteman Orchestra. The music was bouncy but hollow, echoing off the buildings across the street, half-committed to making music while simultaneously declaring that it was too damn hot for Listz.

Vincent's thoughts stampeded through his brain, ramming into one another like overweight men crowding a doorway. More than anything, he wanted to know if he could trust Alexander Smith. He'd taken a gamble with the man and his intelligence. After the fact, Vincent simply couldn't fathom what he was thinking, bringing Smith's warning up in the middle of the meet like that. It was reckless and it might have put both Vincent and Lefty behind the eight ball.

And yet, as Vincent closed his eyes and listened to Paul Whiteman snap his baton to the forced mirth of the ditty, he recognized that if given the choice, he'd do it again. This sort of gamble had been a long time in coming. How long had he attended to the Capo—first under Jim D'Urso, and then lately under Vito? How often had he been forced into a situation he'd rather avoid at their behest, only to receive a begrudging nod at best, and a public dressing down at worst? They'd jerked his dignity from him, dragged it into the back alley, and shot it between the eyes. He'd been called a freak. He'd been treated like he was nothing more than a tool for their use. He had a *handler*, for Christ's sake.

Something had to change. This could be it, the catalyst that changed everything.

But only if Smith was on the up-and-up.

A car careened down the street, sliding to a halt just below Vincent's window. Lefty and another member of the Crew stepped out, rushing for the door to the row house. They looked to be in a hurry, which tied a knot in Vincent's intestines. This was too early. The hit on Masseria wouldn't be until tomorrow night. Was Smith off by a day? Had Lefty's phone call only served to cast the Crew in a suspicious light?

Was that Smith's plan all along?

Vincent pulled himself out of the window and slid it half-shut as knuckles hammered against his door. When he opened the door, Lefty rushed inside, his empty sleeve swiping Vincent's vest as he strode to the center of the room.

"Good evening?" Vincent stated with an interrogative lilt, hoping Lefty's brusque entrance would be curtailed with a whiff of sarcasm.

"Get your jacket," Lefty gasped. His tone wasn't angry, nor annoyed. It was simply direct. Urgent.

"What's going on?" Vincent asked.

"We've been summoned to Havre de Grace."

Vincent sucked in a breath and lifted his chin. "What...happened?"

"They won't tell me," Lefty grumbled.

"Is it Masseria?"

Lefty leveled a weary glare onto Vincent. "Just get your damn jacket, yeah?"

Vincent hopped into the back seat of the car as Lefty rode shotgun. The driver was a young man Vincent didn't really know but recognized from the hotel. The driver didn't have much to say and looked arguably more panicked than Lefty did.

As the car turned down Fayette, angling for the county road north toward Havre de Grace and Vito Corbi's vineyard, Vincent leaned forward over the front bench seat.

"If it was New York, they'd probably have us in bags, by now."

Lefty nodded soberly.

Vincent added, "Gotta be big business, if we're going to the vineyard. Who else got hooked for this?"

"Tony. That's all I know."

"Tony, huh?" Vincent nodded. "Then it's probably some harem scarem over the Bay runners."

Lefty twisted in his seat to face Vincent directly. "Okay, so level with me, huh? What's going on between you and that boat-legger girl?"

Vincent blinked at the question, feeling something cold settle down deep in his stomach.

The driver peered over to Lefty, who turned to bark at the young man, "Eyes on the road, you mook!"

The driver snapped his attention back to the road.

Vincent shook his head. "Nothing."

Lefty squinted. "I gotta know, Vincent. Before we walk

into this…whatever it is. I gotta know you ain't seeing that…" Lefty frowned, clearly catching himself and rethinking his choice of words. "That redhead."

"I'm not." His heart hammered in his chest. What had Hattie gotten herself into?

Lefty fixed him with a glare. "So you're not seeing her is what you're saying? You're not in communication with her? You haven't had any contact with her in months?"

"If I was seeing her, I'd have told you. When have I ever been able to keep a romance under the table with you?"

Lefty stared at him a moment then nodded. "Okay." He turned back around in his seat to glare out his window.

Vincent swallowed hard. That lie wasn't as hard as he thought it'd be. Lefty's nose was usually more sensitive to Vincent's particular vintage of horseshit. But Lefty's concerns worried him.

Because it meant this meeting at the vineyard was definitely about Hattie.

Vincent gazed at the moon in the sky as it ducked behind one of those cigar-clouds, and felt ill as he wondered again what the hell Hattie had gotten herself into.

The car swung onto the drive that lead onto Vito's property, finally coming to a halt at the gravel half-circle drive that wreathed the marble fountain nestled before the stately Italian villa. Vincent and Lefty hopped out of the car, finding several goons ready for them. The front windows of the villa flickered with light. Seemed Vito was in the manse, and not somewhere out in the rows of grapevines. It also seemed that Vito hadn't ponied up to have electric lines run out to his vineyard. Vincent found that odd. The man was all about reform. The new thing. He'd figured Vito would be first in line to get electric light into his palace north of Baltimore.

Then again, as Vincent entered the villa behind Lefty and spied the reproduction marble statues and what was likely genuine Italian furniture in the lavish interior of the estate, he recognized how much reverence Vito paid to the Old World.

Vito stood near an enormous fireplace, its mantel and surround carved out of green marble. The fireplace was absent a fire, and the tall, narrow windows of the gallery stood open to let in the fresh summer breeze off the undulating hills of vines. He was surrounded by a tiny clutch of besuited gangsters, including Tony, who looked sober for a change.

Once Vito recognized the two, he ceased whatever tirade he was inflicting upon the gathering to stand stiff and silent. Stony. His eyes bore holes into Vincent—Vincent in particular.

Lefty continued without a pause, though Vincent hesitated half a step.

Vito lifted a hand in a beckoning gesture. "At last. Come."

The two shuffled forward to join the cadre surrounding Vito. Vincent took in his posture and his expression. The two were difficult to reconcile. At once, Vito's face bespoke pure, seething outrage. On the other, his posture was forward, and he bounced on his feet. Either the man was livid, or excited. Perhaps both at the same time.

Lefty eyed Tony, then turned to Vito. "Are we the last?"

Vito nodded. "Thank you for coming."

"What's the word?" Lefty asked, back full of steel.

Vito gestured to Tony, who ran a hand through his greased hair. "We lost a shipment today." He let the words hang in the air, probably hoping for one of them to draw him out. Lacking that, he continued, "In Rosslyn, Virginia. Right across the river from Foggy Bottom."

Vincent shook his head. "Who was fool enough to run booze that close to the Fed's front door?" Even as he asked the question, the answer landed in his head like an anvil.

Tony winced. "It...it seems that certain individuals... former contractors...made an ill-advised..." He trailed off, struggling for words.

Vito took up the cause. "Two of his nitwit outsiders bungled it."

"The same ones running liquor over the Bay?" Vincent asked.

"The very same," Vito replied, his voice betraying a note of excitement. "A colored driver and a young woman in workman's clothes."

Lefty asked, "How did we receive this information?"

Vito replied, "I have people close to Georgetown. And a few more inside the Treasury." His face eased into a smug grin.

"They were boat-leggers, though. Right? And didn't we just write them off? What gives?" Lefty scowled.

Tony answered, "I want to be clear—Lizzie Sadler was not involved. Not directly. I spoke to her just an hour ago, and she says she wasn't even at her warehouse."

"How bad is it?" Lefty asked.

"We lost twelve crates of West Virginia corn liquor. Busted out right at the base of the new bridge. Right in front of the G-men. The two bootleggers made a run for it and bellied up right in the Potomac."

Vincent felt himself go cold. "Are they dead?"

"No," Tony replied. "No bodies were found. Probably swam off."

Vincent shook his head. "This is nuts. These people..." He took a breath to collect himself. "Based on our experience with this outfit just a couple months ago, these were profes-sionals. They had their business down pat. Are we for sure they were the ones?"

Tony nodded.

Lefty shrugged. "Anyone gets desperate enough, they'll take stupid risks."

Vincent glanced at Lefty, who met his gaze with a raised eyebrow. Fine. Message received.

"According to the Capo's insiders, a checkpoint at the Maryland border noted a truck with a black driver and a white female passenger just an hour beforehand," Tony elaborated. "Said they was carrying olive oil. Point man at the Virginia border said it was olive oil—for a few minutes, anyway. Then one of the boys tasted it and suddenly instead of olive oil, they were staring at a whole bunch of shine."

"Your point?" Lefty asked.

Vito lifted a finger, and everyone drew silent. With a long breath, the Capo said, "The girl used an illusion."

Vincent's heart twisted. Damn. It had probably been too many eyes on the truck, too many senses involved, too much time. And twice within a matter of hours? Gutsy attempt, but clearly too much for Hattie too pull off.

One of the besuited men behind Vito spoke up. "A pincher?"

Vito nodded, his face now fully committed to the eager energy his posture exuded.

"Yes. There is a free-born *stregone* among us. And she was here this whole time." Vito turned to point a finger at Vincent.

Vincent held a breath. But Vito's face wasn't drawn in anger. Instead, amusement.

"And you stood right beside her for several days. It is too bad you *stregone* have no instinct for one another."

"You're sure it was the girl?" Vincent asked. "Not the driver?"

Vito sneered and waved away the comment. "Not possible."

"Because he's colored?" Vincent prodded.

Lefty broke into the sudden tension. "Is there any product left at their warehouse?"

Tony moved to answer, but Vito cut him off. "Who cares? We have in our grasp a free-born *stregone*! And she nearly managed to deliver twelve cases of liquor right under the Treasury men's noses. One such as her would be worth all the liquor in West Virginia!"

Vincent straightened a bit at this comment, hoping it was the value of pinchers in general, and not simply Hattie, that Vito had lassoed onto.

Lefty turned to Tony. "You think Sadler knew what she was?"

Tony shook his head. "She denies it."

"That's not saying much," Lefty grumbled.

Tony shrugged. "She inherited this entire business from Jake Sadler. We all remember Jake Sadler, right?"

Heads nodded.

Tony continued, "If you were to ask me if Jake knew this girl was a pincher, then I'd buy that. But Liz? Nah. She's barely keeping her head above water, as it is."

Vincent breathed through the panic filling his chest. Sure, Tony was doing his best to pull his lover off the tracks. But every word coming from Tony only served to stoke the Capo's fire. A free-born pincher operating right under their noses. Vito would be furious, if this hadn't presented such a rare opportunity.

"Vincenzo," Vito declared.

Vincent stiffened. "Capo?"

"You know this girl. You know her name." These weren't questions, they were statements of fact.

He winced. "Yes. Hattie Malloy." The words felt like treason.

"Then I charge you with acquiring this illusionist."

All eyes turned to Vincent.

"I…" Vincent wheezed.

Vito pressed, "She is a being of power, such as yourself. And we have a fleeting moment, I think. A moment to approach this *stregone*. Approach with open hands. Offer to her this moment, Vincenzo. A chance to join us."

Vincent nodded. Indeed, this was the pitch he'd been refining these past few months, though it was nowhere near as spit-polished as Vito managed on the fly.

"Yes, Capo."

Vito stepped forward to lay both hands on Vincent's shoulders. "You bring me this girl, Vincenzo. You do this, and we will be unstoppable."

Vito's deep brown eyes reached out to Vincent's. He stood in free fall for the barest of moments. The meaty hands on his shoulders sat like blankets. The Capo was drawing him in. This was his chance, even more of a chance than the nonsense with Smith.

But Hattie…

"I will," Vincent intoned, his voice flat and emotionless.

Vito smiled, then nodded. "Go get her!"

The Capo withdrew to a sideboard to pour himself a glass of red wine from a decanter, keeping his back to the rest of them. That was their dismissal.

Outside the villa, standing on the gravel drive, Vincent felt the earth tilt beneath his feet. Never before had the Capo deigned to address him with such familiarity. And Lefty was there, just beside him. It was like Lefty didn't even exist. Of course Vincent was the pincher. The only pincher. And in this sort of affair, the Capo would send a pincher.

Vincent turned to Lefty, who loomed beside him. "So?"

Lefty released a quick chuckle. "So yourself! What's the play?"

Tony sidled up alongside Lefty, eyes expectant.

Vincent straightened his shoulders. There was no avoiding this now. "Tony? Are they at the warehouse?"

"I called Lizzie just an hour ago at her home line." He blushed at the unspoken message there. "Because she, uh… she wasn't at work."

Lefty smirked. "What're the odds that's actually her home line?"

Tony scowled. "I got good odds on that, so mind your own beeswax."

Vincent lifted a hand. "Can you call her again? Get them all in one place?"

"Fat chance," Tony blurted. "She don't know where those two are."

Vincent pinched time…just a second. He took two steps forward, then released the magic. Time slipped back into its normal rhythm, only now Vincent was standing a few inches away from Tony.

Tony gasped and jerked away.

With a somber inflection, Vincent said, "Don't jerk me around. You know where Lizzie is right now. And you know very well that she knows where her people are. This thing maybe went off the rails, but Sadler knew exactly what was going down. They're a tight ship. So, between you, me and Lefty, let's cut the bull. I want you to call Sadler. Arrange a meet. We're gonna bring goons. She needs to know that, so she don't get ideas."

Tony nodded.

Vincent continued, "Tell her we're coming. Tonight. And we gotta talk to Malloy. That's the square deal. If they get hinky with us, let her know there's nowhere we won't go to find her. You got that?"

Tony sucked in a breath, then nodded again.

"So, what're ya waiting for?"

Tony trotted off back into the villa.

Lefty stepped alongside Vincent.

Vincent asked, "What do you think, did I lay it on too thick?"

"I don't know." Lefty snickered. "It sounded pretty good to me."

"What am I doing, Lefty?" He sighed and ran a hand through his hair.

With a spin on his heel, Lefty laid a hand on Vincent's shoulder. "For what it's worth, you seem pretty natural at this. Maybe I misjudged you."

"Exactly when did you misjudge me?" Vincent asked with a laugh.

"All your life."

"Eh, get outta here," he scoffed as they headed toward the car.

Within an hour, Tony had made contact with Lizzie Sadler, and reported that the entire "operation," as he put it, would be in attendance at the Locust Point warehouse.

By midnight, they had three cars and one truck ready to roll to Locust Point. The cars provided the talking heads, and the truck was there to gather whatever product remained in that warehouse. No matter how things went down, the Crew was about to take hold of its own liquor shipping that night.

Vincent wouldn't have been surprised to hear that Hattie was halfway to West Virginia by this point. Last time he'd dealt with her in an official capacity, she was more skittish than a sparrow on a cat's ass. The whole notion of being pressed into the service of the Baltimore Crew sent her into heavy-breathed panic. The word was out, now. Everyone knew what she was. He half expected to arrive at the warehouse to find she'd vanished hours ago.

But then why wouldn't Lizzie have just told them that? Why have them all descend on her place of business like a small army if Hattie was not even in the state?

He mulled it over as the motorcade ran from downtown Baltimore to Locust Point. Hattie knew the conundrum she was in. She knew the consequences of that cock-up in D.C. Surely, she'd have to know. No. Hattie knew they were coming. And for some reason she hadn't run for the hills.

But why?

Vincent considered in a moment of vanity that it was him that had kept her in the city.

He'd tried to talk her into joining the Crew already, and after endless internal debate, he'd decided she was a poor fit. Disastrous, in fact. She was too volatile. Bucked too hard against authority. Hell, every time Vincent met with her to compare notes, he was never sure if the meeting would end in them shouting at each other, or flirting.

The car rammed through a pothole, and Vincent shook his head.

Flirting?

And if he was honest with himself, it hadn't been solely on her side either. Even when they were shouting at each other, there was some sort of electric current between them.

Flirting.

Vincent released a quick chuckle, eliciting a glance from Lefty.

He continued to work on the problem as the motorcade pulled onto Key Highway leading to the waterfront at Locust Point. Hattie knew they were coming. She knew Vincent would be there. Which meant she probably held out hope that Vincent would find some way to let her escape.

His stomach squeezed tight as he realized that wasn't in the cards.

"Hold here," Vincent called out.

The driver stopped the front car along the side of Fort Avenue, easing toward a row of sheds and warehouses. The rest of the vehicles followed suit.

Vincent stepped out to wait for the remainder of the party to gather in a mob before him. Expectant eyes watched as he gathered his thoughts—particularly Lefty's.

"So," Vincent announced, "if what we heard tonight is true, we're about to confront a light pincher." He waved a finger at a few of the gathered gangsters. "That might not mean much to some of you, so let me tell you what we could be up against."

The men shuffled nervously, obviously uncomfortable with the idea of facing someone who would be using magic against them instead of guns.

"Anything you see might be an illusion," Vincent continued. "Anything. You think it's your buddy standing next to you, but it's her, with iron pointed right in your ear. Don't trust what you see, but don't trust what you hear either. If we've truly had a light pincher living here under our noses this whole time, undetected, then she's good. Don't underestimate her."

One of the younger goons snickered. "She's some girl, some river rat who's been running hooch for us. What's there to worry about?"

Vincent pinched time, strolled over to the lad to pull the hat off his head, then returned to his exact position per his practiced method, and released the stream of time. He lifted the hat with a scowl. "She's not just some river rat, she's a river rat with magic."

The lad raised a hand to his head, and finding it bare his eyes widened.

Vincent tossed the hat back to him. "Like I said, if there's really a light pincher in there, then don't trust anything you see or hear. Believe me. All you mooks like to think of me as some sorta freak to laugh at, but I know more about this stuff than you do."

The gathered faces searched for a safe place to look.

Vincent chuckled. "The good news is I'm the freak that's on your side. Bad news is, this individual we're about to approach? Light pincher or not, she is most certainly not on our side. So, I need each and every one of you to listen and listen good. You keep your irons in their sleeves. You hear me? If you pull a gun on this girl, you might be drawing on your buddy. No shooting unless I say so."

Heads nodded.

With a whip of his finger, Vincent turned to Lefty. "You and me and Tony. We'll head up the front, alone while the rest of you stay here."

Tony squinted. "The hell you say."

"Don't give me shit on this, Tony. If she's really a light pincher, then going in there to take her by force is only going to get us killed. Our best angle is to parlay and convince her to come willingly. And I'll do the talking."

Tony nodded, as did Lefty.

"Okay. Hang back, fellas. We'll shout if we need ya."

A couple snickers were his reply.

Vincent turned to the warehouse, adjusted his hat, then stepped forward. Lefty joined him at his right, and Tony to his left.

Tony grumbled, "We couldn't have driven a few more yards?"

"You want to drive into the side of a truck you didn't know was there?" Vincent asked.

"Good point."

They continued up the street until the flickering candle light of the warehouse windows greeted them in the distance. The lane ended in an unpaved lot just before the warehouse, illuminated more by the moon than anything. The geometry of the place seemed grander on foot, as opposed to simply driving in.

Lefty reached over to grab Vincent's arm. Vincent followed suit by holding out an arm to bar Tony.

All of them followed Lefty's nod, to a tiny shadow in the middle of the lot.

"What is that?" Tony whispered.

Vincent shrugged as he took a half-step forward.

It was small, whatever it was. Sitting directly on the dirt of the loading lot. Vincent cast a glance to his companions, then shrugged. He took a step closer to the lot. Then another. Soon, he found himself strolling into the clear space before the warehouse, the moon shining overhead. And that tiny shadow sitting before him.

Vincent approached it and crouched down.

It was cylindrical. A can. The faint moonlight barely illuminated the wording along the paper label. *Bertha's Beans.*

Vincent stood up, he turned to shout, "It's just a can of—"

A shot rang out in the summer night, causing Vincent to clinch his fist. Out of instinct, he pinched time.

Turning against the turbid air of the frozen space, he spied the can of beans. It sat mid-leap, its contents spilling into the air as a bullet rifled its way inches past the exit wound. The slug spun slow in the impossible speed of the time pinch. Vincent straightened up to cast a glance along the line of fire. A plume of fire blossomed from the piles of lumber at the edge of the loading lot, near the harbor.

There was the gunman.

And Vincent froze even as the weight of the magic began to prod his guts, reminding him that every second spent in this pinch exacted a cost on his body. His eyes scanned the entire line of sheds and warehouses surrounding them.

Surrounding.

How many more were there?

This preposterous display was more than a prank. It was a warning—a warning meant for Vincent. Hattie was letting him know that she knew what he could do and she was as immune to his magic as he was to her illusion.

If he could, he would've called out to her in this time pinch. Alas, air didn't move the way it normally did under his ministrations, and so, he was forced into a decision. Release the time pinch and hold off Lefty and Tony.

Or try to get creative.

With a weak draw of breath in the unsteady physics of his magic, Vincent closed his eyes, tried to calm his nerves, then released the time pinch.

CHAPTER 11

The sound of Hattie's gunshot rolled from its subaquatic murk higher and higher until the rushing became the tail end of the bang she'd expected. The slow-billowing plume at the end of her rifle evaporated as time folded back into its normal pace. Of course, Vincent would pinch time. It would have to be a reflex for the man. Hattie had taken precautions—she was under cover, as were Raymond, Liz, and the four Curtis Creek neighbors Raymond had conscripted to help bail them out of this predicament.

The can of beans hopped several feet from its original position, spraying beans into the air in a pinwheel. Vincent stood in front of two men. Hattie recognized them both. There was Tony to his left— Lizzie's side action, and one of the Crew's major players. He was a railroad spike stuffed into a tweed smoking jacket, hard as a nail at the core, but dressed in an unexpected weave of education and refinement that belied his profession.

Then there was Lefty Mancuso, Vincent's handler. That man frightened Hattie more than any of the gangsters she'd met, heard of, or imagined. Pushing fifty, Lefty was a veteran of the War, having given an arm for God and Country. His disability hadn't dulled his aim with a pistol, though. Hattie'd seen that first hand. But the most terrifying aspect of this dark-haired, wrinkle-eyed fellow was his intellect. She could see it in his eyes. They never stopped watching. Noticing. Piecing it all together. Hattie felt certain on a deep level that there was very little she could ever hide from that man.

And he was in charge of Vincent.

The time pincher stood tall in the middle of the dust-paved loading lot. The gunshot hadn't even shaken him. Not surprisingly, he'd led the march with the other two up the drive to the warehouse, leaving the army of goons behind. Vincent knew what Hattie could do to those men, even if she couldn't work her wiles on him. Damned immunity. What-ever cosmic force had saddled the two of them with a mutual resistance to each other's magic was surely laughing its ass off at the moment.

"I'm here to talk," Vincent shouted, his hands raised.

Hattie pursed her lips. Well, here it was. The moment she'd dreaded since she met the man three months ago. In a way, she was surprised it hadn't come sooner. And yet, it felt like she hadn't had any time at all to prepare for this.

With a quick sign of the cross, she hefted the rifle down to the crook of her elbow and stood up to step clear of the lumber surrounding her. Two steps and she was fully exposed.

Vincent's eyes found her immediately.

Hattie kept the barrel of the rifle aimed at a piece of ground halfway between the two of them. No need to act preemptively hostile, but it was best to have the weapon ready in case Lefty took a belligerent notion.

"Evening," Hattie called out. She kept her tone profes-sional. There was no way of knowing how much the Crew knew of their ongoing communication. In case Vincent decided to play this close to the chest, she elected to treat him like a stranger.

Both Tony and Lefty, spotting Hattie with a rifle in her hands, eased hands toward their jackets. But Vincent threw a flat hand behind him, waving his fingers as he muttered something about "keeping it in leather." Tony pulled his hand away. It was Lefty that lingered, eyes hard on Hattie. Once Vincent turned his head and spat something vulgar at the man, Lefty eased his hand away from his jacket.

Vincent nodded to Hattie. "Nice shot!"

"Thank you," she replied in a flat tone. "Thought I'd demonstrate a wee bit of skill, just in case your companions decided this was going to be simple."

Vincent's eyes widened just a bit, and Hattie couldn't be completely sure from this distance, but she detected a slight shake of his head. He was warning her off the attitude. Fair enough. He had a better sense of these men than she had.

"Can we talk?" Vincent asked.

"What'd you think we're doing, then?" she replied.

"Privately?" he urged.

Lefty muttered something to Vincent, who replied without turning. Clearly, Lefty was uncomfortable with the notion. And so, Hattie decided to let them come to their own peace with it before replying.

After several back-and-forths, Vincent called, "How many guns we got pointing at us, if you don't mind my asking?"

"Enough," she replied.

"What's with the bum's rush?"

"Figured you'd come calling. I think maybe there's been a misunderstanding, but you lot aren't known for wool gathering."

"Then may I suggest we take this inside?" Vincent nodded to the warehouse.

Hattie stifled a smile. Yep. He was trying to pull her into a personal conversation, which meant he wanted to get real.

Good. So did she.

"Agreed." She turned to shout to either side of her, "We're stepping inside. Hold your fire. Unless the ugly bastards decide to get cheeky, then have at it."

Hattie spun the rifle and stowed it over her shoulder, watching Vincent as he took tentative steps forward. Technically, one of the Curtis Creek boys could plug him before he even heard the shot, without any chance of him pinching time and avoiding a bullet, but that wasn't why they were here. Hattie wanted—no, she needed—a permanent solution to this mess. Not just for her, but for Raymond and Lizzie.

And Vincent was her only hope.

She strolled ahead of Vincent, keeping a comfortable distance to reinforce the notion they were strangers, and pulled the warehouse door open. It rolled with only a little rust-driven squeal, just wide enough to let them slip inside. Hattie waited a moment as Vincent caught up with her, stepping inside to the space only illuminated by a small flickering candle.

Hattie shoved the door closed, then waited, barely able to make Vincent out in the dim light.

A click sounded in and a feeble illumination added its glow to the lone candle. He watched her over top of the tiny plume of flame rising from his lighter.

Vincent gave her a sad smile. "Well, this is a damned situation, isn't it?"

Hattie let the rifle slip off her shoulder, propping the gun against a stack of empty pallets. "Aye. That it is."

They stared at one another, expressions shifting through uncertainty, concern, and relief that they were finally alone.

Vincent shook his head. "Hattie, what the hell were you thinking?"

She felt her lips tremble at the warm affection behind the scold. "Not much, I'll admit to that. It was stupid but it was the only shot we had at keeping our jobs."

Vincent's face darkened. "There was never a shot. Vito had his mind made before you…" He didn't finish the sentence.

"Before I made it worse?" she offered.

"You've definitely stepped right into the middle of it. Which brings us to the conversation you swore you'd never again have with me."

Hattie rolled her eyes. "Eh, I'm ready for it. Let me have the pitch. Maybe third time's a charm, boy-o."

Vincent grinned, the smile fading just as quickly as it had appeared. "Seriously, though. Vito's got you thumbnailed. And he knows your name."

She searched his face for hope. "Is there any way at all that we can turn this around?"

"I'm afraid not. He's…he's put me in charge of bringing you in."

Hattie stiffened, and her jaw set hard. "You?"

"This can't be a surprise to you. You know he's been chomping at the bit to bring another pincher into the fold." He shrugged. "That's where we are, now."

She crossed her arms. "I'm afraid my answer's the same now as it's been before."

"Hattie…"

"If you think I'm going to make your dreams come true by walking out that door and slipping into your car for a long ride to sign my life away to a monster in a three-piece suit, then you're exactly as daft as you look."

"Don't get all lathered up. You're the one who put us both in this position."

She cocked her head. "We were doing just fine before your boss decided to cut bait. Bloody ignorant of him, if you ask me. He had expertise here. Knowledge of the entire Bay. Every inlet, every outlet. But no. He's decided we're not good enough, so my family and everyone here are left staring into the abyss."

Vincent blinked at the comment. "You really putting the blame for this on me?"

"Not on you," she grumbled. "But you're the Crew's mouthpiece, right? So, you have to listen to me whine on about it."

He snickered, though it rolled out hollow. "Look, I've been working on this spiel a while, now."

"I know. You won't shut up about it."

"Yeah, yeah. So, let me wind up a pitch here. It's obvious your days of shadow boxing are over. Word's out. And you're gonna come on board, or you're choosing a hell of a Plan B."

"Not so obvious," she chided.

"You gonna let me talk, or what?"

She lifted a hand in appeasement.

Vincent cleared his throat. "Any illusion you had of living a free life is over. It's time to start talking nuts and bolts. You know what the Crew's about. You know the water side of the business, but that's just the liquor trade. After this bone-headed Volstead Act gets repealed one of these days, there's gonna be a lot of work to do."

Vincent continued his pitch, though Hattie tuned him out. The inevitability of this situation stuck in her craw. How dare he deflect her right of freedom as an illusion? How presumptuous was he to think that he simply had to wait her out until she made this unavoidable blunder? Her blood boiled, and she balled fists at her sides as he went on about the Crew's businesses and advantages. And through it all, the single thought that truly sent her chest into a twist was that he might be right.

What choice did she really have? Run and hide? Stay and

make them chase her down and drag her in? Or walk willingly into a cage?

Anything was preferable to that cage.

Hattie lifted a hand to halt Vincent's speech. "Eh, boy-o."

He blinked at her, then lifted his chin. "What?"

"I need you to realize something. There's no way in heaven or hell I'm joining the Baltimore Crew."

He huffed. "Okay, okay. Get it outta your system. And when you do, we'll start speaking as adults."

She scowled at Vincent, taking a step back as she unfolded her arms. "Some nerve you got, there!"

"Well, I'm sorry. But you're well past this fairy tale. And don't make this about me. It was you who brought me here. Your screw up."

Hattie thrust a finger at him. "Don't you dare—"

"You're the one who decided to run a truck up the Feds' nostrils. Right? You're the one who assumed she had the stick to pinch an illusion in broad god-loving daylight right on the banks of the Potomac."

Hattie had no defense to that.

He concluded, "I'm not trying to spank you, here. In fact, I'm trying to help you. So, untwist your tongue for a hot second, and let me finish."

She glared at Vincent but chose not to respond.

After a pregnant moment, he cleared his throat to continue. "I can arrange a situation."

"A situation?" she droned.

"For you. And your friends."

That sent a wave of conflict cascading through Hattie's stomach. "What sort of situation?"

"Your boss, Sadler? She's already laid groundwork to step clear of this mess. You probably don't owe her any thanks for that."

Hattie nodded with a leaden scowl.

"And your friend, Raymond."

"Raymond."

"Yes, Raymond. We're always looking for muscle. And that back-bay know-how? I'll bet you short odds Tony's looking for someone with more than half a brain to help run the boys' hooch down the coast."

Hattie shook her head. "You're a daft cock, you know that?"

Vincent grimaced. "Huh?"

Hattie lifted fingers to count off. "First, Lizzie has been a part of your machine for the better part of a year, now. How'd that worked out for her? Second, do you really think a man like Vito Corbi has any interest in bringing a black man into his direct employ?"

Hattie waved her fingers in his face. "And third, it was you said how impossible it would be to work with me. Beyond that, you're laying out how bloody damn magnificent it is to be a slave to the Baltimore Crew, when you don't really believe it yourself." She took a step forward, her voice softening. "I know you think all of this has elevated you somehow, but I have to believe you're still aware of how truly misgiven this life of servitude is. Or maybe not. I don't expect you to understand how I feel. You've never lived a free life."

Vincent stepped away, but she reached out to capture his arm, sliding her fingers down his sleeve to grip his hand.

"I live a free life, Vincent. And I'll do anything to protect that. Anything. Do you understand me?"

His fingers curled around hers. "Please don't make me do this," he whispered.

"I'm not making you. It's a choice you have here."

"Hattie, please don't. Just come with me." His voice choked on the words, and the sound sent a wave of dread through Hattie's frame. What had she said that had upset him so? These were delicate matters, and dear to both her and Vincent, but still, this man for all of his charm and swagger had never revealed such frailty before.

"I don't have a choice, Hattie," Vincent continued. "You'll come with me tonight. One way or another. That's what I'm trying to punch through to you. I want this to be cooperative. I don't want to have to drag you in against your will. I don't want to have to force you into this. Please, just come with me."

Hattie hung her head. "I can't, Vincent."

"What options do you really think you have?"

His voice was soft and gentle. Her chest squeezed tight around her heart. They hadn't known each other very long, to be sure, but their friendship had become something she not only valued, but relied upon. Vincent was the one person who understood her powers, and yet, there was still a gulf between them—her, a free-born pincher, and him, a tool of the mob, a lifelong slave to unworthy masters. No matter how often she'd tried to pry open his eyes, she knew he'd never manage to escape their control. It was written too deep. It wasn't his fault. He was like a child doing what his parents had always told him was right.

It was so tragic that it had to come to this.

She straightened her spine and looked him in the eyes. "Let's go, then."

Vincent blinked in confusion, then sucked in a breath. "Really?"

"Come on," she said, tone even and a little resigned.

He blinked several times, then echoed her posture. "Oh. Are you sure?"

"You said there were no options, boy-o. So, let's stop faffing on and just get this done." She pulled her hand from his, feeling a horrible sense of loss with the action.

He nodded, eyes alive with dubious hope. Stepping

forward to ease the door further open, he gave her a smile. "It's going to be better than you think. Trust me."

Trust him. Hattie bit her tongue. It wasn't Vincent she worried about trusting, but the rest of the Baltimore Crew.

She stepped back out into the sweltering night air. Lefty and Tony remained in their place, hands on their hips. As the two pinchers emerged, their faces snapped tight. Lefty buttoned his jacket with a nod.

Vincent stepped in front of Hattie, almost protectively as they reached the center of the loading lot. With a twinge of guilt, Hattie twisted her fingers together into a claw at her hip, then released them in a sudden motion, pinching light as she did.

Tony and Lefty spun on their heels, both reaching for guns holstered beneath their jackets. Tony covered his head, as he looked backward.

Vincent drew to a sudden halt.

Tony shouted orders over his shoulder as he ran sprinting down the lane. Lefty hoisted his pistol back toward Vincent and Hattie, his eyes wide and wild. As he lowered his gun, he ducked again as Hattie reinforced the illusion with a stronger sound.

"Come on! It's a bushwhack!" Lefty barked at Vincent. And he raced after Tony down the lane, gun held in front of him.

Vincent stood stiff, back to Hattie as the others' footsteps faded and they were enveloped in the silence of night. Voices called out in the distance, near the Crew's motorcade. Slowly he turned to face Hattie, his face drawn in grief.

"What did they see?" he asked.

Hattie focused on the illusion, her intestines groaning as she extended her magic over such a long distance. "Explosions. Near your cars."

He nodded. "That's a hell of a stretch."

A trickle of blood slipped from her nostril.

Vincent pulled a handkerchief from his jacket pocket and offered it to her. She took it, dabbing at her nose as figures emerged from the surrounding crates and sheds—the Curtis Creek boys with their guns trained on Vincent.

He eyed them cautiously. "I suppose you've made up your mind."

"I told you," she gasped, struggling with the illusion. "I'll do anything to protect my freedom."

Vincent nodded, and reached out as she returned his handkerchief.

Raymond approached, his .357 held to the ground but ready to draw onto Vincent. "We gotta go, baby girl."

Hattie nodded to Raymond, then eyed Vincent once more. "This could get uncomfortable for you. You know that?"

"You shouldn't bring these people into it," Vincent warned. "You're going to get them killed."

"Then their blood will be on your hands, boy-o."

His eyebrows shot up. "You really think so?"

"I know so. Godspeed, Vincent Calendo," she declared as she turned to join the Curtis Creek boys.

They walked through the empty lot, making their way around the stacks of lumber for a couple hundred yards until they reached the bend of the Patapsco River, where two boats waited for them. Hattie took a dark-skinned hand and climbed aboard, searching the faces surrounding her.

"Where's Liz?" she asked.

Raymond replied, "She lit out. Told me to tell you she wishes you well, but she don't expect to ever see you again."

Hattie shuddered under the weight of emotion, and the toll that her illusion had exacted on her. She was thrilled that the light pinch had gone off at all. After the debacle in D.C., she wasn't fully confident she could make it happen. Nothing seemed certain anymore.

Except for the fact that she was now on the run, with the entirety of the Baltimore Crew trying to hunt her down and bring her in.

CHAPTER 12

*L*unch at Shakes's Bistro on a typical Thursday was a subdued affair. Four-tops crowded the space along the story-high double windows, afternoon light spilling white and warm onto the lazy diners as they discussed politics or complained about wages, all while pickling their livers with martinis and other cocktails not overtly advertised as a matter of tact.

This was not a typical Thursday.

The entire restaurant had been commandeered by the Baltimore Crew. Men in suits had drawn the tables together to form a long solid surface. Rocks glasses of whiskey and melting ice interrupted a line of half-empty wine glasses. A map sat unfolded at the center of the table. Fingers waggled at one another as Baltimore Crew middlemen suggested plans of attack.

At the far end, Vincent sat slumped in his chair as Lefty lingered at the window, a cigarette in his hand.

"We have to find this Sadler," one of the goons declared. "Take her to the warehouse up off the highway. Take some pliers to her. She'll talk."

Vincent winced. "Lizzie has no idea where Malloy is. She would have made sure of that."

"Then we stake out every road in and out of the city," another man commented.

"She's a waterman. Blocking roads won't stop her," Vincent countered.

"Then she's probably halfway to Cuba, by now," another offered.

Vincent shook his head. "Not as long as the Upright Citizens and the Charleston family are on the lookout. I'm thinking she's holed up in some little unnamed inlet. She'll have to make a move eventually, whether that's to attempt a water escape or come back into the city, and that's when we'll catch her."

Word had already spread that Vito Corbi had a pincher problem—one he intended to resolve. Vito had enough cache with the surrounding families so they wouldn't interfere directly. But they sure as hell would have their eyes open for a red-haired river rat making a break up or down the coast.

Although if Hattie wanted to run for the Caribbean, she'd become a man, perhaps even a Creole. She'd present as anything but what they were looking for. Catching her when she made that move wouldn't be as easy as he was making it out to be, not with Hattie's power over illusions. He was the only one who'd be able to spot her when she was pinching light. He was the only one who fully understood what Hattie Malloy was capable of. Only him.

And possibly Lefty.

Vincent smirked as he pondered that point. Even Lefty had been drawn in by her fake explosions. Lefty knew what she was and what she could do. That illusion must have been very convincing.

Hattie was far more powerful than she gave herself credit for. She had only just begun to understand the extent of her abilities. Those Upright Citizens she'd terrorized into shitting themselves had seen just a glimpse at what he suspected she was capable of. And to date, there was only one man who could see through her mirages.

Vincent stood up as Tony entered Shakes's. The man looked fully sober for the first time in days. Since the ambush at Locust Point, Tony had become a right-hand man of sorts for Vincent in his hunt for the light pincher.

The man had a prime opportunity to dime Vincent out to the Capo over what had happened at Locust Point. It had been Vincent's call to approach the warehouse in a small group, his call to take the conversation private, his failure to take into account Hattie's stubbornness, and ultimately his failure that let her slip through their fingers. If Tony wanted to press the issue on Liz's behalf, or even his own, it would've been child's play. Tony would be heading up this hunt, and Vincent would be where he had always been—the whipping boy called on when magic was needed, and nothing more.

But Tony hadn't dimed him out. And now Vincent stood at the head of this table, with a dozen mobsters looking to him for marching orders.

Vincent nodded to Tony, who approached with outstretched hand. "What's the word?"

"Your source was solid," Tony replied as he gripped Vincent's arm in a vise.

Lefty stirred from his position by the window.

"The Bratva made a move on Masseria, just like you said," Tony continued.

Vincent released a long breath. "What happened?"

"Thanks to the tip, Masseria had men ready. It was a slaughter."

Lefty asked, "Does the Capo know?"

With a grin, Tony replied, "I thought I'd leave that to you two."

Vincent smiled and turned to Lefty. "Feel like taking a drive to the vineyard?"

Lefty shook his head. "Don't milk this. You got a win. I'm sure Masseria will have called by now. Running up Vito's skirt will only make you look like a hanger-on."

Vincent nodded. "And he wants us here, anyways. Good point."

Lefty conceded, "Still, though. It worked out."

"This time."

Lefty scowled. "If you don't trust this Smith character, you need to air that out now. Because after this, I'm betting short odds Vito will want to bring him on board."

"Especially now that Masseria owes us. That sort of marker don't come often," Tony noted.

Vincent shrugged. "If Vito weren't so focused on this light pincher, I'd say yeah." He'd stopped referring to Hattie by name in front of the rest of the Crew. The detachment would be vital toward keeping their trust in his leadership.

Leadership. Huh. What a load of bushwa that was.

"That said," Vincent added, "maybe we can put this new asset to good use?"

Lefty nodded. "You know how to find this Smith?"

"I figured he'd find me once the hit went down," Vincent confessed. "Not like he left me a card, or nothing."

Tony scowled. "You really don't know?"

"He said he'd find me."

Lefty lifted his head with a squint. "Why's this character got you cut from the herd? What's the angle?"

"Wish I knew," Vincent grumbled. He was about to remind Lefty that Smith had approached Cooper first, but decided against it. Why bring that up? Vincent could spot the side-alley entrance to Cooper's poker parlor just two blocks up the street. The man was a toad, a bottom-dweller. No need to give Cooper any credit.

He'd passed on Smith. Vincent hadn't. Time to reap the rewards.

Vincent dismissed the men with instructions to keep a special eye on the smaller docks and inlets, then settled the bill with the day manager. Tony rushed off to deal with his usual duties and Lefty led Vincent to the car, holding the door for him.

"What's this?" Vincent snickered.

"You're large and in charge," Lefty grunted. "Gotta treat you like the Crown Damned Prince, if I want to keep Vito from chapping my ass."

Vincent took the passenger seat, then nodded to Lefty as he closed the door. "Onward, Jeeves."

Lefty swung around to the driver's side, offering Vincent a rude gesture before starting the engine. "You really trust this information broker?"

"No," Vincent admitted. "Should I?"

"Absolutely not. But it's good to hear you're keeping your head on your shoulders." Lefty turned to face Vincent. "All of this is going down fast. Part of me wanted to see this happen a long time ago."

"What about the other parts?" Vincent pressed.

"They're not sure you're ready."

"Ready for what?"

"This responsibility. You've been taking orders for years, but you're in the hot seat now. Everything you do is gonna be under scrutiny. There's something to being able to hoop the pooch and not suffer consequences."

Vincent grimaced. "You think I like living that way? That means I get no respect, no credit."

Lefty snorted. "Credit's overrated, and it don't got no stick. Success means you're the golden boy for a second. Failure on the other hand? That's stays with you. It haunts you. Hangs on your suit like cheap cigars. That's how you'll be remembered, if you let it all go to your head and screw this up."

Vincent nodded. "You're gonna keep that from happening, though. Right? Seriously, because I'm gonna throw you right under the train if this goes sideways."

Lefty laughed. "Good. You're learning. So, we're left with us needing Smith and no way to find him."

Vincent chuckled, a smile drawing wider on his lips.

Lefty eyed him. "Just caught up with last week's funny pages?"

Vincent opened his door and leaned around the front of the windscreen, pulling a tiny white card from the edge of the hood. He sat down in the car, lifting the card to the midday light.

Florid strokes of a pen spelled out an address.

"Looks like we got a date," Vincent said.

They drove to the address, a side lane in a neighborhood off Charles, not far from the Jesuit college. It had only just opened its doors at its new uptown location, and a bevy of lush houses had already sprung up along its periphery—cozy manses for the faculty members and administrators. Smith's note had led Vincent to one of these urban estates, a gothic dark-stoned structure with leaded glass and a short length of well-tended grass separating the masonry from a wrought iron fence.

Lefty snorted. "That's new money, right there."

"Kind of old-fashioned for new money."

"Are you serious? It's god awful." Lefty shook his head. "Only someone with more money than sense would build an eyesore like that."

Vincent smirked at Lefty. "Get a load of you. Looking down your nose at the upper crust. What do you know about money, anyways?"

Lefty swiveled in his seat with a testy glare. "You know I

was born in the Old Country, right? My papa was a man of means before Crispi got his mitts on everything of value. I've forgotten more about airs than you'll ever know, you horse-eating bastard."

"Well, what do you know about that?" Vincent muttered with a thoughtful nod.

Lefty stepped out of the car and shut the door, leaning through the window at Vincent. "Before we come calling on your mole man, here, I gotta lay this out there."

"Here we go."

"You can't trust this fella. He's just come outta nowhere with a cherry piece of intelligence. It was bona fide. That's all you know. A man like this has to have some angle."

Vincent sighed. "You think I hadn't thought about that? Hadn't been turning this around for days, now? Yeah, he's got an angle. My bet is his angle is profits."

"And if it isn't?"

"I suppose we'll never find out sitting out on the street. Come on."

Vincent exited the car and strode for the iron gate. He lifted the latch and held it open for Lefty. The two stepped up the flagstone pavers for the broad, buttressed porch of dark wood beams, then rang the bell. Half-expecting some deep gong or otherwise portentous toll of doom to suit the aesthetic of the house, Vincent nearly laughed as the thing sounded in an asthmatic electric buzz. He pulled his finger away as if jolted by the electricity, then stuffed his hand back into his pocket, avoiding Lefty's glare.

At length, the door opened to reveal Alexander Smith, clad in a light gray suit with a white tie, a folded newspaper tucked underneath his arm. He offered a practiced smile for Vincent, then nodded to Lefty with grace.

"Misters Calendo and Mancuso. Welcome." He stepped back to hold the door for the two men.

The interior of the home was arguably more dismal than the exterior. Dark wallpaper soaked as much daylight as it could before sending the rest into deeply-stained mahogany paneling running the length of the foyer. A spray of flowers sat in a vase near the double sliding doors to a front parlor, filling the space with the syrupy floral charm of a funeral home.

Smith slid open one of the parlor doors for the two, entering the room ahead of them. Vincent exchanged glances with Lefty before following. The parlor was lavish in its floor-to-ceiling bookcases, leather wingback chairs, and a carved wood desk the size of a Ford. As they filed into the room, Smith turned with an affable smile.

"Are you hungry? I could send for sandwiches."

Before Vincent could answer, Lefty replied with steel-jawed charisma, "No."

Vincent added, "We just ate. Thanks anyways."

Smith lingered by a lacquered globe, setting his hand on its apex and spinning it lazily with his thumb. "I'm gladdened to see the both of you. I assume the information I offered has proven…helpful."

Vincent nodded. "We saved a life."

"Which was hardly the point," Smith added with precision. "Corbi is now in the good graces of Joe Masseria, and you've dealt a blow to the Russians which may set their ambitions back a pace or two."

"A lot of mileage out of that blind shot," Lefty commented.

Smith snickered. "If it were anything less, I doubt Corbi would have sent you to summon me. Alas. The cost of doing business. Shall we call it simple overhead?"

Vincent peered at Lefty with a lift of his brow, then replied, "The Capo hasn't summoned you."

Smith's smile thinned rapidly. "Say again?"

"We're not here for the Capo."

Smith glanced back and forth between Vincent and Lefty. "May I ask what brings you here?"

Vincent took a seat in one of the chairs. "Don't get me wrong, the info made an impression. I'm sure Vito's gonna be interested in how this all plays out."

"I'd like to hear that from his mouth." Smith withdrew his hand from the globe, shoving it into his jacket pocket with a scowl.

"That's not gonna happen," Lefty told him coolly.

"We're not there yet," Vincent added. "We may be soon. But I'm here for personal reasons. Well, not personal. It's Crew business, but—"

"Let me guess," Smith interrupted. "This so-called light pincher?"

Lefty took a step forward. "You know about that already?"

With a derisive chuckle, Smith answered, "Of course, good man. It's my damned business to know these things. I recognized Corbi might latch on to the opportunity, though I wondered whether it would be to the exclusion of more pressing matters."

Vincent asked, "Such as the Bratva?"

"Please. The Bratva are essentially beaten. Little more than an annoyance, at this point. No, the issue at hand is the very destiny of the Baltimore Crew. I've opened a door for you lot. Well, you were the ones opening the door, but I gave you the key. I'd hate to see this moment squandered chasing phantoms."

Vincent shrugged. "Well, I can tell you this much. You want an audience with the Capo? You're gonna find a way to put that phantom into his pocket."

"There are some particularly interesting developments

occurring in Richmond at this very moment. I'm certain Corbi would enjoy hearing about it."

Lefty cleared his throat.

Smith rolled his eyes, then sighed. "Fine. Who must I speak to regarding this errant light pincher?"

Vincent stood up. "That would be me."

Smith winced. "You?"

"What's that supposed to mean?" Vincent scowled.

"It's no secret that the Crew holds you in, well...shall we say less than stellar regard?"

"That was then. This is now."

Smith snickered. "Spoken like a true amateur."

"Let's keep the tone civil, huh?" Lefty snapped

"Civil." Smith wandered over to one of the paintings hanging on the wall. It was some god-awful thing with bright colored swirls and what Vincent suspected might be a nude woman if one was looking at a nude woman through twelve inches of dirty glass.

"So tell me, what do you gentlemen think of this?" he gestured toward the painting.

Before Vincent could demand they return to the topic at hand, Lefty spoke up.

"Odilon Redo." He shrugged. "Not one of his better works."

Smith blinked in surprise. "Are you a fan of the French symbolists, Mister Mancuso?"

Vincent's head swiveled to Lefty, uncertain if he'd slipped into a dream state by accident.

"Not particularly, although I appreciate Moreau. His *The Voices* in particular."

Smith faltered for a moment before recovering his composure.

"Helped divert a motorcade of stolen museum artifacts heading over the Pyrenees back in 1917," Lefty added, unusually verbose. "Spent some time with a cultured lady discussing everything from the Impressionists to the Symbolists to cave paintings."

There was something in the man's tone that indicated he'd done a lot more than discuss art with this "cultured lady." Vincent's eyebrows shot up at the rare glimpse into Lefty's past.

Smith clapped his hands twice, then folded his arms. "Civilization brought to the beast in the pursuit of feminine beauty. I say, that is positively maudlin."

Vincent squinted at Lefty. "That turn into something? You and this art woman?"

Lefty eased over to Vincent before popping him on the shoulder. "Keep it professional."

Smith laughed, leaning back against a bookcase. As his laughter subsided, he nodded to himself, then said, "Well, gentlemen. I must say, you are not what I expected."

Vincent couldn't agree more. He'd run with Lefty for the better part of six years, now. And only this past year had he actually discovered anything about the man's life. But they had more pressing matters to attend to than women and art.

He turned to Smith. "Will you help? It will make one hell of a difference in how the Capo considers your proposal."

Smith unfolded his arms, then strode forward to extend a hand to Vincent. "Yes, yes. I'll turn my eyes and ears inward. We'll ferret out this little scamp of yours, and deliver one light pincher safe and sound to the Capo. I only ask for two things."

Vincent took Smith's hand, then froze as the contingency was mentioned. "What's that?"

"First, I want to be there when the delivery of this pincher is made. I want Corbi to know how you came by this knowledge. I'm giving you the benefit of the doubt here, Calendo. Work with me, and I'll work with you."

Vincent nodded. "And the second?"

"Five thousand dollars."

Vincent pulled his hand away. "What?"

"You want me to repeat the number?" Smith cooed in a mocking tone.

Lefty said, "That's a fatter payday than any of us…brutes."

"I suppose I deserve that," Smith confessed. "But still. Can you tell me that Vito Corbi wouldn't pay it, if I brought him his precious light pincher?"

Vincent shifted uncomfortably.

As if sensing the change in atmosphere, Smith held a hand out to Vincent. "Not that I have the first intention of cutting you out, dear Mister Calendo. I have no interest in the glory. I just want the money."

Vincent nodded, then shot a look at Lefty. "What'd I tell you?"

Lefty scowled in return.

Smith stepped forward. "I'll assume that you'll need to make a call, Mister Mancuso?"

"Aren't you the genius?" Lefty grumbled.

"Come." Smith led Lefty back to the foyer. "I have a phone in the office."

Vincent asked, "This isn't your office?"

"Oh, heavens no. This is for entertaining guests. Seriously, my good man…"

Smith brushed past Vincent, opening the sliding door to Lefty and joining him beyond, ostensibly guiding him to a telephone, leaving Vincent alone in the parlor. He wandered around a bit, eyeballing the horrible paintings as well as the rigid leather-bound spines standing at attention along the bookcases. Lots of Latin there.

He walked over to busy himself with the globe. It sat in a finely-rendered frame of cherry wood. The orb bore a paper-and-foil veneer lacquered into place around some damned thing or another, the borders of known countries etched along the surface. Vincent smiled as he recognized some nations that were now long gone, thanks to political matters in Europe. Borders shifted so easily with the application of sufficient force, he mused.

A side door opened behind Vincent, and Smith reappeared. It wasn't the same door he'd taken with Lefty, but was likely a more direct entrance from a room deeper in the house. The man slithered into the room, his face pulled just a bit tighter, his eyes a shade darker. The genial if stuffy demeanor that had greeted Vincent and Lefty had melted away between his exit and his reappearance. In its place was that same steel-cold confidence and intellect that had ambushed Vincent in his own séance parlor.

Smith smirked at Vincent. "How do you intend to do this?"

Vincent stuffed his hands into his pockets to step toward the center of the room, presenting as little threat as possible. "Do what?"

"Secure this light pincher. If I put you in the room with her, I mean. How do you convince someone like that to come to Jesus?"

"Well, you haven't caught me at my best. But I've been known to be pretty damned charming when I want to be."

Smith smiled but didn't laugh. "Charisma alone, then?"

"Maybe it'll be enough."

"Forgive me, but with the specific sort of pressure the Capo is bearing into this matter, do you really want to leave this up to 'pretty damned charming'?"

Vincent scowled. "I suppose you've already put more thought into this than I have."

Now, Smith laughed. He wound his way around the desk to take a seat. "This wouldn't be my first snatch job. The question you have to ask yourself is how do you want things to stand when it's over? This dictates the entire method. If you're comfortable with a hostile cohort, this light pincher dragged into the service against his will, then you may take the shorter, more violent approach."

Vincent tensed. "Her."

"Hmm?"

"She's a she," Vincent stated. "I would have thought you'd have known that, given the nature of your business."

Smith shook his head slowly. "My apologies. My information is fresh, and often times such newness proves incomplete."

Vincent nodded, deciding to let that slide for the moment. "Let's say I'm not interested in a hostile whatever."

"Then it gets interesting. It'll take time, and a slow, practiced hand."

"I got practiced hands," Vincent drawled.

"Is that so?" Smith winked. "Is that why you've failed to collect her, to date?"

"Things went down quick. I made a call. It kept people from getting ventilated."

"Which was likely the best choice available to you." Smith turned toward the sliding entry doors near the foyer, his ears pricked. "If, you'll excuse me a moment." The man rose to his feet, then exited the room.

Vincent grinned. Lefty must have finished his call and was likely sniffing around the house. Hell, he would've done the same. Just as Vincent turned back to consider the carvings of acanthus leaves on the enormous desk, the sliding doors opened. Lefty sauntered inside the parlor with a quick nod.

Smith followed Lefty, as near to the man's elbow as was possible without being discourteous. That condescending manner was back. It gave Vincent pause. Why would he pull down his guard to talk brass tacks with Vincent, when around Lefty he behaved like a snobby aristocrat?

"A practiced hand," Vincent offered with a dip of his chin. "As you were saying?"

Smith's brow eased into a knowing lift. "Such a thing can't be stumbled into. Surely, you realize this? It takes planning, time. Intelligence."

Lefty snickered. "Which happens to be your bread and butter. Go figure."

"Go four figures," Smith jibed. "Which brings me to the question of the moment. Has Corbi agreed to my terms?"

Lefty shot Vincent a quick, reassuring glance, then replied, "One thousand on retainer. Then another thousand upon the delivery of the light pincher."

Smith's grin tightened. "That's less than half what I asked."

"I didn't finish," Lefty snapped. "You'll get another thousand annually for the first three anniversaries of the light pincher's service among the Crew."

Smith rested his fists on his hips. "Three years? Sir, I am not a babysitter. You want me to find this pincher, I'll do it. But you can't hold my information for ransom, all on account of someone's questionable performance."

Lefty replied, "The information alone is not worth five thousand dollars. I think that's the point the Capo's making. Having a second pincher in his service? That is. And if the information doesn't make that happen, you'll have to be satisfied with a small fortune instead of a large fortune."

Smith frowned, pacing a few steps as he pondered the offer.

Vincent, for his part, watched Smith as he moved. There was a current there, one Vincent recognized. A discomfort. A hesitation. Despite this man's spit-shined veneer, a crack was showing.

"Fine," Smith declared with a sweep of his hands. "I accept."

Lefty nodded. "I'll get your retainer by end of day tomorrow. At which point you will offer Vincent a location."

Vincent nodded. "Let me at him."

"Her," Smith corrected. "Seriously, do we have to go over this again?"

Vincent grinned at the man. "I'll need more than a location. You told me I'll need a plan. Something besides my good looks and charisma."

Lefty eyed Vincent. "Charisma?"

"I know words."

"You know enough to order pasta."

Vincent sighed, then faced Smith once again. "We'll continue that conversation later. Because you're right—I'm gonna need a plan."

Smith nodded. "Tomorrow, then. I'll meet you at the Old Moravia." He turned to Lefty. "Unless that will give your boss heartburn."

"It's a free country," Lefty chided.

Vincent and Lefty took their leave of the manor. As they cleared the wrought iron gate, closing it on smooth, oiled hinges with a discreet clink, Vincent stood silent for a moment watching the house.

A thought boiled in his brain. It truly wasn't a thought, but more of a notion. If that. It was a stirring of a notion. A notion about Alexander Smith. Vincent kept it buried beneath the colliding thoughts and questions dominating his attention, because, if Vincent was wrong about this, then he would make things much worse.

Lefty nudged Vincent's arm. "Hey. Where's your head?"

"Oh, I'm square. I was just thinking about buying myself a house like this one of these days."

Lefty snorted. "Right."

"It's not that ugly."

"It's hideous. It's vulgar. Like someone asked himself what would an Englishman have built in the days of Gladstone?"

Vincent followed the other man to the car. "Who the hell is Gladstone?"

boom rattled the glasses inside the old pine wood cabinets hanging on the kitchen walls. Hattie, Raymond and Lizzie sat at a modest square table, worn with years of use and a few intrepid grade-schoolers who felt the need to carve their names into the surface with cutlery. The air was thick, humid and sticky, relieved only by the occasional waft of rain-cooled air rushing through the tiny kitchen window. It'd been a while since Hattie had heard a proper thunderstorm. This one was a dandy—a late summer storm that had slipped in after sunset and was now busily lighting up the sky with lightning as it washed the nighttime air of its soot and harbor stench.

This kitchen was on loan to Lizzie, courtesy of one of her cousins. The tiny shack nestled shoulder-to-shoulder alongside more just like it near the Jones Falls was as safe a space as the three could've hoped for. It had been three days since the Crew had sent Vincent to collect Hattie. Three days of silence. Three days of isolation. Hattie spent that time on the water, floating a skiff on loan from one of the boys at Winnow's Slip. Those were two days of sheer frustration, and she was glad to have had all the space around her on the Bay to scream out loud. This was the nightmare her parents had striven to shield her from. The worst-case scenario. The Baltimore Crew knew what she was. They knew who she was. And they'd chosen the one person in this world who shared her gifts, who shared her unique existence, who had conspired with her to delve into the very nature of their powers, and they'd leveraged him against her.

She hadn't even gone home these past few days. How could she face her father and mother, knowing that their time in the cramped apartment in Hampden was drawing to an end quicker than either of them were physically prepared to cope with? Could they move to another city? Magical elixirs notwithstanding, the physical toll of this situation hung like an anvil over her family's heads.

She would have to tell them. The moment had come. But before she could break the news, forever changing her destiny and the destinies of her parents, she had to deal with Liz.

Hattie glanced up at the woman who sat across the table, arms folded, jaw clenched. She hadn't said a word since they arrived. Raymond had done most of the talking, but he'd run out of chit-chat long ago. Now, the depressing inevitability of the subject was all that remained.

And so, Hattie decided to quicken the end. "I want the two of you to know, I take full responsibility for all of this."

Raymond's bottom lip lifted, the way it always did when he was about to play it casual.

But Lizzie beat him to the punch. "Agreed."

The woman still hadn't made eye contact. She was incensed, that much was clear. Hattie had seen Lizzie angry before. Even livid. Every time, she would fly into a spit-flying rage, shrieking profanities she reserved for special moments in order to flay the object of her wrath by words alone. But this? This was new. It was a dreadful, soft-spoken anger, filled with doom and recrimination. And Hattie couldn't even rise to the bait, since there was no volume to shout over.

Hattie pressed on, "Until this whole bloody mess is dealt with, one way or another—" She spared a half-second to check on Raymond, whose face swelled with alarm. "I resolve to keep my distance. No sense in endangering the two of you on my account." She took a second to compose her thoughts, having suddenly run out of things to say. "I want you to know, both of you, how deeply sorry I am."

Lizzie stood up, shoving the chair into the wall of the claustrophobic room. "That's for the best."

Hattie's boss, or former boss as the posture seemed to communicate, swept behind her chair on her way to the back door.

Raymond half rose from his chair to offer some sort of response, be it holding the door for Lizzie or fetching an umbrella, but Lizzie presented a flat hand to him.

"I've got a lot to deal with. Let's all just…let's figure out our own lives for now."

With that, Lizzie twisted the old brass door knob, jerked the humidity-warped door open and plunged out into the rain. She left the door open, sending more cooling wind into the stuffy room. It would have felt like waves of welcome comfort from the heat, if the icy licks of breeze didn't feel like the lashing of a devil's whip against Hattie's shoulders.

Raymond finally rose all the way to his feet and closed the door. He lingered a second, mumbling something to himself, as was his way.

Hattie ventured a glance at the man as he took a seat once again. "So," she muttered, "I've run short on friends."

"Can you blame her, though?" he asked, voice more assertive than Hattie was ready for.

She shook her head. "I suppose not."

He reached for her hand. "Listen, baby girl, you're gettin' that look. I know that look. Like you're ready to pack your things and run for the hills. How many times we been in this situation, already?"

Hattie thought about it. "Maybe…three?"

"More like ten." He chuckled. "And that's the point I'm tryin' to make. You're special. I know it. You know it. Liz… well, we all know it now. Early on, I weren't sure what you were all about. Gettin' the itch every other month, start to talkin' about movin' west. At first, I thought you were just another hobo on the lam, or somethin'. But when I knew what the score was I realized you weren't wrong to worry. And yet…" He released her hand and lifted a meaty finger to illustrate his point. "Not once has it been the end of the world."

Hattie attempted a smile. "A lot's changed, though, hasn't it? I've managed to keep my head down, to date. But this? There's no coming back from't."

"And how many times have you thought that very thought?" he asked with a waggle of his brow. "I'm guessin' more than twice. You're smart. You find your way outta things. And you're gonna do it again, this time."

She sighed. "I want to believe that."

"That's okay, Baby Girl. I'll do enough believin' for the both of us."

She reached over for his arms, dragging them toward her until she could clutch his neck in a desperate hug. "Thanks for that."

He let her cling to him for a moment, before breaking the embrace.

"Where you goin' now?" he asked.

"Home," she replied. "At least, for tonight."

"Are you really gonna just pull up stakes and leave?"

"What else is there for me here?" she replied. "Our jobs? Gone. Any hope to live a normal life? Gone. There's nothing to stay and fight for."

"You told your folks yet?"

She shook her head grimly.

"Holdin' out hope?"

"More like avoiding the inevitable," she replied. "Alas, it's where I'm bound after I leave here."

He nodded. "You need the truck?"

She winced, reluctant to borrow the vehicle Lizzie had hauled out of the Potomac and Raymond had spent the last two days fixing, but unwilling to walk across the city in the middle of a downpour. "If that's alright with you?"

Raymond laid a hand on her shoulder. "Drop me off at the creek, then take your time. I don't think Lizzie will need it anytime soon."

They ducked out of the shack and into the rain, which had unhelpfully decided to pick up speed. Hattie drove Raymond down the sloppy mud lane leading along the back river toward Curtis Creek, dropping him off farther than she wanted, but closer than a smart person would've ventured with the lane turning to sludge. A three point turn and a tiny slip of the tires, and she was bound back for the city.

Lightning split the sky with a flash of white brilliance. Hattie blinked away the spots in her vision as the rain pounded against the windscreen of the Runabout. There were hardly any vehicles running in the city. The roads were hellish when it rained, and this had turned into a downpour. Fog spread across the inside of the glass. Hattie slashed her hand over the windscreen to clear her vision as she practiced her speech.

"Right... Ma? Da? I've been discovered. No, that's too direct. Ma? Da? Remember that job I ran to Deltaville back in the Spring? Funny thing, that. Ugh!"

She turned a corner onto North Avenue, easing her way around the intersection as she debated simply driving on out of town. Heading west. Anywhere away from here.

She gasped and laid on the brakes as two Fords appeared in her view, both blocking the road. The Runabout slid on the murky street, sidling sideways a little. It was enough to bring the driver's side window in line with the roadblock. Hattie spotted six men in suits, each sporting a Tommy gun.

The Crew!

They lifted their weapons slowly, leveling the barrels at a slight angle to the ground as rivers of rainwater poured from the steel.

Hattie threw the gear into reverse and twisted in her seat, peering through the utterly clouded rear of the truck. It was no use. She'd have to trust there was no one behind her.

She ran the car backward, only to hear engines behind her. Two more cars pulled onto North Avenue, moving to pin her in. With a curse, she hammered down on the accelerator to squeeze between the two, crunching with a jolt into one of the intercepting vehicles.

The Runabout's rear slipped up against the other car's hood, lifting the axle off the ground just enough to rob her of any sort of traction. She was stuck!

Hattie jerked the door open and plunged into the rain at a sprint. A quick burst of gunfire sounded behind her. She ducked and spun around to find one of the goons holding his Tommy gun in the air. Warning shot.

Fine. They wanted to play? She'd play.

Snapping her fingers together into tight, flat blades, she spread the fingers apart one by one. With each motion, she pinched light to create the illusion of another Hattie Malloy. The magic came surprisingly cheap in this nighttime storm. Visibility was low, to begin with. Phantoms of pinched light swam between raindrops—left, right, back and forth. The thugs lifted their weapons, dropping the weight into half-crouches as each leveled their attention onto a separate illusion.

Hattie bolted for the darker side of the street, hoping that any gangster who decided she was the real Hattie was a bad shot.

A spray of brick dust hammered the side of her face as she reached the sidewalk. A line of pock marks erupted along the side of the brownstone in front of her. She ducked with a whimper and waved both hands in front of her face. "Disappear."

She could feel the additional tug of magic in her guts. As light twisted around her, rendering her invisible to her assailant in this dark rain, Hattie ran north. More guns opened fire behind her, taking aim at the phantoms of her making. Half a block. A whole block. It was working. She was going to get away.

Dashing around a corner, Hattie collided into a dark figure barring her path. With a shriek, she threw two hands into the air, shoving at this man's chest. One hand landed against something hard lurking underneath his jacket. Slipping her hand into the jacket, she gripped the iron and jumped back, pulling it free of its holster. Without thinking, in the space between heartbeats, she pulled back the hammer and opened fire dead center at the looming figure barely three feet in front of her.

The gun flashed, then—

A red blossom of fire froze at the end of the barrel as the space between buildings became a column of tiny prisms reflecting the light of the gunshot. The thunder of the gun plunged into a murky thud. The splattering of the raindrops ceased entirely. Each drop of rain hung in the air, the brilliant yellow-orange from the muzzle flash glistening in each.

She sucked in a lungful of impossibly heavy air as she

peered into the face of Vincent Calendo, illuminated by her own gunshot. The bullet hung in the air, inches from his chest, slipping almost imperceptibly forward in this bubble of nearly frozen time.

Vincent took a step to the side, his cheeks slapping against suspended raindrops, shoving them aside like tiny diamonds. His face was leaden. Drawn. Displeased.

Well, she *had* nearly shot him with his own gun…but she'd had no way of knowing it was him.

As she pulled the weapon down, a spiderweb of light laced random branches in the sky above them, winding in treelike tendrils along the route of the street. The lightning crept forward, shoving its surrounding cloud aside to reveal its full brilliance.

Vincent lifted a hand, then snapped his fingers.

Hattie's chest pounded with the gunshot and the explosive thunder overhead as the raindrops fell into their usual gravity. The rush of rain filled her senses.

Vincent glared at her through the downpour. Distant gunshots fell silent as the distraction of the time pinch ended Hattie's illusions. She stood stiff, gasping for air as the gun trembled in her hand, pointed at the street.

"Are you serious?" Vincent snapped.

She didn't reply.

"You almost shot me."

She glared back. "They're shooting at *me*!"

"No, they're not," he chided. "I told them you'd do this. My guess was you'd either make them go blind, or you'd make copies of yourself. I had them ready either way."

"Well, one of them didn't get the memo, 'cause he damned near took my head off back there."

Vincent grew frighteningly still, like a snake about to strike. "Who?" he demanded.

She snorted. "Like I can see anything in the dark with all

this rain. You weren't with them in the cars? You're just standing here? Waiting for me?"

"Figured you'd ditch the truck and bolt north."

"Why north?"

"Because you'd run home," he answered.

Hattie tightened her grip on the weapon. "Don't...don't you dare..."

Vincent lifted his hands. "I have no intention of threatening your family."

She lifted the pistol, aiming it at his impassive face. "Don't you dare hurt them!"

"I swear it," he assured her. "Listen, I'm not here to kick up a fuss."

Hattie released a single disbelieving guffaw. "Evidence to the contrary!"

"It was a show of force," he explained, his empty hands lifted in front of him. "Because I think you've lost sight of the nature of the Crew. We have eyes everywhere and the manpower to cover this whole city."

"I know it well enough."

"Do you? And you think you can escape this?"

She glowered, then lowered the gun once again. "You swear you won't lift a finger against my parents?"

"It's my solemn vow. I have no interest in hurting you, or your family."

"Then you'll step aside and let me go?"

He blinked slowly, then said, "No."

"Then we're at an impasse, I think."

"We're not done with our conversation. The one where I show you how you have no options besides the Crew. None. Vito's got you in his sights. There's nowhere to run. And as I've just demonstrated," he gestured to North Avenue, "I can find you."

She shook her head. "Lucky guess."

"Maybe," he said. "But maybe I'm part of something bigger, like a family with the resources to sniff you out, now that we know who to look for."

Her hands shook, as much out of fear as the chill of the rain. The gun threatened to fall from her grasp.

Vincent stepped closer. "Hattie, I want you to work with me, here. I know this is difficult, but I'm actually on your side. I can make this easier. I've been given special allowances."

"Allowances?" she scoffed.

"To make sure your transition is painless."

Hattie lowered her hands all the way, the gun thumping against her thigh. Why was he being this way? If he'd only try to hit her, or grab her, or anything, then she could just hate him, then she could do what she needed to do. But this? This couldn't be some sort of silver-tongued manipulation—Vincent wasn't devious enough for that sort of mischief. No, he'd only ever been capable of honestly speaking his mind.

Which meant he really *was* trying to help her. Because he saw no hope. No options.

Hattie's stomach twisted into a lead weight as she considered he might not be wrong. She took a step forward, twisting the gun around in her hand so the barrel was outward.

"Can we start over?" Vincent urged. "There's a place set aside for you. The Crew won't interfere until I say you're ready. You'll have food. Dresses. A car at your disposal. Protection. It will be a whole new world, working with us. With me."

She shook the rain from the tip of her nose as she lifted the weapon for Vincent.

In halting tones, she muttered, "Remember."

"Hmm?"

"I want you to remember that vow you took."

As Vincent's brow drew together in confusion, Hattie swung the butt of the revolver against his head. The iron connected with a hard thunk.

With a grunt, Vincent spun, landing on his back in a puddle on the sidewalk. Hattie crouched down beside him, feeling to make sure his heart was beating and his chest was moving. Thankfully she'd just knocked him out cold.

Standing, she took a few steps, then paused to consider the gun in her hand. With a shake of her head, she tossed it onto the ground beside Vincent, then rushed up the street and into the rain-soaked night.

A half-hour's trot in soaking rain brought Hattie to her home street, skin chilled to the point of trembling as she doubled back one more time to be sure she hadn't been followed. Vincent had pledged he wouldn't move upon her family, but that was before Hattie gave him a lick against the side of his face. Was that a deal-breaker? Or would he take it in stride? Hattie couldn't be sure. He was a man, and in her experience, men didn't respond to blows to their ego with considerable aplomb.

She stared down her street. The rows of three-story buildings carved a canyon up the avenue in the stormy darkness. There, just five doors down, was home. The light was still on upstairs. One or both of her parents were still awake. Probably her mother, reading one of her magazines. Since business had improved and Alton had gone to work during the days, Branna had taken to picking up a magazine each week at the newsstand. She preferred Life or McClure's, claiming that politics were a kind of gossip—the kind the Good Lord couldn't hold you accountable for. If Alton were awake, he'd be standing at the window looking for Hattie.

How this had all gone so wrong, so quickly! She'd nearly killed Vincent with that stupid gun. Her face drew into a grimace as the realization landed upon her that she couldn't go home. There was no sense chancing her parents' safety. A sob spilled from her throat. She covered her mouth, but that only gave her license to weep openly, tears mingling with the rain as it pelted her hot cheeks.

That tiny illuminated window was suddenly miles and miles away. Across an ocean. Might as well have been Ireland.

By the time the rain stopped, the sun had begun its cloud-muffled ascent into dawn. The lead-gray sky had adopted a softer tone and Hattie sat beneath a train trellis south of the city, knees huddled up to her chest, eyes drooping in exhaustion, both physical and emotional. Another rumble of chills ran across her shoulders and down her arms. The heat of the air had been sapped by the rainfall, and it would be several more hours before she could feel warm again. Her clothes were still wet. Not simply damp, but wet. And there was nowhere to go. Not home. Not the warehouse. Vincent knew all of her locations, it seemed, and there was truly nowhere left to run in this city where he wouldn't quickly find her.

A boat horn sounded on the Patapsco River, not two blocks away. Hattie lifted her head to listen to the noise of the waterfront. There *was* one place she could go. It would carry as much risk as anything else, but at least it would give her a fighting chance.

With a weak groan, Hattie pulled herself to her feet and trod in water-logged boots toward the waterfront. She found some oyster fishers setting up to head out to the Bay. She must have looked particularly desperate, as they immediately consented to give her a ride wherever she needed.

A few breaks in the clouds revealed tiny fingers of blue sky to the west, and the air had finally shaken its chill. Hattie's clothes had flickered in the Bay breeze for an hour and had become tolerable by the time the oyster boat turned up Curtis Creek.

Raymond stood on the riverbank, already watching for the unusual sound chugging up the creek. They didn't get many diesel boats this far upstream, and Hattie presumed Raymond knew what each one sounded like. His eyes bugged when he spotted Hattie.

She thanked the boatmen with the last of her strength before hopping off the boat and into Raymond's arms, her feet giving way underneath her as she made landfall. Raymond guided her into his home, essentially lifting her off the ground to settle her onto a bed. Nadine shook her head as she checked Hattie's temperature.

"You're gonna catch a damn cold, girl," she mumbled, balancing Dougie on a hip as she felt Hattie's clothes. "Ray, you get on outta here. I gotta get her clothes off."

She handed the child to Raymond and ushered him out of the bedroom. Hattie lodged a thin protest as Nadine worked to pull off the damp clothes and set them flat onto the wood plank floors. The woman handed her a dress, threadbare and full of smoke. But it fit Hattie well enough.

"What're you doin' out there in a rainstorm like that?"

"Running for my life," Hattie rasped.

"What's got a hold of you? Treasury men?"

Hattie shook her head.

"Well, whatever it is, it's probably something to do with that package."

"What…package?" Hattie asked.

Nadine eased her down to rest, and she did. The second her eyes closed, the warmth of the dry clothes and the relative comfort of the straw mattress settled an unshakable wave of fatigue over Hattie. Her eyes closed, and she drifted to sleep so quick that when she awoke four hours later, it made her sit bolt upright.

The smell of coffee and soup filled the air. That was probably what pulled her free of her slumber. She tested her legs.

They were dreadfully sore, but nothing seemed permanent. She sported a slight fever, though. She could feel it in the scratchiness in her throat and the dull ache drifting from her neck down into her chest.

She stood up on unsteady feet, then plodded to the door to open it.

Raymond twisted in his chair to watch as Hattie entered the center room. Dougie gubbed and cooed in his lap, gripping a tiny square cloth and waving it in front of his own face.

Nadine swept from the fireplace to guide Hattie to a chair. The door and windows were open to let in a breeze. The rest of the clouds from the previous night had been banished by the brilliant summer sun, which brought with it the stifling heat that Hattie had prayed for all the previous night.

She cleared her throat. "Thank you both. I was bloody knackered."

Raymond nodded. "Were you up all last night?"

Hattie nodded. "It was the Crew. It was…him."

"Calendo?" Raymond grumbled. "I gotta do somethin' to that man?"

"He's a time pincher, Raymond." Hattie sighed. "Not a lot you can do to a man like that."

"There's a lot you can do," he countered.

With as much of a smile as Hattie could manage, she said, "I gave him a good what-for. Right across the head. Rang his bell and put him out."

Nadine whistled. "You beat a gangster unconscious? Girl!"

"He had it coming," Hattie told her. "Bastard had his boys take pot shots at me. I gave him a good waxin' and ran on."

Nadine and Raymond exchanged glances over tight-lipped grins.

Hattie shook her head. "What's this rot about a package, then?"

Raymond huffed, then reached for a chair opposite Hattie to produce a tiny brown paper-wrapped parcel. It was the same sort of parcel she'd opened before.

"Another one?" She slumped in her chair.

"I didn't open it," he told her. "It was just left on the porch, and look." He lifted it for Hattie to inspect. "It's got your name on it."

Hattie nodded, then reached for the package. "If I'm right about this mystery person, I think it'll have come just in time."

As Hattie tugged at the twine and unwrapped the tiny stationery box, and read the handwritten note inside, she nodded. "Aye. We've got work to do."

CHAPTER 14

*V*incent overshot the restaurant before he realized he'd gone too far. Heading back up the street, he regretted the impulse that had made him ask Fern to meet him for lunch. He was busy, and their last date hadn't exactly been enjoyable.

But he needed this. He needed some time away from the stress of trying to find Hattie before Vito lost his patience with the delay. He needed something to keep his mind off the look in Hattie's eyes when she realized she'd almost shot him.

He needed to be with a well-mannered woman who wasn't going to knock him upside the head with a pistol and leave him lying in a puddle.

This wasn't his usual lunch spot. Fern had chosen a cafe he'd never been to before, probably for that very reason. She had moved along the periphery of the Baltimore Crew for so long she knew the usual haunts the gangsters tended to patronize and after one too many rotten eggs, Fern seemed ready to put some distance between her life and the Crew.

Which might present a problem for Vincent if this thing between them ever went anywhere.

He stepped past the maître d' with a curt nod and proceeded into the front room. Half the tables were empty, making it easy to spot Fern at a window near the far corner. Her back was against a wall, her eyes watching the passersby. Vincent wove around empty chairs to join her. As he reached her table, he knocked on the wood with his knuckle.

"Daydreaming?" he asked.

She jerked out of her reverie with quick gasp as she peered up at Vincent. "Oh! Sorry. Yes, I was just enjoying the —what is that?"

Her eyes widened as she stood up, tossing her napkin onto the table and reaching for the shiner that took up a good bit of real estate around Vincent's left eye. He tried to pull away, but her grip was too firm. She jerked his head back to face her, fingers probing his sore cheek.

"Hey!" he hissed. "Take it easy."

"What in God's name happened to you?" she asked, voice distant, eyes scanning his face.

"Took a dirty shot, was all. I'm fine."

Her fingers pressed into his face, making him yelp.

She shook her head. "The bone isn't fractured, which is one thing you have going for you." She pulled back and shook her head. "Bruiser!"

He smiled as she kissed him on the cheek, then he stepped around to pull her chair for her as she took a seat once again. Vincent settled across the table, removing his hat to set it onto a nearby chair post.

"Surprised you didn't see me on the street," he said.

"I was on the watch for someone who didn't look like they lost a fight with a slab of pig iron. Any blurred vision?"

He shook his head. "I'm fine."

She leaned forward with a mischievous smirk. "What's the use in twisting time if you can't dodge a punch?"

"You have to see it coming to do anything about it. I'm not a mind reader, you know."

"Hmm. More's the pity."

She returned her attention to the menu sheet settled before her on the white linen tablecloth as Vincent sighed. Fern seemed in a better mood today—more relaxed then she'd been before. It'd been nearly a week since he'd seen her, and he hoped that fact wasn't contributing to her disposition.

"So, what's good in this joint?" he asked, reaching for his own menu.

"Poached quail's egg on a bed of tomato salad and a baguette," she read aloud. "Broiled white fish with potatoes and asparagus."

"Ever been here before?"

She shook her head distractedly. "*Ragu napoletana*. That sounds good. Or, the beef tips."

"Bit heavy for lunch, huh?"

She dropped the menu and shot him a tentative smile. "I'm hungry today."

"Wow," he muttered, thinking back to their awkward date at the Old Moravia Hotel. "Glad to hear that. Beef tips it is then."

He waved over the waiter and ordered for the pair of them.

"You wanna take in that John Ford movie later?" he asked.

Fern wrinkled her nose. "I don't know. He's so depressing. Doom and gloom...it's too nice a day for that sort of thing."

Vincent nodded without enthusiasm. The weather had improved over the storms of the previous night. The shift was jarring, making the failed confrontation with Hattie feel like a dream, like it had been weeks ago. The throbbing beneath his eye reminded him how recent it truly was.

Fern waved a hand at Vincent. "Hey. Where'd you go, Buster Brown?"

"Hmm? Oh, sorry."

"Do you have a headache? You feeling at all like you're going to pass out on me?"

He smiled, enjoying this side of her when she was all business, like a nurse. "I'm fine. Really."

"It's probably too late, but maybe I could slap a steak on it," she mused.

Vincent lifted hands in mock defense. "Hell no! Last thing I need is another woman hitting me in the face with something!"

Fern blinked in shock, all the animation draining from her face, her laughter abruptly ending in a squeak.

"A woman?" she gasped.

Vincent winced, realizing his mistake. "It's...not what you think."

Fern straightened in her chair and stared at Vincent, wide-eyed and still.

Vincent searched for a life raft. "There's a pincher out there that Vito wants brought in. She's a woman. I'm in charge of the war party."

"War party?" Fern asked.

"She's a pincher, Fern. You, don't go after people like me without a serious effort."

She bent her head to inspect the tablecloth at length.

Vincent sighed. This had gone south in a hurry. Fat damn mouth! Coulda had a nice meal for a change, but now Fern was on the defensive, curling into herself over... Over what, exactly?

"Say?" he asked. "Where's the funeral? What's with the

rain face?" He added with a coy nod to the windows. "Thought it was too nice a day for this sort of thing."

Fern shook her head. "I'm fine."

"Every time someone says they're 'fine,' that usually means they're anything but."

Fern shifted in her chair, still staring intently at the tablecloth. "I said I'm fine."

Vincent crossed his arms with a frown. "I don't want you to get bent outta shape, thinking I'm chasing some ankle."

Fern rested her hands flat against the table, peeking up at him from under her lashes. "I know what you were doing," she replied in even, low tones.

"Just my job," he clarified.

"Right. Just your job." She fanned her fingers in and out before adding, "Can we please talk about something else?"

"Sure," he muttered.

Food arrived after a short space of silence, but the task of eating did little to freshen up the atmosphere.

Between bites, Vincent decided to take another stab at conversation. "Some weather we had last night."

Fern nodded. "Our roof leaks. We could hear it in the attic."

"You want me to get that looked into?"

She paused with her fork midair and slumped just a little. "No, Vincent. We can manage."

"Didn't mean nothing by it."

Fern peered out the window as a tiny smile lifted into the corner of her mouth. "We're not as helpless as you'd like us to be, you know. All of us up by the Hill. Those girls in the house, they can do just about anything, handle just about anything. Not just the roof either."

"I'm sure you have…" He hit the brakes on his thought before expressing it. He was about to speculate on their ability to perform roof repairs. But, as Fern's eyes met his,

Vincent suddenly realized the true source of her suddenly withdrawn mood.

He was such an idiot. Here he sat with a black eye, telling her a woman gave it to him, when she'd just ended a relationship with a member of the Crew who'd treated her like a punching bag.

It wasn't jealousy that had soured Fern's mood. It was the notion that Vincent had set upon a woman in the service of the Crew. The fact that Hattie had come out on top in this particular situation was beside the point. Fern must have played out the entire scenario in her mind, and in each possible walkthrough Vincent was every bit the predator she'd come to expect from Vito's men.

"I didn't hit her, Fern. I swear I didn't lay a hand on her. We were having a conversation, mainly me trying to convince her to come with us, then she cleans my clock and takes off."

She picked at her food a moment then nodded. "Okay."

"Okay, you believe me? Because I don't want you thinking I'm like that."

"I believe you," she said, a bit too fast for the words to sound honest. Then she gave him a practiced smile. "So the roof leaks, but we've got it all in hand."

Vincent set down his utensils desperately hoping they could somehow get back to where they were when he'd first come in. "That's good to hear, because you know? I think I caught a drop or two just outside my kitchen. Say," he teased, "if I round up two or three of your friends, think you could patch up my roof for me? I got lily hands." He waved his fingers with a grin. "They ain't seen real labor my whole life."

Fern stared at him a moment, her expression unreadable. "Thinking about you up on a roof...that's amusing."

There was something odd in her voice, and Vincent

wasn't sure if she was taking a jibe at him for his lack of skills in manual labor, or insinuating something else.

"You ever see a man fall three stories and break his neck? Because that'll be the long and short of it if I have to get up on a roof."

She stabbed at her beef tips, with more energy than was necessary, but her expression remained numb. "I'll remember that."

Vincent returned to his meal with renewed calm. She was talking. And joking. At least he thought she was joking. He'd struck a nerve, but this wasn't anything he couldn't come back from.

"Buster Keaton's got a new one showing at the Palladium," he offered. "Less war, more yuks."

She shook her head in amusement, a light finally sparking in her eyes. "You realize the name of the movie is The General, right?"

"It's about a train called The General."

"It's about the War between the States." She lifted a finger. "And how do you know what the film's about? You've already seen it, haven't you?"

"So have you," he replied with his own finger lifted across the table. "Isn't that right?"

She scowled, then released the pretense to laugh into her hand. "It was awful."

"Was it?" Vincent groaned. "I love Keaton."

"I think it may be time for the fellow to retire. These new talkie shorts have us expecting more."

"If you like shorts."

She feigned shocked embarrassment and fanned herself. "My dear sir!" she gasped.

"I bet if you..." Vincent's words rolled to a halt as he peered out the window.

At a figure.

A man, smiling and offering a nod as he proceeded toward the restaurant entrance.

Fern gave him a puzzled look. "What?"

Vincent gathered himself, suddenly aware of the shift in his own demeanor as Alexander Smith entered the dining room to approach their table. Shooting Fern a quick glance, Vincent tried like hell to communicate his apologies to her before the man spoke.

"Mister Calendo," Smith declared in his impossibly modern accent. "I fear I've interrupted your liaison."

That son of a bitch. Vincent gritted his teeth and thought of more diplomatic responses. "If you were so damned afraid of it, you'd have shoved on down the road."

Smith's face cracked into a farce of a smile. "Such quick wit. That's why I like you so very much, Mister Calendo."

Vincent checked Fern, who sat as still as a statue.

"What do you want, Smith?" Vincent growled, trying to reclaim his personal time.

"Your undivided attention," Smith proclaimed.

"It can wait," Vincent grumbled.

"Time is of the essence, I'm afraid."

Vincent lifted a hand to stop Smith, but the man was indefatigable.

"Mister Calendo, my investment in this particular endeavor hinges entirely on your success. As such, I must insist we speak now."

Vincent's nerve's crackled with a desire to take action—to stand up with enough force to shove the chair well clear of the violence before Vincent popped Smith a solid right cross against his jaw. Or a jab directly onto the front of his nose, sending it sideways and sullying that smug bastard's face for the rest of his life.

All of these were simply fantasies. But the truth of the matter was that Vincent needed Smith. And Smith knew it.

Fern reached into her lap to pull her napkin to her lips. She dabbed her mouth twice, then folded the cloth four times to drop it onto her plate. Vincent sucked in a breath to implore her to stay even as she rose from her chair.

She announced in a tired, worn voice, "Business. I understand. Good day, gentlemen."

Vincent sat stony, even as she gathered her belongings and swept past them toward the front of the café, and out the door. He wanted to flag her down, but any attempt to hold her attention would register as weakness in Smith's eyes. That would not do.

Damn it all…why was it so hard to have a simple meal in this city?

Once Fern was clear of the restaurant, and the remainder of the patrons had returned to their own business, Vincent gestured for the chair opposite him.

"Have a seat."

Smith took Fern's seat, folding his legs and hands into a tidy knot at the center of his mass.

"Vito is aware of last night's incident," Smith stated in the emotional fervor of a woman informing her husband that the cat had shit in the kitchen again.

"Yeah, I know," Vincent grumbled as he tossed his napkin onto the table, shoving his plate of risotto aside for the bus boys to dispose of however they deemed fit. "This long game sounds more and more like a waste of time, if you ask me. And I recognize you didn't, so I'll just ask myself. Vincent? Did last night seem like a good use of our time? Why, no Vincent. It did not."

Smith's eyes narrowed at the sarcasm, and once Vincent had expended his breath, the man replied, "You're a fool."

"It's been said before."

"What do you think has transpired in the interim?" Smith

pressed. "While you've elected to take casual meals with women?"

Vincent balled a fist in his lap but kept it beneath the table top.

Smith waved a hand at the window. "Your quarry has had time to calculate your move. If this young woman is half as smart as I'm giving her credit, she'll realize that she cannot return to her home as long as you've drawn real muscle into this task."

Vincent squinted, his arms tight around his chest.

Smith eased his tone. "Listen, it doesn't take a genius to recognize that you have some history with this light pincher."

"That's none of your business," Vincent snapped, instantly regretting the show of emotion.

Smith's grin was feral. "I assure you, Mister Calendo, I have no interest in your private dalliances."

Vincent choked over the word, even as Smith continued.

"But, your Capo's patience wears thin, and you've given the impression that this Hattie Malloy is your...your *friend*. That you have her best interests in mind."

Vincent sneered. "What if I actually do?"

Smith's face drew into a mask of bafflement. "Do you? Oh, well. I fear I must prevail upon your inner sense of unambivalent rectitude."

"You gonna speak English anytime soon?"

"It's all horse apples," Smith snarled, his face finally betraying a hint of actual humanity. "You and your righteous attempt to keep this woman safe. You *had* her. But instead of grabbing her and hauling her off, you as good as let her go. A long game is one thing, but you're stalling."

Vincent shook his head. "I told you I want her to come willing. That's smart. It's got nothing to do with whatever you're imagining my feelings are for Hattie."

Smith interrupted, "You're on a first-name basis with the target, then?"

"Why are you here, Smith?" He snapped, done with this conversation.

"To move us farther down the board. I know where she is."

"You know where Hattie is?" Vincent repeated.

"That's why you pay me, Mister Calendo. To know things."

Vincent shoved his seat away from the table and stood, straightening his suit. "Where is she?"

"I'll require the retainer," Smith replied, his face easing into the exact ferret-snipe cartoon that Vincent had anticipated.

"You want your money, huh?"

Smith watched with eagerness. "The retainer, as agreed upon."

Vincent exhaled. "I'll have it within the hour. Now… where is Malloy?"

Smith smiled. "Are you familiar with her pilot? A certain Raymond Bowles?"

* * *

LEFTY FLAGGED Vincent down in front of the Hole, a warehouse in Fell's Point that the Crew used to store and package incoming booze from the Alleghenies. Vincent adjusted his hat as his driver dropped him off in front of the tiny brick-veneered face of the building. It was easy to miss, by design, tucked between a meat hanger and a packaging plant.

Vincent nodded to Lefty as they turned for the entrance. "Our man inside City Hall bring the map?"

"He did," Lefty replied hesitantly.

"And Smith's money?"

"They're pulling it together."

Vincent blinked at Lefty as the man lingered a half-step. "What's in your cheese?"

Lefty cleared his throat. "I just don't like that all this intelligence is coming from one person."

"What, you want us to check it out first? Kinda defeats the point."

"I know," Lefty grumbled. "I just don't trust the man."

"Every slice of ham he's given us has panned out, hasn't it? The only reason we don't have Hattie right now is..."

After a pause, Lefty finished the statement. "You?"

"Look, I get it. Smith's a mercenary. He's not one of us, and you don't like that. But his motivation is pretty simple. Cash on the barrelhead."

"Sure there isn't some other agenda?"

Vincent shrugged. "If he was asking for five dollars, I might wonder. But he's asking for a thousand times that. It takes big plums to give a man like Vito a price tag that huge."

Lefty lifted his hand. "I suppose so."

"What's the word at the Moravia?" Vincent whispered. "With Vito?"

"He hasn't said much," Lefty replied, taking a step closer. "But between you and me and the fence post, I'd watch your step."

Vincent nodded. "You're the army man. It should be you heading up this war party not me."

"Yeah, but it was you who lit the fire. You can't hand it off just because it's burning your shorts."

Vincent nudged him with a smirk, then sighed. "Seriously, though. You got anything for me? Advice? Kicks in the ass?"

Lefty nodded. "I know Smith's got you sold on this 'long game' bushwa. But we both know you don't have many more free passes left. So if it was me, I'd close the deal.

Better to gamble on forgiveness than permission, at this point."

Vincent reached for the bruise on his cheek, tapping it gingerly. Lefty was right. Hattie had made her feelings on joining the Crew willingly abundantly clear. She was never ambivalent on the subject. What she'd lacked was the understanding that it would be inevitable. Dragging this out would only prove painful for the both of them.

This time there would be no talking. This time, he was dragging her kicking and screaming out of there if he had to.

Vincent clapped Lefty's shoulder, then nodded to the door to the Hole.

As he pulled the door aside and stepped into the darkness, he saw a line of nearly thirty men scattered between cars that had backed into the space into a tidy phalanx. He stiffened briefly, surprised at the numbers gathered. After the last debacle, he'd assumed Vito would have pulled resources away from this snipe hunt.

All eyes turned to Vincent as he wove around the front car to present himself to his war party.

With a wave of his hand, he asked, "Where's the map?"

A slight fellow in a black coat and bowler hat stepped forward with a large roll of paper beneath his arm. He presented it to Vincent without a word spoken.

Vincent nodded to the man, then unfurled the map, laying it flat against the hood of the nearest car. The war party slipped around the hood, three deep in places, to observe as Vincent took in the terrain.

"Curtis Creek is where we're headed. My source places our target here," Vincent jabbed the map, "where Curtis meet the Back Creek. This is a waterman we're dealing with, so we'll need a boat here at the mouth of the creek. Maybe two." He peered over his shoulder at Lefty. "Can you get on the horn with Tony, see what he can spare?"

Lefty nodded.

Vincent eyed the rest. "Some of you were with me last night. You know what you saw, or think you saw. We're hunting a light pincher, gentlemen. Which means you can't trust your eyes or ears. If she catches you coming, you'll see what she wants you to see. This time, there will be no negotiations."

Vincent wound around the front of the car to poke several spots on the map.

"There's only so much she can do before she taps out. That's her weakness. And she can't pull the wool over your eyes if she don't know you're even there. We'll break up into small groups, light on our feet. Four men each. Fan out here, here…and here. Two more teams up the road in case they find a way to make a break for it by car. If she hits one group with one of her illusions, we'll have three more hanging back." He spied the mouth of the river. "And I definitely want two boats. One upstream, one right at the Bay in case they make a run by boat."

Heads nodded. Feet shuffled. Mouths drew into tight agreement.

Vincent waved his hand over the map. "But all of this? It's just our fallback plan. I'm hoping we won't need any of it."

A voice called from the group, "What is the plan, then?"

"I go in alone," he replied. With a lift of his finger to his black eye, he added, "I've got some payback coming."

A spattering of snickers washed over the crowd.

The same voice asked, "We goin' tonight?"

"Actually, no. The last two times we tried to move on this woman, both times were at night. That was a mistake. It might sound backwards, but we do better in broad daylight. Her magic costs more during the day."

He didn't feel like going into specifics, as much because he didn't want to lay out the particulars of pincher frailty for a group of armed men, but also because he wasn't sure they'd even understand.

With a heavy nod, he concluded, "We hit the target today. As soon as I get confirmation our boats are in place."

He turned to Lefty, who shrugged. "Better beat feet, hadn't I?"

Lefty withdrew to find a phone as Vincent corralled the men away from the map. With a broad wave of his arms, he said, "This isn't about taking down a hostile. We're bagging a live target. You read that?"

Heads nodded.

"But she won't be alone. She'll be protected, like before. Broken up into packs of four, we're whittling down the chances she'll turn our own guns against us. But we have to beat her reaction time. We move fast, we take her unharmed. Anyone else gets the draw on you..." He squinted. "You take them out. There's no room for failure this time."

* * *

THE CALL to Tony went through, and he assured them he'd have two boats ready at the mouth of Curtis Creek, out of line of sight one from the other, per Vincent's instructions. Lefty had led the motorcade from the Hole down the county lane toward the patch of reeds and low-hanging boughs filling the plot of land along the river. The summer heat beat down hard onto Vincent's hat as the first party slipped into the grass alongside the lane, ready to shoot out the tires of any fleeing vehicle.

They proceeded on foot, slicing off groups of four as they went, each spreading in a semi-circle around the line of shacks huddled onto pilings half over the river. Smith had given Vincent specifics—the third shack from the road, the one with a white oak hanging over its back porch. It was easy enough to spot. A thin plume of white smoke rose from the stove pipe jutting from its roof. Someone was cooking.

They were home.

Vincent spied one of his groups poking through the tall grass nearest the first shack. He waved them back until they'd disappeared once again. There could be no warning from neighbors, most of whom had probably taken up arms in their first showdown at Locust Point. He'd given orders to eliminate all obstacles who weren't Hattie Malloy. If at all possible, he wanted those obstacles to keep their heads down and their children from becoming orphans.

With a quick double and triple-check, Vincent peered at Lefty, who gave him a reassuring nod. He reached into his jacket to pull his pistol.

"Show time," Vincent whispered, and pinched time.

The sweltering summer breeze pulled to a halt, and the whispering of leaves in the enormous white oak fell into silence. Otherwise, the quality of light and the tableau set before him seemed unchanged. Odd how his time pinches always seemed more dramatic at night.

Vincent wasted no time lingering in this time bubble. He shoved through the murky air toward Raymond Bowles's shanty, taking an angled approach. The second he pinched time, he'd announced his presence to Hattie. That was as much for her as it was for her companions. This was his final nod of conciliation, the last chance for her to recognize she was under attack, and to keep Raymond and his family from getting caught in the crossfire.

Vincent reached the side of the shack and pricked his ears for any shuffling, muddy noises from Hattie. Sound didn't carry very well at all inside a time bubble, but the tiniest of noises was all he needed to hear to know she was on the move.

Silence.

He stepped onto the rear porch as the range of the bubble tore at his guts. This was a big pinch for Vincent…he'd pay for it later. But it was worth it.

With his back against the crooked slats of the porch wall, he stole a peek through the single window. The interior was dark. Impossible to tell who was where.

A wave of nausea slipped up his gullet, and he choked it down before he gave away his position. He couldn't creep around like this, not in the time pinch. The time for her to respond had passed. Time for action.

Vincent swam forward for the door, reaching for the makeshift leather strap door latch, and jerked it open. It hung up on the warped floor boards of the porch, scraping with a faint grind as he kicked it completely free. Gun up, he ventured inside.

His eyes adjusted to the low light.

A long table stretched out before him. Four chairs. Plates. Cups. No people.

The stove sat to his left, the warmth reaching out through the frozen time to greet the side of his cheek. A pot of water sat simmering, its surface a still landscape of undulating bubbles. There was no meat. No vegetables. This wasn't any sort of soup or stew. No meal, really. Just water.

The tiny space left no room for hiding, save for a single door leading to what had to be the bedroom. If Hattie had a surprise waiting for him, it would be there.

The pressure of the time pinch ground his insides. A cold sweat broke out across his forehead. He was tempted to drop the time pinch and call out to her. But that would only endanger the Bowleses. No sense in that. No sense in tarrying at all.

He strode across the room and nudged the door open with his foot, watching for an attack from within. He knew guns wouldn't work in the time bubble. Only a bludgeon or a blade. The door eased open an inch. Then two. Then a full foot.

No reprisal.

Vincent swallowed hard against a lump of bile as he stepped into the tiny bedroom. A single bed, neatly made, lay in the corner. A bassinet stood beside it. No blankets. No child.

Vincent turned a quick circle, then holstered his pistol as he released the time pinch. The rushing of leaves returned, joined by the soft bubbling of the water pot on the stove. He peered beneath the bed. Nothing. He returned to the main room and paced a slow circle, mopping his brow and forcing his stomach to calm down.

The shack was empty.

This wasn't just poor timing. The baby's clothes and blankets were gone. Someone had lit the stove but only left a pot of water on. The smoke from the stove pipe was an invitation. A decoy.

How had she known? Was Smith's info finally wrong?

Or did she have an insider among the Crew?

Vincent paused by the table as he spotted a tiny folded piece of card stock. It had a clean edge and a ragged edge, as if torn from a larger sheet. He reached for the paper and snatched it with his thumb and forefinger, unfolding it with a lift of his thumb.

A tiny, messy scribble greeted his eyes.

Too Slow, Boy-o.

Vincent sucked in a breath, then smiled.

Conflicting emotions flooded his chest, washing away the sickness of his ambitious time pinch—primarily dread of what Vito would do now that he had, once again, failed to secure Hattie Malloy. He was running short of chances, and soon the Capo would decide Vincent wasn't up to the task. The men he'd gathered would once again return to the city empty-handed, eyeing him with the old disdain he'd endured all these years. Lefty would be dragged down with Vincent in this whirlpool of failure.

But yet…he also felt a sense of relief that Hattie was still out there.

And that someone clearly was helping her.

CHAPTER 15

The words of the note flashed behind Hattie's eyes as she stepped through the revolving brass door to the Old Moravia Hotel.

They are not *more powerful than you.*

That was one of several lines from the note that had shaken Hattie to the core as she'd read it. This second missive was as verbose as its predecessor was terse. Raw emotion poured off the page as Hattie had read it in Raymond's home. Whoever this secret benefactor was, they had pulled out the stops on this attempt to reach out. The entire page was scribbled in jagged slashes of ink, instructing Hattie on several points.

First, stop thinking of Vincent Calendo as a superior. The message went on to envelope the entirety of the Baltimore Crew. The sooner Hattie accepted that she was equal to, perhaps stronger than, those goons, the sooner she'd realize she didn't have to play the role of victim.

Second, the benefactor urged Hattie to stop reacting, and take the fight to the Crew. This meant going on the offensive. Sucking up her fear and plunging close to their heart, where they'd least expect to find her. Use her powers. Don't fear her own strength.

Know herself.

Hattie'd read the note in a moment of desperation, which was probably the best timing possible. As she'd sat in Raymond's house, shivering from her night in the tempest after hammering Vincent across the brow with his own gun, she'd been ready to surrender. Then...this. It was a rifle shot of clarity for Hattie, slicing through decades of bias and dread served to her by her parents. *The establishment wants to use you. They are to be feared. You will never be as strong as they.*

But what if she *was* stronger?

That was the thought that had propelled Hattie through a few hours of fever and coughing as she gathered the Bowleses to relocate with a relative. She'd instructed Raymond to put his family first. It seemed raggedly obvious to Hattie, but Raymond's dogged sense of loyalty often clouded his judgment. He always did best when she gave him marching orders, rather than improvise as they went. As such, Raymond remained at arm's length with his family, and Hattie prepared to go on the offense.

Once the cough had cleared, Hattie put herself out on the water in Raymond's boat. Where else could she feel so distinctly herself? The note sat in her hands for hours as she drifted on the Chesapeake, sun beating down onto her pale skin, warming the depths of her that had been chilled simple hours prior. That time served her well. Whoever had sent her the note understood.

They understood what it was to be a free pincher.

And that made all the difference.

As such, Hattie did the unthinkable. She approached Lizzie Sadler for help. The woman was the last person Hattie would've imagined approaching for a handout, especially since Hattie was singly responsible for ending her entire business—her dead husband's business.

But instinct was at play, here. Hattie had buried it too long, and she felt for some time now that Lizzie was on Hattie's side more than just as an element toward profit. And that instinct paid off.

There was a solid half-hour of top-volume screaming. Another of soulful remorse and recrimination. And then Lizzie Sadler emerged from the funk and reached for Hattie's hand. She gripped it tight, assured her that Hattie was not the real villain here, and offered her a hundred dollars to take the fight to the Crew.

And now, as the sun set over the western suburbs and the city lights began flickering into life, Hattie Malloy stood inside the marble-paved lobby of the Old Moravia Hotel, the seat of the Crew's power, decked in a brand-new evening gown with a beaded bandeau around her head.

Into the lion's den.

Never before had she played at such high stakes. Hattie had bought the gown with the offered money. She'd even laid out for the face makeup, seeking some direction from the helpful ladies at Stewart's Department Store downtown. They'd assured her that, despite whatever urgings toward modesty her father had saddled her with, the tune of the day was a short hem, bobbed hair and makeup.

Hattie already had the short hair. The women at Stewart's supplied the rest.

The gown was a silver-and-gold sleeveless sheath, perfectly molded to Hattie's slim figure. Fringe dangled barely to her knees as she stepped into the lobby, a glossy curl of her light red hair plastered in exact geometry against her cheek…just like a movie star.

Since she'd gone to all the trouble to gussy up in proper clothes and presentation, all she'd have to do would be to pinch light enough to keep from being recognized. It was a persistent, annoying use of her power, but in this swell of a crowd milling about, engrossed in serious conversation, very few bothered to take notice. It was the paradox of the city— so many eyes, so little attention. Thus, the cost of her magic was surprisingly cheap.

Hattie took careful steps on her new heels, wobbling on the balls of her feet as she attempted to perfect the casual stride the rest of the women in this building seemed able to execute in these ridiculous shoes. She'd taken several practice laps around the Locust Point warehouse under Liz's tutelage. They'd only achieved minor success, and daylight came at a premium. By the time Hattie made it to the lobby bar, she was already exhausted physically. She couldn't afford to exhaust herself mentally. That was the trap that would get her killed.

A young buck in a suit approached as she reached the bar. He was barely twenty if that, his straight ebony hair slicked back with a handful of pomade. His face was bizarrely smooth and free of blemish, and his brown eyes wide and full of admiration. He was a youth in every sense, and Hattie had found her first test of the evening.

"Heya, toots," he barked as he sidled up alongside her at the bar. "You, uh...you here with a Mister, or what?"

Hattie focused on her face, allowing the light pinch to evolve into something more forgettable. Time to test out her accent.

"Oh, my brother just told me to meet him here. You know him? His name's Carmine." She affected a faint nasal twang, ignoring most of the R's and keeping her syllables choppy.

The youth scowled, then shook his head. "Oh, uh...hey. Yeah, sorry. Don't know him. But, I'm sure he's around. Keep your eyes open. He'll probably show up once he's, uh...done with..." The young man didn't even bother to finish the sentence before sweeping away to find another young woman with a curvy frame to set upon. Implying that she was a gangster's sister was a sure bet to dismiss all interest, assuming the goon in question wanted to keep his chest free of bullet holes.

Bolstered by her first face-to-face encounter with the Crew, Hattie decided to order a gin and tonic from the barkeep. He poured her drink into a tidy highball, and when she tried to pay for it, he gave her a condescending wave of the hand, encouraging her to "forget about it."

And so, she did.

Now, drink in hand, Hattie began the real work of the evening.

"You heard how it went down?" one of the young lions groused into the ear of his compatriot as Hattie passed by. "Calendo had about thirty boys ranged up military-style. Broken up into groups. Borrowed two boats from poor old Tony."

His friend laughed. "Yeah, and made a big deal about it all like he was Alexander the fuckin' Great, or somethin'. So, what's he find? And empty shack. Took them about an hour just to get to the shack. And that's all there was."

His friend asked, "Didn't he get clobbered on his face just the night before?"

"Yeah!" A spate of stifled laughter choked the two men for a moment. "Yeah…oh, sweet mother Mary. That freak's on a short leash, now."

"That idiot has been face-to-face with her what, two or three times? Why can't he just whack her on the head and bring her in. She's just some dame. Not like he can't grab her and stick her in a sack or something."

Hattie swallowed her gin hard, then kept walking as if she hadn't heard a thing. As she moved about the room, more voices colluded one with another, all spelling out the same story.

"The pincher's burned his last grace with the Capo."

"He's probably gonna get sold to the New York boys."

"Good riddance, if you ask me. Him and that one-arm cripple oughta take a dirt nap."

Hattie's heart grew heavy as she reached the front windows, her highball still mostly full. It wasn't personal. She was trying to survive. To stay free. If Vincent found himself in an intolerable position because she'd found a way to do just that, wasn't that simply making her case?

But then again, he'd never laid a hand on her, or tried to use force, and clearly that's what the rest of his mob would have done. It made her feel guilty and even more conflicted that Vincent was risking ridicule and scorn all because he wouldn't resort to violence to bring her in. Hearing these things said about him stung. Why would a group like this be so quick to turn on their own?

The answer was frustratingly clear. He was a pincher. He wasn't to be trusted. Just a weapon to point at the problem. Not a person with feelings. She'd seen it the past spring, as they dealt with this very same quest. Only then, they were hunting a fictional pincher on the Bay. Now, the pincher was very much real.

And she was winning.

Her thoughts occupied her as she turned from the windows, full of memories of Deltaville, when she and Vincent had stood together in some bizarre triumvirate of power with the demon that had set up shop on that muddy slip of land piercing the Bay when she stepped directly into Lefty Mancuso.

Her drink slipped its brim, sending several drops of gin onto Lefty's suit.

He sucked in a breath and stepped clear of her with remarkable grace.

Hattie clenched down on her light pinch, feeling the increased weight of the illusion as a man who would ordinarily recognize her face now stood directly before her, peering into her twist of magic.

"Oh," she declared in her faux Carolinian drawl. "Gracious me! I do apologize."

Lefty stood stiff for a moment, his eyes orbs of stone staring a hole through her soul, until he reached for his lapel and offered a handkerchief.

"My fault entirely," he grumbled, offering her the cloth over the back of his hand in a baroque gesture of manners.

She took the kerchief and dabbed a perfectly dry spot on her collarbone before offering it back to Lefty, per the delicacy of the moment.

"You'll pardon me," she cooed as she attempted to side-step the man.

He lifted a hand, not to grab her, but to capture her attention before she fled. "Excuse me...have we met before?"

"I don't believe so, sir." She offered him a semi-flirtatious glance that put extra load on her light pinch but would hopefully send the man who was oddly averse to such dalliances into retreat. "I think I'd remember a polished man such as yourself?"

The predictable flood of discomfort and courtesy fluttered over his face, and he tried his best to smile. "I'm sure a man like me would rather be forgotten. Good evening, madam."

She nodded, then turned to curtsy as she passed. "Mademoiselle."

He offered an ameliorative grin as he withdrew on his way toward the bar, and she was clear of the greatest danger in the room.

That was assuming Vincent didn't show up. Now that Lefty was here, she had to wonder. The man was Vincent's handler, after all. Vincent seldom went anywhere without Lefty. But, could the converse be said to be true?

Considering the ill winds blowing against Vincent in the room as it was, Hattie prayed he would stay home and keep his head low—for his sake, *and* for hers.

Another half-hour of wandering and adjusting the light load on her facial illusion offered more of the same. Voices throughout the room questioned Vincent's ability to lead. His right to lead. Whether or not this woman was a pincher at all, or just a member of a rival gang intended to keep them off balance. There was even one conversation questioning Vito Corbi's blind dedication to catching her. Simply by refusing to be captured, Hattie had accomplished what groups like the Bratva or the Upright Citizens had failed for so long—she'd driven a dagger into the heart of this gang's fortitude.

She smiled to herself as she drained her glass and set the highball onto a rail just shy of the main lobby. She'd read the lay of the land. All she lacked was a sense of their next move, which was the entire purpose of her being here.

With a sigh, Hattie turned back for the main bar area, looking for the best faces to shadow as she attempted to glean their forthcoming play on her freedom. She chose Tony, Liz's contact and the man responsible for robbing them of their business. He was a book-smart man, if anything could be said of him. Educated, head filled with facts, figures and theories, but when it came to the common-sense side of the equation, his slide rule never quite lined up. But he was on the inside, close to the decision makers. Aside from Lefty, who was too dangerous to linger around, Tony would be the best shot.

Hattie wove her way around the islands of four-top

tables, leather-upholstered wingbacks, and potted palms until she spotted the original lad who'd propositioned her at the bar. He waved her down with three men in tow.

Uh oh.

"Hey, uh…you?" he blurted with a flailing of his hands. "Come here, will ya?"

She offered a courteous grin and steeled her illusion, now wearing heavy after Lefty had forced a greater cost onto her magic. She nearly launched into her Southern drawl before remembering. Brooklyn, not Carolina.

"Yeah?" she called. "What is it?"

He ushered her to join his fellows, which she did while keeping an eye on both Tony and Lefty.

"I'm looking for him," the boy explained with a wave to his friends. "But I couldn't tell. Was it Abruzzo or Battaglia?"

She lifted a brow. "Huh?"

"Carmine," he sighed. "Your brother. Is it Carmine Abruzzo, or—"

"Tanzi," she blurted.

"Carmine *Tanzi*?" he repeated, his eyes drawn into a question. "I don't know no Carmine Tanzi." He turned to the others. "You know any Carmine Tanzi?"

The first shook his head dismissively. The second, however, gave it some thought before snapping his fingers.

"Hey…yeah. I think I met him up by Dundalk ways."

"Really? What's he into?"

"I think it was him. Up by the seaport. He's got the harbormaster in his pocket, runs cash to him every other week so he keeps his trap shut."

The original lad nodded thoughtfully. "Oh, yeah. Tanzi. I think you're right."

Hattie stifled a smirk as the two led themselves down the primrose path.

"So," she asked in all her nasal glory, "you boys gonna buy a girl a drink, or what?"

They stood stiff for a second. "You, uh…" The lad asked in a whisper, "Sure Carmine won't get the red-ass?"

She shoved her hands onto her hips. "Well, maybe you should worry I might knock your block off. Like that Calendo fella what got his clock cleaned by that Irish girl."

The men erupted into earnest guffaws, and she soon found herself with three different drinks lined up at the bar, all purchased by different men ready to roll the dice against the temper of the fictional Carmine Tanzi.

It was enough to bring her closer to Tony, sitting at the bar, nursing his drink the way he had in weeks past. The sauce had hit him hard, and he nodded dumbly as a man grilled him on the nature of the Bay trade. This man stood out from the crowd, as Hattie gave him extra scrutiny. His fashions were far more conservative than the zoot suits surrounding her. His face was sharp, nose aquiline and fierce. His eyes were piercing. His hair a fine medium brown rather than the uniform coal-black Italian stock surrounding them.

Who was this man?

Hattie took a drink and backed up to Tony, nodding and pretending to engage the gang who'd decided Carmine's sister was "alright."

The well-polished man said, "Rest assured, my good man. This is simply a temporary setback."

Tony blathered in full gin-soused fury, "It's over! He's gonna get a call to the vineyard, and then that'll be the last we hear from him."

The man lifted a flat hand. "Your Capo has entrusted this task to Vincent specifically because it would not be easy."

*Your…*Capo? So, this man wasn't a member of the Crew. Who was he, then?

Tony shook his head with undue vigor. "The boy's three for three. Robbed me of two boats when I coulda made a run down for the Carolinas. Good haul, too."

The outsider rolled his eyes. "I'm sure your problems will present their own solutions. But you should listen to me now. Calendo needs support from the inside, if he's going to survive this."

Survive? Surely they meant politically, as in Vincent's status with the Crew and not actual survival. Hattie's brows knitted, wondering if the stakes in this really were life and death for Vincent. Couldn't be. Vito would hardly off his only pincher over a failure to bring her in, would he?

"Ha! He's dog meat, Smith. No one can save him. Not even Lefty."

So, the outsider's name was Smith.

Smith ran a hand over his face in a self-calming gesture. "Perhaps we should have this conversation when you're dry and straight on your feet."

"Good luck," Tony grumbled.

Hattie smirked.

"Speaking of which," Smith added as he shifted away from Tony to stare at the main lobby.

Tony turned to follow Smith's gaze. "Holy shit."

Hattie gripped her glass even as her companions turned back to the center of the Old Moravia lobby to find Vincent Calendo striding into the space.

She turned away from the lobby, nursing her glass. Damn it all. Vincent could see through her illusions, no matter how strong they were. That annoying fact remained true for both of them, even though the mechanism of this condition yet eluded the two of them.

Hattie slipped from her bar stool and eased around Tony and this Smith character, edging her way deeper into the bar as Vincent stepped in. His face was firm and resolute, fully aware of the gossip that had buzzed in this place prior to his arrival. He seemed to have made a choice to defy it. All of it.

Lefty wound his way toward Vincent, chin held at a defiant angle to anyone casting a salty glance in their direction. After a quick conversation, Vincent and Lefty turned to approach Smith and Tony. Which was Hattie's cue to move through the crowd. She did so pulling extra weight onto her own illusion. By the time she reached the main lobby, her stomach was flipping somersaults, and a sweat had broken out on her forehead.

Finally, clear of the bar area, she paused for a second to steal a glance at Vincent. He remained upright and proud, despite the space the others had put between him and themselves. She smiled to herself, oddly gratified that he hadn't been cowed by these two-bit hoodlums.

Not yet, anyway. If Vito decided to weigh in, that would be the end of Vincent's moment. That might be the end of Vincent. And that thought made her resolve waver.

But for now, he was holding his own and Hattie had information. A large shipment bound for the Carolinas was held up thanks to Vincent's hunt for her hide. That shipment had to be lingering in the Bay somewhere.

Hattie stepped back out of the hotel, sweeping around the corner to a shadowed alley where she'd stashed the dented Runabout she'd borrowed from Liz, then steered the Ford south toward Locust Point.

No one was guarding the warehouse. The Crew was sure that Lizzie had folded up shop, and that this would be the last place Hattie would choose to show up. They were wrong. The warehouse door remained cracked open, and a dull orange light emerged from the crack, twinkling in the darkness of night from the flame of Liz's lantern within. Hattie drove up to the front of the warehouse, intending to report then leave. No sense in borrowing trouble from fate.

She killed the motor and dove out into the balmy night air, slipping through the warehouse door to find Lizzie standing arms crossed…in front of a man.

He wore a finely-tailored suit. Very money, very conservative. He turned to face her with an annoyed lift of his brow. Sharp features. Aquiline nose.

Smith!

Hattie froze, then backed away a step.

Lizzie nodded to her. "Malloy! Come on in. I want you to meet someone."

Hattie turned toward the door, spying the car outside. There was no way possible that Smith had beaten her here! She'd left him in deep conversation with Vincent and company. And no one knew the back roads to Locust Point better than Hattie Malloy!

This was impossible!

Lizzie sighed impatiently. "Well?"

Hattie stepped cautiously into the warehouse, hands stiff to her sides.

Smith turned fully to greet her, extending a hand.

She did not take it.

Lizzie glared at her, silently searching for an explanation for her impoliteness.

Hattie drew her lips together into a scowl, then said, "We've met."

Smith's eyes clamped into a squint, before he nodded. "At the hotel."

"Aye," Hattie replied in her native accent. "You've made good time here, haven't you? Better than me."

Smith smirked. "I suppose that merits an explanation."

"What are you, then?" Hattie demanded. "Some sort of pincher?"

He did not answer.

Lizzie shook her head, peering at Smith. "What's this about?"

Smith reached into his jacket to produce a folded piece of cardstock. "I've come to offer you a tangible means to strike back at the Crew."

He held it at arm's length at Hattie.

Lizzie reached out to pluck it from his fingers, and read the note. "Kent Island. Fifteen barrels." She looked up from the paper. "What the hell is this supposed to be?"

Hattie offered, "The Carolina shipment."

Smith nodded with a sharp grin.

Hattie continued, "He's handing us the location of a major shipment outbound for the Carolinas."

"Who are the greatest source of competition south of Virginia for the Crew? Now that the Upright Citizens are floundering, the Greeks are your primary rivals," Smith added.

"You mean Vito's rivals," Lizzie corrected.

"No," Smith chided. "*Your* rivals. The Crew has proven it can't compete with your structure. Vito knows this. It's only his damned foolish pride that prevents him from acting on it. You push him hard enough, make Tony look the fool, and Vito will adapt. He'll improvise. He'll find a reason to bring you back into the fold."

Lizzie sneered. "Not as outsiders."

As she tossed the note onto the ground, Hattie reached down to snatch it up, pocketing it as if it were only ever meant for her. By Smith's expression as he watched her do so, Hattie felt sure she was right.

"Outsiders notwithstanding," Smith continued, "there is only so much business on the East Coast which Atlantic City hasn't already cornered. Vito is in a moment of temporary advantage, now that Richmond is focused on their internal issues. He has the good graces of Masseria. The man must push his advantage to the next level, if he doesn't want to slip into irrelevance yet again." Smith eyed Hattie. "But instead he is chasing after phantoms."

Lizzie tossed her hands into the air. "Why do you think I give a good God damn about Vito Corbi?"

"Because he was your sole client," Smith replied. "You need him as much as he needs you. Which is what brings me here."

"What *does* bring you here?" Hattie asked.

"I have several interests at play, my dear Miss Malloy. One of which is Corbi's acquisition of a certain light pincher."

Hattie took a step away.

He lifted a hand. "Which is, admittedly, a very minor interest. More than anything, I need the Baltimore Crew to falter."

"Why?" Hattie snapped. "What do you get out of this?"

Smith's grin was sharp enough to cut glass. "Money. If they want to succeed, they need you and they need me, and we'll both be in a position to demand top dollar for our services."

Lizzie stepped between them. "So, this shipment?"

Hattie considered the situation as Lizzie and Smith conferred.

"Fifteen barrels," Smith declared. "Find a way to secure that load at the expense of the Crew, and you will find yourself in possession of significant leverage. Do as you will with it. Sell it on the open market. Or, offer it back to Corbi with your regards. In either event, Tony will look the fool. Which will, in turn, deflect the heat from Calendo, and restore Corbi's faith in your organization as the fool-proof method for shipment."

Lizzie squinted at Smith. "What're you asking for this information?"

"Nothing," he replied. "I told you. We have interests in common. You have a chance to get your business back. I have a chance to prove that they need my services as well." He peered over Liz's shoulder to Hattie. "And you stay one step ahead of the hunt."

Hattie frowned. Was it him? Had he sent he letters? She stepped forward so that both could hear her whisper and she could gauge Smith's reaction. "Know thyself?"

Smith looked to the ground, eyes alive with thought as his lips pulled into a satisfied grin. "Always…sound advice." His eyes lifted to meet hers. "My dear light pincher."

CHAPTER 16

It was busy at the hotel, even for a Saturday night. Vincent hadn't counted on this. It took a good hour's bootstrapping just to haul himself up the street and through the front doors. But now that he was here, and more pairs of eyes were suddenly glued to him than he was expecting, there was no backing down. He stepped into the bar area of the Old Moravia, head held high, meeting every cross glance with a challenge. The Crew kept their distance, and that was fine for him. It was still better than it used to be.

He spotted Lefty, Tony and Smith colluding at the end of the bar. By the time Vincent joined them, a sizable bubble of space had grown around them, affording the four a little privacy.

Lefty nodded to Vincent. "Decided against sleep?"

"Yeah," Vincent replied, "for the rest of my life."

Tony sighed and offered a demure toast with his gin.

Smith spun on his barstool to face Vincent. "Bold move to come here after our last outing. Bold...and smart. Don't let these peons keep you thumbed under. Once you let them, it'll never end."

Vincent shot Smith a testy glare. "You gonna crack wise with me after everything that happened? You made me look a total fool."

Smith lifted a hand. "I admit my information wasn't as timely as I'd hoped. But it *was* correct."

"Fat lotta good it did me," Vincent grumbled.

"Still, though," Smith offered. "That's one hiding hole denied your quarry."

Lefty sneered. "She could be anywhere at this point, though. Halfway to Philly. Or West, where we got no one."

Smith reached for his wine glass with a cocksure smirk. "Oh, is that a fact? You have such little faith."

Vincent shook his head. "No. Not good enough. Going out and finding her again won't erase three foul balls."

"Oh, dear Mister Calendo. I don't mean to leave you on the spit like this. Listen—since my last directive proved fruitless, I'll give you one for free towards making amends. I don't know exactly where your light pincher is, but I do know this. She hasn't left the area. In fact, she's still in the city, using her abilities to blend into the population." Smith added with a waggle of his finger against the stem of his goblet, "In fact, she could be in this very room and we'd have no way of knowing it."

Tony grumbled, "Yeah, right. That'd take brass balls."

Vincent grinned, then considered the remark. He took a long, slow glance around the bar area, catching a glimpse of every face in the room. No matter how hard Hattie pinched light, he'd see through it.

No dice. "She's not here."

Smith lifted a brow. "How would you know?"

"I'd know," he assured the man with an arched brow.

Though he nodded, Smith seemed unconvinced. Vincent held his gaze for a moment, chasing down his thoughts on Smith. What did he really know about pincher affairs? How familiar was he with the ins and outs, the costs and limits, the nature of the magic and how they related to one another?

Smith added, "Regardless, she will turn up soon enough. A solid source of mine suggests she has a family in the city."

"No," Vincent blurted out, then withdrew a half-step.

Lefty eyed Vincent with a wrinkle of his brow but said nothing.

"Yes," Smith countered, "I am sure of it."

Vincent stuffed his hands into his pockets, then said, "They're off limits."

Even Tony turned around for this.

Vincent continued, "If she had family in town, that is. There's no way I'd leverage them."

"That's not your call," Lefty stated.

Vincent shook his head and fixed each of them in turn with a hard stare.

Smith let the tension linger for a moment, then said, "I'm here to give you information. Not strategy. As it is, your latest plan of attack was well thought out."

"Not good enough," Vincent grumbled. "Obviously."

Tony added, "No, it was tight."

Vincent peered over at Tony.

The man lifted his glass. "I heard how you had everyone spread out. Thought of things from this illusionist's angle. These palookas are giving you the business over it, but that just shows what they know. If she'd been there, you'd have nabbed her."

Vincent nodded to Tony, a clutch of emotion twisting a knot in his throat. Those words felt like a balm, that recognition he'd craved for so long. It meant something.

Lefty clapped Vincent's shoulder. "No plan of attack survives contact with the enemy."

"We shoulda been so lucky." Vincent chuckled.

"Vito hasn't called you out onto the carpet yet. Maybe

you've been at this too long. Give yourself a break. Go home. Make some pasta. Get some shuteye."

Vincent stared at the ceiling in resignation. "Not much I'm gonna do here, right?" He looked back to Smith. "You still on retainer? You gonna ring my bell the second Malloy pops up?"

"Naturally," he replied with a lift of his glass. "In the meantime, I intend on some rest, myself."

"Sure." Vincent turned to Lefty. "You hear any rumblings from the vineyard, maybe give me a couple steps before you drop the hammer on me, huh?"

"No promises."

He left the hotel in a stew of emotions. The more his compatriots tried to make him feel better about his failures, the worse he felt. Granted, if Vincent actually laid hands on Hattie, he wasn't sure how much better he'd feel about it. Black eye notwithstanding, he truly didn't want her taken like this. He'd held out hope for so long that she'd come around and eventually embrace the situation, that she would work with him willingly, keep her family safe and fed, find a place of belonging. But after all that had happened, he realized she would die before serving the Crew.

And that was what depressed him more than failure. This would likely end with one of them dead.

He made it home and did as Lefty suggested, made some pasta *aglio e olio*. The moonlight streamed through his open window alongside the tinny strains from his neighbor's phonograph. As he ate his lonesome dinner, Vincent considered his fortunes. The Capo had yet to put a bag over his head, shoot him, and dump him in the river. Hattie Malloy was still kicking around out there—a mixed blessing, but still. Lefty hadn't soured on Vincent just yet, though he seemed miffed that Vincent knew Hattie's parents were in the city.

For the very moment, all Vincent could do was wait. Lefty was right. He needed to relax and clear his mind.

After dinner, he remained near the window, chair kicked back on its rear legs as he propped his weight on the back of his head against the wall. The music ran out, and the neighbor took a couple minutes to flip the record.

Vincent's eyes drooped, and he shut them for what felt like half a second.

The chair dropped back onto its front legs, sending Vincent tumbling forward. He jumped to his feet, catching himself on the table as he released a sharp gasp. It wasn't a half-second after all. The music had stopped again and was unlikely to continue as it was well past midnight, and his neighbor was probably asleep.

Vincent shook his head and tried to laugh at himself, but he couldn't summon the mirth.

A knock at the door sent Vincent into a secondary panic, enough for him to instinctively pinch time over most of the city block. He released it immediately, still shaking off the cobwebs from his unintentional nap.

A second knock, then a voice called through the door. "Heya, Vincent. You still up? Saw your light on."

It wasn't Lefty, as was expected with a sudden late-night drop in. No, this voice was different.

Tony.

Vincent reached for his gun on the counter, easing toward the door. Why was Tony here so late? Or, at all? Was this the hammer he'd been waiting to drop? Had Vito sent Tony with a crew of men to take Vincent down?

There was an easy way to tell.

Vincent pinched time again, with a much smaller radius than he'd just done, and eased his door open. All he found in the hallway was Tony, standing straight with one hand in his pants pocket. It looked like he'd sobered up at some point during the evening. There were no gunmen backing him up. Maybe this was simply a social call after all.

As relief swept through Vincent's chest, he holstered his gun and decided to have a little fun. He closed the door, stepped directly behind Tony, then released the time pinch.

Tony huffed, shaking his head as he rubbed the back of his neck.

Vincent smirked. "I'm still up."

Tony nearly jumped out of his skin, throwing himself at the door to Vincent's apartment with wide, wild eyes. He caught his breath, releasing it in a spate of profanity.

Vincent chuckled—there was the mirth.

Tony gave him the bird. "You ass."

"Hey, it's after midnight," Vincent said, opening the door to his apartment. "What's got you on my doorstep so late?"

Tony followed him in, still grumbling to himself. Vincent offered him a pour of something clear, strong, and illegal across state lines. Tony waved him off.

"Keeping your wits tonight?" Vincent asked. "So, what about it?"

"I figured you was here alone. Probably letting all of this eat you up."

"Actually," he said, recorking the bottle and sticking it back into the cabinet, "I was sound asleep until you arrived."

"Horse apples."

"So, you want to play cards, or something?" Vincent prodded.

"I got a call from my boys out by Dundalk port."

He nodded. That was where most of Tony's boat-leggers had been running hooch from the Hole out to the water.

"Something go wrong?" Vincent asked. "Or right?"

"Didn't sound like a beach blanket picnic, so yeah. I'm afraid something's gone wrong."

"That's why you're here?" Vincent asked. "You need my help."

Tony shrugged, then nodded noncommittally.

Vincent set down his glass to fetch his coat and hat. "Let's beat feet, then. We're burning moonlight."

Tony hopped behind the wheel as Vincent climbed into his car, and they made their way to Dundalk Port without any obstacles. The whole way, Vincent considered Tony. This situation was odd, but not necessarily worrisome. Tony was in a pickle, arguably as bad as Vincent's. He was charged with Vito's other pet project—the assumption of all liquor traffic within the organization. And though Tony had "managed" Lizzie Sadler and her boat-leggers to date, he truly had no experience with large-scale distribution of illicit goods across state lines, no knowledge of the Feds and their favorite pinch points and shakedown schedules, no lay of the land, the Bay, and all of its endless inlets and outlets. Tony may have been a college man, but this sort of business required more horse sense than anything a book could teach.

Which was why Sadler had thrived.

But those days were gone now, and Tony probably saw something in Vincent he could relate to. The same sort of pressure. The same alienation.

Tony broke the silence to make conversation as he drove. "I hear Vito hasn't kicked up any fire and brimstone over that Curtis Creek bust."

"Not yet," Vincent agreed. "Though someone could dime me out at any moment." He turned to Tony. "Someone who had two good boat crews sitting in the water getting a sunburn for nothing."

Tony sneered. "You think I'm a rat?"

"You don't owe me nothing, Tony. Why would you keep it under your hat like this?"

He shook his head. "Let's call it professional courtesy."

"I like the sound of that."

"Listen, Vincent, a lot of the guys are just getting their kicks on you. But they ain't no one to go bend the Capo's ear. Hell, watching you fall on your face is about the only sport they got, anymore. Ever since we dealt with the Russians last year, and the Richmond boys are cooling their heels." He wagged his finger back and forth between the two of them. "People that matter, though? Close to the top? Me, Lefty... We know how easy it is for the right plan to go sideways. And we don't put that on you. This girl's as slippery as a greased eel. I mean, she was under our noses the whole time. How often did I see her in that warehouse, and never knew? Blended into the background, that one did. Hell, I barely noticed her. If I'd run smack into her on the street, I'm not sure I'd have known who she was. This isn't your fault. The girl's smart, she's got magic, and she's good at staying hid. Not your fault at all."

"Yeah, but will Vito see it that way?"

"Heh. Hopefully you'll have her before he finds out."

Tony pulled the car down a hitch lane toward the port, easing between warehouses alongside ships and boats of various sizes and registries. A group of men lingered by a fishing boat with a fresh coat of paint. They waved him down as he parked.

As they stepped out of the car, Tony buttoned his jacket and started barking immediately. "Alright, so what's the beef? It's half past a monkey's ass out here."

They guided them toward the boat, empty aside from a couple dog-eared Crew members who looked like they'd just had their dog shot in front of them.

A short man with curly brown hair spilling out from underneath a cabbie cap hopped off the boat and ushered the rest away. "Heya, boss."

"Curly? You got heat out on the water or something?" Tony prodded.

Curly sighed and crossed his arms. "We got hit. Right past McHenry."

Vincent scowled. "That's barely clear of the city."

Curly shot Vincent a vicious glare. "What do you know about it, you freak?"

Tony pulled his hand back, then slugged Curly across the jaw, sending him to the ground. The muffled conversation on the boat fell to absolute silence, leaving only the sound of water lapping against the boat and Curly groaning as he nursed the side of his face.

Tony cracked his knuckles. "Mind your p's and q's, pal. He's got more right to be here than you do."

Curly scowled at them, still sitting on the ground rubbing his jaw.

With an impatient wave of his hands, Tony grunted, "So, what happened?"

"Boat," Curly spat. "Came up on us outta nowhere. Maybe eight men with tillers. Had us dead to rights. Took the shipment, then left us in the wash."

Tony groaned, "The whole shipment?"

Curly nodded.

Vincent stepped forward to offer a hand. After staring at it for a second, Curly took it as Vincent helped him to his feet.

Tony paced a circle. "How many barrels?"

"Fifteen."

Vincent asked, "Where were they bound for?"

"Charleston," Curly replied. "The Greeks were supposed to meet us at Newport News."

Tony shook his head, his eyes searching the ground for something to say.

And so, Vincent kept prodding. "Tell me about the boat. Did you get a name?"

"Yeah…" Curly turned to the boat. "Hey, Carmine! You get the name of those sons a' bitches?"

Carmine called, "Blanco Forte, or something."

Vincent stiffened. "*Bianco Fiore?*"

"Yeah, that's it!" Carmine chimed.

Tony squinted at Vincent. "That mean something to you?"

"It does," Vincent replied. "They're a band of righteous types. Lynch mobs on boats. Real Confederate cut to their patriotism, if you take my meaning."

Curly shrugged. "They just marched us behind the engine house and carted off all the goods. Wasn't no violence."

Vincent cocked his head. "Did they give you the business over your Roman stock? Call you Wop or Guinea, or anything like that?"

Curly shook his head.

"What're you thinking?" Tony asked almost out of desperation.

Vincent eyed Tony, then Curly, then turned to face the water. This was a bit far north for those Fiore thugs, especially given the current unsettled situation in their territory. And the timing of it all was a bit…convenient.

Fifteen barrels that never made it to the Carolinas? That would be enough to ripple the water between Baltimore and Charleston. It would likely kick off an exchange of words between them and the Crew, maybe more than just words. It would come at a time when Vito was looking to expand, not contract. Plus, the Crew would need to divert manpower to chasing down those decentralized Fiore idiots. All this right when Vito was poised to expand and show his power, right when his focus was on consolidating his business in house and adding a pincher to the Crew.

And Tony was in hot water as it was. Something like this

would go a long way to pulling Vincent's ass out of the fire. Tony knew it, too. If he returned to the vineyard with little more than "thugs took the hooch," he'd be looking for a new line of work in short order.

However...

"Doesn't sound like the *Bianco Fiore*," Vincent declared, still staring over the water. "They're out for blood, not booze. May come a day when they decide Sicilians aren't their sort of complexion, but today isn't that day."

Tony asked, "If not them, then who?"

Vincent turned to face Tony. "Richmond."

"Richmond?" Tony parroted. "How do you figure?"

"Something Smith told me when he tried to talk me out of siccing him on Malloy. He said the Upright Citizens were up to something. There's always been some overlap between the gangsters and the bigots down that way, and they haven't shied away from using those thugs to do their dirty work before. If someone were trying to rebuild on the sly, it'd be a good tactic to slap the words *Bianco Fiore* on a couple boats, then put a hit out on your boys here. They stand out."

Curly sniffled. "Says you."

"No," Tony admitted, "he's right. You wouldn't know these hooligans from the Upright Citizens from the Feds. You nearly got pinched by the G-men just two days ago. Remember?"

Curly turned away.

Vincent offered, "I know Vito's eager to keep the trade inside the family. But Sadler's people knew the Bay. They knew every inch of the coastline. They had friends in every fueling stop, every speakeasy, every fishing camp, every hobo village. And they knew the difference between some sheet wearing reubens on the water and the Upright Citizens."

Tony lifted a hand. "I get it, I get it. We were better off."

Vincent nodded.

With a sigh, Tony said, "That's gonna be a hard sell with Vito."

"Tell me about hard sells some more."

Tony smirked, then chuckled. "Yeah, I suppose you're savvy as much as anyone. It helps being able to take the Richmond boys to Vito, instead of this bag of sorry bastards." He nodded to the crew on the emptied boat.

"He's gonna lose his mind, one way or another."

"Yeah, but at least he'll focus that at Richmond, and not me." Tony grinned. "Thanks for that. You, uh…you didn't have to volunteer that info."

Vincent slapped his shoulder and turned back to the car. "Let's call it professional courtesy."

CHAPTER 17

The eastern sky was a shimmering cobalt as the low-hanging clouds over the peninsula glowed pink.

Raymond eyed the color and grunted, "Best hurry this up. Get these babies under cover before daylight."

He growled as he hoisted a barrel of purloined moonshine from his boat, aided by Hattie Malloy who threw her shoulder into the work.

"We will," she huffed. "How…how many more…left?"

Raymond settled the barrel onto the pier at Winnows Slip, caught his breath, then counted the remainders still on the boat. "Shit. Six."

Hattie leaned against the engine house and stared at the sky. "Can I catch my breath, then? I'm knackered."

Raymond shook his head. "We stop moving now, we're gonna get sore. Then we won't move anything."

With a beleaguered nod, Hattie wound her way to the fore and began walking the next barrel toward the rail as Raymond lugged his into the warehouse they'd rented from the locals. Half an hour later, both had cleared the last of the barrels and lay sprawled along the warped wood planks of the pier as footsteps clacked from within the warehouse.

Lizzie Sadler emerged into the breaking dawn's light like a conquering general. Her face was the picture of satisfaction.

Hattie grunted, "It was a good haul."

Lizzie crossed her arms and cocked her hips. "Couldn't have done it without a light pincher."

Raymond lifted a hand. "And a pilot."

Lizzie smiled. "Yeah, you. Couldn't have done it without the both of you."

She ushered them into the warehouse before too many locals emerged to stick their noses into their business. Inside the ill-lit building, Hattie hopped onto the top of one of the barrels, patting it with her palm. "Those daft buggers seemed eager to hand these over. I bet with a little more persuasion, I could've talked them into unloading them for us."

Raymond grumbled, "They must not get paid so good."

Lizzie scoffed, "Are you bucking for a raise there?"

He lifted his hands, head hung in exhaustion. "I'm too tired to buck anyone."

"Well there's a first," Hattie jibed.

Admittedly, she was as worn out as Raymond. Though he did the lion's share of heavy lifting, it was no easy task maintaining an illusion as detailed as the one she'd pinched for the Crew's boat-leggers. Eight men with guns. A boat with *Bianco Fiore* scrawled across the transom. She'd remembered the precise look of it from earlier that spring, when she and Vincent had a run-in with that lot. The details helped, but she had to keep the pinch up for as long as it took to help Raymond unload the barrels. She felt no small measure of pride that she'd pulled it off. Perhaps her practice was paying dividends after all?

After a brief rest, Raymond departed to head back to his

family, leaving Lizzie with Hattie. Lizzie slipped her hands into her pants pockets to step into the center of the warehouse.

"You think they took the bait, then?" Hattie asked.

Lizzie shrugged. "That depends on your friend, the time pincher."

"He's no friend of mine," she snapped.

A razor-sharp smile lifted onto Liz's lips. "I suppose you believe that."

"What's that mean?"

"Come on, Hattie. I've been dealing with the Baltimore Crew since Jake was alive. They want something, they take it and damn the consequences. Anyone else was after you, they'd have taken a cudgel to your head and had you tied in some basement before you knew what was happening. The only reason you're walking free right now is because that boy is too sweet on you to muscle you around."

Hattie swallowed hard, feeling that familiar ache in her chest. "I know. I mean, not that he's sweet on me or anything. He's just not the sort to be violent toward a woman or a woman friend, or..."

Liz's eyebrows shot up.

"He's not...it's not..." Hattie scowled. "Anyway, it was a good plan to hijack these guys at Fort McHenry."

"In truth, it wasn't my plan at all."

Hattie hopped off the barrel and approached. "Was it Smith?"

Lizzie nodded. "He knew where they were going to be and when. The man has the pulse of the Crew, I'll give him that much. He's a man in the know."

"Aye," Hattie grumbled. "He's a crafty one."

"But, as I said, it all depends on how well you know this Vincent Calendo. Too much of this hinges on him connecting the dots from *Bianco Fiore* to Richmond."

"Oh, he'll follow the bread crumbs." Hattie lifted a finger. "And what about your part? Do you really think Tony will go to Vito, hat in hand?"

With a proud cackle, Lizzie replied, "I know that man. He'll jump at the chance to get the business back in our hands."

"He doesn't take well to pressure, then?"

"Well, it depends on what you're pressing." Lizzie snickered. "And how hard."

Hattie grinned and shook her head.

"Hattie," Lizzie said after a moment of composure. "I wanted you to know…I was furious with you."

The shift in conversation knocked Hattie mute.

"What you did. How hard you pushed for it. How very thorough you were in lousing it up. It felt like…"

"Betrayal?" Hattie finished.

"Like I was watching my own daughter piss away her livelihood, as well as mine. I know you fight a battle every day to stay free, despite your condition."

Hattie wrinkled her nose at the phrasing, as if she were a leper.

Lizzie continued, "And though I see that, I feel there are more mundane concerns you should be attending to. There's more to living than living free."

"I disagree," Hattie blurted.

"Hear me out. What's the use in freedom if you spend it constantly on the lam? Looking over your shoulder, waiting for someone to drop a hammer on you. Ever heard of the Sword of Damocles?"

Hattie waved her off. "I read books, you know."

"Fine, then. You get what I'm saying."

"I don't think I do. You're saying I should surrender to the Crew, so that I can live comfortably? Is that the short of't?"

Lizzie frowned. "Heavens, girl. It's like you're not even

listening. What I'm saying is you can't only fight for freedom. You need something to live for. Family."

"I've got one of those."

"Industry."

Hattie cast a glance at the barrels surrounding them. "What do you call all this, then?"

Lizzie lifted an eyebrow. "Love?"

Hattie's stomach dropped like a lead weight. "How about I stick with family and industry."

Lizzie stepped forward to lay both hands on Hattie's shoulders. "Listen to me. I've been fortunate in life. I've had one great love. A magnificent man who never raised a hand against me. Who not only listened to me, he *respected* me. He believed I could contribute to his business, and he brought me alongside him. He saw me as an equal, as a partner, as someone who was just as smart, just as strong as he was. There will never be another man like that, as far as I'm concerned."

Hattie dropped a sorrowful gaze to the ground. "Jake was one of a kind."

Lizzie lifted Hattie's chin with her finger. "And yet, here I am. Knocking boots with a gangster." She stepped away. "Don't think I don't see how the both of you look at me sometimes. You and Raymond. When Tony's driving off, and you act like you just showed up. Like I'm sullying our temple with another man's affections. Like I'm...replacing..." Her voice failed her.

Hattie reached to lay a hand on Liz's back. "No sense in you being lonely, Liz. We don't judge you."

"Oh," Lizzie sniffled. "I'd like to believe that. But let's be honest."

Hattie nodded. "It seemed quick, how you two fell in together so soon after Jake's death, but that's not my business."

"There's a reason I'm telling you this." She turned toward Hattie, eyes rimmed red with tears. "I would never betray Jake's memory. But, Jake is *gone*. And he's not coming back. There is simply no point in living my life a grieving widow, when all it does is to rob me of this painfully short time we have on this Earth."

Hattie considered the woman, standing so strong and yet filled with such fragility. "You'll see Jake again someday. God willing."

Lizzie released a bitter laugh. "Right."

"Don't you believe in Heaven?"

"You can believe what you like, girl. But I'm living for here and now. The hereafter can wait. But you? You shouldn't wait. Your years are getting behind you, and before you realize it, you'll be as old as I am, wondering when you were supposed to start living. I don't want that for you."

She placed a hand against the side of Hattie's face, and Hattie reached for it, pressing it hard against her cheek. "When you feel something for someone, when there's that spark, that tiny shoot breaking through a frozen ground, then let it grow. Let it bloom. Nourish it, because that's one of the things that makes life worth living."

She leaned her forehead against Hattie's and the two held there, letting the moment linger between them. Then with a sigh, Lizzie stepped away.

"So," Hattie said with a clearing of her throat, "what's next for us?"

"Smith says we should look west, now that Tony's looking to the Bay."

Hattie frowned. "West? You mean?"

"West By God Virginia," Lizzie declared in a hokey accent. "He says that he agrees with your original plan, by the by. Take the fight to the bootleggers."

"I think I've shown that to be a poor plan," Hattie grumbled.

"Well, maybe yes and maybe no. Smith knows the contacts in the hills. Moonshiners who produce for the Crew."

"And?" Hattie pressed.

Lizzie shook her head. "That's all he gave me. There's going to be another meeting, two nights from now at Locust Point."

"Is that safe?"

"The Crew won't be looking for us there. Smith assured me of that."

Hattie covered her mouth with her hand as a dark thought crossed her mind.

Lizzie picked up on it, cocking a brow. "What?"

"Do you really trust that man?"

"I most certainly do not."

"Then why put so much stock in his schemes?"

Lizzie marched for the warehouse door, urging Hattie to follow. "Because, my dear protégé, the first step in surviving men like Smith is to understand that they always have an agenda. And that agenda shifts like the wind."

Hattie emerged into the morning light as Lizzie shut the warehouse and locked it.

That sentiment was well and good, but Hattie left Winnows Slip wondering if a wind like Smith's was something they could weather without flying apart.

CHAPTER 18

$\mathcal{A}$ knock on Vincent's door pulled him from his thoughts. He withdrew from his window, setting his coffee onto the table before stepping for the door, hand on the pistol in his jacket. He pinched time to crack the door open. This time, it wasn't Tony looking for him…

It was Fern. What in the world was she doing here? He hadn't had a spare moment to speak to her after the aborted lunch at the café, and for her to show up on his doorstep like this…

He released the time pinch, forgetting to close the door and "reset," and as the flow of time resumed, Fern started.

Vincent winced. "Sorry about that. Is something wrong? Has something happened? Did Cooper…?"

She shook her head. "No! Nothing's happened. I just needed to talk. I just…" Fern lifted a hand to her cloche as if to ensure it was properly seated on her head for no particular reason, then let her fingers trace an uncertain path down the side of her face. "I wanted to…"

Vincent eased the door open to invite her in. She was

clearly struggling with a thought, and her anxiety filled him with dread.

Before he could formally invite her inside, she dropped her clutch onto the floor of the hallway and leaped through the door, grasping the sides of Vincent's face to pull him into a kiss that had far more to do with desperation than desire. He held stiff in her embrace until she was done, then pulled away, his eyes wide.

"What's wrong?" he demanded.

"Nothing, I just…" She leaned into him and he backed up a step.

"Are you alright?" he asked.

She stiffened, then twisted away from him. "I'm sorry."

"Fern?"

"I'll go."

Vincent reached for her arm, guiding her back to face him. "Hey, what's going on? You can't just show up here, kiss me, then leave."

"I'm fine," she protested with a sudden air of forced calm. "I just… I was thinking about you. And I decided that I wanted to see you. Is it a bad time? Should I leave?"

"No, of course not. I'm glad you came by."

He wasn't glad, he realized. He was perplexed and confused—and not just about her vague reasoning for the impromptu visit. Having a beautiful woman appear at his door and throw herself at him should have been the highlight of his day, heck, his month. Instead he found himself mildly annoyed and dreading the stress that seemed to come every time he and Fern shared a moment together.

Vincent pulled a chair at his table for her, and after a moment's consideration on whether to sit or flee his own apartment, he gestured toward the kitchen. "Coffee?"

"No, thank you."

Vincent sat across from her, wishing he had something

stronger in his own coffee. "So, you wanna level with me? What's going on?"

She spread her hands out on the surface of the table and closed her eyes, taking a long breath. "I saw Cooper today."

Vincent balled his fists. "Where?"

"One of Tony's boys twisted his ankle on some run gone wrong."

Vincent nodded. "I know about that."

"Tony picked me up to come take a look, wrap his ankle. Make sure it wasn't broken. When I got there…"

"Cooper was there?"

She nodded.

"Did he touch you?" Vincent asked.

"No. He didn't say a word. He was just…there."

"Why?"

"I don't know. Neither did Tony. He just watched, like a buzzard."

"I'll have a word with Tony," Vincent offered.

Fern's hand shot across the table to latch onto Vincent's. "Please don't!"

Vincent sucked in a breath.

She added, "I just want him…away. Away from me."

"Well, sounds like he won't stay away unless someone reminds him that you're off limits."

"Don't. He'll come after you. He'll say something and get you in trouble."

Vincent shook his head in frustration. "He's part of the family. We have people who can back you up, now. Look what happened last time."

She squeezed his hand. "I feel safe with you. When you're *you*, I mean. And not…" A tear dropped from her eyelash.

"Not a pincher?" Here it was again, as it always was.

"Not a *gangster*," she corrected.

He blinked at the comment. "I don't read you."

"All of you are dangerous." She pulled her hand away. "When you're dealing in guns, guts and greed. I've seen all of you, at some point. Bullet wounds. Broken arms. The Crew is no family, Vincent. It's a meat grinder. I grew up in the belly of that meat grinder. It's all I know, but the thought of spending my life like that...that I might say the wrong word at the wrong time and get someone I care about killed, or myself beat to a bloody mess. I don't want that."

"It's a tough life, sure, but you're safe. Protected. We take care of our own."

Fern sighed. "Until you don't." She folded her hands in her lap and dropped her eyes. "I enjoy spending time with you. It was a long time since anyone saw me as a person and not just a dame." Her eyes met his. "Which scares me, because I think I could fall for you. But..."

Vincent's heart skipped two full beats, then returned hammering against his sternum in double-march step. This should have thrilled him, but instead he was mentally counting the steps to the door.

"But what? You're afraid I'll get hurt? That I'll make a wrong move end up at the bottom of the river?"

"I wish it were that simple," she said, wiping a fresh tear from her eye.

Get myself beaten to a bloody mess, she'd said. "You're afraid that *I'll* be the one doing the hurting," he stated, realization settling over his brain.

She shot him a look filled with apology and nodded. "When you're around the others, you're different. You're like them. When that man came into the café, you changed. I don't want you like that. I want the other Vincent."

He clamped his lips hard on an angry reply. There was no other Vincent. It was all him, and the thought that she didn't want half of who he was bothered him almost as much as her insinuation that he might eventually beat her.

"I've seen good men change," she continued. "They wilt under the strain of this family's violence. Corbi is no different than D'Urso. Same machine, chewing up men to turn them into killers." She added with a scowl, "I hate it so much."

Vincent forced a smile. "I don't doubt that, but no matter what I do for the Crew, you're safe with me."

"You say that, but I feel like…" She took a breath, then tried again. "I feel like you've been sucked into this pincher hunt, and it's changing you—changing you for the worse. You're ready to set into this person, to put the same chains on her that you've forgotten are on your own wrists."

He scowled. "Now you sound like Hattie."

Fern looked away.

Vincent shifted in his chair to peer out the window. It was a sunny day out. There were no immediate plans. He was waiting to hear from Smith, but who knew when that ghoul would appear. And as much as he wanted to return to his peaceful morning, he didn't like the thought of her leaving like this.

"Want to go to the park?" he asked.

Fern lifted her chin to look out the same window. A smile crept across her face. "It's a pretty day."

"It is. I could buy you an ice."

She blinked as sunlight filled her eyes. "We could feed the ducks."

"That sounds nice."

They remained seated.

Fern turned to Vincent. "Be honest with me. Is there any way at all that you'll ever escape the Crew?"

He stared at her. "What?"

"Can't you just leave? Run away?" She reached for his hands again. "If we get in a car, we can just drive west. Get away from everyone. Go somewhere quiet. I'll get a job working in a department store, and you'll find something that doesn't involve taking a lead pipe to someone's legs or shooting someone. Eventually we'll get a place with a little garden out back where the kids can play. You'll read the paper in the evenings and smoke a pipe while I darn socks."

"I don't smoke," he commented, feeling oddly terrified at the scene she was painting.

"Then don't smoke." She leaned in closer to him and for a second he thought she was going to kiss him again. "No more guns and blood and broken bones. No more black eyes or worrying over who might knock on the door in the dead of the night."

"I'm a pincher, Fern. I'm part of the Crew. This is what I do, this is what gives me purpose. I can't just head west and get a job…welding or something. Lily hands, remember?" he joked, trying to force some levity into the conversation.

"You could be a clerk, or a salesman," she urged. "I think you'd be a good salesman. And you'd be home at five every night and I'd have dinner ready for you."

She smiled, her eyes sparkling with happiness at the idea, but in Vincent's mind the whole thing sounded like his worst nightmare.

"I need to have purpose. Sitting in an office adding numbers all day? Selling…what? Selling furniture or men's suits or newfangled coffee makers? There's no purpose to that. I'm a pincher."

"Then don't be a pincher," she urged. "Just be a man. Just be a normal man and find purpose in a normal job with a normal family and a wife who takes care of you."

Don't be a pincher. She really thought it was that simple? And that he'd find purpose in this horrible boring life she was envisioning for him? Did Fern know him at all?

No, she didn't. Not like…not like someone else did.

"Leave with me, Vincent," she urged. "I can't do this alone, but with you, I think I can."

Vincent closed his eyes and thought. Beyond the horror of the picket-fence fantasy she was spinning, he knew there could never be a life like that for a man like him. Pinchers were always tools for the men in power. No matter how far away he ran, someone would want to possess him. What's more, he didn't want to run. As much as he detested the violence, he understood it. The blood came with the life. The Crew was where he belonged, even if they didn't see him as an equal. To simply drive west without a plan? Without support? To live a life without *purpose*?

And then there was the whole niggling suspicion that her affections were more about having someone save her than any budding heartfelt emotions for him.

A noise from the front of the apartment jerked Vincent from his musings. He opened his eyes to find Lefty standing in the doorway holding Fern's clutch. They'd left the door open, and her purse on the floor.

The maelstrom of uncertainty inside Vincent's chest stilled upon seeing Lefty. Fern pulled her hands away. She stood, eyes hooded, lips tight.

"I think I'll go," she muttered.

Vincent nodded. "I'll talk to you later. Maybe...maybe we'll catch a movie next weekend," he offered half-heartedly.

She lingered a moment, then turned for the door.

Lefty held out her clutch. She took it with a quick nod. "Thank you."

Lefty watched as she withdrew down the hallway, heels clicking down the stairs. Once Fern had gone, he eased into the apartment.

"I don't know what I just walked in on—and I don't wanna know."

Vincent stood up. "Vito call a meeting?"

Lefty nodded. "Let's go."

Even as he snatched his hat to move for the door, Lefty held out a hand. "You solid?"

"Solid."

* * *

Turned out, Vincent got plenty of sunshine after all as he stood shoulder-to-shoulder with several Baltimore Crew auxiliaries and hangers-on, all gathered outside the villa at the Havre de Grace vineyard for the meet. Vito's voice carried through the open windows and double doors as Vincent looked on. He caught bits of the tirade, in particular the points where Vito got his blood into a lather.

"...the uncultured swine of Richmond...cripple their entire family...a war for all memory..."

The Capo was in rare form. His voice possessed a sort of Roman quality of oration as he held his vowels at the right moment, took breaths between cheers of agreement, angled his tone up and down to sway the emotions of those gathered. This was Vito on a good day. It was what he'd been preparing for, a chance to prove himself. Tony was right. Most of these young bucks had settled into peacetime and had grown disgruntled because of it.

"...to prove once and for all that we are heirs to greatness!"

There it was. Vito's credo. Prove ourselves.

The diatribe lasted another twenty minutes, during which the message met with occasional applause and cheers. In truth, however, the picture Vito painted for the gathering was blithe and reductive. All they had to do was to assert themselves, take the fight to the Upright Citizens, and then the rest of the East Coast families would fall into line. It was a load of bushwa, but it sold.

Once general marching orders were announced, the

upper echelon exited the villa, waving over heads at their point people, gathering flocks to prepare for war.

Lefty eyed Vincent from the open double doors and beckoned with his finger. Vincent nodded and pressed his way through the mass of suits until he found himself inside the villa. Only a handful remained, most of which conferred in a tight huddle with the Capo. Vito's eyes lifted to find Vincent, and he brushed the rest away with a grumble. They made a quick exit, and as a valet closed the doors behind them, Vito turned for a sideboard and poured himself a goblet of red wine.

Lefty took position directly beside Vincent. Tony leaned against the wall between windows, his face sharp and clear. Looked like he'd kept his sails furled for this meeting.

"Vincenzo," Vito muttered, "I hear things. Things I do not like." He turned to face Vincent. "I do not relish the thought of failure."

Vincent said nothing.

"Particularly now, when we have been insulted by the Virginians." He waved the goblet at Tony. "Had Antonio not seen through their deceptions, we may have continued hemorrhaging into the Bay."

Vincent cast a glance at Tony. His eyes had drawn just a little wider, filling with alarm. He'd taken credit for Vincent's deductions, but seemed unprepared for the moment. With a few words, Vincent could call him out on it. Right here, in front of the Capo. It might come off as petulant. It might even cost Vincent yet more face in Vito's eyes, but it would dash Tony's newfound esteem.

But Vincent found no joy in that. He'd given Tony that insight, that the *Bianco Fiore* boat was actually the Upright Citizens trying to pull a hoodwink. He'd done it to help Tony.

"I have a lot of respect for Tony," Vincent replied. "He has some thoughts on the boat traffic situation which, well...I think we should hear him out."

Tony gave him a slight nod of thanks.

Vito waved off the comment. "Yes, yes. He's already made a diplomatic gesture of showing me the error of my ways. Perhaps not as diplomatic as he thinks he was, but I understand. But we are not here to discuss our failures on the water. We are here to discuss *your* failures—" he pointed his glass at Vincent "—in finding my pincher."

Vincent bowed his head. "I apologize for the delays. Smith and I had agreed that a slow hand would be the smart way to approach her."

"Slow hand?" Vito spat. "Three failures to secure the light pincher is not a slow hand. It is a disgrace."

"Capo, if I may," Vincent urged. "Each one of these moves, these failures...they are part of a plan."

Vito squinted, took a sip of his wine, then gestured for Vincent to explain.

"See, you're looking to secure a pincher. Not just physically, because she'll be a fly in the ointment if she's forced, more trouble than she's worth. No, we have to capture her mind. This woman is convinced that she's better off out there on her own. What we've been doing is to surround her with the force of the family. Demonstrating that there are no options. Showing her that there is nowhere to run. And when she accepts it, she'll come to us." He added with a nod to Lefty. "It'll save us time and resources in reeducating her."

Lefty spoke up, "We may not have time to send her upstate if Richmond is pressing us."

Vito frowned, then paced toward the doors. "You're telling me, then, that you are doing this the correct way. Not the fast way."

"In so many words," Vincent admitted.

"You think me careless, then? So eager to snatch this

quarry that I'd be willing to endanger my own long-term goals?"

Vincent froze. Vito's tone was sharp and testy.

Lefty said, "Capo, I—"

Vito lifted his hand, and Lefty shut up.

"It takes a man of uncommon, callous disregard for his own well-being to accuse his Capo of imprudence." Vito smirked. "I need such men, for it is true. I have been reckless. Reckless with our water distribution." He nodded to Tony. "Reckless in trusting this information broker, this outsider. Reckless when I was so quick to dismiss the contractors who have served us in a period of expansion, perhaps even responsible for that expansion. If you are telling me, Vincenzo, that I have offered you nothing more than complaint and castigation, then perhaps it is time that I offered something more."

Vito snapped his fingers.

A valet opened a side door. Footsteps echoed from the terrazzo hallway, clopping louder and louder until a man entered the room.

Vito declared, "Allow me to rectify this oversight. You need assistance. You shall have it."

Vincent stiffened as Loren DeBarre gave him a wink.

Lefty squinted at the down pincher from Philadelphia. "What brings you to Baltimore?"

"I do," Vito snapped. "I've been in continual contact with the family in Philadelphia ever since your meeting. They are as alarmed to hear of these stirrings from Richmond as we are. They represent a threat to traffic all the way to the Delaware River."

DeBarre offered, "Sabella's got a real itch about it. We figured if the liquor down in Baltimore was getting squeezed, our beer would be next." He peered at Tony. "By the way, Billy McCoy sends his regards."

Tony smiled and nodded. "Tell him I got a case of grappa for him next time he wants to lose a hand of poker for me."

Vito grumbled, "Enough."

The room fell silent.

With a measured glance at Vincent, Vito concluded, "War is upon us. The time for slow hands has come to an end. We need this light pincher. Make it happen."

He drained his glass and took a seat behind his desk, their cue to exit.

Outside, Vincent offered a hand to DeBarre, who shook it with verve. "Glad for the help, DeBarre."

The polished man shrugged. "I have experience in this sorta thing. Brought Arnoud on board just last year. I think a little girl with a bag of tricks will be small potatoes compared to him."

"You might be surprised," Vincent muttered.

Lefty asked, "You familiar with this Alexander Smith character? He's an informant who fell from the sky with all sorts of useful tidbits he's willing to sell us."

DeBarre shook his head. "Never heard of him."

"Doesn't surprise me," Lefty grumbled, turning to Vincent. "This long game of his is getting us nowhere. I don't think I have to tell you, this may be our last chance."

DeBarre nodded. "Assuming she hasn't flown the coop, yet."

"Smith says she's staying put" Vincent told him. "Probably trying to find some way to turn this around."

DeBarre asked, "You know this girl? I think someone said something—"

"We worked together briefly last spring," Vincent hastily interrupted. He eyed Lefty, who slipped his hand into a pocket with a pointed glare.

"What's the next step?" Lefty asked, as if he knew exactly what step he would have taken. "Thoughts, DeBarre?"

The man stared out over the vineyard, tapping his chin with a finger. "You think she's trying to play your Crew, huh? Stay a step ahead and look for a way to stay in the city?"

Vincent nodded.

"Why's she so dead set on staying in Baltimore?" DeBarre asked. "Anyone got a read on that? Does she have a job here? Family?"

Lefty sniffed and lifted an eyebrow Vincent's way.

"She's a stubborn Irish woman, is why," Vincent offered.

DeBarre smiled. "I like her already. Fine. We know she's keeping an eye on your Crew. So, you stop looking out there at the city, and you turn your eyes onto your own. She's staying close to you. The harder you look, the less likely you are to find her."

Vincent nodded. "Right. She got nabbed the first time trying to bootleg a truck through D.C."

DeBarre laughed. "That took guts. Hell, who is this girl? Can I have her?"

Something hot boiled in Vincent's stomach. No, DeBarre most definitely could not have her.

With a breath he cleared his head of the sudden murderous thoughts. "She took a chance, thought her powers were stronger than they were." He eyed a cart of barrels sitting outside the winery. "If she makes a play on us, it'll be the shipments. That's her wheelhouse—that's where she's got connections and experience. Probably over the water since —" he caught his breath "—since she knows everything about running hooch for the Crew over the Bay. For the *love of God...*"

"What?" Lefty urged.

"We're already a step behind. And she's already pulled the trigger on us." He turned to Tony. "Sorry, Tony. I may have been dead wrong."

"About what?" Tony asked.

"Richmond. They weren't the ones who knocked you over the other night."

"Who, then?" Tony blurted.

"It was her," Lefty grumbled.

Tony shook his head. "But, there were eight gunmen on that boat."

DeBarre snickered. "That's what you get for taking on a light pincher. You said she spins illusions, right? Mirages?"

Tony groaned. "We...uh, we have to tell Vito."

Lefty reached out to grip Tony's arm. "Like hell, you will. You do that, and he'll have us all at the end of a rope."

Tony pulled away. "So, we're just gonna let him take us to war with the Citizens?"

"You're damn straight. Let it be for now, and we can reel this in later, when the timing's such that we won't get strung up for our mistake." Lefty turned to DeBarre. "And you'll keep this under your hat. Capiche?"

DeBarre shrugged. "I have no quarrel with that. Our beer's safe on the rivers, and now Corbi owes us one. I don't see a problem here."

Vincent rubbed his face, half-terrified that he'd just sent the Crew to war with the hamstrung Upright Citizens, and half-amused at how well Hattie had played him. It had to be her. Only she would've known Vincent would misread the *Bianco Fiore* like that.

"We have the advantage again," Vincent declared. "Only the four of us are savvy to Malloy's plan. We keep it that way, and she'll make another play for our hooch. When that happens..." He rammed his fist into his palm.

"That's a hell of a gamble," Lefty said.

Vincent replied with a smirk and a nod to DeBarre, "Sure, but Hattie Malloy ain't the only one with an ace up her sleeve."

CHAPTER 19

"What is the purpose of this?" Hattie mumbled as she rubbed her face.

Smith eyed her from across Lizzie's office, arms crossed, fingers tapping his biceps. "You have the Crew looking to the Bay. Now we hit them in the mountains. Corbi is convinced he's locked down the bootleggers coming out of West Virginia. With his focus pulled to the east, we strike west."

Hattie sighed. "I'll ask the question again, if you like."

"Well, perhaps I don't understand the question," Smith spat.

"The entire purpose of me doing any of this is to get Lizzie back her work and cross me off the Crew's wish list. I don't see how harassing some bootleggers makes either of those things happen."

Smith pinched the bridge of his nose, then uncrossed his arms to gesticulate. "The *purpose* is to take down the Baltimore Crew."

Hattie turned to Lizzie with a cocked brow. "Is that what we're about, then?"

Lizzie scowled. "Not as such." She looked to Smith. "The Crew is our sole source of income. Let's not lose sight of that."

The Crew *had* been their sole source of income. It had always seemed too much of a risk before, but with the events of the last week, Lizzie had come to the decision that putting all her eggs together wasn't wise. The Crew would be their priority, but there were a hundred small-time moonshiners with product, and slipping a few cases here and there on the boat would only add to their profits.

Smith waved a hand. "No, no. Of course. By 'take down,' I simply meant to reduce their sense of grandeur. Deflate Corbi's ambitions of becoming a dominant force. They'll be a more reliable source of income when they aren't trying to rule the world."

"So what about me, then?" Hattie pressed. "My name is on their lips. How am I supposed to do my job if they're trying to kidnap me all hours?"

Smith stepped to the center of the office, addressing them both. "This is all about leverage, ladies. We position Corbi back into a posture of weakness, and you can demand damned near anything."

"Have you *met* the man?" Hattie drawled, remembering her conversations with Vincent.

"Have you?"

Hattie frowned. "Weak posture, and then?"

"One step at a time," he cooed with a calming gesture. "Moving forward, you'll work with the Crew as a contractor. They'll accept that as the limit of the bargain."

Hattie shook her head. None of this made one lick of sense. This Smith man was twisting them all about for his own agenda, and she got the feeling that she going to be left holding the bag at the end of the day.

"The entire point of this was to preserve my freedom. I'm not bargaining for any sort of position with these brutes. I'm not working for the Crew. None of what you're proposing benefits me one bit."

Lizzie said, "But, you're working for the Crew already. You have been for years."

"Not as a slave."

"That's not what Smith is saying. Things go back to the way they were. The only difference is that they know what you are. You won't be the priority anymore, these other things will."

Hattie put her hands on her hips. "Honestly? You think that's how this will really turn out? It's daft, this plan of yours."

Smith declared, "Which is worse? Playing a long game with the Crew, or finding yourself in one of their reeducation camps?"

She blinked. "The what, now?"

Smith's face adopted a sinister cast. "The New York families maintain facilities upstate. Secluded locations with armed guards, and specialists who are masters at picking apart a person's mind, their free will. There they reduce a pincher to a honed weapon of war." He stepped toward Hattie. "Why do you think the notion of a free pincher is so inconceivable for your friend, Calendo?"

"He went to one of these camps?" Hattie choked out.

"The poor boy practically grew up in one. He's known nothing else."

"His family agreed to this when they sold him? They *let* him go to that sort of place?"

Smith shrugged. "I don't have that sort of information. For a price, I could find it for you."

Hattie sneered. "No, thank you."

Smith nodded with amusement. "Then you'll do it? I have a driver ready to take you to Shepherdstown."

Hattie checked with Liz, who stood with stiff lips and narrow eyes. "Liz?"

"It's your decision," she stated. "These moonshiners are criminals. Most of them are uneducated. They're a dangerous crowd."

"I can handle dangerous," Hattie offered. "It's the end result that has my blood up. We talk them into bypassing the Crew, and it'll bring violence. I'm not sure I can convince them of the virtue of crossing Vito Corbi."

Smith said, "That's your end of it, my dear. Your give. The take is a weakened Baltimore Crew."

Distract the Crew with the Upright Citizens and renegade moonshiners out west, and hope it took the heat off her at least temporarily. It wasn't a great plan, but it was better than nothing. Hattie paced for a moment as she thought it through, then nodded. "Fine. But I want Raymond to drive me."

Smith grinned. "Don't you trust me?"

"Not even remotely."

Lizzie shook her head. "I have Raymond on the water today. Sorry."

Hattie eyed Smith, who stood impatiently at the door to the office. "Shall we, then?"

Smith had a Model T waiting outside the Locust Point warehouse. The man next to it was enormous, in a coat and cabbie, face haunted by a five o'clock shadow although it was barely even noon.

Smith saluted the driver as he peered from the window. "This is Serge. Serge, this is Hattie, your ward for the day. Now, I don't want you jabbering away at her the whole drive."

He nodded, and stared forward waiting for Hattie to get in.

"Charming fellow," she grumbled.

"He's a professional," Smith chided. "I encourage focus in all of my hires."

Hattie climbed into the passenger seat with a sigh. This day trip was going to be a barrel of monkeys.

* * *

SERGE PROVED to be as laconic and focused as Smith implied. They drove two full hours before he so much as cleared his throat. Hattie eyed the man once or twice, but otherwise contented herself to watching the farms roll by as they headed into the foothills of the Alleghenies.

A fox ran across the road, pausing in confusion as the car barreled forward. Serge laid onto the brakes, snarling, "Chyort!"

Hattie gripped the window as the car lunged forward. The fox doubled back and disappeared into a thatch of tall grass as Serge shook his head and hammered the accelerator.

Hattie smirked. "Damned fool animal doesn't know better than to cross against traffic."

Serge didn't respond.

"So, where are you from...Serge?"

The man glanced over at her, then grumbled in a voice thick with a muddy European accent, "Frah-nce."

"Ah, I see. Know more English than you can speak, then?"

He shrugged.

A few minutes down the road, she added, "I've always wanted to see Paris."

"A dirty city," Serge offered.

"Hmm?"

"Filthy."

Hattie snickered to herself as the road crossed the Potomac into West Virginia.

The hand-off occurred just outside Shepherdstown. Serge pulled up alongside a jalopy with rust holes along the fenders. Two men eyed them from inside the truck. Serge stepped out of the vehicle to open Hattie's door. The moonshiners sat motionless as Hattie emerged into the balmy summer air.

She gave them a smile and a wave. "Afternoon, boys."

At the greeting, their expressions erupted into broad smiles. The driver stepped clear of the truck and pulled off his hat to reveal a shaggy mop of dusty blond hair. His smile was a castle of broken, gray teeth.

"You're Miss Mallory?" he asked in a looping drawl.

"Malloy," she corrected with a polite nod. Hattie turned to Serge. "Are you stayin' put, or are you scurrying off back to Baltimore?"

Serge eyed the two men, crouching down to take in the passenger, then offered a nod before climbing back into his car to make a tight turn and drive away.

"Not much of a talker," the driver said.

"Aye, that's the gospel."

He extended a hand. "I'm Tom Ed, by the by. Tom Ed Greely."

She shook his hand. "Hattie Malloy."

Tom Ed bowed down to shout into the truck, "Hey, boy. Get your hide outta that seat and say hello to our guest."

The passenger emerged, almost a head shorter than Hattie. He didn't look a day over fifteen.

"This here's Shane. He's my boy."

Hattie nodded to the youth. "I appreciate your patience with me. This can't be easy for you. I feel I'm barging in."

Tom Ed snickered. "Aw, hell miss. I'd sell my still to spend a day with a pretty lady like yourself."

Hattie blushed, and tried not to chuckle. She knew this fellow was laying it thick just to make her feel comfortable, but she wasn't used to compliments. Oh, she'd been called all sorts of things by city men, usually unsolicited and accompanied by some waggle of the brow or an ironic sneer. But this man—this father who looked to be not much more than thirty years—was a stranger to all guile. His words rang clear as a church bell on a crisp winter morning. His life was too dangerous to waste time with games. When he spoke, it seemed as if she could mint the syllables and save them in a bank to earn interest. As such, when he called her a "pretty lady," it made Hattie feel small and grand all at the same time.

"Get your butt in the back," Tom Ed hollered to Shane, who hopped over the side of the truck in a single leap. The father held the door for Hattie as she slipped inside, the springs of the bench seat squeaking even under her slight weight.

They continued on up the road past Shepherdstown, steering up the hill on an unpaved lane largely overgrown with brush. Likely by design.

"I gotta say," Tom Ed offered as they rounded several switchbacks to climb into some haggard wilderness that seemed to punish the truck as they pierced deeper, "I was surprised when old Tony rang us up to fill us in on this little situation."

Hattie stifled a scowl. It wasn't Tony that had made the call. It was Smith. But Tom Ed probably had never taken a direct phone call from Tony, nor was likely to tell the difference even if he had.

"Oh, aye. The Crew is developing its network of distributors." She worked over the syllables with deliberation, trying to be clear without talking down to the man.

To his credit, he nodded and continued piloting the truck through impossibly dense brush. "I heard about what happened to them Dryfork boys."

"I'm sorry?"

"Dryfork Brothers. Couple months back, they tried going 'round the Crew. Made runs straight north to Pittsburgh. They caught hell for that."

Hattie sucked in a breath, remembering the story Vincent had told her about the incident. "Well, it's a new world now. Isn't it?"

Tom Ed shot her a quizzical glance. "Where you from, if you don't mind me asking."

"You've caught the hint of Irish music in my words, have you?" she jibed.

"Irish, huh? I know some Irish down by Weston."

"Moonshiners?"

"Yup. We keep an eye out for one another. Unless they cross over into our territory, then..." He chuckled. "Then we keep two eyes out."

After a full hour easing through low-hanging branches and ferns, the truck finally emerged into a clearing. At the center was a log-walled shack with a stone masonry chimney jutting from an uneven gable. The structure appeared ready to blow over at a small breeze, yet seemed ageless having stood at this spot for a hundred years.

"Alright, then," Tom Ed declared as he killed the engine. "I know you're a lady of manners and all that, but you wore overalls. Too late to plead innocent—we're puttin' you to work!"

Hattie beamed. "I wouldn't have it any other way, friend."

Shane leaped from the back of the truck and bustled for the side of the cabin to pull a tarp off a squat copper kettle with a short, conical chimney. A thick stove pipe ran horizontally from the cap of the chimney to a secondary chamber. A tiny spigot sat about a foot off the bottom of the chamber.

"Is that it?" Hattie asked in a reverent whisper.

"The still? Yup. For what it's worth. If I got my hands on some copper, I'd build me a nice coil. Maybe a taller chimney with chambers for my gin and vodka."

"You make gin?" she asked. "And *vodka?*"

"Depends on the season. Just right today, we're about to cook up some corn mash. Next week, I oughta get some peaches from a buddy down by Shenandoah. Gonna mash that into a brandy."

Hattie sighed. "Peach brandy? Sounds divine."

Tom Ed laughed. "Well, don't get too excited. You ain't tasted it yet."

Hattie regarded the man as he plodded over to help his son stack short hand-hewn lengths of firewood beneath the still. He had a habit of deflecting all compliments to him and his craft. It bordered on false modesty, but the setting reminded Hattie that he was a man not given to false courtesies. Perhaps he felt genuinely uncomfortable receiving any praise, while at the same time waxing effusive over his love for the avocation?

"Shane? Grab that bucket and get us some water."

The boy snatched a tin bucket and trotted into the woods nearby.

Tom Ed turned to Hattie with a lift of his brow. "The key to a proper moonshine is a good clean source of mountain water. It ain't just the taste. The minerals help the mash turn a product without bitterness."

"That a fact?"

"Yup. That's why you don't see no decent 'shine from over your direction. Gotta get the water from the mountains if it's gonna taste worth a piss."

Hattie threw in a hand to stack more wood beneath the still. Tom Ed lit the logs with a dried-hay fire starter, then gestured for her to help roll a barrel from a lean-to beside the cabin. The work wasn't easy, but more leisurely than what she'd endured with Raymond just the day before.

Shane returned with the bucket of water, adding it directly into the still. It popped and hissed as it hit the pre-heated tin. As a plume of steam rose from the opening in the still hatch, Shane ran off for more.

"What's the water for, then?" Hattie asked.

"This mash," Tom Ed explained, "has been bubbling away for about a week, now. If I start pouring this right into the still, it'll caramelize some of the corn. We don't want that."

"Doesn't sound so bad," Hattie offered.

"Yeah, well. Trust me. It's less sweet, more scorch. Anyways, we'll get a good boil inside before we decant the mash."

Hattie helped Tom Ed pour the slurry of fermented corn and water into a series of buckets as Shane ferried in more mountain water. At last, the time came to begin pouring in the mash. They took it in turns, trying to get as much of the bubbling sludge into the still as quickly as possible. By the time the barrel was half empty, Tom Ed and his son hoisted the barrel over their shoulders and poured the remainder directly into the still, straining off the hunks of grain as they reached the bottom.

The process took the better part of an hour, and another before Tom Ed seemed to relax.

The chamber popped and hissed. Hattie kept her distance, remembering stories of exploding stills that circulated the docks in her trade. Tom Ed smiled at her.

"Don't you worry none. This old girl's so full of leaks and holes, nothing's gonna pop on you."

"What's happening now?" she asked with a nod to the chamber.

"Well, the mash is about to boil. That steam rolls on up into the chimney." He ran a finger along the stove pipe angling down into the top of the adjacent chamber. "The steam collects up in here and drops down. The 'shine gathers before the water hits it."

"So, you're boiling and dropping it back out."

He nodded, knocking the side of the chamber to listen to the quality of the sound. "The first runnings are poison. We throw them out. Then we take it in stages. I like to gather it in quarts, but Shane here says we're just borrowing trouble."

Shane demurred as Hattie cast a glance in his direction.

"Why so many pours?" Hattie asked.

"Each gets a little better," Tom Ed replied. "Until it don't. There's a sweet spot—the reserve."

"Aye, I hear all the besuited orangutans in the clubs go on about Reserve this and Reserve that."

Tom Ed released a belly laugh that lasted a full minute.

"Oh huh, yeah," he finally managed. "They think it's the cream of the crop. Well, I'll tell you a secret, lady. We call it 'reserve' for a reason. We reserve the best of the runnings for ourselves! The rest get sold to Corbi and those orangutans!"

"I see. You wouldn't happen to have any of that reserve handy, would you? For educational purposes, you understand."

Tom Ed's face drew into a knowing smirk. He nodded with a lift of his finger. "After we're done playin' with fire. Deal?"

"Deal."

The distilling process took up the majority of the afternoon. Tom Ed countermanded his son's wishes, and took the time to collect the entire runnings in a seemingly endless array of quart-sized mason jars. He dipped a finger into each one to taste-test. Once his face soured, he summoned Shane to collect the remainder in a large bucket, which was tossed into the grass nearby once the still had cooled. Four quarts of moonshine were declared reserve, and capped and stored away inside the cabin. The rest were carted to a wooden bench beneath the lean-to for packaging.

Hattie helped as each mason jar was waxed and stamped with a tiny iron press bearing the Greely Family sigil. The act seemed oddly medieval.

"Don't you sell barrels of this?" Hattie asked as her fingers grew sore.

"Aw hell," Tom Ed replied. "We could if we didn't care about what we did. The Dryforks? They just ran shitloads of this through their rickety old outfit. Barrels on barrels of rotgut. Sold it pennies on the penny, if you take my meaning."

"But the Greely Family moonshine is the sort you serve at a self-respecting establishment?" Hattie asked.

Both Tom Ed and Shane paused, waves of discomfort and embarrassment washing over their faces. Hattie swallowed hard. She didn't mean offense. Truly. There was a degree of quality to this particular product that she'd found alluring. Even though she worked on the water most days, she was at heart a city girl. And she'd grown accustomed to certain contexts which these men had no experience with.

"I didn't mean..." she added.

"Naw," Tom Ed muttered. "You think we're a cut above, and I do appreciate the sentiment."

"Well, you clearly are," she replied. "Damn the rest of't. I think the attention you give this is admirable."

Shane nodded, and said, "One of these days, that there Volstead Act's gonna get repealed. Then we'll wind up in the best restaurants up and down the East Coast."

The boy declared it like a manifesto, chin high and hands

balled in fists.

Hattie said, "I hope so, boy-o."

Tom Ed scowled and shook his head. "Well, that's a nice fantasy."

"You don't agree?" Hattie prodded.

"Listen...here in West Virginia we've been dealing with a local prohibition since 1914. And now these biddies from the sewing circles and preservation societies, and whoever else done talked all of Congress into gettin' righteous in the other states as well. This is the new normal, miss. Everything about this country's gone all to hell. A man can't lift a finger without some wrinkle-pussed hag declaring it a sin, and some slick-as-shit senator tryin' to tax it."

Hattie smiled. "Aye, that's about the long and short of't."

"So, we do what we do, and hell with 'em. We don't need no fancy white-linen restaurants. No senators. No governors. We do our best, and we go to bed knowing that's what we done."

After the packaging was done, and Hattie's arms and back were throbbing form the awkward posture, they stepped inside the log cabin. Though there was no fire, the entire building smelled of smoke. Hattie was ushered to a kitchen table inside while Shane took a brown paper-wrapped bundle of smoked jerky from a cabinet, and his father slipped a jar from beneath a floor board.

Shane pulled a hunk of jerky clear from the hock, strings of meat splaying free and filling the room with a delightful odor of venison.

"Brought this one down myself," Shane said as he handed Hattie the jerky. "Just last March. Got him right up the hill yonder. Eight point buck. Pow!" He made a shooting motion with both hands in a thumb-and-index-finger rifle.

As Hattie tasted the jerky, Tom Ed slid a thimble-sized glass in front of her, brimming with an amber liquid. The venison was earthy, with a little spice and a note of rosemary to compliment the gamey twang.

Hattie nodded to Shane. "It's quite good."

Tom Ed tapped the table. "You asked, and here it is."

She lifted the shot glass to inspect the liquid. "What's this?"

"That right there is some applejack we cooked up last fall."

"What's an applejack?" she asked, sniffing the liquor.

"It's like an apple brandy, but with some spices thrown in."

Notes of cinnamon, allspice and vanilla flowed into her nose along with a fumey head of booze. She crossed herself and took a hit of the applejack.

She winced as the fluid spilled down her gullet like molten lead.

"Oy, sweet Jesus!" she grunted.

Shane snickered.

Tom Ed asked, "How's that finish?"

Hattie tried her best to speak in a concerted tone, but her throat was wrecked. "Burns like Old Scratch!"

Tom Ed nodded. "I told you, don't judge a liquor before you taste it. Now..." He reached into his coat to produce a flask, filling the shot glass with a darker liquid. "This here's the real reserve."

Hattie glared at him. "Did you just poison me, then?"

"Heh...no. That's what we sell the Crew. This here? This is what I drink Christmas morning after all the kids get their stockings."

Hattie eyed Shane. "You've got a large family, then? Brothers and sisters?"

Shane shrugged. "Got two kids of my own."

Hattie's mouth dropped open. "That a fact?"

Tom Ed nodded. "Working on number three already. And thank God for it." His face lengthened as he stared up at the ceiling. "Shane's mother passed on in childbirth. He never knew her." After a moment of profound silence, he smiled and slapped Shane on the shoulder. "But the boy's got himself a good girl. A fine wife. She keeps him happy, and that keeps me happy."

Hattie sipped the "true" reserve, and closed her eyes as her mouth filled with a swirling bouquet of sweet and sour apple, cinnamon, clove, and a hint of orange peel. The flavor hit her throat along with the fumes, all transporting her to a Thanksgiving dinner some several years past, when Alton and Branna had invited neighbors for dinner. They'd brought a jam with the same flavors and aromas which they spread over the slices of hen. It was home in a glass.

"That's…"

Tom Ed nodded. "That's why I do what I do."

The sun began to set, and with rested bones the trio collected several pallets from behind the cabin to load into the truck.

"So," Hattie offered Tom Ed with a gathering of strength. "When it comes to what you sell the Crew, how's that work?"

"Oh, they dictate the price. I sell it to them and that's that."

"Are the prices fair?"

He released one dry chuckle. "They're what I'm given."

"You mentioned the Dryforks—they made arrangements with Pittsburgh?"

Tom Ed waved his son away to get the truck started. With a conspiratorial huddle, he replied, "Best we don't discuss that sorta thing in front of the boy."

"Why?"

"He's young. He don't see the point in the Crew to begin with."

Hattie sucked in a breath—this was it.

"Well, if you don't mind me sticking my nose in. What *is* the point of the Crew?"

Tom Ed eyed her with disbelief. "You're on the inside, yeah? What's this, some kinda test?"

Hattie lifted a hand, resting it slowly on his arm. "Not a test. Honest to Jesus. And I'm not truly on the inside. I'm just a boat-legger trying to expand her horizons."

"Yeah well, this sorta talk gets back to Corbi, and they send guns up into the hills."

"I know that's what happened to the Dryfork Brothers," she said, "but if they hadn't been…" She let the words hang.

Tom Ed bobbed his head for her to continue. He was on the hook.

"Well, between you and me? The Crew had an insider."

"With the Dryforks? That's crap."

"No," she urged. "It's the truth. Only reason they ever got caught was because they weren't as tight as you and your son. You said it yourself. They ran their operation like a factory. Lots of opportunities to miss the obvious."

Shane said behind her, "There was only the family. Couldn't have been an insider. Unless…"

Hattie turned to inspect the lad. His eyes were wide and expectant. "How far is it from here to the Pennsylvania border?" she asked.

Tom Ed shook his head, but Shane answered before his father could shut it down. "About half an hour outside of Shepherdstown."

"Oh," Hattie said with a display of surprise. "That's a short hop. I thought it was dangerous."

"It is," Tom Ed declared, swinging around to the driver's

seat to end the conversation. "No one crosses the Crew without ending up like the Dryforks."

Shane lingered beside Hattie. "Pa?"

"What?"

"The boys up by Pittsburgh pay two dollars."

Tom Ed sighed and hung his head as the door swung open. "That ain't the point."

"The Crew pays us seventy cents," Shane added.

"Yes, they do."

"Think you're gonna buy up any decent copper with that sorta change?"

Tom Ed lifted a finger at his son. "Listen, boy. We don't sell to the Crew because it makes sense. We do it because we ain't got no choices."

"But, what if we did?" Shane pressed. "Word is the Crew's got problems on the water."

"You're gonna bet your life on that being enough?" Tom Ed spat.

"Well, see, the Dryforks were stupid. They got pinched because they went all in. I'm sayin' we run high-payday runs up to Pittsburgh, but we run the white lightning on over to Baltimore. Looks aboveboard. No one gets the wiser. I've thought this through."

Tom Ed nodded at Hattie. "And here you are, with your master damned plan, hosing it off in front of one of their own."

Hattie shuffled on her feet, projecting an air of guilt. "Actually, boys…"

They both clamped their jaws shut and stared at her.

Hattie continued, "Truth of the matter is, I've got more than one iron in the coals. You think a waterman can keep her family fed from the Crew's table scraps?" She shook her head.

Shane whispered, "You runnin' on the side?"

"I'll trust you with that if you can trust me."

Tom Ed stood in misery, eyeing his son. "What, you wanna do a run around to Pittsburgh? To the Philly boys? You ever meet Bill McCoy? This isn't smart, not if we want to stay above ground."

Hattie smiled. "It *is* smart. What you've laid out just now? Selling controlled product across the state line? That's almost precisely how we make ends meet on the Bay. Maybe more than just meeting ends."

"You do okay?" Shane pressed.

She nodded, then feigned a pretense of self-conscious panic. "But, don't listen to me prattle on like this. Your business is none of mine." She lifted her hands. "I've a bad habit of inserting my opinion."

Shane shushed her, though Tom Ed simply stood motionless, eyes hard.

The son offered, "Well, look. It's just talk. Right?"

Tom Ed nodded. "Ain't no one got killed in these hills for just talkin'."

Hattie winced. If only the same were true in the city.

As the moment threatened to pass, Hattie dug deep for one final gambit.

"Shane, you have a little one on the way?"

He nodded.

"What if..." This was a huge thing she was offering, but somehow in the last few hours, this trip had become more than just putting a spoke in the Crew's wheel. It was about taking the wheel off their axle. It was about ensuring people got a fair deal for their hard work. It was about taking the bloodsuckers out of the mix.

What she was about to propose would be part of a long game—a very long game, but if she could pull it off, then the world would be a better place, at least this corner of the world, anyway.

"What if I helped you? If I were your eyes and ears? What if I were to use special skills that I may or may not have to keep you safe? Would that change your mind?"

* * *

THE SUN DIPPED below the hills west of Cumberland, bathing the landscape in shadows lit from above by a still-bright evening sky. The tone of the trip was far less sagacious than when she'd joined the Greelys on their climb up the hill. Now, they were in business—and a deadly business at that.

They'd stopped in Shepherdstown to use a friendly telephone. One call was made to Shane's contact in Pennsylvania. It seemed the Greely scion had done more than simply "think this through." Tom Ed remained at the wheel, and as if acknowledging her complicity in this turn in their fate, they'd relegated Hattie to riding in the bed of the truck in place of Shane. Three crates of fruit brandy rattled behind her—product of decent quality. Far better than they'd send the Crew. It was meant for a family wedding, according to Tom Ed, but Shane talked him out of it. Selling this brandy could but them the copper they needed, maybe add a second still, maybe add a second truck.

But there were risks if they made this sort of thing a regular occurrence. Setting these men into a discreet side business with Pittsburgh would set them against Corbi. And if they weren't careful, it would end in bloodshed.

The sky darkened as they made the trip toward the Pennsylvania state line. This was a bit of a dog leg in Smith's plan. He'd meant to arouse a distraction among the distillers in the West Virginia hills. But this? This had escalated farther and faster than Hattie had anticipated. A man like Smith should have seen this coming, she mused as the truck kicked on its headlamps.

Indeed.

A man like Smith was a master of options. Planning, strategy. That's all the man was—a ghost of gambits. So, why had he pushed so hard for Hattie to run this thankless errand? Her powers were wholly unnecessary for the job. If anything, Lizzie would've been the better choice here. But that was never on the table, it seemed.

Nor was having Raymond drive her to the job in the first place. How would that have played with the West Virginians? Hattie wasn't sure how welcome a black man would have been on that hillside. She had no way of knowing for certain. Too often, bigots were as charming as peacocks as long as it was a fellow peacock they were crowing to.

As the sky darkened, so did Hattie's thoughts.

What if there was more than Raymond's complexion at play? Smith might have had his eye on Hattie, ever since her training day with Raymond where she'd nearly killed herself with her own magic. What did that mean? If it was he who'd sent her the notes, then he'd helped her. He'd endeavored to keep her one step ahead of the Crew at each turn.

Excepting, of course, for those steps when Vincent was out in front of her.

She stiffened her spine, peering around the cab of the truck with a squint.

She'd relied on Smith's information as if it were exclusive to her interests. But what did Smith want, after all? She'd pieced together more than one suspicion regarding his "condition." In the back of her mind, the man was looking out for a fellow free pincher. Clearly, he had a knack for being in more than one place. Either that was superior skill at names and dates, or something more magical.

But what if that cursory instinct had been dead wrong this whole time? What if Smith's motivations were far more cynical? Far more mercenary?

Where would he find a grander payday? If he wanted money, hauling her in was the big score. If he truly wanted to bring down the Crew, not just weaken them, but bring them down, then the best way to do that was take away their advantage. With her and Vincent dead, there would be no magic within Corbi's quick reach, and he'd be vulnerable, just another mob with guns.

Hattie nearly shouted for Tom Ed to stop the truck but swallowed her words before she made a scene. This was raw speculation. Hattie was prone to this. God knew she'd twisted her guts into knots over nothing more times in the past than she cared to admit. Still, she adopted a standing posture, eying the road ahead as the headlamps illuminated each curve.

Her instincts proved annoyingly astute as the truck whipped around a grove of black walnut trees. The head-lamps caught a reflective surface, sending a flash at Hattie's eyes. It might only have been visible from her elevation, and Tom Ed may have missed it. But there was no mistaking… there were at least two cars huddled behind those trees.

With a wide, grasping motion, Hattie reached into the air rushing over the truck and pinched both light and sound. She clamped her eyes shut, whispering, "Disappear."

When she opened her eyes, she spotted a line of three cars and a mob of at least a dozen men with guns, all eyes forward on the road. Among them was Serge, Smith's driver.

Hattie snarled as the truck whisked past the hit squad under the protection of her light pinch. The drain on her was enormous, but she stoked the furnace in her chest with a newfound hatred for not only Serge, but Smith as well.

She was never meant to bring these men safely to Penn-sylvania. She was meant to fall, along with these moonshin-ers, in a hail of bullets. Smith had given, then he'd taken. What would the payday be for wrangling these errant bootleggers, she wondered? What would he offer Lizzie once the news of Hattie's demise reached Baltimore?

Was Vincent next?

Hattie slumped into the bed of the truck once it was out of earshot of the ambush and released her light pinch. Never had she assumed that she'd meet a greater bastard than Elmer Capstein.

She was wrong.

CHAPTER 20

*V*incent spread some fig jam onto his toast as Tony spouted off in his mid-Sunday manner, railing against the families to the south who had just challenged the Baltimore Crew. Lefty exchanged glances with Vincent as Tony continued on, the two recognizing how much drama he'd pumped into the speech. Tony knew there was, in fact, no war with the Upright Citizens. At least…there was no actual pretext for war. And yet, the battle was coming.

"People are gonna die 'cause of this, Lefty," Vincent whispered."

The man narrowed his eyes. "Don't do anything stupid. Half these goons are itching for a fight anyway. Gives 'em something to do."

"But the other half? And these Virginia mooks who aren't gonna know what's going on when we hit them?"

"You wanna stop this? Bring in that girl and tell Vito this was all her doing."

Vincent caught his breath at the thought of what Vito would do to Hattie. "He'll… he'll…"

"He'll nothing. Maybe smack you and Tony on the

side of your heads for being such rubes and getting taken in. He's not gonna string her up for trying to save herself. In fact, he'll think she's even more valuable if he knows she pulled one over on us and managed to pin the blame on the Citizens. Proves she's got skill, guts, and smarts."

Vincent took a bite of his toast. Lefty was right. This game of cat and mouse had to stop. He needed to bring her in before they launched a full out war against the Upright Citizens, and before she got them—him—into who knows what other sort of trouble.

DeBarre strode into the middle of Shakes's, the man the picture of comportment, his suit buttoned down, his hair greased into submission. Nothing was out of sorts for the man. It was another sunny Sunday afternoon. If anything, he was a tourist, simply holding back to collect the obligation that Corbi would owe Philadelphia once Vincent found some way out of this mess.

"There is, as far as we know, only one pincher in Richmond," Tony declared. "She's a glass pincher—which, if you bother to use your imaginations, is a hell of a weird thing. But that said, she's fallible."

A few grunts and snickers rose from the long table as Tony leaned back in his chair to take a long pull from his mug of coffee. The man was still dry, as far as Vincent had seen. Good for him.

DeBarre took a seat next to Lefty. "Still rattling sabers?"

Lefty nodded. "That's all right now. Trying to hold this off best as we can."

"Still no word from your mystery man, Smith?" DeBarre asked with a lift of his brow.

Vincent shook his head. "He's gone to ground. I expect he's greasing wheels with that retainer Corbi cut him a few days ago."

DeBarre snickered. "You Baltimore men have a strange way of doing business."

Vincent lifted a glass to toast. "Here's to improvisation as a business model." He and DeBarre clinked glasses and shared a nod. Lefty sat between them, sullen as usual, sipping a glass of water.

A youth stepped into the bistro, eyeing the gathering with confusion until his gaze landed on Vincent. He approached like a mouse at a cat convention, and pulled his hat off his head.

"Uh…excuse me, sir? Mister Calendo?"

Vincent leaned back to greet the youth. "That's me."

"A Mister Smith wishes to see you?" he said in the manner of a question. The lad was barely over eighteen, and was visibly trembling from the upper echelon represented in the room.

Vincent nodded. "He can come get a plate of eggs with the rest of us."

A few gangsters nearby chuckled, though the lad remained stiff.

"He…requested that you, uh…like, just come out and talk to him alone?"

Vincent twisted in his chair.

The youth appeared close to fainting.

Lefty grumbled, "The man's got a full-blown fetish for privacy. Better bring some napkins with you."

DeBarre released a laugh, and took a long drag of his drink.

Vincent nodded. "Fine, fine. Give me a second."

Once Vincent had extricated himself from his lap napkin, the gathered company, and had drained his glass, he marched through the dining room toward the concierge station at Shakes's. The youth nodded for the door.

"What?" Vincent blurted.

"He's up the alley, sir. Please...please don't ask me to go with you. He told me—"

"I get it," Vincent grumbled, fishing out a coin to tip the youth.

He stepped out into the bright sunshine of a Sunday afternoon, scanning back and forth for Smith, and finally spotting a figure huddled next to a row of refuse bins near the side entrance, up an alley wide enough for a truck to cart produce up to the kitchens.

With a roll of his eyes, Vincent marched up the alley, away from the street, behind the row of bins where no one could witness the skullduggery intended forthwith.

"All this side-stepping, I better get some solid info this time, you son of..." His voice trailed off as his eyes landed upon a figure shorter than Smith, though bedecked in a full suit. Trousers. Shirt-sleeves. Vest. Jacket. Fedora.

All of it tailored to fit. And all dressing the slight figure of Hattie Malloy.

She peered at Vincent from behind the bins, a literal white flag in her hand. She gave it a wiggle as he stood gobsmacked.

"Top of the morning, boy-o."

Vincent's blood dropped into his shoes.

"You..." He took a few hurried steps backward.

The light pincher reached for her hat to pull it closer to her brow, further occluding her face. "One word that I'm here, and I'll disappear."

"I'll know better," he reminded her.

"Aye. But the rest of your sorry lot will be none the wiser."

This was the first time he'd seen Hattie since she'd whacked him with his own pistol and run off into a stormy night. Vincent crossed his arms with a smirk, his eyes trailing her from shoes to lapels. He'd seen her in baggy homespun pants and a loose shirt. He'd seen her in a dress. But this snug-fitting suit…it was scandalous. It was lurid. It was as sensual as if she'd stood before him in a dressing gown.

"I gotta tell ya," he muttered, "this look makes an impression."

She rolled her eyes. "Get your mind out of the gutter."

He lifted his fingers to his chin. "What? Me think indecorous thoughts?"

Hattie snickered. "Indecorous? What, have you been reading, all of a sudden?"

"I read," he countered, marching around her like a lion sizing up a zebra. "Trousers, huh? I've seen you in working pants before, but this is something…"

She lifted a hand. "It's a disguise, ya daft bastard. Don't take a shine to it. Barking up the wrong tree, if you are."

"Am I really? Because I think you should wear this again sometime. Maybe when we're somewhere a bit more comfortable than the back of an alley."

"Vincent!" she squeaked. "Focus!"

She was adorable when she was flustered like this. Vincent held up his hands in a gesture of surrender. "You have to give me a moment. Didn't expect to see *this* today."

"No, I suppose not." Hattie adjusted the jacket. "It's just that, in broad daylight, this is easier to—"

He lifted a hand. "No, I get it. Cheaper magic."

She nodded, then took a deep breath. "We need to talk."

Something tightened deep in his chest. The moment he'd wished, but never dared wish for, had finally arrived. She was giving in. Willingly. Excitement bubbled through him. As much as he'd claimed he could never work with her, he was unexpectedly thrilled at the prospect.

And he was happy to just see her. Alive. Unharmed. Wearing an indecent outfit.

"Well, thank God. You've finally come to your senses, have you?" he retorted with a bend in his knees.

"You…alright there, boy-o?" she mumbled.

Vincent composed himself, brushing off his sleeves. "Oh, yeah. I was just thinking that the Crew couldn't handle yet another war against some city or another."

She shot him a puzzled look. "Aye. I suppose not."

"I figure we should talk terms before we end up sending men south. That business with the *Bianco Fiore*. That was your idea?"

She squirmed, then replied, "It was a group effort."

"A group, huh. Your pals at Locust Point?"

Hattie squinted. "Vincent?"

"Hmm?"

"I'm done playing games with you."

He pulled his face into a frame of sobriety, nodding with a cleansing breath. "Yeah, okay."

Hattie continued, "I know you have a man who's feeding you information."

"The one you're trying your damnedest to impersonate? Yeah. You're a sight prettier than he is, though."

Hattie's expression seemed unchanged. "You should know—he's double-dealing on the Crew."

Vincent's smirk melted. "What?"

She nodded. "He's been in contact with me from the beginning. I've received handwritten notes."

Vincent's stomach dropped. "Notes?"

"Aye. You think he's working to bring me in? He's working to keep me free. Actually I think lately he's working to see me dead."

Vincent scowled. "The hell you're saying?"

Hattie withdrew, urging Vincent to follow. He complied, now almost entirely concealed from the view of the street.

"Did this Smith urge you to set upon Raymond's home?" she asked.

Vincent held a breath, then simply nodded.

"What did you find there?" she prodded.

Vincent reached into his jacket to produce the note. Waving it in the air, he enunciated with an astonishingly poor Irish brogue, "Too late, boy-oh."

Hattie grinned. "Know why that was the case? Smith tipped me off." She produced another slip of paper, brandishing it in the air.

Vincent glowered. "That makes no sense."

"Oh? Well, then. After you rummaged over the creek like a feckless toad, you braced yourself for a drubbing at that hotel."

He filled in the blank. "The Moravia?"

"Would it shock you to hear that I was there?" she asked.

Vincent soaked in the words. "You...were there?"

"Aye."

"I don't believe you," he mumbled. "I would have seen you...noticed you."

"You sidled up to the bar with your one-armed keeper, Liz's paramour, and that shiftless peacock, Smith."

Vincent took another step back. "Uhh..."

"I was there," she urged, closing the distance between them. "Before I ran out so you wouldn't spot me."

Vincent's guts pulled inward, cold chills sweeping across his back. "Why would he play both sides? That makes no sense at all."

"It does, if you know how to milk Vito Corbi. There's money in the chase, it seems. So, he keeps the chase alive."

Vincent scowled as he crossed his arms. As he leaned against the side of the building, that scowled eased. His brow crept higher as he began snickering.

Hattie shook her head. "What's so amusing to you, then?"

He waggled a finger at Hattie. "Oh, you are too good at this, Hattie Malloy. I respect it, but for the sake of all that's sacred, ease up on the war drums, huh?"

She rolled her eyes. "You don't believe me?"

"Smith is a sharp-minded businessman. And yes, I think you've hit the nail on the head when it comes to his motivations. But double-dealing on Vito? That's…" He devolved into unrestrained laughter.

"Stuff it, Calendo," she growled. "I'm telling you the truth. He sent me to West Virginia."

Vincent wiped a tear from his eye as he caught his breath. "That a fact?"

"Aye. I was sent to sow discontent among the moonshiners. And I did, but all too well."

Vincent shook his head in amusement.

She marched toward him with a finger jabbing into his chest. "More of the same, too. The idea was to pick apart the Crew's distribution network, drive the wedge deeper. Smith gets more money for more information to solve the 'problems,' and with all the distractions, I'm less of a priority. Only, I was played the fool. The entire trip was a suicide run."

Vincent's mirth faded. "What are you talking about?"

"Smith had men," she explained. "Waiting. For us."

"A bushwhack?"

"I was meant to die last night, along with those bootleggers."

Vincent shook his head. "That doesn't make sense. You're worth more alive to him than dead. If all he wants is money, he wouldn't kill you, and he sure as heck wouldn't kill a bunch of moonshiners that he could rat out for cash."

She reached out a hand to grip his arm. "That's because he wants more than money. The easiest way to take down the Crew is to hack at their income stream by messing with their liquor distribution, and to take away any magical advantage they might have."

"You don't work for Vito yet," he countered.

"But I'm within his grasp." Her eyes searched his. "Kill me, so I'm no longer a factor. Kill you. Throw the Crew into a war with Virginia, and screw with their income. They'd be vulnerable."

"And Smith wouldn't get a dime," he retorted. "Hattie, this makes no sense. One man isn't going to take down the Crew. Smith is playing this for money. It's not about power. It's about money."

"But if it's not?" She tugged on his sleeve. "You need to keep your eyes open boy-o, because I really don't want to hear that you took a slug to the head."

"This…this is going to be difficult to prove," he told her.

"I know it, but I'm not here to prove anything to you. I'm here to warn you."

Vincent sighed. "There's no way in God's green hell I'm taking this to the Capo. I'm on a limb as it is. Telling Corbi that Smith's playing both sides will only get me sent…" He didn't finish the statement.

But Hattie did. "Upstate?"

Vincent squinted and backed away a step. "How do you know about that?"

"God's truth?" She raised her eyebrows. "Smith told me."

"Smith told you about upstate?"

Hattie checked over her shoulder again. "There's more."

"Lovely."

She pursed her lips to think for a moment, sending nervous energy through Vincent's gut. Finally, she said, "I think Smith's a pincher."

The words sliced through his brain before they could register.

She continued, "That night when you were at the hotel? Smith was there, yes? You were conspiring with him and your cronies while I was hot-footing it back to my warehouse. Only, by the time I got there, I found Lizzie huddled with the man. He'd been there for an hour."

Vincent nodded absentmindedly. "I've seen him do things. Easy to miss, if you're not paying attention. It's like he can be in two places at once."

She nodded with a muffled smack of her fist into her palm. "That's it. I'll gamble he's some sort of place pincher."

Vincent scowled. "That would come in handy for a man in his line of work."

"Don't you see what this means?" Hattie's voice was breathless with excitement. "Your boss wants another pincher. You *have* one. Give him Smith."

Vincent frowned. "What, this is all about finding a replacement?"

"What else?" she demanded. "I'm the one hunted. I have to find some way to survive this, or you'll never leave me be. Fate's just dropped this arrogant bastard directly into my hands. I'm happy to hand him over to you."

"And I'm back to being out on a limb."

"Get your handler involved. He'll know how to spin the yarn."

Vincent rubbed the sides of his face, twisting away from Hattie. "Hell."

"Think about what he's doing to you. Not just me. He's using you, boy-o. Just as surely as he's used me."

"No," Vincent told her.

"No?"

Vincent took a deep breath, then made eye contact with Hattie once again. "Vito's not looking for any old pincher, he's looking for Hattie Malloy. He has a name pinned to his little crusade. I can't simply hand over an alternative and expect he'll be satisfied. All that'll do is to give him three pinchers to obsess over. He'll still want you too."

Hattie's face drew into a mask of despair. "You...you won't even try?"

"What good would it do? Either I hand him a place

pincher who will fight me tooth and nail, and I'll still be on the hunt for Hattie Malloy. Or I call Smith out, am proven wrong, and I lose every last inch of credibility I've gained since this all started."

"Really?" She rolled her eyes. "Credibility? Is that what you think you have, then?"

"You're pitching off center, Hattie. I don't *want* Smith to be my partner."

She snorted. "I don't half blame you, but it's a far sight better than anything else you've got."

"I disagree."

"Do you?"

"Yeah. I've already got someone I want to work with."

"Your one-armed friend?"

"No," Vincent snapped. "You! I want to work with you! We've got a synergy together. Things fall into place when I'm with you. I'm stronger when I'm with you for some strange reason. And besides that I…I like you. I like being with you. You're smart and funny, and when we're together everything just feels right. I want *you*. I want…" He caught his breath, suddenly realizing what he'd been about to say.

Silence fell over the alley as both of them straightened a little.

Hattie made a half-turn, hiding her face beneath the brim of the fedora, hiking her shoulders up a little so that the collar of the oversized jacket covered her chin.

Vincent's blood ran cold, and he also turned away.

After a minute Hattie asked, "What about your brunette?"

He peered at Hattie over his shoulder. "My what, now?"

"I don't remember her name, you git."

"Are you talking about Fern?" he asked.

"Fern. Do you think she'd enjoy hearing you talk like that? Saying those things to me? Think she'd like us working side-by-side like that, day in and day out? Nights. Sometimes overnights? Because if I was someone's girl, I wouldn't like that one bit. No, I wouldn't like that one bit."

There had been a harsh tone to the last sentence, as if she were saying the words through gritted teeth.

"She knows business is business." He winced remembering the conversation with Fern in his kitchen. The woman didn't like his sort of business. And no, Fern probably wouldn't like him running off with Hattie every day, fighting by her side, laughing, flirting.

Flirting. Oh. Damn. He really needed to have a conversation with Fern sharpish, because it was blindingly clear where his fancy lay.

"Business?" Hattie snapped. "Thinking she might have a different idea of business then you do, boy-o. You seriously think she'd be okay with this?"

The ground dropped from underneath Vincent's shoes for the barest of moments. What was this? Where had it come from? Vincent wasn't aware that Hattie even knew about Fern. And yet, here she was…

Was it jealousy?

Could it be?

Vincent released a held breath with a nervous smile. "I don't honestly know."

"That's a hell of a way to court a woman, then."

"There's no courting." He shrugged. "There no nothing. So, don't get green over Fern."

Hattie spun on him. "Green? You think I'm jealous of your evening girl?"

He whipped his chin up. "What…what did you call her?"

"I'll call her whatever I bloody well please."

"You're ranting."

"I'm what? Ranting?" She pushed him in the chest with barely enough force to nudge him back onto his heels. "That's for rummaging around Raymond's. He's got a baby, you know. And you brought an army with you. What if something'd happened to the child?"

"I wouldn't let that happen."

"So confident, are you?"

Vincent took a step into Hattie. "Now, wait a second. Aren't you the one who shot at me, then cocked me across the face with my own gun? And when it comes to armies, what would you call those rifle-toting watermen you surrounded me and Lefty with?" He waved a finger back and forth between them. "I know it's easy to feel like a victim, but in this whole deranged fiasco, I'm the one who's getting rolled here."

"Is that what you call it?" Hattie jibed. "Sitting safe and sound in your flat, drinking your expensive whiskies and eating beef. Strolling into the Old Moravia for jazz and gin and sandwiches, bemoaning your fate because some upstart little Irish girl won't play with you?"

"Now you're *definitely* ranting."

She tossed her hands into the air. "Fine. I came as a courtesy. If you want to piss all over it, I won't stand here and watch you do it."

"Oh, don't be so damn righteous! Leave it for the Pope."

Hattie reeled back and slapped him across the jaw.

Another pall of silence fell over the two of them.

Vincent reached up slowly to rub his face. With a quick sniffle, he muttered, "That's two I owe you. Three if I count the time we first met."

Hattie stepped away. "You're a bastard."

"Maybe. But you're the one pointing the entire family at Richmond. You have to stop this nonsense before people get killed."

Hattie stood stiff, her back to Vincent. "Tell that to Smith."

"You really think he's a pincher?"

"Aye. And so do you." She glanced over her shoulder. "I'm not letting him get the better of me. Not after he's tried to have me killed. I suggest you watch your back around him as well."

She bustled around the bins and out onto the street, probably disappearing with a pinch of light as far as anyone else could see.

Vincent lingered, stewing in a whirlpool of emotions. His face stung, but it was fairly innocuous. Nothing like getting hit in the head with a pistol. What truly stung more than anything was how quickly he'd lost control of the conversation.

I want you. Did he really say that? And the way she'd reacted.

His intestines tied and untied themselves several times over before he brushed off his sleeves, straightened his hair and replaced his hat, and returned to the interior of the restaurant.

Lefty was on his feet by the time Vincent stepped into the dining room. The man intercepted Vincent, corralling him close to whisper, "What was that about?"

Vincent knew in an instant that Lefty had suspicions. The man could read him like a street sign.

"I think we need to take another look at Smith," Vincent whispered.

"To be fair," Lefty said, "I was telling you this a week ago. But fine. What's crawled under your skin?"

Vincent stared out the window at the passersby. Was Hattie still out there, watching? Or had she put as much space between her and Vincent as was humanly possible?

It occurred to him that he and Hattie had crossed a point of no return. Up until this point, it was all like a game. A deadly one, but still, it had been a game with rules. A back and forth. But Hattie would never come around. He not only understood that, he believed it. People were going to die if this didn't stop right here and right now.

It wasn't a game anymore. It wasn't just about him and Hattie anymore. The lives of the Crew, the Upright Citizens, those moonshiners in West By God… If he was going to keep people alive, if he was going to expose Smith for a double-dealer, then he was going to have to break the rules.

She'd never forgive him for what he was about to do. Never. And that thought settled like a lead weight in his chest.

"Get the car," Vincent muttered. "And a couple of the boys."

"What's up?" Lefty prodded.

"Make sure they're packing."

Lefty grabbed Vincent's arm. "You gonna level with me here, or what?"

"Bring DeBarre. Just in case."

"In case of what? Where are we going?"

Vincent glared at Lefty. "We're going to bag a pincher."

CHAPTER 21

The mosquitoes had a taste for blood, and they seemed to have been starved for weeks. Clouds of them hung beneath the boughs of oak trees at Winnow's Slip. Hattie swatted them away as they buzzed her face beneath her bangs. Raymond plodded behind her, his feet clomping down onto the weathered pier boards as they approached the warehouses.

"So, you want me to break his legs?" he grumbled.

"If you can get a hold of the man, sure."

"They were his men?" he prodded. "You know for a fact?"

"I saw the driver," Hattie declared, turning a corner to the boat launches. "Serge. I spent three silent hours with the man. I know it was him."

Raymond muttered a spate of incoherent profanities. "Gonna kill him. I'm gonna break his legs first, then kill him."

"Be careful," Hattie urged. "I think he's a pincher."

"What kind?"

"I suppose I'd call him a place pincher. He can be in two places at the same time. Maybe more. If you grab hold of the

291

bastard, he might be standing behind you holding a gun to your head." She paused to glance over her shoulder.

Raymond did the same.

"What's that mean to us?" he asked.

"It means we have to be careful. And take nothing for granted."

"I heard that."

They passed the first two warehouses, stopping at the third where they'd stored the liquor they'd stolen from the Crew. The door stood ajar, lock hanging from its hasp.

"Looks like Lizzie's beaten us here," she muttered, stepping into the darkness of the building's interior.

It took a moment for her eyes to adjust to the low light, but when they did, she found something confusing.

It was less a "something" and more of a "nothing."

Lizzie leaned against the far wall, arms crossed, eyes hard.

There was nothing else in the building.

Raymond groaned in confusion as Hattie stepped toward Liz.

"Where's the scratch?" she asked.

Lizzie shook her head. "Gone."

"You moved it?" Hattie prodded, already knowing the answer.

"It wasn't me."

Raymond huffed. "Well, what the hell?"

Hattie replied, "It was Smith. Probably had this planned all along. Send me to West Virginia to get slaughtered along with the moonshiners. Meanwhile, he cleans us out and hands the liquor back over to the Crew. He comes away with another feather in his cap. Probably a bonus."

Lizzie offered, "Or he could've sold it to the Carolinas. Either way, he gets paid."

The three stood in silence for a moment.

"So," Raymond finally asked, "what now? We got a plan? Some way to hit him back?"

"Best thing we can do is to try to clue in Corbi's men. Turn them against Smith," Lizzie suggested with a shrug.

"Already done," Hattie said.

"When?"

"This afternoon."

Lizzie squinted. "You spoke with Calendo?"

Hattie nodded.

Raymond peered at Hattie. "He believe you? About Smith?"

"I honestly don't know. The man's as focused as his goblin of a boss. I thought bringing another pincher to the table would've taken the heat off my neck. I'm not so sure. Might have made things worse."

After a moment of silence, Lizzie pulled herself off the back wall. "Listen, I think we've run out of plays, here. I appreciate what the two of you have done, but—"

Hattie blurted, "Please don't."

Lizzie held up a silencing hand. "But it's time we cut our losses."

Raymond asked, "What's that mean, exactly?"

"It means your family has already been moved to a safe place. It's time you joined them."

He scowled. "Now, that's just my cousin's place. He can't hole us up forever. We got a home."

Lizzie shook her head. "The Crew knows where you live. As long as you're associated with Hattie, you and your family will be in danger." She added with a sheepish dip of her chin. "I can help you out."

Hattie crossed her arms. "So, after all this I have to run?"

"More than any of us. We've discussed this—"

"We discussed the absolute worst case scenario."

Lizzie raised her hands. "What would you call this, then?"

"I…we still have friends, here. Elements inside the Crew who are sympathetic. Tony."

"He won't defy the Capo. Not for me, not for anyone."

Hattie replied, "He already has. Right? Do you think we'd have gotten this far if he hadn't kept his silence? Or at least, not been as effusive as he could."

She shook her head. "I don't know what he has or hasn't done."

Raymond grumbled, "Well, maybe you should ask him before we go packin' our bags."

"I'm sorry," Lizzie snapped. "But I'm not waltzing into a room full of gangsters to beg for our jobs."

"It's more than a job," Hattie insisted. "It's my family."

"Your family can move easier than anyone. There's steel work in St. Louis. You could move to New Orleans. Or Seattle. Somewhere the fingers of the gang families can't reach you."

"Da's older and not in the best of health," Hattie grumbled. "It's not the destination that's the bloody problem. It's the moving." She took a breath. "Besides, Vincent may be a bastard, but he won't touch my parents."

"You seem certain of that."

"He made me a promise. For all his faults, the man is true to his word."

Lizzie shook her head. "That's fine for him. But what about his boss? What happens when he bypasses his pincher and sends someone less scrupulous after you?"

Hattie had no answer.

Raymond asked, "What about you, Lizzie? Where will you go?"

Lizzie cackled. "Me? I'm not going anywhere. No reason to. I've got most of my money tied up in the warehouse, and the rest tied up in three shipments of liquor the Crew never paid me for. As long as they're in arears, I'm staying put." She added with a leaden tone, "I've got no one to lose, anyhow."

Hattie glared at Liz, and her expression easing as the truth of her words settled. She cast a glance to Raymond, who'd stuffed his hands into his pockets as he stared at the floor.

"Is this really happening?" she whispered. Had it really come to this? She'd gone from determined to ride it out, to take the fight to the Crew and stay strong, to fleeing the city in a mere two days. But was there really any other option? Her parents were safe, but if she stayed, she'd take Lizzie and Raymond down with her, and the noose was tightening around her neck. No, the only two options really were either to flee, or to give in and surrender herself to the Crew.

And only one of those was really an option.

Hattie sighed, then stepped over to Raymond to wrap her arms around him, giving him a tight squeeze.

He unwound one of his tree trunk arms to slip over her shoulder.

"Thanks for all the rides," she mumbled, a catch in her throat threatening to blossom into a sob.

He patted her back, sending jolts through her chest. "You done good, baby girl. Go get yourself safe, you hear?"

She nodded and wiped her eyes as she stepped away.

Lizzie spread her arms for a hug, but Hattie cocked a brow at her. "Are you serious?"

With a dry snicker, Lizzie offered a hand to shake. "Thought I'd try."

Hattie shook her hand, then held it tight.

"Oh, hell with you."

She pulled Lizzie close and gave her a hug.

When they parted, Lizzie gave her a nod. "I have friends at Penn Station. I can get you and your parents onto a train bound for Missouri. Or wherever you like. You'll have to pay, but my friends can keep it anonymous."

"Thank you." Hattie wiped her eyes again and took a long sniffle. "Well, I suppose I'll have to go break the news to Ma and Da."

"Need a hand?" Raymond asked.

"No, you've got your own boom to drop."

"Borrow the truck?"

"I'd rather walk," she replied. "I've a lot to think on."

He nodded.

And, with nothing left to say one to another, Hattie turned for the door and stepped outside.

The heat of the day had eased with an easterly bringing some rain-cooled air off the Bay. Thick clouds billowed to the east, with a distant rumbling of thunder serenading her steps as she marched up the street toward the city. It would be a long hike. Hopefully, long enough for Hattie's weeping to run its course. Her shoulders jerked in sobs as she took slow, plodding steps.

The injustice of it all swept through her, stoking a fury within. Against Smith. Against the Crew. How dare they put her in this position? How dare they ruin lives for their thirty pieces of silver?

As she growled and took running kicks at rocks, the indignation subsided. This was the way it had always been. The kings of men used pinchers for their own ends, and they crushed the small people underfoot if it afforded them the tiniest privilege. Today was no different. Only thing was, today would be her last day in Baltimore.

By the time the wharves along the city-side harbor had lumbered into view, the sun had dipped behind the thickening clouds overhead, sending the city into a shadow in tones of gray. She took in each of the familiar buildings as she wound her way towards North Avenue. The old market.

The florist she liked to visit. The Fontainebleau. They would soon be memories.

The street car had stopped running, so Hattie had another half hour's walk to Hampden to work out how she would break the news to her parents.

There seemed to be no other choice. Which was difficult to wrap her head around, since Hattie wasn't entirely convinced of that fact. It felt needlessly defeatist. Sure, she'd been handed several hard blows from Smith and the Crew, but was it really the only option? Having cried her nerves raw on the walk through the city, she grew to realize there would always be another option as long as Vincent Calendo was in the city.

She'd really laid one on him earlier that morning. He'd been an ass. Well, if Hattie was honest with herself, he had simply been steadfast. She still felt it in her bones that Vincent could help her. He'd helped her so far. He'd never lifted a hand to hurt her or bring her in by force. He'd promised not to involve her family. In his own way, he *had* helped her. Maybe between the two of them, they could come up with a solution to this.

Hattie climbed the stairs to the apartment, suddenly unsure what she'd even tell her parents. Her brain was in a fog, her heart playing tug-of-war against her battling convictions. As she opened the door to her apartment, she found Alton sitting at the kitchen table, a glass of whiskey in front of him. Before she could muster a trite chastisement for her father, her eyes swept along the table to find Branna seated beside him, her eyes low and hard. Hands flat against the table.

The door closed behind Hattie. She peered over her shoulder to find Lefty Mancuso shutting the door with a gentle click.

"What's all this?" she gasped.

Branna muttered, "Hattie? You should sit down."

Hattie stepped fully into the kitchen directly behind her father. Vincent sat at the far end of the table, his pistol resting on its surface.

He nodded to her with heavy-lidded eyes. "If you would."

"Vincent? What are you…"

In a split-second, Hattie realized how very wrong she'd been about him. No, he wasn't on her side. Not at all. He was, as he always had been, a tool for the mob.

"You promised."

Her voice was barely a whisper. Vincent flinched, then his expression hardened and he gestured for the chair opposite Branna. "Please."

Hattie reached for her father's shoulders, a hundred plans for escape cascading through her brain. But before she could land on a single illusion that could blind the one-armed thug behind her, and find a way to side-step Vincent as he saw through her powers, Alton lifted a hand to rest onto her fingers.

"Aye, 'Attie. You best do what the man says."

All of the steel in her bones melted in an instant.

With a quick squeeze of her father's thin shoulders, she stepped around the corner of the table to pull out a chair and take a seat.

It was over.

CHAPTER 22

*M*isery filled Vincent as Hattie slumped in her seat. She wouldn't look at him—not after that initial moment when the pain and betrayal on her face had nearly ripped him apart.

This was a horrible, horrible mistake. If he'd had the power to reverse time, he would have instead gone to Vito, told him about Smith, that the Upright Citizens were not involved in any of this. He would have taken whatever punishment the Capo deemed fit, even if it cost him his own life, anything rather than have her look at him that way.

But it was too late for that now.

The silence that fell over the room ground his brain into a fine paste. He did his best to maintain a calm exterior, all the while his soul withered and caught flame, reducing itself to ash in a moment of guilt-driven self-immolation.

Hattie sucked in a breath and stared at the table. He knew she'd be angry. He'd crossed a line, passed the point of no return. He'd tried his best to plan for every eventuality, knowing her propensity for lashing out. This was her weakness. Her Achilles' heel. This was her family.

Vincent broke the silence. "I know how you like to call the play on the fly. So, before you try to figure out how to escape this, you should know that I have a man in one of the back rooms. I won't tell you which. I also have a man on the street, watching both the windows and the door. I won't tell you where."

Her glare was intense as she finally met his gaze.

He continued, "I truly didn't want it to come to this."

"You gave me your damned word," she snarled. "You made me a promise."

Her words speared him through the chest, but all he could do was nod. "I did. I know I did. But that promise I gave? I can no longer honor it."

She waved a hand at him and looked away.

Vincent leaned forward. "You said it yourself. This isn't a game. Not anymore. I can't afford to play by the rules, now." He jabbed his finger into the table. "There's column A, where you stay free. And there's column B, where you work for the Crew. That's it. I'm here trying to keep everyone alive, which is, unfortunately for you, column B."

Hattie glared. "How can I trust a word you say? You've broken your oath. You're nothing to me, now. Nothing."

"Oh, grow up!" Vincent snapped.

Branna pulled her hands off the table. Lefty took a step forward.

Hattie's mother thrust a crooked finger at Vincent. "Don't you dare raise your voice to my child, you bastard!"

Vincent eased away from the table, lifting his fingers in apology, if not surrender. Hattie's father shuffled in his chair across the length of the table eying him with more curiosity than fear. He had since Vincent and company had knocked on the door, muscled their way in, and situated the couple in their seats to wait for Hattie's return.

"'Ere," Alton murmured. "Settle down, Branna."

She spun on her husband. "Don't tell me what to do. They come in here, waving their guns—"

"Ma!" Hattie shouted, causing everyone to jump a little. "Hush."

Branna complied with a smoldering glare at her daughter.

Hattie turned back to Vincent. "You're waving guns at my parents, then?"

"I didn't—" Vincent grumbled, but Hattie interrupted.

"I see your true nature now, Vincent Calendo."

Vincent scowled as the knot in his stomach unwound a bit in indignation.

"Oh, don't get so righteous," he blurted. "We're both doing business. I'm just doing it in broad daylight, while you're running hooch over the water in secret. At the end of the day, we're in the same line of work. So, don't come at me with this moral high ground. I told you how this would end. I gave you chance after chance after chance to accept it. You wouldn't. So, now we're here."

"She's not a bloody gangster," Branna snarled.

Vincent turned to the woman, taking a calming breath. "Ma'am. Your daughter has been running illicit liquor across state lines for the better part of two years. She knew what she was doing. She knew who she was doing it for." He turned to Hattie. "I did my best. If you don't believe that, then you're the problem."

Hattie slapped the table.

Lefty reached into his jacket toward his holster, but Vincent shook his head to wave him off.

"You can't give me an ultimatum and then blame me for refusing it. I'm not the problem," she snarled.

"No?" he replied. "You're not the one who drummed up some sort of damned war between Baltimore and Richmond? One which I'm trying to stop by bringing you in?"

Hattie rolled her eyes. "I wasn't the one who told your

boss that it was the Upright Citizens who stole his moonshine."

Vincent fixed her with an even stare. "No, that was me. But you led me directly to that conclusion, didn't you? You knew me well enough to realize that I'd get all clever and try to save the day. You *played* me, Hattie Malloy. And I think I'd like to hear you admit that."

With a tiny smirk, she replied, "I suppose so."

Branna shook her head. "What in blue blazes are you going on about, girl? Do you know this man?"

Alton chuckled, and all eyes turned to him. "Well of course she does, Branna. This is him. The one she told us all about." He leaned toward her in a conspiratorial whisper. "You know, the one like her."

Branna shook her head. "I haven't the foggiest idea what you're talking about."

Vincent sucked in a breath and eyed Hattie. "You told your *parents* about me?"

Hattie swallowed hard but didn't reply.

Alton gestured at Vincent. "He's that time pincher, Branna. This all makes complete sense now."

"How? How does it make sense?" Hattie squawked.

"Well," Alton suggested with a bob of his head and a vague gesture of his hand. "He's got that Valentino look about him. Eh? Not an Irish lad like I'd hoped for, but he'll do."

Hattie looked mortified, then grimaced and made a slicing motion with her index finger across her neck.

Alton chuckled and nodded to Vincent. "Can I offer you some whiskey, lad? I don't have much, but I feel impolite not to offer't. We should be havin' a chat too, y'know?"

Vincent waved off the offer, wondering what in the hell the old man was going on about.

Branna slapped the table. "Don't treat this animal like a person, Alton!"

The old man's eyes took a hard edge. "Eh, now. May be easy for you to think that. But our 'Attie has a family, no?" Alton pointed to Vincent without breaking eye contact with his wife. "What sort of family has he ever known?"

Branna replied through tight lips, "I don't...bloody...care."

Alton straightened and smiled at Vincent. "So, boy-o. Did you ever know your parents, then?"

Hattie winced. "Da? Best leave that alone. He doesn't take well to that line of questions. I know."

The old man squinted at Hattie. "How well do ya know him, then? Sounds to me like the two of you are closer than just friends here."

"No!" Vincent blurted out. "I mean, we've been through a tough spot together, that's all."

Hattie flinched, and he wondered if he hadn't said the wrong thing yet again.

"She's a pincher," Vincent added. "Aren't many of us around." He cast a glance at Hattie. "When I meet someone who understands what it's like to be...well, me? It means something."

Hattie ventured a glance at him before returning her gaze to the table top.

Alton pressed, "So, you never had a family then?"

"I have a family. A big one, too."

Branna groused, "That's no family, though you enjoy calling it one. It's a gang of outlaws, is all it is."

"She has a point," Hattie muttered. "*They* don't consider you a part of their family." She looked up to him. "Do they?"

"I never knew my birth parents," Vincent answered Alton, toward avoiding the comment. "I grew up in a private school and relocated to Baltimore when I was of age."

Hattie blanched. "That private school of yours. That...that upstate school?"

Vincent's hands balled into fists.

She continued, "What did they do to you there?"

Before Vincent could answer, Alton asked, "Do you even know if they're still alive? Your parents?"

Vincent took in several breaths, then glanced up to Lefty, who stood restless by the door. The handler's face was alive with calculation and alarm…as if these were questions Vincent need never ask, much less know the answers to.

The sight of Lefty's face centered Vincent, and he eased his hands open again.

"Your parents will be taken to the Old Moravia Hotel," he told Hattie. "We have a luxury suite prepared for them. If they haven't eaten yet, we can have dinner brought up for them."

Alton smiled at the notion, while Branna's eyes hardened into glass-cutting diamonds.

Vincent continued. "They'll go on ahead of us. They'll be safe."

Hattie added with bile, "As long as I come quiet-like?"

"Something like that."

Alton slapped his hands together and chuckled. "Well, as fate would have't, we haven't eaten yet. What do those poor buggers down in that hotel cook up in the middle of the evening? Oh, I do hope they have some lamb. It's been a stone's age since I had proper lamb."

Branna clamped her eyes shut, her cheeks glowing red. "Alton, in the name of all that's Holy, shut your gob!" Then she opened her eyes and glared at Vincent. "Where are you taking my Hattie?"

He responded in a low, even tone, "I'll accompany Hattie personally to meet with the Capo."

Branna thrust her finger right back at Vincent. "You can do what you like to me and my husband, but you won't so much as lay a finger on my daughter!"

Hattie reached across the table to lower her hand. "Ma. It's done."

"How can you be so resigned?" Branna spat. She then turned to her husband. "And you! Acting like this is nothing more than a free meal for you. Shame on you."

The man leaned back in his chair to fold his arms. "It's all gonna work out fine, Branna."

The woman sat stunned, shaking her head. "Fine? You think this is going to work out fine?"

"Aye. It's gonna be fine. This gent here, he's been decent with us. He'll make sure our girl is safe."

"He's the enemy!" Branna blustered

"Aye, that he is. But there's plenty a those. If you're given a chance to make peace with the villain of your choice, you should thank the Holy Mother she saw fit to deliver a lesser one."

Vincent couldn't stop a tiny grin from blossoming on his face. This old man seemed oddly calm and comported, considering the circumstances. His attitude was as disarming as it was unexpected—which was probably the point. He trying to save his girl from further suffering.

His wife, on the other hand, sat appalled. "I can't believe what I'm hearing."

Hattie shoved her chair a couple inches away from the table. "Fine. They go to the Moravia. As hostages for my cooperation."

She paused, obviously waiting for Vincent to defend the accusation, but he refused to rise to the bait.

"Then you parade me in front of your boss like some trophy," Hattie continued.

"That's not my intention."

"Oh? Then tell me what will happen."

He shot a look at Lefty, whose face remained stony. "I'm not entirely sure. It'll be what Vito says it'll be."

"That's supposed to give me comfort?"

"No. But I can tell you this. He's moved Heaven and Earth to bring you into the fold. And as long as you come with me, you won't get sent upstate. Which means, assuming you act civil, you'll be given resources. A place to live that's a sight better than this. And you'll have me to watch over you."

Hattie's mouth twisted. "Listen here, Calendo. I may go along with this, as you have my parents under the point of a gun. I may play the part of the docile light pincher, as you'll have a knife at my family's throats. But I will never, ever, be your friend. You'll only ever be the lying bastard who delivered me into slavery. So, chew on that while you go on about how close you'll be."

Vincent shook his head. "You know, every time you say that word, slavery, it's like you're smacking me in the jaw again."

Alton snickered. "She do that a lot, then? Smack you in the mush?"

Vincent rubbed his jaw. "More than you'd think."

"You'd be surprised," Alton quipped, taking a sip of his whiskey.

Hattie's last nerve seemed to fray loose, and she spun on her father. "Da! Why are you acting this way? We're his property, now. Don't you see that?"

Alton set down his glass, then reached over to smooth Hattie's arm. "Ah, my dear sweet girl. Only, you're not really a girl, are you? You're a grown woman, now. Responsible for herself. You know, getting yourself in and out of the shite you do. Our days of protecting you are long gone. You've been the captain of your own ship for longer than either your mother or I are willing to admit to."

Hattie wilted under her father's touch.

He continued, "In fact, you're the one taking care of your parents. Making me well again." He waggled his brows. "If you think I hadn't seen you slipping me something in my morning tea all these months, then your estimation of my eyesight is simply insulting."

Hattie released a single laugh.

Alton gripped her fingers in both hands, pulling her forward. "Live your life, girl. That's all that matters. That's all we've ever wanted for you. I know, I know, we've been on and on about these damned crooks and their moonshine and Tommy guns, and how you should stay clear of that world. Fat lotta good that's done ya, eh?"

Hattie shook her head as tears streamed down her cheeks. "I've done just fine, Da."

"The only reason they're here is because this lad thinks *we're* the means to getting your cooperation. But he's wrong. At least, he ought to be wrong. And if he had a brain under all that hair, he'd know it."

"What are you saying?" Hattie gasped.

"What I'm saying," her father replied in a firm tone, "is that you have to get on about your life, 'Attie. You want to do that with these gangsters? I'll support you. You want to be your own woman somewhere else? Then you go do that, and hang the rest of these bastards. And us with them."

Vincent sat stunned by the man's words. How could anyone feel so selflessly devoted to another? Was this what family was meant to be? As opposed to the continual betrayal and belittlement he'd equated the word with?

In an unexpected rush of motion that set everyone in the room, including Lefty, to high alarm, Hattie released her father's hands and reached over Vincent's pistol to grip the sleeves of his suit. Her face blazed with desperation.

"Will they be safe?" she rasped. "Truly safe? From everyone, including all of your bastardly goons?"

Vincent nodded. "You have my word—"

"Your word means nothing," she snapped. "I'll never trust

you'll keep your promises because one word from your boss and those promises will go right out the window. You can say what you want about protecting my parents, but you won't—not the first moment that promise conflicts with what the Crew wants. If anything, you've just proven that to me."

Vincent swallowed hard. He'd already surrendered the integrity of his own vows. He was a traitor to Hattie. No oath would hold meaning from this day forth. "I promise you that I'll put a gun to the head of anyone who so much as looks at your parents sideways."

"I'll need more than that," she insisted.

He replied in a volume low enough that only she could hear him, "What do you want from me?"

"I want Smith's head on a bloody pike, is what I want!"

Vincent clenched his hands into fists. His stomach twisted into a knot. Glancing over to Hattie's parents, he saw they were as shocked by this sudden declaration as he was. Only, Vincent knew precisely what she was saying —and why.

He cleared his throat with a pointed glance at Lefty. "I'll see what I can do."

Hattie sat back as her grip on his suit relaxed.

"Your parents, and your associates as well…they will all be safe," he added. "I swear it."

Hattie peered at Vincent with an otherworldly intensity. This was deeper than any oath he'd made before. This was beyond any loyalty he'd ever shown to the Crew. This was a life-bound debt.

She nodded. "I'll hold you to that."

"Then…we're solid?"

Hattie dropped her hands to the table. "Feed my parents. Take me to your goblin."

Vincent sucked in a breath of sheer hope, then nodded. "Okay."

He raised his hand, and Lefty stepped forward to urge Alton and Branna to their feet. He murmured assurances of his gentility as the gunman who had roosted inside Hattie's bedroom emerged, pistol in hand.

Alton lumbered to his feet, catching as his hip gave him a complaint. Hattie rushed to his aid, kicking the chair aside as she got to her feet. Once she'd aided her father to standing, they both peered at Branna.

She remained seated.

"Ma?" Hattie put a gentle hand on her shoulder. "It's decided. Either you smooth the way for us, or you add to the suffering."

Branna's face pinched tight, then eased into a sorrowful release of will.

"I…oh, fine then."

Lefty corralled Hattie's parents quickly, speaking in short but polite tones as he urged them to pack only what was necessary for one day. At the end of the second day, they'd be afforded certain luxuries and accoutrements—assuming Hattie complied as expected with the Capo's direction.

It was enough to send them downstairs within ten minutes' time. Lefty paused by the door frame leading to the stairs. He shot Vincent a dubious glance.

"You're taking her in alone?" he whispered.

Vincent replied, with Hattie busied behind him with her own packing, "It's safer this way."

"Because her illusions don't work on you?"

"That's the long and short of it."

Lefty shook his head in contemplation. "That's a weird thing. I don't like that that's a factor."

"Well, what you like don't matter a hill of beans, does it?

Get her parents to the hotel. I'll take her to the Capo. It'll all be over come sunrise."

Lefty reached to grip Vincent's arm. "You're certain she can't weave her magic over your mind?"

Vincent blinked, then realized Lefty was talking about Hattie's illusion abilities. "I'm certain. She's tried time and time again. No, I'm set."

Lefty escorted Hattie's parents to the car downstairs, set to deliver them to a suite in the Old Moravia Hotel overlooking the city. It would be a nicer evening than Vincent had ever enjoyed, to be sure. Silk sheets. Champagne. Caviar —whatever the balls *that* was. And most importantly, the entirety of the Baltimore Crew protecting them.

It was the wild card, Alexander Smith, that put the hook in Vincent's plans. What if Hattie wasn't simply being hysterical? What if Smith truly was double-dealing? Would that matter at the moment?

The clear answer was a resounding "No." Vincent had Hattie Malloy. And she was coming quietly. The matter with Smith could wait.

He escorted Hattie down the flight of stairs to the street, once her parents had been carted off under Lefty's ministrations. She preceded Vincent with limp posture, seemingly resigned to her fate. Vincent kept an eye on her nonetheless. He'd been sucker punched by Hattie one too many times to really trust she wouldn't try something, even if simply out of spite.

Outside, a figure leaned against the Alfa Romeo, rolling a cigarette.

Vincent sighed. "You're supposed to be two doors down."

DeBarre smirked and licked the wrapping paper. "I wanted to meet her. Is this your light pincher?"

Hattie stiffened as he slipped the cigarette between his lips and offered her a hand to shake. "Loren DeBarre."

She glared at his hand without response.

As he pulled it back, he shook his head. "Yeah, that'll be her alright."

Vincent grumbled, "I told you to not to show your face. Her magic still works on you."

DeBarre shrugged, then stiffened. His eyes bugged, and he took a step back. Just as Vincent was about to turn to check over his shoulder, DeBarre released a belly laugh that echoed off the surrounding buildings.

Vincent peered at Hattie, who smirked up at him.

"What are you doing?" he muttered.

DeBarre pointed at Vincent's face, tried to catch his breath, then burst into more laughter. "She... you...you're a..."

"I'm a what?" Vincent snapped.

"You're Josephine Baker," Hattie replied as she moved for the passenger side door.

Vincent rolled his eyes, then waited for DeBarre to compose himself.

Finally, DeBarre said, "You're gorgeous. Hey, can you keep him this way?"

"I'll meet you at the hotel," Vincent grumbled, moving around to the driver's side.

"Yeah, yeah. One more stop, then I'm skedaddling back to Philly. Hate to think what Arnoud's done to my city."

Vincent slapped his shoulder. "Drive safe."

"You too."

Vincent climbed into the car and cranked the engine. He sat as the motor rumbled, hands on the wheel, staring forward through the glass. Hattie joined him in his silent repose.

"I'd like to think of this as a beginning," he told her.

She continued to stare straight ahead. "Just drive the bloody car."

He engaged the gear, easing the Alfa Romeo up the lane, turning at the next intersection.

The thunderstorm that had been brewing over the Bay finally decided to waltz across dry land. Rain spat upon the glass of the windscreen, and soon the inside had fogged over enough for Vincent to reach forward and wipe it clear with his sleeve. Puddles gathered along the sides of the streets, which were mostly empty. He kept the car toward the middle of the road to keep the wheels from rutting into the mud. All the time, he kept Hattie solid in his periphery. Night. Rain. Fog. These were all means for her magic to come dirt cheap. It wouldn't be hard for her to play with light here. But he wouldn't see it. This was the safest way to move Hattie Malloy—him at the wheel, and no one else.

What would working with Hattie be like, now? She had clearly written him off as an enemy. The thoughts darkened his mind, so he decided to try to break the mood.

"Josephine Baker, huh?"

"What?" Hattie snapped.

"You know, I saw her once. Up in New York, when I—"

Out of the corner of his eye, he spotted a truck pulled to a halt just past the nearest intersection.

Vincent laid on the brakes, sending the Alfa Romeo fishtailing one way, then twisting almost straight again in a rush of rainwater and mud. The car slid to within inches of the truck.

Their heads jerked forward, then back again as they came to a full stop.

"Shit!" Vincent spat, reaching for the door latch.

His vision filled with light as he looked to his left. Two headlights, then an eruption of motion and noise.

Vincent pinched time out of reflex. Shards of shattered glass sprayed into the cab, slicing his cheek as they dangled in midair, reflecting the headlight beams of the car that had just rammed into his door. The raindrops hung like tiny prisms out in the street, nearly indistinguishable from the glass. A bend of steel edged toward his forehead, already sent shooting for him before he'd pinched time to its slow grind. The momentum of the impact sent Vincent sideways toward the door frame, even in the slowed bubble of time.

As the steel of the door frame made contact with the back of his head, its imbued energy sank into Vincent's body, knocking him instantly unconscious.

CHAPTER 23

A dull throbbing ache pounded through Hattie's head as she came to. A wall of wood spread away from her face like a vertical fin. It took a moment before she realized that wall was, in fact, the floor. Her cheek pressed into rough-hewn planks, and as she struggled to right herself, she noted that her wrists had been tied behind her back. With a grunt, she struggled against the rope, the scratchy jute digging into her skin. Whoever had crafted this knot had meant business.

With a few swings of her torso, she managed her way to a sitting position. Her eyes made out shapes in darkness. A low-hanging gable of rafters sat at a lazy slant overhead. Several posts held up the roof along the length of the stuffy space. She appeared to be in an attic. A tiny L-shaped banister stood at the far end of the attic, cordoning off what must have been disappearing stairs. Four louvered ventilation windows lined one wall, one of them with the slats completely broken off. Faint moonlight streamed in through them. The storm had cleared, making her wonder how long she'd lain here.

The air was heavy with the fishy rot of the harbor, but this was no warehouse. Old furniture and a few steamer trunks sat at the far end of the dark space. They had to be in the city, probably atop one of the three-story brownstones near Canton. Just to Hattie's right, a figure lay slumped against one of the support posts.

Vincent.

He had four times the rope invested in his immobilization than Hattie. Whoever had waylaid them with that car in the middle of a stormy night had made precautions for the man. They must have known who he was, and what he could do.

Meanwhile, Hattie sat there in a simple wrist knot, as if an afterthought. Was she simply collateral damage? A hapless bystander in some sort of mob hit? The odds stacked in favor of that conclusion, and she pursed her lips to glare at the lump taking shallow, unconscious breaths before her.

That rat bastard. He'd sold her family out, then got her caught in the middle of Crew intrigue before she'd even officially joined. Hattie scooted across the planks toward a nearby post, trying to get to her feet. Unfortunately, her ankle sent a spike of pain up through her leg as she tried to put weight on it. She slid back down the post with a quiet gasp.

Even if she could find a way to free herself, it wouldn't save her parents. At this point, she needed Vincent alive and intact. Otherwise, no one would believe her.

And her parents would be dead.

Hattie spun on her butt to slide toward Vincent. She jabbed his thigh with her foot once. Then twice.

The air shuddered. Going thick, then thinning out again in flashes. It was his power. She recognized the dizzying sensation of slipping into the time bubble, but it was only in jerks and starts. She gave him a solid kick, and the air solidified. She panicked for a split-second, gasping against the air.

Her lungs wouldn't move. Her muscles were frozen. Her mind was free, but everything else in the world seemed truly trapped in time. Then the time pinch abruptly released as Vincent sucked in an enormous gasp, his body jerking against the rope.

"Get a hold of yourself!"

His wide gaze darted around the attic for a few seconds. He'd just emerged from the moment of the crash, Hattie deduced. The shift for him was sudden and jarring. Perhaps that was the way it always was, when a person is taken down in the middle of a time pinch?

His breath came in ragged gasps until his nerves calmed enough for him to close his mouth and breathe through his nose. Shoulders bobbing, he tried to move his arms.

"What…where…" he wheezed.

Hattie squinted at him. A sheet of dried blood covered half of his face from a cut along the side of his temple. "Oh, Jesus," she grumbled. "You look like hell."

He scowled. "Thanks. Where are we?"

"Search me. An attic, apparently. Did you get an eye on whoever hit us?"

Vincent shook his head. "Felt like it was deliberate. They wanted to take us alive."

"Aye," she sneered. "A lot of that going around."

He glared at her. "Not helping."

"Why should I help you, then? Do I get a bonus, or something?"

Without replying he pinched time, struggling against his bonds for a moment before releasing the pinch. The cut on his head broke open and a fresh drop of blood oozed sluggishly down the side of his face.

"I'm trussed up like a damned pig here. They came ready for me." He looked her over. "You, though?"

"It's painfully clear to me that you're the one who got me into this mess," she snapped.

He nodded. "Yeah, well it looks like you're gonna have to be the one to get us out of it."

"Who do you think put us here?"

Vincent shushed her quickly, eyes looking up into space as he bent an ear toward the banister. Muffled voices sounded from below the planks. "I think we're about to find out."

The attic ladder creaked against long steel springs, dropping through the floor of the attic, sending flickering gaslight into the room from below. The stairs clunked once, then twice as they were straightened, and heavy steps took the climb into the attic. A head emerged, followed by its enormous frame. Hattie recognized the figure.

Serge. Damn Vincent for not listening to her. Damn him for not taking care of this before he'd stormed her parents' house to haul her in.

"It's Smith," she muttered to Vincent as Serge cleared the landing.

"Indeed," a voice called from the darkness behind them. Hattie twisted to find Alexander Smith leering at her from the far corner of the attic, stepping from behind a stack of boxes and old furniture.

Hattie glared at Smith as he marched between her and Vincent.

"*Sergei,*" Smith called. "*Pochemu zdes' Irlandskaya devchonka?*"

Serge...or apparently Sergei...replied with a simple shrug, "*Ona byla v mashine.*"

Vincent coughed. "Once again for the English speakers in the room?"

Smith stepped forward. "Allow me to introduce myself in

earnest, Vincent Calendo. My name is Alexandre Dmitrevich Sokolov. I believe you knew my brother, Yakov?"

Vincent stared up at the man. "Shit."

Hattie peered at Vincent. "What's this about, then?"

"He's Bratva," Vincent grumbled. "Always was." He glanced up at Dmitrevich. "And here I thought we were done with you."

"It seems not." Dmitrevich crouched in front of Vincent. "Though we've taken great pains to make it appear as such."

"You got pretty good English for a Ruski."

Dmitrevich snapped his fingers. "Sergei?"

The brute stepped forward, wheeled an arm back, then sent a hammer fist directly into Vincent's jaw.

Blood sprayed Hattie's face, and she squawked as she scuttled away.

The air stiffened as Vincent pinched another time bubble. Hattie sat in her spot watching as he lurched forward and back again, struggling against the rope. After he'd expended his energy, both physically and magically, he released the bubble.

Dmitrevich turned to Hattie. "Apologies, miss." He glanced back to Vincent, then stood, a smirk on his face. "I saw the stutter, my friend. You'll have noticed that I've taken precautions against your time twisting."

Vincent rolled his tongue, then spat a gob of blood onto the floor. "Guess you want me to shut my trap?"

"That would be best for now, although you're going to die tonight whether you continue to hurl insults at me or not. You see, you are no longer necessary for my endeavors."

"Endeavors, huh?" Vincent grumbled. "Pitting Hattie against the Crew? Setting me and Corbi against her. Playing both sides while we chip away at one another? That took some brain power, I'll give you that."

"Well," Dmitrevich declared with a clap of his hands. "You

could hardly expect us to do nothing after you killed dozens of us." He paused and stated with dead sincerity, "After you killed my *brother*."

"That was business, Smith," Vincent replied. "The Bratva knew that going in. We all knew it. And as for your brother…he would have been fine if he'd kept his mitts out of the till."

Dmitrevich nodded. "Yes business is business, but my brother? Well, I guess you wouldn't understand my family's feelings on that matter. You're a pincher who's never had a true family—a family of blood." He made a fist in front of Vincent's face. "Real blood. Blood that is shared in our veins. But then, what would you know about that?"

Dmitrevich continued, "But until my mother came to visit the Great Damir, and he offered her such valuable advice, our course was uncertain."

Hattie blinked at the pair of them. "Who's the Great Damir?"

Dmitrevich chuckled. "Oh, you're unaware of your companion's night job? He runs a scam on little old ladies." He made a walking gesture with his fingers. "Leads them into a world of mystery and forbidden knowledge. Plays the part of an Arab, complete with costume and makeup." Dmitrevich fixed his gaze back on Vincent. "It's disgusting."

Hattie lifted a brow at Vincent.

He shrugged. "It's a hobby."

"So, this is true?" Hattie asked. "You did this?"

"I—" He searched for words, then just nodded.

Of course he did this. He'd confessed it all to her in halting tones at that café a week ago—he'd told her about the young Russian who'd started it all, as well as his feelings of guilt in the matter. She'd given him some ease after he'd told his tale, and now she was regretting that.

"You're nothing but a murderer."

Vincent squinted. "It was business, Hattie. It was a rival mob. It was business."

"What sort of business?" she spat. "The business of *murder*? That's what I'm meant to serve? That's what you and your pig of a boss are expecting me to do?"

Dmitrevich eyed Hattie. "I see you've joined his little gang."

"Not that I had any choice in the matter," she replied. "Much like you gave me little choice when you sent me into your suicidal errand two days ago."

Dmitrevich nodded. "Apologies for that. You've wound up in the center of this predicament. Caught in the crossfire, perhaps? I hadn't accounted for you in my initial plans, to be honest, but you pulled that stunt in Georgetown, and incited Corbi into a crusade. I had to adjust."

She spat at him. "Well, you can go straight to hell."

Dmitrevich nodded. "In time, as will you. But for now, the two of you must wait. Purgatory, I suppose, has become an attic."

"Let her go," Vincent urged. "She's got nothing to do with any of this. She's just a boat-legger, some Irish girl caught in the middle of it all. Let her go."

"She's a pincher."

"One who hates the Crew. Let her go and she won't stand in your way. Hell, she'll probably work with you."

Dmitrevich laughed. "I doubt that. Not after she's watched us paint the floor with your brains. No, she stays here for now until I decide what to do with her and until the time comes to take your life."

"Why the wait?" Vincent glared at the man. "Part of your endeavor?"

"I take a long view, Mister Calendo. You have one purpose to serve yet—but for that, I await a last guest." He snapped his fingers. "Sergei? *Svyazhite devchonku.*"

Sergei strode toward Hattie. She kicked at his ankles to no avail as he gripped her by the arm and dragged her to the post Vincent was bound to. He untied her wrists, jerking them around to her front, then stringing the rope beneath her armpits and through Vincent's bonds. He made several passes around her chest, tight enough to hold her fast, but not enough to constrict her breathing. She squirmed as the wooden post dug into her back. Sergei finished by re-tying her wrists at her lap, cinching the rope beneath her breasts to hold her hands tight to her sternum.

"I'm sure the two of you have much to discuss. I shall return shortly."

Dmitrevich waited for Sergei to precede him, and the two descended into the building below, closing the stairs behind them.

Hattie gasped against the ropes. "Another fine mess, Calendo."

"You're blaming me for this?"

"Well, you're the one who killed his brother. Now I'm paying…" she grunted as she twisted her wrists "…for it."

"If it means anything, I wasn't the one who actually pulled the trigger."

The rope around her wrist slackened as she twisted her wrists into an X. "It doesn't."

"Listen, I've been trying to do right by you. But this…this is just old business that you shouldn't be a part of. It stinks, and I'm sorry. I'll do everything I can to get you out of this alive and get you back to your parents." He jerked against the rope, as if he were trying to edge around the post enough to look at her. "I'm sorry, Hattie. I'm so sorry for this—for all of it."

"Aye, I suppose."

Were they really going to kill him? Of course they were.

This is what these gangs did to each other. They were going to shoot him right in front of her.

And as hurt and angry as she was, even with the pain of his betrayal still sharp in her chest, she couldn't bear the thought of him dying.

Not that he needed to know that.

"So, you're not mad at me?" he asked.

"Furious. "But we'll have to work together if we're to survive this."

He sucked in a breath. "Listen, it's me they want. You're not family, not part of the Crew and Smith knows that."

She shook her head. "Smith won't let me live. He's tried to kill me before to keep me out of the Crew's hands. Once he finds out your gang has my parents, he'll know that I'll do whatever your boss commands."

"Then he won't find out about your parents." She heard him scoot against the post. "They're gonna kill me, but I'll do anything I can to get you out of this mess. Anything. So if I say and do stuff when they come back…well, don't think I mean it."

Everything in her chest hurt, and it wasn't just bruises from the car accident. All he could talk about was her safety, saving her life. Was that guilt over his breaking his promise to her? Or was it something else?

And here she was, thinking only of how she could get *him* out of this with his head in one piece. She glanced around the room, at the banister, at the angles of the roofline, at that window with the broken slats and got an idea.

"They're *not* going to kill you. I won't let them kill you. I lost Valentino earlier this week. I'm not losing you, too," she told him, forcing some lightness into her tone.

She heard the smirk in his voice. "Valentino took a bullet to the head, did he? I thought he died from some infection after a surgery. Wasn't aware he was courting you, either.

Took his death personally, did you? I'm feeling a bit jealous over here."

She laughed. "More like *I* was courtin' *him*—me and a million other love-struck women."

They both chuckled then fell silent, the seriousness of their situation settling back in.

"I betrayed your trust," he said softly. "I'll go to my grave regretting that. I know it's too much to ask that you forgive me, but know that I'll die wishing I'd not done what I did, wishing things hadn't ended like this."

She felt as if a giant lump had somehow lodged itself in her throat. "You're *not* going to die. I've got a plan. It'll all work out, but you've got to have faith in me."

She looked around the room once more. That window with the slats broken off...if it overlooked the water, she might recognize enough of the waterside and landmarks to know where they were, even with only a quarter moon and the city lights to aid her eyesight. And then...and then she'd need to get to work. Wiggling from side to side, Hattie fished her hands toward the dip in her blouse. Her fingers caught hold of the tiny glass dram tucked in her brassiere and tugged it free. It had survived the crash without shattering and spearing her through the heart. Small miracles because she was going to need it after the insane pinch she was about to perform.

"Of course I have faith in you," Vincent told her. "So we have a truce?"

"More like a detente, but you probably don't know what that word means."

"Funny."

She pulled hard against the bonds, holding her breath as the rope dug into her ribs.

"What are you doing?" Vincent asked.

She pulled again, trying to get sufficient slack in the rope to raise herself high enough to look out the window. "Just need another inch."

"Again…why?"

"I'm going to try something. Breathe out on the count of three, eh?"

"Why?"

"Just do it," she grumbled. "One. Two. Three."

Vincent exhaled and Hattie lunged forward, muscles aching as she lifted herself along the post. He released a panicked grunt as they slid down, settling at an angle to each other, shoulders nearly touching.

Vincent huffed, "You trying to kill me?"

"Not yet. Not with rope."

"Why not rope?"

"Too slow. I like things quick and painless."

He nodded. "Don't think I don't appreciate that."

"Okay, here we go."

"You gonna fill me in, or what?" he asked.

"I think I know where we are. Canton, near the waterfront, a bit north of the harbor by my reckoning. I'm pretty sure which block too, judging by the lights outside."

"Yeah. I heard a ship's bell outside when Smith, or Dmitrevich or whoever, was giving me the business." He peered over his shoulder. "What's your play?"

"I'm going to try a light pinch."

"To what end?"

"Getting our hides out of this attic," she groused. "If we're where I think we are, then we're about eighteen blocks east of the Old Moravia Hotel."

"Huh. You can pinch light over a distance like that?"

She paused. "Well, we're about to find out."

"Ever do something like this before?"

"Not really."

He twisted more, trying to make eye contact. "You sure that kinda reach won't kill you?"

"No, but if the magic don't kill me, then these Bratva bastards will. Besides, I have a card up my sleeve."

Hattie closed her eyes. She pictured the building they were held in, what she saw in this room plus what she'd seen in that brief glimpse out the attic window. Then she envisioned the city, itself. And west, toward downtown. The Old Moravia, lit from within with electric light and a few flickering gas lamps. A jazz band playing. Gangsters huddled in the lounge. Lefty. That pincher from Philadelphia.

Then she pinched light.

Immediately, the magic hammered in her chest. It was enough to draw a yelp from her throat. The draw was intense, stabbing into her and through her. Her insides felt lengthened, jerking out through the soles of her feet. Her entire body began to tremble, soon jerking in spasms, blood bubbling up with each breath.

But through the agony, she maintained focus. This was her only shot, the one illusion that might be able to save them.

Just as she felt her lungs shredding, she popped the stem out of the dram, and moistened her tongue with the Aqua Vitae.

The calming warmth spread through her mouth, but even though it had begun to do its work, Hattie's brain fuzzed. The ropes pulled tighter and tighter as she lurched against the beam.

And as her light pinch fizzled into the aether, she blacked out.

CHAPTER 24

Whatever Hattie had done was enough to knock her out. Vincent nudged her again, whispering over her shoulder.

"Malloy? You with me?"

No response. She'd slumped against the ropes away from him, and all he could see was her shoulder and the tangle of her legs on the floor. He could feel by the periodic ebbing and tugging that she was still breathing, but that was it. That light pinch she'd pulled had to have been far outside the limit of her abilities.

But was it enough?

Vincent had been laid low by his own powers more often than he cared to admit. Every time, he'd needed help to recover. If he couldn't get her out of this attic and into friendly hands, Hattie might not survive this.

Struggling against the bonds had proven useless. That thick son of a bitch, Sergei, had a remarkable talent for knots. They crisscrossed beneath Vincent's arms at the shoulder, and retied at the small of his back. His wrists had been bound between his legs in a sort of sitting hog-tie. The odds of muscling his way out of this were long, and pinching time wouldn't help, either. If he couldn't wriggle his way out of the ropes in regular time, trying to do so in frozen time wouldn't be any better.

He'd have to try to think his way out of this instead—which seemed just as pointless as fighting against these ropes.

Footsteps clopped on the floorboards behind Vincent, and he froze. Was this part of the illusion Hattie had spun?

The steps came to a halt behind Vincent.

"Now," Dmitrevich's voice slithered from the shadows, "let's see what this card up your friend's sleeve is."

Vincent glanced over his shoulder to find Dmitrevich slipping a tiny glass bottle from Hattie's unconscious hand. He sniffed it, then held it up to the moonlight slipping in from the tiny windows.

"How..." Vincent glanced back at the still-closed stairs. "You're a pincher. Aren't you?"

Dmitrevich wove around the post, dropping the stemmed cap of the bottle back into place. "I'm sure I have no idea what you're talking about."

"A place pincher. You can be in two places at once." Vincent squinted. "So, the Bratva has their own magic after all."

"What do you think your friend accomplished with her illusion? If anything."

"I don't have a clue," Vincent grumbled.

"Clearly. Not very forthcoming, is she?" He held up the bottle for Vincent. "What is this?"

"Laudanum? How should I know?"

Vincent knew very well what it was, and he was surprised that Hattie had found the mythical water pincher, as well as somewhat hurt that she'd kept that a secret from him.

Dmitrevich stared at him for a long moment, eyes peeling

aside Vincent's words, searching for the lie. Then he simply shook his head. "So many secrets between the two of you." He pocketed the dram. "Not much of a relationship, is it?"

"We don't have a relationship, you mook."

"Lies, lies. Although, it won't matter much longer." Dmitrevich lifted his head toward the outside wall.

The sound of an engine outside met Vincent's ears, followed by car doors.

With a grin, Dmitrevich said, "That would be mother."

He marched toward the disappearing stairs and clopped his heel against the floor three times before shouting, "I'm up here."

Before long, someone pulled the stairs open, spilling more light into the attic. Dmitrevich stared down the opening, his face brimming with satisfaction. Figures emerged up the stairs. Dmitrevich reached down to offer a hand to a frail, elderly woman dressed in black. One of her feet slipped on the stairs, and he reached with both hands to steady her.

Dmitrevich blurted in a spate of sharp Slavic syllables, "*Ostrorozhno, Mama.*"

"*Sasha,*" the crone replied. "*Ne kudakhtai'.*"

Dmitrevich guided the elderly woman forward to face Vincent as Sergei and two more gunmen followed her into the attic. She had a bent frame and long, stringy white hair flying at strange angles from what was probably an updo that was over a week old. Her eyes were sharp, deep, and filled with anger.

The old woman hobbled forward, trembling step after trembling step, until she reached Vincent's feet. She then grunted as she bowed down at an awkward angle, bringing her face closer to his.

Dmitrevich announced, "Vincent Calendo, this is my mother—Yulia Gennadevna Sokolov."

With a dry voice, she asked, "Do you recognize my face?"

Vincent shook his head. "Lady, I gotta tell you, if I did I woulda said so by now."

She squinted one eye, then reached into her clutch to produce a sepia tone photograph of a young man in a lopsided cap. Yakov Dmitrevich.

"Now?" she droned as she dropped the photograph into his lap.

"I meet lots of old ladies. Don't take that the wrong way."

"You speak for the dead," she muttered. "And you lie. You take my son's life, and then you take my money to put words in his mouth." She spat in Vincent's face.

Dmitrevich chuckled.

Vincent nodded. "Right. So, this is just straight vengeance? That's the part I have to play in your long view?" He twisted to face the man. "Why bring Malloy into this? Just let her go, and do whatever you're gonna do with me."

Dmitrevich replied, "Unfortunately, I can't let her go. You see, you piece of filth, I'm not content to settle for avenging Yakov's blood. Nor is the Bratva. We have entire generations of dead sons to avenge. Like you said—a long view. And having a free pincher roaming around the city—especially one whose parents are in the control of Vito Corbi—isn't in keeping with my plan."

Vincent twisted to face him. "So, those dead sons you set up to get massacred by Masseria's boys? What were they? A down payment?"

Yulia turned to her son. "*O chyem on govorit?*"

He waved her off, choosing to answer Vincent directly. "There is a difference between family and Bratva. That difference means being willing to sacrifice with full forgiveness."

"Sacrifice?" Vincent laughed. "That's what they signed up for? Did they even know? I'll bet you told them they were part of some grand scheme. A play for the power in New

York. They went after Masseria's family thinking it was a big damn deal. And they never knew they were sheep led to slaughter by their own blood."

Dmitrevich called over his shoulder, "Sergei?"

The brute stepped up and hammered another strike into Vincent's face.

Vincent went limp for a moment, then sputtered back to consciousness with a stream of blood rolling from his lips.

Yulia gestured toward one of the gunmen. *"Day mne pisto-let. Ya sam zastrelyu etu sobaku."*

The gunman reached into his jacket to produce a pistol, but Dmitrevich pushed his hand down. "Not here. I don't want the mess in my attic. Take them to the harbor. We'll do it there."

Vincent shook his jaw, then rasped, "Fine, fine. But do you have to kill the girl too? What is she to the Bratva, anyhow?"

Dmitrevich stepped away from his mother, turning to face Vincent. "You have leverage on her parents. She's clearly joined your merry band."

"We don't have her parents. We lied to gain her coopera-tion. She's not a part of the Crew, and she won't lift a finger to help them…or me. Let her go. If you people are about to make a move on Corbi, then she's already out of play anyway."

Dmitrevich crouched down. "A move on Corbi? You think that's the extent of my plans? No, no. We are moving on several cities, my friend. Masseria in New York. The syndicates in Philadelphia. Atlantic City. Pittsburgh. Even your friends down in the Carolinas."

"Total war, huh?"

"Yes. And I can't have any of you pinchers wandering in and out, causing trouble. Not tonight. Not ever."

Dmitrevich straightened up and motioned for Sergei to untie the two.

"Wait," Vincent blurted.

Dmitrevich held a hand to Sergei.

"You want to know what's in that bottle?"

Dmitrevich smirked. "I do, very much.

"It's an elixir."

"Go on."

"It's called Aqua Vitae. It's supposed to heal wounds. Extend life. An honest to God fountain of youth. She, and only she, knows where to get more of it. You kill her, and you'll cook the goose that lays the golden eggs. Maybe it's just me, but I'd say you want to keep her handy. Especially if you're gearing up for a prolonged battle with the entire Eastern seaboard. Just think, instant cure for gunshots or stab wounds. You'd have an invincible army with that stuff—but none of that will happen if you kill her."

Dmitrevich pulled the bottle from his pocket and inspected it.

His mother reached for his arm. "Lies."

The man peered dubiously at Vincent, then just past him at Hattie. "A fine yarn, my friend. But it doesn't appear to hold water. Your friend is still—"

"She's awake," Hattie spoke.

Dmitrevich sucked in a breath. "Clever. Well, Mister Calendo. You've made a compelling argument for sparing her life. I regret to say it will not spare yours."

"That's fine," Vincent stated.

Hattie whispered, "Hang in there, okay? Shouldn't be much longer."

He peered at her over his shoulder. She shot him a weak grin.

"Just don't tell anyone when this is all over, okay? I have a reputation to protect."

"Enough," Dmitrevich grunted. "Sergei…"

As the brute moved to untie his handiwork, Dmitrevich released a gasp.

Vincent watched as the man stared at the tiny bottle in his hand. Actually…it wasn't in his hand. It sat in midair an inch or two over his fingers.

"What is this…?" Dmitrevich shouted.

Vincent glanced down to his lap, where the photograph of Yakov Dmitrevich lifted an inch into the air.

His stomach fluttered, as if in freefall.

In a sudden, baffling flurry of motion, Dmitrevich, his mother, and the Bratva thugs flew into the air, slamming against the gabled rafters.

Blood rushed into Vincent's head as he looked up at the ceiling…as if lashed to the beam upside down.

Down was suddenly up. Hattie grunted, then shouted in panic.

In an instant, the situation switched again. Vincent and Hattie eased back against the floor as their captors dropped several feet. The old woman released a blood-curdling shriek as she landed on her frail arms. Dmitrevich scrambled as his head hit the floor boards. The bottle slipped from his fingers, rolling along the planks toward Vincent.

"Bozhe moy!" Dmitrevich shouted, reaching for the bottle.

Vincent lifted his leg and captured the dram beneath the meat of his calf, just as gravity shifted again, this time sending anyone not tied to the post tumbling along the floor toward the street-side wall where they landed with more grunts and cries of pain.

Hattie gasped. "What's happening?"

With a smirk, Vincent replied, "It's DeBarre."

"Right," Hattie said between breaths. "Down pincher. Handy."

Gunfire erupted downstairs. Shouts of alarm. Footsteps. More gunfire.

Amid the commotion downstairs, gravity returned to normal.

Dmitrevich got to his feet, pulling his injured mother upright. He barked commands in rapid fire Russian as Serge drew his weapon. Then he eased Yulia toward the stairs, where she paused to shoot Vincent a withering glare before Dmitrevich urged her out of the attic.

Vincent lifted his leg to check the bottle. It was still there, undamaged.

The two sat catching their breaths as the din slowly subsided beneath them. After the last gunshot had been fired, and an engine had chugged away out front, two shadows appeared at the opening to the stairs.

Vincent smiled as Lefty hoisted himself into the attic.

"Jesus, Vincent," he said. "You look like hammered crap."

"I feel like it." Vincent glanced past Lefty at DeBarre. "Thanks for that."

"Hope I didn't bruise you up."

Vincent shook his head. "We were tied in place. Speaking of which…"

Lefty stepped forward and produced a switchblade, snapping the edge into view to begin sawing at the rope. Before long, he had Vincent free. DeBarre wound around the post to assist Hattie, taking her arm as she stumbled to her feet.

Vincent took his time, running a hand over his jaw and tonguing a loose tooth. He reached beneath his leg for the bottle, and finally took Lefty's hand to rise to his feet.

"I believe this is yours." He held the bottle out to Hattie. "Bit miffed you didn't trust me enough to tell me you'd found him."

She took the dram, avoiding his gaze. "I made the right

choice, given how untrustworthy you've shown yourself to be."

He winced, realizing that he probably deserved that. Hattie bent over and plucked the photograph of Yakov Dmitrevich off the floor. "This was him?"

"Yeah," Vincent replied.

Lefty said, "Alright, you gumballs. Someone wanna tell me what this is all about?"

Vincent nodded. "Smith."

"What about him?"

"He's Bratva."

Lefty scowled. "Well, isn't that a kick in the shorts?"

"His real name's Dmitrevich. You remember that clutch of Russians we hit last year? His brother was one of them. And he's out for revenge."

Hattie added, "Not just revenge. The Russians are about to hit every major city on the East Coast."

Vincent nodded to DeBarre. "Including Philly."

DeBarre's face darkened. "You're sure of this?"

"Yeah, I'm sure. How the hell did you find us, anyway?" Vincent asked.

Lefty nodded to Hattie. "Well, this one comes rampaging through the hotel lounge shouting about you getting trapped in a building down by the water. Next thing I know, we're here, one minute standing outside the building, then up in the attic looking at you two tied to a post."

DeBarre added, "Only, we're the only two who saw any of this."

"I figured it was one of your illusions," Lefty said. "Handy work."

"Aye," she grumbled. "Just don't ask me to do it again."

Vincent asked, "Are you ship shape? That had to have taken a lot out of you."

Hattie nodded as she tucked the bottle of elixir in her shirt. "Right as rain."

Lefty turned toward the stairs. "If the Bratva are about to move on the Crew, then we better get on the horn with Vito."

DeBarre followed him. "And I need to call DeSanza and McCoy. They'll be the first ones these bastards hit."

Hattie grabbed Vincent's arm as he turned to go with the others. "If…if they launch an attack on the Crew tonight, where would they hit you?"

Vincent replied, "Probably the Old Moravia."

Her face paled. "Isn't that where you took my parents?"

Vincent stiffened, then exchanged a quick glance with Lefty. "We need to get to the Old Moravia. Now!"

They hurried down the attic stairs and through the well-appointed brownstone. Once they reached the street, Vincent waited for Lefty to indicate which car was theirs. They piled in with DeBarre behind the wheel. The wheels spun and the car whipped around to return to the hotel.

As they rushed along the night-emptied streets, Lefty turned to him, "Where's my auto?"

"You probably shouldn't ask that sort of question at this hour."

"I loaned it to you on specific conditions—"

"The Bratva smashed it with a cheap quality Ford, Lefty. I'm fine, by the way. Thanks for asking."

The last few blocks proceeded quickly, and in sullen silence.

DeBarre laid on the brakes, sending the car into a fishtail a block before they reached the Old Moravia.

"What's wrong?" Vincent demanded.

DeBarre lifted a finger. "Listen."

They all held a breath.

He added, "Do you hear that?"

Lefty nodded.

As did Vincent.

"Are we too late?" Hattie whispered.

They exited the car, plunging into the humid night air punctuated with the sound of a machine gun exactly one block away.

CHAPTER 25

A half-circle of Bratva foot soldiers gathered around parked cars and trucks, spraying the face of the Old Moravia Hotel with Tommy gun fire, their faces illuminated in muzzle flashes, revealing a halting arc of angry, sneering visages hell-bent on murder. The hotel, for its part, returned fire of its own. Several of the second and third-floor windows had been smashed or shot out, now home to the flares of automatic gunfire sending hot lead down into the Bratva's cover.

The war had begun.

Hattie clutched her hands into fists as she spied the upper floors of that building. Her parents were inside, somewhere. Besieged.

DeBarre shouted to Vincent as they huddled behind the corner of a nearby building, "Where's the nearest telephone?"

Vincent nodded forward. "The hotel."

"Oh, lovely!"

Vincent shrugged. "I know you didn't sign on for this, but it looks like helping us is your quickest way to helping those back home."

DeBarre checked the scene of carnage down the street, then nodded. "Alright. I'll assist you." He winked at Hattie. "Besides, us pinchers gotta stick together. Right?"

Hattie grinned. "I've heard pinchers say otherwise."

"Then they're bastards."

"I'll drink to that, boy-o."

DeBarre smiled. "I'll hold you to that, doll!"

Vincent scowled at the two. "Alright, focus people."

Lefty nodded. "So, okay. You just put it out there. We have three pinchers right here. Surely, you mooks can pull some magic and get us inside that building?" Lefty eyed Hattie. "Sorry for calling you a mook."

"I've been called worse," she replied. "But I don't see much point in helping any of you, at this point. My parents—"

Vincent pointed down the street. "Your parents are precisely why you *should* be helping us!"

She stowed her indignation. Right. Vincent was absolutely correct about that.

"I, uh…I suppose I can make us invisible. Not sure I have the juice, though." She'd exerted a lot of energy on that last pinch, and wasn't sure the physical aid the elixir gave her extended to renewing her magical abilities. But it had been a while. Surely she was recovered enough for a quick, tight pinch.

"I might be able to hold it long enough to get inside the building," she told them. "Don't figure any of you can make us bulletproof?"

Vincent shrugged. "Get me close enough, and the pair of us can drag these two inside before the time pinch gets too expensive."

Lefty lifted a hand. "*What? 'Pair* of us'?"

Vincent brushed him off. "Trust me. So, what do you say? How solid do you feel? I know you took a big hit already this evening."

Hattie wrinkled her nose. "I'm fine. I've seen to it. But...I don't know. There might be a problem. Won't know until I try."

Vincent squinted. "That elixir helped though, right?"

Lefty gruffed, "What elixir?"

Vincent waved him off again. "You're sure?"

"As sure as I can be." She turned to the car. "Only, it'll be best if we all get in the car."

"Why's that?" DeBarre asked, trotting up next to her.

"It's the economy of the thing, boy-o. Easier to shroud a single car than four individuals. Less motion. Easier to pinch."

DeBarre nodded with an approving glance. "Smart."

Vincent pushed between them to open the car door. "Yeah, great. Let's get moving."

Hattie eyed Vincent as he held the door for her. He seemed...testy. Oh. Well, wasn't that just funny? With a smirk, she stepped inside. "Thank you, Vincent."

He closed the door with a petulant slam.

Lefty took the seat beside her rather than Vincent, who manned a Tommy gun alongside DeBarre at the wheel. Lefty turned to face Hattie.

"This is a gamble," he grunted.

"I'm aware of that."

"Just wanting to get a read on the moment, is all. I don't know you. With everything that happened at your parents' house, putting my life in your hands fills me all kinds of dubious."

Hattie patted his knee. "I got nothing against *you*." Then she returned her focus to the light pinch at hand.

DeBarre started the motor, then craned his neck toward Hattie. "We good?"

She closed her eyes, then lifted flat palms over her face, picturing the entire vehicle. That was her gamble. One vehicle. One moving body in motion. One bubble of light to pinch.

"Let's go," she whispered.

The car lurched forward in a jerking motion, spinning around the corner as the thin rubber wheels slushed against the grime of the street. DeBarre wasn't playing around.

Hattie waved her hands in front of her closed eyes, chanting, "Disappear. Disappear. Disappear!"

The car continued.

She braced for the impact of the magic on her constitution. This wasn't an overly expensive magic. One vehicle in the middle of the night, amidst the utter chaos transpiring in the center of the block. As the car approached the hubbub, the cost would get higher and higher. That was when she'd urge Vincent to pinch time so that they could haul the other two into the relative safety of the Old Moravia.

The tendrils of magic, the cost of subverting the natural order that inexorably came to exact its toll were strangely absent.

"Guys? Uh, guys?"

The sound of gunfire rose in her ears.

Still...no tug on her insides. Even the smallest of light pinches, the tiniest glamour which she employed in her practicing, were palpable on some level. She could always feel the magic. But not now.

"Guys!" Bratva gunmen turned in place, their guns aiming now at their vehicle. "Vincent, now!" she shouted.

The car's front wheel popped, sending it dropping forward and to the left as the windscreen shattered from gunfire.

As Hattie lifted her hands to block her face, the tumbling motion of the car as it sliced to the side and tilted toward an end-over-end collision with the Bratva barricade came to a halt.

She removed her hands and breathed thick air into her lungs.

Vincent jabbed his finger at Lefty with a panicked face.

Hattie nodded, then reached over Lefty's lap to open his door. She shoved on the man's frame as Vincent climbed over DeBarre to unwrap his fingers from the steering wheel.

Hattie slithered over top of Lefty, electing to pull him from the car rather than to push him. She'd deduced that, even though time had come to a seeming standstill in one of Vincent's pinches, the items in motion still possessed all of their original momentum. If she ran Lefty into anything moving at high speed in real time, that could do as much damage as if they hadn't pinched time at all.

Hattie paused as she moved to place her foot onto the street outside of the car. She peered back at Vincent, who was gesturing madly for her to avoid touching the street. With a stiffening of her spine, she nodded. This inability to communicate verbally inside a time bubble was really starting to annoy her.

Fine. No touching the street or anything outside of the car.

She pulled herself onto the roof of the vehicle, already canting to the side. As she planted her feet against the sides of the car frame, she reached between her legs and jerked Lefty clear of his seat, hauling him into thin air, where he lingered, easing through the time-thickened space as if falling through quicksand.

Vincent appeared outside the opposite window, dragging DeBarre higher into space than she had. He gave her work a quick inspection, then nodded. He lifted a hand of five fingers, then folded one down. Then another.

Countdown.

Vincent braced himself with a hand on DeBarre's collar,

giving him one final jerk in the opposite direction of the car's motion.

Hattie did the same with Lefty, course-correcting him backward against the momentum that would return in…

Two fingers.

She repositioned her feet, twisting for a good jump point.

Vincent lifted a single finger.

She nodded.

And with a shove of her legs, Hattie launched herself into the air.

The time bubble dissipated, with the hail of gunfire re-erupting in her ears. Her motion backward in space immediately collided with her original momentum, spinning her in a somersault until she landed on her back, tumbling forward on the street a few feet. The result would have been far more violent if she hadn't shoved herself backward, as was evidenced by the car itself, now spinning along an oblique axis, shedding fabric and glass in fine arcs as it tumbled into the first of the Bratva barricades.

Hattie pressed hard against the street. A hand clamped down onto her shoulder. She peered up to find Lefty nodding to her. He jerked his head for a side-alley alongside the hotel, where Vincent was already heading alongside DeBarre. Taking Lefty's hand, she rose to her feet and the two sprinted for cover.

Hattie and Lefty swung into the alley just as the gunfire returned. The bricks behind their heads spattered in shrapnel as bullets hammered the front corner of the alley. Lefty held a hand behind Hattie's head as they rejoined the others.

DeBarre reached out to arrest her motion, gathering her at the waist in the crook of his arm, and nodding to her as she caught her breath. Vincent pushed between them to peer around the corner between bursts of gunfire.

"What happened?" Lefty demanded pushing his face close to Hattie's.

Vincent pulled his head out of view before a fresh salvo of bullets peppered the opposite wall of bricks. "I'm guessing we didn't pull off that light pinch."

Hattie scowled at him. "Nothing gets past you, does it?"

DeBarre shoved Lefty a foot away from Hattie. "Okay, let's calm down. Did you have enough time?"

Hattie nodded. "Aye. It was…it just didn't…"

Vincent asked, "Was it like Georgetown?"

With a considerable effort, she nodded again. "Only worse. There I felt the illusion sputter. This was…this was like going numb."

Lefty spat onto the ground. "Perfect. Fat lotta good this'll do us."

"I didn't fail on purpose," Hattie wailed, tears of frustration threatening to fall from her eyes. "I've only just pulled off the longest distance light pinch I've ever even done. Trust me. I'm not…I didn't…"

Vincent offered as she struggled for words, "You're probably still tapped out from that. Let's go easy on her, fellas."

Lefty squinted at DeBarre. "Hey. Can't you use your powers on these blockheads?"

"No can do, boss."

"Why not?" Lefty demanded.

DeBarre pointed at the sky. "You see a roof over our heads?"

"Does that matter?" Vincent asked.

"Sure does," DeBarre replied with a nod to Hattie. "She wanted a single car instead of four people, right? Well, if I don't have a ceiling to pinch these guys at, the down pinch drain'll kill me. You register that?"

Vincent nodded. "You need a limit."

Hattie shifted enough to catch a glimpse at the Bratva

battalion. A clutch of gunmen were making their cautious way around the barricades.

"Eh, gents? They're looking for us. Best find a solution sharpish."

DeBarre sidled alongside Vincent as the two conferred. Then DeBarre stepped away, his face swarming with doubt.

"It could work," Vincent insisted.

"Fat chance," DeBarre replied.

"I know, I know. It's a big maybe," Vincent offered. "But we're all about to get ventilated with bullets. So, one way, we all die. The other, we're rolling the dice that it'll work."

DeBarre spat, "And only I die."

"If you got a plan, we gotta move," Lefty snapped.

DeBarre waved him off. "Okay, yeah. Kinda want to see if this crazy idea plays out, anyways."

Hattie asked, "What are we doing, exactly?"

Vincent ushered her and Lefty forward. "Listen. DeBarre's problem is that he needs a limit to his down pinch. So who's to say whether or not a time bubble constitutes a limit?"

Hattie sucked in a breath, then muttered, "Oh. He's definitely going to kill himself."

Vincent scowled. "I'm serious. Everything I've ever seen about my time pinches says that all rules are off the second you pinch time."

Lefty asked, "How can he even use his powers if you pinch time?"

"Right, that's the trick," Vincent grumbled. "He'll have to commit to the down pinch. Send them flying. Then I'll pinch time and create a boundary for him. Once these goons are moving, the time pinch will take over. When I release it, DeBarre will have to somehow knock it off."

"Yeah, he's definitely going to kill himself," Hattie repeated.

DeBarre shrugged. "Hell with it. Let's give it a go."

Lefty jerked his pistol from his jacket, sending two shots into the head of an interloping Russian gunman. "Better make up your minds, folks."

DeBarre nodded to Vincent. "Now."

With that, DeBarre clenched both fists, then spun around into the clearing of the alley. He released a war cry that sent bolts through Hattie's limbs. It was a moment of sacrifice. Of gamble. Of pure power.

The whole block lurched underfoot for a half-second before Vincent reached for DeBarre's fists, clamping his hands down on top, and sending his own powers into the twist of nature.

The moment wasn't like anything Hattie had experienced with Vincent before. Her feet lifted off the street. Her stomach rushed toward her throat. As she blinked away the time-thickened air she was used to under Vincent's powers, she realized that everyone...including Vincent...had been captured in DeBarre's down pinch.

A rush of panic filled Hattie's throat.

Vincent fumbled about his waist for a moment as a trickle of blood emerged from his nostril. This was too large a space for him, she realized, or perhaps too many pinches in too short a time. Whatever the economics, it was proving too costly.

He whipped his belt free of his trousers and sent the free end sailing through the thickened air for Hattie. She reached out to catch the buckle in the flat of her palm then moved in tandem with Vincent to angle his belt around Lefty's chest, just below the shoulders.

Vincent coughed and said something to Hattie, blood spraying in a slowly spreading mist, his words lost to the time pinch. But it was something important enough for him to try.

What had he said?

As Hattie sucked in as much air as her lungs could draw in order to reply, Vincent snapped his fingers.

The upward motion of the down pinch continued as the thinness of air resolved, and the sounds of nature returned to its fluid state. No more gunfire. Instead...screams of panic.

Hattie rushed into freefall, her hand still clamped onto Vincent's belt, feet slamming against a fire escape, digging painfully into a gap between the wrought iron railings.

Vincent hammered against a flagstone sill, his hand reaching to grab the edge as the rest of his body threatened to hurtle farther into space. With a grunt, he jerked against the belt.

Hattie did the same.

Lefty hit the contracting length of leather at that moment, his arms now flailing in confusion. The leather slapped hard against Lefty's shoulders, smacking him in a downward force.

That force traveled up the belt to both Vincent and Hattie, now roughly ten feet off the ground, jolting them a little higher. In a split-second of freefall, Hattie caught Vincent's eyes.

They were calm. Serene, even. In control. This was Vincent in his element, where he was absolutely confident in his abilities. Suddenly Hattie realized that no matter what he'd done earlier tonight, she still trusted him to keep her safe—trusted him with every ounce of her being.

Then without notice, gravity slipped its fingers around Hattie, sending her earthward in a nauseating tumble. The three of them hit the ground hard, grunts rushing from their lungs. Lefty coughed and gagged, the wind knocked out of him. Hattie tumbled sideways, spreading the impact on her legs through her hips, lower back, and ultimately to her shoulders as she collided with the side of the adjacent building.

Once she'd hissed against the pain and determined up from down, she peered over to the others. Vincent was already on his feet, but his face was filled with panic. On the ground just before Vincent lay DeBarre. His arms flailed at his sides, alternately pounding against the ground and reaching for his chest. The man coughed and retched, blood foaming from his mouth.

The magic had taken its toll.

Hattie slipped the dram from her blouse, and with the tiniest of prayers to whatever God cared to listen, called out as she tossed the bottle to Vincent.

The tiny, fragile vial of Aqua Vitae slipped through the air, landing in Vincent's steady fingertips.

He pulled the stopper, dangling a drop overtop DeBarre's lips holding one of his flailing arms with a knee. A single mote of the elixir slipped from the glass stopper, and fell into DeBarre's mouth.

In a second, the spasming stopped. The man sucked in a hard breath, then released it with a chest-crushing cough. Hattie stepped around DeBarre, peering out onto the street, which was oddly empty.

Then a car landed with a crash.

And another.

One by one, the barricades crashed back to Earth, followed by the sick-wet slops of Bratva gunmen slamming against the pavement. Hattie covered her mouth in horror as bones splintered out of skin and blood sprayed against the adjacent buildings. The entire force of Russian attackers fell hard against the street as if they'd been hurled from a five-story building.

DeBarre, for his part, had settled into a peaceful repose with Vincent hovering over him. She stepped alongside

Vincent, peering down at DeBarre as he took in short, shallow breaths.

"Is he…alive?"

Vincent nodded. "This saved him." He held the dram up for Hattie.

She took it, tucking it away once again.

DeBarre opened his eyes, reaching up for Vincent's hand. He struggled upright, shaking off the effects of the elixir like dew on his brow.

"Wow," he muttered. "Thought I wasn't gonna make it outta that one alive."

Hattie squirmed. "I have an elixir I gave you. Physically, you're all healed up, but it doesn't do anything to restart your powers. You might not be able to down pinch for a bit."

"How long?" DeBarre asked.

"I don't know. A few hours maybe? No longer than a day, from what I can tell."

DeBarre snickered. "Oh, hell. I can handle that."

He got to his feet, and the four gathered together to take in the carnage in the street before the Old Moravia. Shadows sliced out along the pavement as men emerged from the hotel's entrance.

Vincent stepped free of the alley, hands held high. "Hey boys! It's me. Hold your damned fire."

A lone figure strode forward, holding his hands high to stave off the rest of the Crew. As he turned, Hattie recognized the figure as Tony.

"Vincent! Lefty!" he shouted. "Damn, boys! Was this all you?"

Vincent nodded. "With some help from my friends."

Lefty pulled Tony closer. "Have you seen Smith?"

Tony nodded. "Sure. Ducked into the hotel right before these beet-eaters hit us. Why?"

"Because," Lefty replied, stepping forward, "Smith is one of them."

Tony blanched. "The hell you say."

"It's true," Vincent said. "All his information was just a scheme to infiltrate us."

Tony cast a dubious eye at Hattie. "What about this one? You brought her on board entirely due to Smith's information."

Vincent caught his breath and shot DeBarre a quick glance, full of some hidden meaning, before turning back to Tony. "It was all a hoax. All Smith trying to destabilize the Crew."

"You expect me to waltz in there and tell the Capo that everything he's been scrambling over these past few weeks is horse apples?" Tony asked incredulously.

"That's exactly what I expect."

"He's not going to hear that well," Tony muttered.

Vincent scowled. "Smith's outed himself as the enemy, and he's in that hotel right this second. We'll deal with the personal fallout later. The Bratva's hitting every major family on the Eastern seaboard. We gotta secure this block and get DeBarre back home."

They hurried past the men, sprinting over ruined Russian bodies and through the entrance to the hotel. What had once been the center of culture and opulence, a refined oasis of jazz music and ice-cold gin, was now a war zone. Tables had been overturned. Men in suits stood behind them with Tommy guns and pistols. The wounded had been gathered behind the lobby desk, a tiny swarm of women attending to them. Several wounded gangsters sat at angles against the marble-clad walls as men and women attended to their injuries.

Hattie spotted an elegant, slender woman with brunette hair in an elegant marcel wave. She wrapped gauze around the arm of one of the gunmen, her eyes lifting briefly to meet Hattie's.

Fern.

Hattie shot a quick glance at Vincent, but he didn't seem to notice the woman. As they stepped past the gathered bodies, Tony gestured for a door behind the lobby desk. "Through there."

"Is that the stairs?" she asked.

"No," Tony replied, shooting a tense expression at Lefty.

"Oh," Hattie grumbled. "Right, then. Let's get this over with."

Tony held open the door as Hattie stepped inside. Vincent, DeBarre, and Lefty followed, but Tony remained outside. The room was cramped, two tables occupying most of the space. A map of Baltimore lay spread out across both tables, several red lines and black X's indicating…something. A pitiful electric bulb illuminated the map from the center of the room, but otherwise the surrounding walls were shrouded in darkness. Leaning against one of these walls, arms crossed and thumb working his chin in contemplation, was Vito Corbi.

His eyes glanced across the pool of electric light at Hattie.

She stepped up to the tables to take a wide stance, one hand gripping the other behind her back.

Vito unfolded his arms to crack his knuckles. "So. This is Hattie Malloy?"

Vincent nodded.

Vito took a roundabout path through the room as he sized her up. "You're young."

Hattie did not respond.

Vito added, "And elusive. I'm glad to finally meet you."

"You, as well," she replied.

Vito's bushy eyebrows lifted. "You a Mick?"

Hattie balled her hand behind her back. "I was born outside of Dublin, but lived in the States most of my life."

He scowled. "Had that long to lose the accent, but you didn't. What does that tell me?"

"It tells you," she offered, "I'm not ashamed of who I am."

A grin crept onto his cracked lips. "Good answer." He turned to Vincent. "Vincenzo, I would say that I'm pleased you've finally found a way to fulfill my request, but my patience is simply gone."

Vincent replied, "Yes, Capo." He added with a cautious tone, "There is something you should know."

Vito lifted his chin and gestured for Vincent to continue.

"Alexander Smith, the information broker whose services we've secured."

Vito corrected him, "Who services *you've* secured."

"Yes. Turns out he's an infiltrator for the Russians."

Vito's eyes narrowed. "What?"

"All of this, from Masseria," he gestured to Hattie, "to her. It was a scheme to stretch us out and catch us off guard. They're hitting everyone, too. Not just us. New York. Philly."

Vito slammed his fist into the closer table, sending a thud echoing off the walls. "This…is…unacceptable!" Vito shook his head and paced a circle before stopping in front of DeBarre. "My apologies, friend. You have business to tend to, if what Vincenzo says is true."

DeBarre replied, "I believe it is, from what I've seen."

"I'll have you brought to a telephone." He snapped his fingers.

DeBarre turned for the door, then stopped to exchange another quick glance with Vincent before turning to the Capo.

"That Smith character, he came close to embarrassing you."

"How so?" Vito grumbled.

"Beyond the obvious, I mean. It took real planning to set up an innocent girl like this."

Vito stepped past Hattie. "What girl is that?"

DeBarre nodded at Hattie. "Every little coincidence he'd stitched together to make her look like some sorta light pincher? It took balls and brains. Anyways, I wish you luck."

Vito glared at the man. "She *is* a light pincher."

DeBarre cleared his throat as he stretched his arms. "She was set up to make you look like a fool, sir. We sure coulda used her help out there, but she couldn't do any magic. Not even when her life was in danger. Not even when those Russians were trying to put a bullet in her head. Clearly she's not capable."

Hattie bit back a grin, forcing her expression back into a neutral mask as Vito stepped in front of her, inspecting her face. Then he turned to Vincent.

"Which is it? Is she a pincher or not?"

"I'm ashamed to admit that I was fooled, Capo," Vincent bent his head. "I believed Smith. I caught her and was bringing her to you when we were waylaid. But in all honesty I've got to tell you that all the times I've been face-to-face with her, I've never seen her perform any magic. It's always been heresay. It's always been Smith's word I've relied upon."

Hattie held her breath, afraid to look at him. What was he doing? He'd surely suffer for this. He'd be sent upstate, or beaten, maybe even killed. Why was he doing this for her?

Vito snapped his chin at DeBarre. "You agree?"

DeBarre simply replied, "She can't cast any sorta magic. Saw it myself. Smith put her into a position to get caught by the Feds, then by you. Hell, I wouldn't be surprised if Smith was actually the light pincher himself."

Vito swirled to face Lefty and Hattie stiffened, knowing the man's words were going to carry more weight than any of the others in this room. "You doubt her abilities, Alonzo?" he asked.

With a sigh and a slight bow, Lefty replied, "I think she's just a girl who got caught in the middle of all this. A remarkable girl, and maybe one of the best boat-leggers we've hired. But there's nothing magical about her that I've seen."

"So," DeBarre offered, picking up Lefty's cue, "that would have been embarrassing once the rest of the families found out she wasn't no pincher."

Vincent nodded with fervor. "Which was probably all part of Smith's plan to begin with."

Vito scowled as his face turned red, then he turned away.

Lefty added, "She played the part good and well. I'll give her that. And who can blame her, what with us pulling guns on her parents and all."

DeBarre shook his head, gesturing for the front of the hotel. "Does it look like she had anything to do with this?"

Lefty nodded. "Girl's just a girl."

Was this truly happening? Why would these three suddenly jump in to save her from the Capo like this? Especially DeBarre. She'd just met him. He'd nearly died...

But then, that was it. She'd saved his life with her Aqua Vitae. And now, he was helping to save hers.

Vito spun on his heel, and everyone froze. He lumbered forward, working his hands in and out of fists. Finally, with a groaning sigh, he declared, "Get her and her parents out of here. We don't have time for this nonsense."

"Yes, Capo," Lefty replied, jerking Hattie away from Vito before the man flew into an ensuing rage.

Hattie trotted out behind DeBarre.

Once the door had closed behind them all, Tony stood with a twist in his brow. "What's the word?"

DeBarre peered around the corner to the lobby desk. "That the phone there?"

Tony nodded.

DeBarre smiled and rubbed his hands together. "Gents, it's been a gas. But I'm afraid I really must make a phone call."

Vincent reached out to shake his hand. "Thank you for your help."

"Hey, don't forget. All you palookas owe us Philly boys big, now. I will be calling to collect." DeBarre turned to Hattie. "If you find your way up the Delaware anytime soon, and you run into Bill McCoy, you tell him that Loren says you're off limits, and then maybe swing by the cannery to share a glass of something with me."

Hattie smirked. "I might do that."

DeBarre shook Lefty's hand with a nod, then withdrew to the lobby desk.

Lefty turned to Tony. "Anyone spot Smith yet? Or... Dmitrevich? Whatever."

Tony replied, "Not yet. Man's a ghost."

Vincent said, "He's probably still in the building."

Hattie declared, "Which means my parents might still be in danger. Come on, boys. We're not done."

Vincent pulled his piece, inspected the rounds, then nodded. Lefty flipped his pistol overhand to do the same. The four rushed up the stairs as Tony led the way. Tony shoved the stairwell door open, holding it for the others.

Hattie moved to sweep around Tony, only to be held back by Vincent. "Wait!" He pointed to a body on the floor, then trained his gun up the hallway.

Hattie's stomach dropped. "Who...is that?"

"Looks like Curly," Vincent grumbled.

He lifted his fingers and gave them a snap. Time wound to a halt. He reached for Hattie's hand, pulling her forward toward the door left ajar behind Curly's body. She shoved it open to find the room in ruins. Tears threatened to fall from her eyes, but instead they simply lingered in a cloud around her eyelashes. Rubbing them clear, she stepped into the room.

There was no blood, which was a good sign. The bed was mostly made, though the blankets had been twisted, as if someone had struggled there.

Vincent tapped her shoulder, then pointed to the far corner.

Hattie would've cried out if she could in the time bubble. She shoved forward through the time-stiffened air, reaching out for Alton, who sat in a chair, hair a mess, eyes haunted.

Vincent released the time bubble, and the sudden thinning of the air sent Hattie stumbling forward, nearly tackling her father as she wrapped her arms around him. Alton sucked in a gasp of alarm.

Hattie stroked his head. "Da!" His arms trembled, and she realized it wasn't just from her sudden appearance out of thin air. "Are you hurt? Where's Ma?"

Alton's face twisted in grief. "They took her."

CHAPTER 26

*L*efty shouted "Vincent!" as he crouched over Curly.

Vincent rushed for the doorway, kneeling to find Curly's eyes open, though tight with pain.

"He took a bullet in the gut," Lefty grumbled. "I sent Tony to get someone." He pulled a handkerchief and balled it, sliding it over the wound. As he pressed down, Curly released a quick shriek.

"Who did this?" Lefty asked the man as his cries weakened.

"That…creep. The one that was whispering all that stuff to Vincent." Curly coughed again, then whispered, "I came to tell them to get packed. You know…so we could move the parents." He coughed again and nearly gagged. "I walked in on Smith. He had the old man…out. Turned and drew on me. Then ran."

"Someone was guarding the floor?" Vincent urged.

"Yeah," Curly replied. "Cooper."

Vincent eased away. "Is it possible…Cooper's involved with Smith?"

Lefty swore under his breath. "He's Crew. May be a pill, but he's one of us. No way he'd turn coat."

"I'm not so sure," Vincent mused. "I saw Cooper and Smith at the bar together. It was the night before Smith found me up by the grocer's. They looked to be in cloaks and daggers, if you take my meaning. Smith told me he'd propositioned Cooper before he came to me." Vincent sighed. "Maybe Cooper took him up on it, after all, and all the rest was just the plan?"

Lefty squinted, mulling it over. "You're suggesting Cooper's working for the Russians?"

"It makes sense. Where do you think Smith was getting all that info? We know he's Bratva. He's no info broker. Everything he knew he either got from Cooper, or me, or Hattie."

"But what's the motive?" Lefty asked. "For Cooper? It's a death sentence."

"He ain't the sharpest knife in the drawer. You know that. And he's been real sore ever since we dressed him down in front of Vito."

Lefty smirked. "I did shoot him in the foot."

"He changed his name, his church… I think he's been on the way out for a while, now."

The stairway door opened, and a small team of gangsters streamed into the hall. Fern raced through the center of them, barking out orders as she shoved Vincent aside with her knee. She had Curly's shirt cut off, and pressed a handful of hotel towels against the wound.

Vincent motioned for Hattie and Alton to exit the room, guiding them away from the pool of blood that had gathered in the hallway carpet.

Hattie whispered, "Is he alive?"

"Hanging on, but just barely." He nodded to Alton. "How are you? Are you hurt?"

Alton shook his head. "He gave me a wallop, but it's nothing I haven't had before. It's Branna I'm worried about."

"We'll find her," Hattie told him. "Won't we boys?"

Vincent looked to Lefty.

"No," Lefty told him. "After we take care of these Bratva fools, maybe we can go look for her, but not now. Capo isn't gonna send his manpower after some Irish woman, especially when we just convinced him this one isn't a pincher."

Hattie tried to push past them. "I want to speak to Corbi. He was supposed to protect my parents and he failed. I'll hold him responsible."

Lefty held out his hand. "Probably not a good idea. He just ordered you out of the hotel."

"Hell with him!"

She shoved past Lefty and Vincent reached out to grab her, gripping her upper arms in his hands. "Stop. You're gonna get yourself killed. Lefty's right. Corbi isn't going to give a rat's ass about your mother. Storming down there and yelling at him is only going to get you a bullet in your head."

"It's my mother," she snapped. "Those Bratva bastards are probably holding her as a hostage. Your boss won't trade for her and they'll kill her once they realize she's of no value to them. I have to find her. I have to save her."

"Hattie, Vito will never allow it."

"He promised to protect my parents," she snapped, trying to yank her arms free of his grasp.

He gripped her tight, giving her a little shake and in the process pulling her against him. "No, *I* promised to protect your parents." He waited until that sunk in. "And I intend to do so."

"Vincent," Lefty warned. "Not gonna happen. You're needed right now. These Russians have only retreated. They're regrouping and they'll be back. Vito needs you here, to defend the family. Your family needs you."

"I made a promise, and I'm keeping it. I'm not asking, Lefty," he replied, his eyes still on Hattie. "I'm telling."

There was a moment of silence, then Lefty sighed. "Been nice knowing you, pincher."

"Does that mean you're not coming?" Vincent looked over at his handler.

"Course I'm coming. It's my job to make sure you stay outta trouble, you mook."

He looked back to Hattie, his eyes meeting hers before he let go of her arms. "Soon as we get outta here, we'll find a way to track down where they're keeping your mother. And we'll get her back. Okay?"

She stared up at him, her eyes huge. Then she nodded. "Okay."

Vincent led the way as they headed downstairs, stepping into the lobby to find the circus had achieved a degree of order. The firefight in the street was over. The last of the Russians had either fled or had been shot. Wounded were gathered in tidy rows while the able-bodied lingered in clutches, eyes peeled on Vito.

The Capo loomed in the direct center of the lobby, orbiting the space below the grand chandelier as he ranted and raved about the lack of preparation, the wounds incurred, the insults borne from this attack. No one offered a response.

Tony met them at the bottom of the stairs. "Best to stay around the edges. He's in a mood."

Corbi stopped his tirade midsentence and scowled over at them. "Get over here. I need you both. Now."

Vincent caught his breath. "Capo—"

Vito lifted a fat finger at Lefty's face. "Can you not control him? Throw those Irish out, and get your pincher ready. We are at war." He turned to Vincent. "And you, Vincenzo. The day I have the greatest need of you, you've shown me your true value. Rather, your lack of value." His face darkened. "You get taken by these Russians and need to be rescued. You have given me false information, caused me to waste resources and look the fool. You are worthless to me. Worthless."

Vincent drew a breath to respond, but Vito turned to dismiss him, addressing Lefty. "Alonzo, you will escort him. See that he makes it home, and stays there. I shall make a call to Ithaca in the morning. Do this...and perhaps you will prove your worth."

Vincent nearly lost his breath at the comment. Even Lefty seemed shaken.

Ithaca?

He stood motionless as Vito bellowed for a clear path to the elevators. It was over. All of it.

But before he came to terms with that, he had a promise to keep.

"Come with me." Vincent slipped through the crowd, slicing through until he reached Tony, perched on the desk not far from DeBarre. "Tony...where's the war party going?"

"What?" Tony muttered, looking for a way to avoid Vincent's company.

"Corbi's gathering the troops, right? Going to hit back at the Russians. So, where is everyone going?"

Tony mumbled, "Uh... Washington Hill."

"What's in Washington Hill?"

"Word around the room is that's the last known head-quarters of the Bratva," DeBarre spoke up.

Vincent nodded, then held his gaze with DeBarre. "Why are you still here?"

"Can't get through to Philly."

"Are they getting hit, you think?"

DeBarre nodded. "Arnoud's probably on the case. I'll bet he is. And I almost feel sorry for those bastards." DeBarre's eyes narrowed, and he leaned forward to whisper, "Ithaca, huh?"

Vincent couldn't answer.

DeBarre added with a chuck to Vincent's shoulder. "I'll see what I can do. Maybe there's a buyer down in Atlantic City who could use you."

Vincent turned away. "I suppose we'll see."

"What's this that about, then?" Hattie asked.

"Not now," he grumbled. "One thing at a time. Let me figure out how to get your mother back first, then I'll…" His voice trailed off. Vito was sending him upstate. Disgraced. He'd be traded…if he was lucky.

Tony shook his head. "We're already heading to Washington Hill. If Smith is there…"

Lefty said, "Fat chance of that. They're going to find an empty building. Smith probably planted that little nugget to send the whole Crew on a snipe hunt."

Hattie threw her hands in the air. "Well, someone has to know something!"

DeBarre stepped forward. "Excuse me, miss? But, I think your father's trying to say something?"

She spun on DeBarre, then lowered her hands. Turning to Alton, she noted his profound discontent. "Da?"

"So…" he mumbled. "It's a thought."

Vincent prodded, "What is it?"

"There's more than one Russian over at the mill, is all. We take breaks together at times. I kinda struck up a friendship with them. They're the only ones who bring proper tea to work."

Vincent asked, "And you think they'll know where the Bratva are holed up?"

Alton shrugged. "We're not an upright bunch over there. I'll wager ya someone knows something."

Lefty shrugged. "As good a lead as any."

Vincent eyed DeBarre. "Loren? If you're not on the road for Philly, we sure could use a hand."

DeBarre reached into his jacket to produce a comb, ran it through his hair twice, then replied, "The enemy of a friend is most definitely my enemy."

They stepped around and over people to reach the street, still spangled with bodies and ruined vehicles. The Baltimore police had gathered at a distance, dealing with the public as they streamed from the surrounding buildings in small groups. Luckily this was downtown, and not around any neighborhoods. And the police knew better than to interfere with the families when the war drums were pounding.

DeBarre guided everyone around the corner and down a block, gesturing toward his car as the sky above began to thin into a deep blue of dawn. They stuffed into the vehicle as best they could, shoulder-to-shoulder.

DeBarre asked, "So, where to, gents?"

Alton replied, "Bedlam, son."

The Down Pincher turned in his seat with an incredulous wince.

Lefty clarified from the front passenger seat, "Bethlehem Steel. It's on the water. Take a right up here, then keep on."

As they drove east out of the downtown area, Vincent did his best to give Hattie space on the seat. But there wasn't much room. His leg pressed against hers. She didn't seem put out by the confines of the car. Rather, she was preoccupied with her hands, making quick gestures with her fingers.

Alton patted her knee. "Don't you worry, girl. We'll get your mother soon enough."

She shook her head distractedly. "It's not that. I'm just..." She peered at Vincent. "Can you see...oh. What am I talking about? Of course, you wouldn't see it."

Alton added with a lift of a crooked finger, "Was it a canary?"

She beamed at him. "Aye. That, it was. And this?"

She made another gesture.

He frowned. "It was like a cat, but…"

Her hands lowered to her lap in defeat.

"Your powers—are they coming back?" Vincent asked.

"A bit," she replied. "Can't be sure how much."

By the time they'd reached the steel mill, the eastern sky was a rosy pink. A steam whistle sounded somewhere within the hulking plant, enormous gables of steel and tin slicing against the dawn sky, with chimney stacks sending plumes of soot skyward. The entire mill yard was immense, littered with hunks of coke and pig iron, a constant puddle of rusty water gathering into sluices of mud between the street and the gate.

They exited the car, gathering in a line as an army of workers bustled in and out of the gate during the shift change.

Alton lifted a finger. "There. Those three with the beards."

Vincent nodded, and DeBarre and Lefty rushed forward to intercept them before they were lost in the stream of egress.

The bearded fellows drew up, hands held up to their shoulders as their lunch pails dropped to the mud. They released a flurry of pronouncements in their native tongue, ceasing only as Alton stepped forward next to Hattie. Their eyes eased as they caught sight of the old man.

"Alton!" the tallest of the three shouted. "Is good!"

Alton nodded and stepped forward to shake their hands. "God's health on ya, Vasily."

The other two lowered their hands.

"What is this?" Vasily asked with a nod to the gangsters. "You are, as they say, hoodlum now?"

Alton laughed. "Lord Jesus, no. But they're lending me a

hand. And not to put too fine a point on it, I'm hopin' you'll do the same."

Vasily turned to take Alton's arms into his hands for a quick shake. "For you, my friend, anything."

"That's good, lad. Because I need to talk to your young friend, here." Alton pivoted to the shortest of the three, a man of barely twenty. His beard was remarkably full, disguising the youth in his features.

Hattie strode up as Vasily urged the lad forward. She reached for his cap, jerking it off with a quick snap. "Eh, then. It's you, after all!" Hattie chuckled. "Aye, last I laid eyes on this one, I put a snake in his hand."

Vasily's eyes drooped. He turned to the young man. "You know this girl?"

He shook his head. Hattie cocked a brow and he nodded sheepishly.

Alton reached forward, gripping the young man by the arm. "Last night, my wife Branna was kidnapped by the— what's the word you fellows used?"

Vincent replied, "Bratva."

"Aye, that's it. The Russian mob," he added with a sudden gravity to his typical sing-song casual tone, "They have my wife, Vasily. She has no part in any of this nonsense. They don't know it. And I'm afraid they're going to do her some insult. So, if you'll be very kind, my friend," he jerked the lad in front of Vasily, "you'll muster some cooperation from your wayward youth, here."

Vasily leveled a glare onto the lad. "Of course my friend. And what's this about a snake?"

* * *

DeBarre rubbed his chin as the five stood across the street from McGillicuddy's Quality Meats. "You wouldn't expect to find Russian gangsters housed up in a place with the name of McGillicuddy."

Lefty grumbled, "Which is precisely why they're here."

Vincent commented, "And they don't know that we are. We get one shot at this, and if we louse it up…"

Hattie frowned. "We're not lousing it up, so don't bother painting the picture." She turned to her father. "Da? I need you to stay here with the car. Don't stick your head up, getting it blown off."

Alton cocked his jaw. "Oh, and I'm supposed to let my girl go running into a hornet's nest then?"

Lefty sighed, then stepped alongside Alton. "I'll stay with him. Cover the exits in case things go—"

"They won't," Hattie urged with a testy tone.

Alton regarded Lefty with amusement. "Hey, now. Aren't you the one who kidnapped me only yesterday?"

Lefty shuffled on his feet. "And I'm sure this will go just as smooth."

Hattie squinted at DeBarre. "No, it should be you."

DeBarre lifted a brow. "How's that?"

"You should stay, she urged."

"Why? You don't think having a third pincher with you would be, well…valuable?"

Vincent picked up the line of thought. "Have you tried to do a pinch recently?" After a blank stare from DeBarre, he explained, "The Aqua Vitae. We used it to keep you from gutting yourself from your own down pinch. Remember?"

He grumbled, "Oh, right." With a nod to Lefty, he chimed, "Sorry, old-timer. You pulled active duty on this one."

Lefty smirked. "Story of my life."

Vincent, Hattie, and Lefty stepped across the street.

"Do we have a plan?" Hattie asked. "Just wondering, is all."

Lefty inspected the wide three-story packing plant in front of them. "One loading dock up front, and a street entrance. Not a lot of windows. Probably more points of entry in the rear."

Vincent shook his head. "We strike quiet and dig deep. Get to Mrs. Malloy before they know we're here. Anyone Hattie can't shroud us against, I'll deal with outside of time. Lefty will be our check valve. Anyone gets past us, he drops. But that means we're blown, so that's gotta be our last resort."

Lefty nodded acknowledgment.

With a decisive wave of her hand, Hattie pinched light around them, rendering them invisible. Lefty stumbled for a moment, then pressed on.

They proceeded for the front loading dock, climbing a short flight of stairs to a covered truck loading canopy. The overhead door was down and locked. Vincent tried the employee's door to the side. The bolt slid open, and the door eased against the hinges into the building. With a nod, Vincent opened the door all the way and the three stepped inside. They found a warehouse area, poorly lit, with neatly arranged crates and packaged goods lined up behind the overhead door. Hattie released the light pinch, giving Vincent an apologetic shrug. He nodded in approval. That was smart. Conserve her powers while they could.

Lefty pulled his gun and gestured with it toward the far end of the warehouse. A long metal wall separated the warehouse from the interior of the packing plant. Two guards stood near the wide sliding doors, each brandishing a Tommy gun.

Vincent whispered to the others, "I'm on it."

He crouched along the shadows near the crates as far as he could. The guards, immersed in a conversation in Russian, finally noticed his approach when he was only about twenty feet away.

With a snap of his fingers, he pinched time between him

and the guards. Swimming forward through the time bubble, he set a flat palm beneath the jaw of the first guard, then rammed his head against the wall behind, leaving it in place. He turned and gave his partner the same treatment before releasing the time pinch.

Both of their heads hammered away from the walls, knocking the men unconscious in a split-second. Vincent took their guns, then turned and gave the others a thumbs-up.

The sliding door creaked loud against its rail, and they paused to check for alarm within. As there was no indication their cover had been blown, they pulled the door wide enough to enter. A spray of ice crystals rained on them as they eased the door against its frozen rail.

Vincent's breath rose in puffs as the air dropped to arctic temperatures. Rows upon rows of hanging pork bellies ran down the length of the enormous cold box. A series of gigantic ice cubes stood in a wall before a row of fans, sending frigid air through the insulated space.

"Probably no guards in here," Vincent whispered. "I wouldn't stand guard in here if I had a choice."

They wound their way past the carcasses of meat slung onto iron hooks. When they reached the far end, all they found was a wall. After a bit of searching, Lefty found another sliding door on the right-hand wall. Vincent and Hattie gave it a gentle shove. Though the rail wasn't quite as loud as the first, it still sounded a grinding peal as the wheels ran against ice and corrosion.

On the other side were four young men.

Hattie waved her hand in front of her face then marched out of the cold box. None of the Bratva soldiers raised their guns. Instead, they simply turned to her and muttered something in Russian. Vincent had no idea what they were saying.

Hattie, however, seemed to have no problem. She announced, *"Ya ostavil moy koshelek na komode tvoyei materi."*

The young men released a belly laugh and waved her through. She continued on. Vincent and Lefty advanced behind her. Vincent gave the nearest Bratva a quick salute. The young man nodded, then returned his attention to his compatriots.

Once they'd rounded a corner, Hattie slumped, holding the wall to catch her balance. As she gasped for air, Vincent reached out to lay a hand on her back.

"You alright?" he asked.

"That wasn't easy," she gasped. "Wasn't sure…it'd work."

"What did you tell them?" Lefty asked.

Vincent nodded. "Yeah. I didn't know you knew Russian."

She smirked. "I don't. But I spent some time practicing in the market."

"Practicing?" Vincent asked.

"Never mind. There were some Russian boys I followed for a while. I picked up a phrase here and there. No idea what it means, though."

Lefty nodded. "Well, it worked. Nice job."

She straightened up, chucked his shoulder, then continued forward.

They poked their heads into several rooms, finding most empty. Ultimately, they reached a flight of stairs, and made their way to the second floor. This was apparently the nerve center for this Bratva cell. Dozens of men gathered in several rooms, mostly with guns out and at the ready.

Vincent eyed two hallways spreading out in two directions. Taking a chance, he motioned toward the east, then gave them a flat palm to stay put. With several breaths, and a snap of his fingers, he pinched time. As quickly as he could, he shoved his way down the hall, peeping into every door possible. Nothing but Russians. The last door down the hallway was locked.

The time pinch sent tendrils of nausea through his abdomen. This was taking too long. He jerked hard on the door, shoving into it with his shoulder. But time bubble physics didn't accommodate the way he'd expected. All he did was push his form against an immovable plane, knowing he'd pay for it the second he dropped the time bubble.

And that time would have to come soon, as his throat began to throb, and a cold sweat erupted over his forehead.

He abandoned the locked door to shove his way through his own time pinch back to the stairwell. By the time he'd made it back, he was already grimacing from the pain in his guts. As the time bubble released, he fell against the wall of the stairwell, sliding down to sit and rest.

Hattie crouched beside him, "Thought you'd never make it back. You think she's behind that door?"

Lefty shook his head. "What are you talking about?"

Hattie explained, "There's a door at the far end. It's locked, by the looks of it."

Lefty squinted. "I don't understand. How can you—"

"I'm immune to his magic," Hattie explained. "And vice versa."

"That a fact?" Lefty muttered.

"Wouldn't happen to know how to pick a lock, would you?"

Lefty holstered his gun and wiggled his fingers. "I make do pretty good, but that's a skill that takes two hands."

She nodded. "Aye, I suppose so. We'll have to break the door in."

Vincent lifted a hand as he caught his breath. "Not sure your mother's...behind that door."

"Can't know until we check," she replied, spying the hallway.

"Loads of Russians between here and there. You got enough magic left to get us there and back?"

She smirked at Vincent. "You got enough gas to get to your feet?"

He reached for Lefty's hand and stood up. "Just give me a minute."

"We don't have a minute," Lefty whispered as footsteps sounded on the stairs below them.

A flutter of panic spread through Vincent's chest, the adrenaline sending energy through his body. He peered down the stairwell, gritting his teeth.

Hattie peered at him expectantly. "Well?"

"Well?" he repeated.

Lefty urged, "Do something, folks. Right or wrong."

Hattie reached out and thumped Vincent's chest with the meat of her fist. "Let's go."

She threw open the door at the top of the stairwell and waved her hands, shrouding them in another pinch of invisibility. Vincent followed, with Lefty bringing up the rear. She rushed down the hall, footsteps pounding against the floor. Vincent couldn't tell if she was also muffling the noise, but if she was, this expensive light pinch wouldn't last long. None of the hostiles in the surrounding rooms appeared to notice.

At the end of the hallway, she came to a halt by the locked door, holding herself up against the wall.

She motioned to Lefty with a finger-gun, pointing to the door.

Lefty nodded and pulled his piece.

As he took aim at the door, Vincent eased away toward Hattie, asking, "You covering this sound?"

She nodded.

"You got enough to hide a gunshot?"

She shrugged.

Lefty took aim at the latch, then pulled the trigger.

The shot rang in Vincent's ears, unmuffled to him by Hattie's light pinch. The wood of the door beside the latch splintered in a tiny hole.

Hattie nearly fell to her knees, jerking backward as the gunshot pressed against her illusion. Vincent steadied her, noticing a trickle of blood emerging from her nostril.

Lunging into the door, Lefty pushed it open as a few bits of ruined lockset dropped to the floor. He caught the door with his gun hand, hooking the revolver around the edge of the door to ease it wide.

Vincent checked back down the hall. Still no response.

Hattie whimpered as she held onto the illusion. With wild, desperate eyes, she shook her head at Vincent.

Nothing left.

Vincent nodded for her to release the illusion.

She drew in a ragged breath as her powers released. Lefty lifted his head in response to the change, and Vincent gave him a reassured nod.

They crept into the room, sliding through the opened door to find a narrow, wood-paneled storage room that had been cleared of everything but a chair. That lone chair held Branna Malloy, bound at the wrists but otherwise unmolested.

Dmitrevich stood behind the chair, arms crossed, deep in conversation with his mother, Yulia. They exchanged rapid bursts of Russian, Yulia thrusting a finger at her son, then out the tiny square window toward the city. Dmitrevich shook his head and unfolded his arms, revealing a coil of rope left over from binding Branna's hands.

Dmitrevich's eyes widened as he saw them and Vincent snapped his fingers.

Still weary from the last time pinch, the pressure of the magic immediately hammered him in the guts. He pushed forward to snatch the rope from Dmitrevich's hand. He whipped coils of rope over Dmitrevich's head, ringing the jute over his arms. He threaded the rope over itself a few times, giving it a hard tug before knotting it.

And with the last of his strength, he released the time pinch.

Dmitrevich heaved a hard breath as the rope pressed suddenly against his chest. He flailed backward, tripping over his own feet to fall against the back wall.

Lefty rushed forward, training his gun on Dmitrevich. "Keep it tucked in, pal."

Hattie pushed past Lefty to lay her hands on the sides of her mother's face.

Branna muttered, "Hattie? What are you…?"

Hattie's fingers flew over the knots at her mother's wrists. Vincent watched as she tossed aside her mother's bonds. Hattie's face peered at him over her mother's shoulder—flushed, tear-strewn not from relief, but from anger. A storm of vengeance brewed beneath her scowl, and as lightning flashed in her eyes, Vincent considered how strangely calm he felt.

It all seemed tied together, now. Done. The Bratva had torn him and twisted him, to be sure. But the urge for reckoning was oddly still within his chest. His thoughts returned to the more mechanical issues. The thugs still down the hall. The fallout with the Capo. DeBarre and Hattie's father sitting in the car on the street below.

Vincent eyed Yulia, standing a pace from Lefty, her face more a match for Hattie's than his own. Separating the two would be a wise move—now, before more blood was shed.

And before Hattie did something she'd regret.

Vincent stepped between Lefty and the Malloys, looming over Dmitrevich. "We're done here."

Dmitrevich said nothing. But the man's own calm

demeanor caught Vincent by surprise. No anger. No regret. He was missing something.

And it dawned on him just as Vincent turned to Lefty. "Careful. He's a pincher. He could be standing behind—"

No sooner had the words left Vincent's lips than a figure filled the frame of the door Lefty had shot open. A mirror image of Dmitrevich took a single step into the room, lifted a gun and pulled the trigger.

It was one of Vincent's reflex pinches that hurled the room into a time bubble. These were uncontrolled moments, unstable fractures of time erupting from Vincent's panicked brain. Time shifted in fits and starts. The muzzle flare from the gun rippled and bloomed as the blast of powder peppered the air. The bullet itself eased in jerking motions through the twist.

Vincent eyed the path of the bullet, then twisted on his heel, pushing himself toward both of the Malloys. He hadn't had enough strength left to completely stop time. The bullet was traveling too fast, the pinch unraveling quicker than he could move through the thickened air. He met Hattie's startled gaze and with a backwards shove pushed her clear, then turned to pull Branna with the last of his strength.

The woman spun in a lazy half-circle through midair as she eased away from the path of the bullet.

As Vincent struggled to catch his balance before the unstable time pinch dropped, he swung an arm high.

Too high.

The bullet, slithering through the time bubble, shot forward several inches.

Vincent's arm made contact.

In a fraction of a second, the full force of the bullet impacted his arm, spinning him against the wall in a spray of his own blood as the time pinch released.

CHAPTER 27

The blast of a gunshot. The thickened air of a time pinch.

Hattie struggled to catch up with the sudden appearance of Dmitrevich's second self, turning to her mother as the bullet slid through this strangely tenuous time pinch. Vincent must be too weak—or this was an instinctive action, and something he couldn't quite control.

Before she could react, Vincent sent an elbow into her sternum. She coughed out a breath as her feet caught Dmitrevich on the floor. She slid into the air, not quite in the grip of gravity, but unable to right herself.

A wave of relief rushed over Hattie as she watched her mother slide away from the bullet, then the time bubble released without warning.

She fell over Dmitrevich, her head smacking the floor at Yulia's feet. A warm spray covered her arm.

Blood.

Vincent lurched against the far wall, sliding down in a limp heap. Was he shot? How could that be possible?

Lefty lowered his gun a few inches, turning toward Vincent.

In that moment, Yulia rushed Lefty, the toe of her shoe catching Hattie in the temple. She blinked at the impact, a moment of dizziness resolving as she opened her eyes to find Yulia covering the others with Lefty's gun.

"Now…you." She motioned to Lefty. "Step back."

Lefty complied, his hand opened in surrender.

Dmitrevich twisted beneath Hattie as his doppelganger strode into the room with a sneer, reaching down to jerk Hattie away.

Yulia moved the gun back and forth between Lefty and Vincent who remained on the floor. "I kill you all!" she hissed. "For Yasha!"

Hattie reached up with pleading hands. "Please. My mother has no part of this!"

Yulia snarled, "I do not care. A blood price will be paid."

She cocked the gun, now aimed directly at Branna.

"Why?" Hattie shouted at her. "We're not even part of the Crew! She's my mother, let her go!"

The old woman stared forward, eyes hard and cold. Lost in her own world of pain, so deep she didn't care who she murdered. She only needed to kill. To feel.

She was a woman lost in her grief.

Hattie sucked in a breath, patting her pockets until her fingers landed on the photograph she'd snatched from Vincent in their attic holding cell. A photograph of the woman's slain son.

Yakov Dmitrevich.

How much power did Hattie have left? It had to be enough. Whatever was left…it was her last hope.

Hattie held up the photo. "Madam!"

Yulia cast a glance over her shoulder to spot the photo of

Yakov. Her brow lifted, eyes filling with a stream of pinched light that Hattie sent her. Illusions. Fantasies.

Standing alone in a room with her son. Holding a grandchild. Hearing that grandchild play an upright piano as the family gathered around. Hot tea in some hands, vodka in others. The fragrance of spicy pipe tobacco and the sound of laughing children. Faces alive with smiles. Family. All alive, thriving, growing, as Yulia sat in a rocking chair, simply watching.

Hattie poured everything she had into the illusion. All senses. Sight. Sound. Smell. Taste. Touch. The immersion had to be complete. Just as Hattie had lost herself in her own fantasy of her vision of an idyllic past, this woman must latch onto a false future that might have been.

Blood streamed from Hattie's nose as her insides ground and twisted. She'd passed the point of damage. This magic… this would kill her.

One of the Dmitrevichs turned back to Yulia, who had dropped the pistol.

"*Mama?*" he muttered. "*Shto ne tak? Shto proiskhodit?*"

The second Dmitrevich squinted at his mother, then back at Hattie. He lifted his heel to send his foot into Hattie's midsection.

She wheezed, her chest heaving against her own lungs as the wind left her. Blood sprayed the floor, and she retched. The light pinch dropped immediately. Hattie struggled for air, and when it finally came, she barely had enough strength to turn her head.

Yulia sat on the floor, eyes distant, a thin smile spreading across her face. She muttered and cooed, finally humming some low, baleful lullaby from her homeland.

One of the Dmitrevichs crouched beside her, tapping her cheeks. The one that had kicked Hattie free of the light pinch watched with dread. "It's the girl. She's an illusionist."

The other turned to snarl at Hattie, "What are you doing to her?"

Hattie shook her head just a little. "Nothing now. It's done. It's done, and she's not coming back."

She wasn't pinching anything at this point. The fantasy had taken hold, and Yulia was keeping it alive. That deep need to see her son alive again, that same force that had driven all of this violence, was now pulling her deeper and deeper into the fantasy Hattie had molded into being.

The new Dmitrevich lifted his gun and faced Hattie. "Stop it now!"

Hattie shook her head. "Too late."

He cocked the pistol. "Did you not hear me, girl? Stop what you are doing to her. Stop it."

Thuds shook the floor. Shouts from the hallway. More thuds…screams of pain and panic.

"Drop the iron, Smith," Lefty growled. He'd retrieved the gun Yulia had dropped and now had it pressed against the back of one of the Dmitreviches.

The gun-wielding Dmitrevich clenched his jaw, sending a vein in his temple twisting back and forth. His fingers tightened around the pistol.

"Don't know if this'll kill you both," Lefty added. "Be happy to find out, though."

Dmitrevich sighed, "*Nyet.*"

His fingers withdrew from the pistol…which hung in midair. Then, with a sharp jerk, it flew up onto the ceiling.

A voice called from the doorway, "I'll do you one better, Lefty."

DeBarre stepped into the room, taking in the carnage.

Dmitrevich, the one still on his feet, threw a swing at DeBarre.

With a flick of DeBarre's finger, the entire man dropped to the ceiling, and then back to the ground.

Lefty clubbed the other Dmitrevich with the butt of his pistol, sending him to the ground as well. With a heavy breath, he said, "You were supposed to stay in the car."

"You're welcome."

"Guess you got your mojo back?"

DeBarre nodded, frowning as he spotted Vincent slumped against the wall. "What happened?"

Lefty stepped around DeBarre, and pulled Vincent away from the wall. "Not sure. It went down fast."

Hattie tried to speak, but it only came out as a bloody gurgle.

DeBarre rushed to her, easing her to her feet, and bringing her to the chair.

"Easy," he muttered as he settled her down. "Looks like you had a day."

Hattie attempted a smile, unsuccessfully.

DeBarre gave her a wink and wiggled his fingers. "Powers came back. Hauled ass inside the second I was sure."

A new set of hands landed on Hattie's shoulders. She looked up to find her mother weeping over her. She pulled Hattie into a folded hug, crying as the terror of the moment passed.

Vincent stirred with a groan as Lefty applied pressure to the gunshot wound in his arm. "Aww…Jesus."

Lefty chuckled. "You baby. The man just winged you."

Vincent opened his eyes and sucked in a breath as Lefty shifted his grip. "What…where are we?"

DeBarre patted Hattie on the knee before withdrawing to help Vincent to his feet. "Baltimore, you pin cushion."

Vincent shook his head. "What are you doing here?"

"Saving your ass."

Lefty nodded. "Took the rest of the building out. I think we're gonna have to pay him, at this point."

Vincent smiled. "Ain't that our luck." His smile faded as he regarded the battered pair of Dmitreviches lying on the floor. "I'll be damned. I was right."

DeBarre nudged the nearer Dmitrevich, who stirred with a moan. "Still alive."

"Good," Lefty groused. "Vito's gonna want to take his time with this guy."

"Sure it's just one guy?" DeBarre asked as he examined the second.

Vincent answered, "He's a place pincher. He can be in more than one place at a time."

DeBarre shook his head. "Knocked this one out cold. How's he keeping the pinch this long?"

Vincent scowled. "Good point. What then?"

"Twins?" Lefty asked.

Hattie leaned forward to examine them. With a clearing of her throat and a couple tries, she said, "Could be."

Vincent frowned. "When Hattie and I were tied up in that attic, he just popped out of nowhere. I could've sworn..."

"Perhaps they planned this, all of this, together?" Lefty offered. "If so, one of them could've been hiding the whole time, just waiting to hear what you had to say behind their backs?"

DeBarre nodded. "Smart. Devious and convoluted, but smart."

Hattie gripped her mother's hand tight as a wave of nausea racked her body. Once the threat had passed, she released low, slow breaths trying to get a rein on her body.

"What exactly did you do to that old bag?" Lefty asked with a nod to Yulia.

"Gave her what she wanted. The life that was robbed from her."

A voice cackled in the hallway, "The 'ell is all this riot?"

Branna huffed. "Alton Malloy! You get right in here this instant!"

Hattie's father shuffled into the room, his eyes wide, face pale from the carnage outside the room.

DeBarre lifted a hand to stifle a chuckle, then declared, "You're supposed to stay in the car, old-timer!"

Lefty shot an elbow into DeBarre's side. "Lot of that going around, you useless gorillas."

DeBarre began policing bodies while Lefty left the building to phone the Old Moravia and fill in the Crew on the developments. Vincent pulled off his jacket and made a field dressing with a strip of one of the Dmitreviches' shirts, twisting it around his arm wound with a little help from DeBarre. Once that was done, they tied their captives more thoroughly and set them against the far wall.

Vincent paused as he finished a knot in the rope and turned to Hattie. "How are you?"

"Bloody damned knackered."

"I hear that."

Vincent stood up, wincing and hissing at the wound in his arm and Hattie hid a smile.

"Oh, Jesus," she teased. "Are you five years old?"

"Alright. Don't give me the business. This hurts like hell."

"Aye, and if your fairy godmother came down and kissed it, you'd bleed rainbows and rock candy, wouldn't you?"

Vincent sucked in a breath to defend himself, until he spotted the grin on Hattie's face. "Brat."

Hattie blinked at that. "Hey. Only one person calls me that, and if he were here—"

"Is Raymond safe? His family?"

She replied after a pause, "Aye. Tucked away from your hordes and goblins."

They stood awkwardly for a moment.

Vincent offered, "At least he, well, one of these guys, scared you all off before we got there."

Hattie nodded, reaching into her back pocket to pull out

the same note that was left for her at Raymond's house. Vincent reached for it and she released it into his grip.

Unfolding it he frowned down at the bold writing. "Wait." He stretched to collect his folded jacket, pulling a tiny card from its pocket. "The handwriting isn't the same."

Vincent held the tiny card up to the light. Hattie leaned in, her arm brushing his good shoulder, to peer at the two pieces of paper. The first, her note—warning her in quick, sharp strokes of the pen, *The Crew is coming for the Bowleses. Show them you are smarter.*

The second—a tiny business card with the words in florid, looping calligraphy, *Nice pinch. Let's talk after.*

"Do you think they were each written by a different twin?" Hattie asked.

Vincent shook his head. "Why go to all the trouble of perfecting your mannerisms, your habits, and your appearance, but have such completely different handwriting?"

"So…so they didn't send this?"

"No, I don't think they did."

Hattie took the note from him, trembling a little as she returned to her parents.

Alton lifted her chin with his finger. "You with us, girl?"

She couldn't answer. Because, no matter how invested Vincent, DeBarre, and Lefty were in keeping her identity as a pincher safe from Vito Corbi, someone else out there had been watching her.

And this person knew exactly what she was.

CHAPTER 28

*D*eBarre kept the engine running as Vincent and Lefty escorted the Malloys back to their apartment. Both Vincent and Hattie held back from the rest as they climbed the steps, both of them exhausted from the use of their powers. Alton held the door open for his wife and daughter.

Hattie turned to face her father. "Can I have a moment, Da?"

He nodded and guided his wife to the kitchen. "I could use some tea, Branna. What d'ya say?"

Vincent glanced at Lefty over his shoulder.

Lefty returned a weary grin, then said, "I'll wait for you downstairs." He added halfway down the hall, "Don't take forever, huh?"

When he was out of sight, Vincent turned to Hattie. "Listen," he said with a shuffle of his feet, "I want to apologize again, but you'll probably just bust my balls and make me regret I ever met you in the first place."

"Try me."

"I'm sorry. For diming you and your family out to the

Crew. For getting you and your family caught up in the middle of all this. I know you're ready to spit nails over this whole thing. Ready to maybe never see me again, and I get that."

She closed her eyes and took a deep breath. "Here's the truth of things as I see't. We were both in an impossible place. No choices. Lives were at stake, and I can't really blame you for thinking that was more important than my freedom. Still, we were set against each other, and you broke a promise to me. That's going to stay with us for a while, I imagine."

He nodded.

"Don't go making yourself a martyr, Vincent. You and I will be just fine as long as your boss leaves us alone, especially if Lizzie gets her business back."

"I'll talk to Tony and Lefty before I get sent off, make sure that happens," he offered.

She winced. "Are they…do you think he'll really send you off? Sell you?"

He sighed. "Maybe. I didn't just screw up, Hattie, I defied my Capo. Maybe us finding and taking out the rest of the Russians will even things up a bit, but maybe not."

They stood in silence for a while, Hattie staring at her feet.

At length, Vincent asked, "Sooo…where do we stand?"

"I don't know," she chimed. "Where did we leave off?"

"Hunting down a Hell pincher."

She looked up at him and nodded. "Aye. That."

"Look…if I'm still here when all this blows over, then maybe we can talk about that Hell pincher up in Pennsylvania?"

She nodded, extending a hand to Vincent.

He reached out, gripping it gingerly.

"Sounds like a plan," she said. "But you should understand one thing, right now."

"What's that?"

"Things will never be the same."

She turned, stepped inside the apartment, and slowly closed the door. Vincent ran his hands over his face, cleared his throat, then turned back for the stairs. As he reached the top flight, the door opened again.

"Eh, there. Time pincher."

Vincent peered around the banister to find Alton hobbling forward with two shot-glasses pinched between his fingers.

"So, it dawned on me that I offered you some whisky and never followed through." He held one of the glasses for Vincent. "That's bad luck, don't you know?"

With a tired smile, Vincent took the glass.

Alton raised his own in a toast. "To all the right bastards getting what they're due!"

They downed the whisky then Alton collected both glasses with a wink. "You need a place to run, boy, you come to us. We've a lifetime of raising a magical person, and there's room here enough for another."

Vincent nodded deeply as Alton returned to his apartment, then headed down the stairs. Lefty lingered by the door, giving him a leering smirk.

"Is she gonna be a problem?"

Vincent cocked a brow. "How could she be a problem?"

"We're entering some choppy waters here, Vincent. I need you focused."

"I *am* focused."

"You're focused right now on that Irish chippy upstairs, but I need your focus where it'll do us some good."

"Shut up."

Lefty chuckled. "The hotel's crawling with the G. Entire outfit's relocated."

"The vineyard?"

"No," Lefty replied as he held the front door to DeBarre's car open for Vincent. "Not the vineyard."

"Where?"

"Poker hall."

Vincent lifted his face to the sky. The morning light had matured into a broad bolt of yellow, spilling in from a cloudless blue sky.

"Listen," Vincent whispered, "keep what you know about Cooper under wraps. Got it?"

"What's the play?" Lefty asked as DeBarre did his best to eavesdrop from inside the car.

"Just...cool the spool. I got something cooking."

"Won't get the two of us killed, will it?"

Vincent shook his head. "No. Might even help."

As they climbed into the car, DeBarre turned to Vincent with a grin. "And just what are we getting killed over this time?"

Raymond slipped two fingers into his mouth to release a shrill whistle as one of the Crew's trucks backed into the warehouse. The driver stopped the truck, and two more errand boys hopped out to open the tailgate to unload the crates of wine onto a neatly-stacked pallet.

Raymond shot Hattie an approving nod. "I like it when they do the liftin'."

"I bet you do," she said with a smile. "Don't you worry, though. I'll make sure you do all the lifting when we make the delivery."

"What, you don't need the exercise?"

"Hang that! I've had enough exertion to last the rest of the year."

Lizzie barked at the errand boys as one let a crate slip. The box only fell a few inches, but the rattling of the bottles was loud enough to draw a spate of profanity from Liz's lips.

"She's in a mood, isn't she?" Hattie grumbled.

"We're gettin' behind," Raymond replied, guiding her away from the activity. "Looks like another week of late nights."

Hattie sighed. "Fine."

She put on, but the work was highly welcome. The money came at a good time. Cutbacks at the steel mill had dried up Alton's wages. At least he'd have his health. Hattie kept the dram of Aqua Vitae at home, now…resolving never to use it for her personal purposes. The cost, she'd discovered, was too high.

Liz, for her part, hadn't missed a single beat getting the warehouse back into the swing of things. With that had come the return of her less-than-charming business demeanor. Which, in and of itself, was a welcome sight. When Lizzie was polite, she was worried. When she was calm, she was unpleasant. Better the devil Hattie knew.

Hattie wandered out into the night air with Raymond. The heat had come in full force, as had the fireflies which flickered in and around the crates surrounding the Locust Point warehouse.

"You wanna practice some more?" Raymond offered. "Your hoodoo?"

Hattie smiled. "No. I think I have a handle on it."

"You're just worried you'll get locked in again. Hey, that's fine. I don't cotton to all that heavy witchcraft."

She jabbed his ribs. "You're happy enough when I use it to save us from snooping eyes on the water."

"Yeah, well…a flim-flam here and there. That's alright. It ain't so unnatural."

She stuck her tongue out at him.

"Well, then," he declared. "We'll run this latest haul on out to Winnow's when they get it packed up. And you're helping me load it!"

Hattie smiled. "Long nights."

"Long nights." Raymond sighed as they reached the Ford Runabout. He lifted a chin. "Looks like your little bird left you another note."

Hattie half-snickered at the comment before she realized he was actually serious. She turned toward the front of the truck to find another note, crisp and white in the moonlight, tucked beneath the windscreen wiper blade.

A jolt ran through her.

Raymond shook his head. "Probably some secret damn admirer. You gotta get yourself figured out, girl."

He trotted off to give her a moment's privacy and Hattie stood stiff, arms to her sides, staring at the tiny slip of cardstock on the glass.

This wasn't Dmitrevich. Nor was the note at Raymond's house. Nor, likely, was the note bearing the admonition "Know Thyself." Whoever had sent those messages was still watching.

She turned in a circle, eyes on crates and stacks of lumber. Nothing but fireflies and evening breeze. The rushing of the wind sent a chill deep into her core.

Finally, mustering the strength to face it, Hattie reached for the note. She jerked it free of the wiper blade and unfolded it.

She read the message, scratched in jagged slashes of ink.

Soon we shall met.

Hattie folded the note and tucked it into her overalls.

To the north, the lights of Baltimore flickered across the ripples of the Patapsco inlet. The city, so filled with souls and stories, had for so long been both her home and her prison.

Now, there was one more soul with eyes on her. What would it mean?

She cleared her throat, pulled her bangs away from her eyes, and marched back to the warehouse. There would be time to meet this mystery person later. For now, she had work to do.

Want more? Clip Joint, book 3 in the White Lightning Series releases November 13th!

ACKNOWLEDGMENTS

A huge thanks to our copyeditors Kimberly Cannon and Jennifer Cosham whose eagle eyes catch all the typos and keep Debra's comma problem in line, and to Damonza for cover design.

Special thanks to all our readers who have individually followed us to Hel and back, and enthusiastically cheered us on during our first collaborative project. May there be many more ahead!

Debra and J.P

ABOUT THE AUTHORS

Debra lives in a little house in the woods of Maryland with her sons and two slobbery bloodhounds. On a good day, she jogs and horseback rides, hopefully managing to keep the horse between herself and the ground. Her only known super power is 'Identify Roadkill'.

A Louisiana native, J.P. relocated to the vineyards and cow pastures of Central Maryland after Hurricane Katrina, where he lives with his wife and son. During the day he commutes to the city of Baltimore, a setting which inspires much of his writing.

For more information:
www.debradunbar.com/white-lightning or
J.P. Sloan's Author page
Debra Dunbar's Author page

ALSO BY DEBRA DUNBAR

<u>White Lightning Series</u>

Wooden Nickels

Bum's Rush

Clip Joint

***

<u>The Templar Series</u>

Dead Rising

Last Breath

Bare Bones

Famine's Feast

Dark Crossroads (2019)

* * *

<u>IMP WORLD NOVELS</u>

<u>The Imp Series</u>

A Demon Bound

Satan's Sword

Elven Blood

Devil's Paw

Imp Forsaken

Angel of Chaos

Kingdom of Lies

Exodus

Queen of the Damned

The Morning Star

* * *

<u>Half-breed Series</u>

Demons of Desire

Sins of the Flesh

Cornucopia

Unholy Pleasures

City of Lust

* * *

<u>Imp World Novels</u>

No Man's Land

Stolen Souls

Three Wishes

Northern Lights

Far From Center

Penance

* * *

<u>Northern Wolves</u>

Juneau to Kenai

Rogue

Winter Fae

Bad Seed

ALSO BY J.P. SLOAN